The Warriors of Transcendence

Erez Moshe Doron

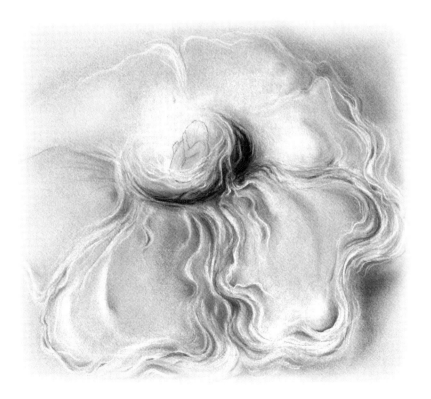

Copyright
©
2008
by Erez Moshe Doron

Lev Hadvarim
The secret of small things

P.O.B. 160 Mevo Choron 99765, Israel

972-2-5667567

www.levhadvarim.com
www.tmurot.net
levhadvarim@gmail.com

All right reserved, including the right to reproduce this book or portions thereof in any form whatsoever.

Registered by "Miraz" Center for counseling and rights registration Inc.

Registration number 00211007280703

Design and Layout:
Eye See Productions
972-2-5821453

Cover Illustration, maps and illustrations:
Chava Doron

Editor: Ellen Kraft Jaffe

ISBN
978-965-91342-0-5

Printed In Israel 2008

THE WARRIORS OF TRANSCENDENCE

Erez Moshe Doron

Translated from the Hebrew by
Deenah Rachel Misk

Contents

Prologue	9
City of Steel	15
A Farewell	23
The Wall	43
The Memory Shield	53
Legend of the Wings	67
The Memory Master	79
A Lost Vessel	91
The Obliterated One	101
A Mission	109
Encounters on Green Isle	119
Conspiracies at Obliterator's Peak	137
The Essence of Soul Concentration	145
Shadow Valley	155
The Marker of Tumult	165
All Waiting Shall Be Fulfilled	173
Abyss of the Shadows	181
The King's Cloak	187
Loneliness is not Always Pain	197
Fire Mountain	205
Tzalaii's Trial	213
Seven Gates	221
A Different Time, Above Water	239
Archives	247

Journey to the Tower 259

The Heart Is the Key 269

Good Depth in Exchange for Evil Depth 281

Ten Days in the Tunnels of Time 287

An Initiation Discussion 313

Melodies of the Master 323

Battles in the Green Lowlands 329

Silver Swords 337

Enigmas of the Wastelands 347

The Thousandth Leader of the Deathliners 361

The Imposter 375

The Game of Forces 391

The White Emperor 403

Into the Mountain Core 417

The Crown of Darkness 429

Whispers 445

Trapped in the Valley of Silence 457

A New Dawn/ Epilogue 469

Glossary 477

Prologue

*In the "Archives of the Tunnels of Time," Sixth Millennia,
it is written:*

*"Before all beings were emanated and creatures created,
A superior light permeated existence.
Whence it became His will to create the world
This light was pushed aside.*

*In the vacant space of His light did roam
a great gust of wind, over water with no end.
A fire was set ablaze in the world, hidden away.*

*As if placed in an invisible hand,
Life giving paths were formed,
Chords created to contain the water,
Trails made their way through heavy, murky waters
The keys of fifty gates were molded.
The creatures were destined to meet their Maker.*

*Opposite them
Creating distance to gain closeness
And concealing in order to discover,
Evil was created.*

*In time, his name became known amongst men as
"Khivia."*

Eons passed. Khivia's mark, engrained in every creature, was yet to be discovered. He lingered, waiting for the right moment to break through the desires of man, and reign with his help. He waited until the arrival of the six thousandth year, while the kingdom of the Ancient Progeny flourished. Only then did he unleash his webs, already spun in the days of old.

The five great cities, inhabited by millions, spread out into the Land of the Southern Cliffs. Elegant towers and steeples, adorned with precious stones, crowned their streets. The city dwellers wore beautiful golden cloaks, and their faces expressed splendor. The mightiest of knights were their heroes. Most impressive and wise were their kings and noblemen. Grace and truth lit their paths. Lovely and gracious were their actions.

Khivia became envious of their blessed plentitude. From his throne on the Mountain of Ohn, he began whispering impure thoughts of despair and weakness into the river sources. The rivers carried these thought into the homes of the city dwellers that drank from their waters incessantly and became contaminated by them. Spirits raged, minds withered, hearts filled with uncertainty. The faith of the inhabitants of the great cities weakened, and they became distrustful of the King, thus leading to the deterioration of the ancient kingdom. The King's seven advisors, too, drank from the contaminated waters and became poisoned by Khivia's venom, which clouded their thoughts. They weakened the King's spirit by informing him of evil rumors about civil wars, which they alone had caused by their internal disputes.

Ultimately, the King was murdered in his sleep by his councilmen. That very same night, Sword carrying legions from the North invaded the land. In the duration of several short weeks they managed to demolish the beautiful cities to their core and slaughter most of the inhabitants. Only several thousand succeeded in escaping to the Northern Forest and distant beaches of the King's Sea, where fourteen villages were built.

It was then that the Master of Transcendence appeared, circling Ohn Mountain with clouds and blocking the powers of the mountain dweller. Khivia, who had hoped to become ruler, was forced to go into hiding in the depths. But yet his whispers did not cease.

The annihilators of the ancient cities left nothing of worth, as Khivia made it clear that it was his intention to eradicate all memories of the Ancient Progeny from the heart of man. The large remaining stones were taken from the heights of the Southern Boulders to the valley of the Green Lowlands, and were used to build a new City. It took fifty years to construct the City, inhabited at first by two hundred thousand men. Its builders and original inhabitants were young men who were taken captive from the great cities. Their power was great but their memory short, since they too were poisoned by the contaminated waters. Just a few generations later, the inhabitants of the new City knew nothing of their actual origin. They were convinced that they were descendents of Emperors, when in fact they were their slaves, soldiers born to serve a master whose name they did not know.

The Towered City was comprised of seven levels, each one controlled by a designated Emperor.

Their power is described in the *Archives of the Tunnels of Time*:

"Earth controls the base. Its power is derived from Jupiter. It is governed by instruments of percussion. Its tools are made of steel. Color of flame: gray. Symbol: A sword.

Water controls the second. Its power is derived from Saturn. It is governed by stringed instruments. Its tools are made of mercury. Color of flame: Sapphire. Symbol: Grape Cluster.

Wind controls the third. Its power is derived from the stars. It is governed by wind instruments. Its tools are made of lead. Color of flame: White. Symbol: Split Wood.

Fire controls the fourth. Its power is derived from Venus. It is governed by bowed instruments. Its tools are made of tin. Color of flame: Crimson. Symbol: Flame."

Less was known of the remaining levels:

"Sun controls the fifth. Its tools are made of copper. Color of flame: Emerald.

Mars controls the sixth. Its tools are made of gold. Color of flame: Violet.

The Moon controls the seventh. Its tools are made of silver. Color of flame: Indigo.

Ruler of all levels- The Master of Ohn."

The poisoned waters infected the earth, and the country's beauty faded. All attempts by the Emperors to preserve it went up in smoke, until it was transformed into a white, barren desert. Trees that once bore fruit in the Green Lowlands became parched, and in their place grew new crops around the tower. Fruits of Oblivion.

Hundreds of years passed. The Emperors still reigned over the vast City, but they themselves were unfamiliar with their roots of origin. Though Khivia had granted them with eternal life, as they sipped the strengthening and supernaturally powerful blue potion, they had simultaneously become sterile. Contrary to them, the Descendents of the Emperors who were the original City builders were propagating.

It seemed as though the Emperors' rule extended, uninterrupted, over all occupied lands. But during the last millennia clear signs were observed, indicating that the Master of Transcendence had begun drafting warriors.

The thousands of villagers from the shores of King's Sea were not trained in warfare. If the Descendents of the Emperors were to envelop them in an attempt to conquer their lands- all fourteen villages would surely succumb, as the cities of the Ancient Progeny had centuries earlier. It was only because the Descendents of the Emperors feared the Masters powers that they avoided an open attack. They had other strategies.

It was different in the Land of the Northern Forest. The entire area was covered with vast tangled forests, and conquering it would be slow and agonizing. Headstrong warriors continued to battle against the Descendents of the Emperors, even initiating heroic attacks that nearly reached the walls of the Towered City.

These were the "Storm Dancers," trained by the Warriors of Transcendence. A seemingly innocent ceremonial dance led to a violent attack, disturbing the tranquility and peace of the Descendents of the Emperors, and discouraging their victories.

The dwelling of the Master of Transcendence was unknown, but a legend pervaded the earth: "A unique being shall arrive, destined to dispel all fear and cleanse the world from terror." These words instilled anxiety in the hearts of the Descendents of the Emperors and hope in the hearts of free men. Spoken by them both, ever so softly and with conviction, were the words: *Legend of the Wings*.

And Khivia continued to spin his web…

Chapter One

City of Steel

City of Steel

The wind grew strong at Sea Point high above the Northern Forests. Woodland animals nestled deeply into their underground abodes. Waves of yellow leaves were carried through the trees, swept up into the air, swirling violently before descending to rest on the damp earth. Rain struck the wide treetops, drenching the trees, pouring down onto the earth in great torrents. The raging storm reverberated throughout the woodlands like the sound of a multitude of winged creatures in flight. A bird, gone astray, attempted to find its way through the downpour, searching for sanctuary among the rocks.

Finally, a ray of sunlight burst through the dark clouds, illuminating the forest. A deer hiding under the trees shivered in an attempt to dry itself, lifting its head to receive the unexpected gift of light. A lone wolf howled.

From an aerial view, the trees on the great mountain peak appeared as a cult of crowded, haunted men, arms raised seeking refuge.

On a clear day the border of the Wall would have been visible, but now a heavy fog obscured the peaks. Beyond the mist, faintly visible sections of the Green Lowlands sprawled out into the distance. In its center lay the Towered City like a massive, silent beast.

The rain finally ceased and the air cleared. The sun painted the blackened City walls in streaks of yellow. At the unfathomable height of the tower, the plethora of windows seemed to reflect a red color. Down below, on the lively market street, there was an unusual commotion caused by the presence of the secret of strength of the Sapphire Level. Weary to the point of collapse, a pale, emaciated man was seen running for his life. He wore an old and dirty light-blue garment upon his clammy body. It was obvious that escape was impossible and his frantic flight only delayed his inevitable doom. Subsequently, stalls were overturned, fruit was squashed and utensils shattered and scattered, but the over-excited bystanders were not disappointed by the damage. Many had looked forward to this special moment expectantly aware that the Emperors would, from time to time, express their generosity towards the Towered City's inhabitants by providing a hopeless, convicted creature to cause their blood to stir.

The spectators were unaware of the nature of this man's crime and the rationale for the killing game was irrelevant to them. Merchants, dwellers of the street and passersby, stared at the fleeing man, taunting him, ridiculing him. Excited spectators crowded the windows on all the levels of the tower. To their surprise, they realized that the frantic runner was not even being pursued. From what was he fleeing? The dark, smooth stones made running difficult causing him to stumble and fall from time to time, to the amusement of the crowd. Reeling around, he resembled a drunkard as he swayed from side to side, eventually losing his strength and dropping helplessly to the ground.

Six men in the crowd arose and approached the prone man. Taller than all the others, their stride was proud and confident. Their white garb distinguished them from the other warriors. Their faces were stern, their eyes harsh and alert, their capes marked by sapphire-colored flames.

So! Warriors from the Saturn Level really were on the base.

The reality of this rare spectacle caused a breathless excitement in the crowd. Even the arrogant, shaven-headed soldiers fell silent.

"Mother, who are they?" asked a young boy of six, while nestling closer to her. In the stillness, his whisper seemed amplified, as if he had shouted.

"They are the WireArchers," replied a warrior in shiny black leather garb.

An old woman watched from a distance. She alone knew that the man's sole crime had been his successful resistance to obliteration attempts. Even the most headstrong prisoners could be obliterated with ease, but a few, such as this man would not surrender. A strength ingrained in certain souls was able to resist total obliteration. An inner will-power continued to exist in spite of the dark shadows that blurred the mind.

The six WireArchers, their cloaks rustling, formed a crescent-shaped enclosure around the criminal. Their severe and emotionless faces terrorized the trapped victim. His sporadic, labored breathing was all that could be heard now in the silent marketplace. The six WireArchers emitted a loud wail, which grew continuously stronger. Their cloaks darkened, and the sharpness of their features faded. Simultaneously, from deep within themselves, they released a peculiar substance as the unfortunate captive shrunk into a fetal position. From their outstretched hands, they exuded thin, shiny white strings that were flung onto the prisoner, forming a net. The strings enveloped him, painfully welding onto his skin like smoldering, sharp, metallic wires.

"You must not watch this!" exclaimed the mother, shielding her son's eyes while, at the same time completely mesmerized by the sight herself. An expectant silence permeated the area, extending to the terraces above. Those who stood in close proximity to the prisoner began to retreat, as his moans grew deeper and his breathing became more shallow. Soon, he made no sound at all.

An ear-shattering noise like an explosion of thousands of glass shards, emanated from the prisoner's body. His face began to dissolve and the color of his skin paled. His eyes were shut and his facial features became distorted as his body disintegrated leaving only the residue of a grayish glass powder. The wire coils encircled the powder, causing it to heat up and change color, transforming it into blackened ashes that were carried away by the evening breeze.

Suddenly, the pent up tension in the hearts of the spectators erupted wildly. The audience roared and swayed, applauding, whistling and tossing objects onto the now empty killing ground where nothing remained of the captive.

The extraordinary skills of the WireArchers stirred the blood of the onlookers. Most felt fully prepared to participate in the Unification ceremony. The young mother attempted to pull her child away protectively, but the boy was drawn to the young warrior who had responded to his earlier inquiry. He approached the warrior in a childish attempt to learn more about the spectacular net.

"Why did he not escape through the net?" he asked gleefully, as if he had merely witnessed a game.

A crooked smile distorted the warrior's face. Upset and agitated, as if offended, he responded, "Foolish child. That net cannot be severed!"

"Of course it can!" replied the child, innocently, "Even a child can tear a net like that!"

"In order to release the net, one must kill all of the six WireArchers who created it," clarified the soldier. "If this is not done, the trapped prisoner is turned to dust."

"And who can kill a WireArcher?!" inquired the child.

"No one on earth," replied the proud warrior with the conviction of a true believer. The boy's eyes glimmered. "WireArcher," he repeated the word, joyously rolling it over his tongue. Maybe he too would merit to join their ranks when he grew up. "And how can one become a WireArcher?" he asked.

But, alas, the warrior had vanished; the child's question remained unanswered.

Warriors from all the surrounding areas were beating on drums. Swarms of natives gathered from all the lower levels. The evening breeze had swept away the stench of sweat and fear. The lingering aroma of herbs and spices had also faded from the marketplace, but the visual intensity of the killing game, the images of the man's death, were felt by all of the spectators. The sound of drumming was faint at first, distant and as light as the evening breeze, carrying a message: The dwellers of the Kingdom of White Fire are destined to be consumed by the great fire, burning at the pinnacle of their tower. The drums grew louder, rough and metallic, eliciting excitement in the hearts of the people. The pulsating rhythm opened passageways in their minds, and they soon began to transcend, in unison. Darkness deepened. Echoes arose. The streets of the marketplace became deserted. All that remained was the dance of the transcending fire, the dance of unity, burning, blurring the borders that had once separated the leather-clad warriors from the colorfully-dressed merchants.

Carrying all to the heavens, drowning all in an abyss, the fire took life and transformed it into a deeper and more thrilling substance.

Chapter Two

A Farewell

A Farewell

All was quiet in the house. Not a sound was heard in the village, only the bark of a lone dog. Despite the early evening hour, the villagers had already returned to their homes. Ulu's abode was located on the seashore and the comforting, familiar scene of the fishermen's boats secured to the stone pier brought a contented smile to his face. The wooden gate to his courtyard was easily opened and as Ulu closed it behind him he felt the familiar warmth emanating from his home. As common in all villages, his home was a simple cabin, built of unadorned, wide wooden planks. Through the open window, Ulu sensed the welcoming aura emanating from within. He knocked on the door, the door of his own home, before entering.

Ulu, of average height, wore a simple light blue cloth garment. His round face, pale blue eyes, and cheerful features, were framed by curly, blond hair. His slow and careful movements revealed his contemplative nature.

Rising from his resting place to welcome his master, Ulu's dog nuzzled him affectionately.

The large living room was decorated with colorful rugs and fabrics. The fresh scent of fields in bloom permeated the atmosphere, blending with the earthy aroma of the hot soup cooking on the stove. It was an innocent evening in a quiet and noble, simple village, reminiscent of earlier times, safe and serene. Ulu's wife emerged from the kitchen, a smile softening her features. Like her husband, she was of average height. Her dark hair was gathered and held in place by a simple straw clasp and her lively, dark eyes, were as youthful as ever, unchanged since her youth, when she and Ulu had first met.

"I knew you would come," she said, simply, although she hadn't been informed of his imminent return. Nonetheless, she knew… "Like always, when the winds begin to sing, I listen and I can hear your footsteps."

Outside, they could hear the sound of the sea breeze. Had she really heard his footsteps in the wind?

A long time had passed since he had been home. *Much too long*, he thought, relieved of the sadness he had felt.

Home! Ulu, accustomed to frequent journeys, fully appreciated his home, a precious place to return to. He entered his children's room and caressed their faces. They hugged him in their sleep, but it wasn't long before they sensed his presence and awoke to greet him. The children embraced him, jumping up and hopping about, chattering and giggling, sharing news of their home-life.

"Father!" Three-year old Shaii jumped into her father's arms, followed by five-year old Dorrianne. Ulu happily produced two carved wooden flutes from his bag, gifts for his two young daughters. He had carefully chosen this particular item in order to re-enforce his children's belief in his occupation as a merchant of handicrafts and musical instruments.

"Father!" said twelve year old Saag, the eldest, as he embraced him, "Father, you have returned!"

"Yes, I have. And I have brought you something, too," said Ulu as he handed Saag an intricately carved white, wooden horse.

"Thank you, Father, thank you. We have three new puppies," Saag reported.

"In just one more week we will be able to eat the apples from the tree!" exclaimed little Shaii. "Yes, and just yesterday we planted carrots in the vegetable patch by the fence! Do you want to see it, Father?" asked Dorrianne.

"Tomorrow, my precious, we'll see it tomorrow," smiled Ulu as his wife joined the reunion, reveling in the happy family scene.

Ulu, presented with his daughter's handicrafts, listened as she explained her creations. He had a love for artistic creation, and the children enjoyed creating small objects for him, each according to his own ability.

"We made this cabin with Mother," continued his eldest daughter, as she presented a miniature model of a wooden cabin.

"It is our home," said his youngest daughter. Saag just hugged his father and smiled. The dog, hearing loud voices in the middle of the night, entered the room and began to bark affectionately at Shaii, wishing to join the celebration.

"It's not for you, silly, it's for Father!" announced Dorrianne, and everyone laughed.

An hour later, they were all fast asleep. Smiles adorned their slumbering faces.

In the morning, after a festive breakfast, they went out into the garden. The apples on the tree seemed to have a lavender hue. The green grass in front of the house contrasted with the orange-colored flowers near the door. After visiting the new carrot patch and listening to his little daughter's enthusiastic explanations, Ulu sat with his wife on a huge, old tree trunk, watching the children at play. The sun spread its rays generously over the world. A light breeze carried the smell of fresh fish from the dock. Saag pushed Shaii and Dorrianne on their swing.

For a moment Ulu thought he and his wife might be able to have a quiet conversation, but the children began to play a new and rambunctious game. Saag had fastened glittering strips of material to his blue clothing. Brandishing a long staff, he spoke to his sisters arrogantly.

"I am the great Emperor!" he announced.

Ulu's smile abruptly dissolved as Shaii and Dorrianne bowed down to their brother. He touched their heads as if pardoning them and allowed them to resume an upright stance. Just then, Dorrianne concealed herself in the bushes for a moment, before reappearing as a new character in the game. From the folds of her blue cape, she drew out a sharpened stick, and briskly approached the *Emperor*.

"Who are you?" the *Emperor* questioned the approaching challenger, mockingly.

"I am the Warrior of Transcendence," answered the child intently, approaching her siblings, her sword drawn.

Ulu's eyes narrowed in great concern. While focusing on this curious game, he glanced quickly at his wife, sitting by his side. They had been together for fifteen years, and she knew the inner perceptions of his heart. He was surprised to see that his children knew so much about the external events taking place in the world. Perhaps his wife was aware of the source of their newly acquired ideas.

"The village children are fond of this game," she whispered apologetically, as if she inwardly distrusted this seemingly innocent, popular pastime.

In the meantime, the threatened *Emperor* retreated to the garden fence, alarmed.

"Oh, no! Not the Warrior of Transcendence!" he exclaimed as he raised his arms for protection.

"That is nonsense. I don't want to play this game with you any longer!" complained little Shaii. Ulu guessed that she was unhappy with her insignificant role in the game.

"What's wrong?" asked Dorrianne.

"You are no Warrior of Transcendence!" the child asserted.

"Who told you that?" asked Dorrianne, insulted, pointing her staff towards the child who challenged her authority.

"You don't look like a Warrior of Transcendence," Shaii persisted courageously.

"How do you know what a Warrior of Transcendence looks like?" Dorrianne retorted, defending her position.

The little girl raised her voice, "I know that a Warrior of Transcendence doesn't even need a sword. He triumphs with his mind."

Ulu took a fallen branch, carrying it like a sword, as he turned to Saag, in obeisance, like a soldier facing his commander. Ulu was a master of self control and so his children did not suspect his investigative objectives as he joined their game. "Please explain to us, honorable *Emperor*, how to recognize a Warrior of Transcendence."

A serious look appeared on Saag's face. The soldier's obedience flattered him, and he replied solemnly, "It is hard to say. They can appear in various disguises, so one must be cautious of them."

"Yes, one must be cautious of them," echoed Shaii in adoration of her big brother.

It is of utmost significance, thought Ulu, *that Saag has chosen the role of Emperor. Why had his son assumed such a powerful position? He had always been a delicate, dreamy child...*

"I humbly request orders to engage them in battle," offered Ulu, in his role as the Emperor's 'soldier.'

"You? But are you prepared?" asked Saag, toying with his imaginary sword.

"And who is prepared?" probed Ulu.

"Only the Emperor, of course," answered Saag, arrogantly.

Someone has definitely touched the child's soul, thought Ulu, in alarm.

"I wish you luck," he said to the *Emperor* and everyone laughed as the suspense lifted and the game came to an end.

As he always did during his days at home, Ulu occupied himself with the various chores that awaited him. He strengthened the wooden fences, examined the vegetable patches and spent as much time as possible with his children. The sun dyed the sea red as the wind grew chilly. One night, after the girls finished their dinner and climbed into bed Ulu told them a bedtime story.

"…and then," Ulu concluded their bedtime story in a festive manner; "the King glanced at him and said, *Well, my prince, you have demonstrated your loyalty to me. From now on you shall reside in my palace, eat of my bread and drink of my wine. You shall remain close to me forevermore.*"

Dorianne said, "I love your beautiful stories of the Ancient Progeny, Father, but have you ever seen them?!"

"Tell us," added Shaii.

Ulu smiled, "Now you must sleep. Tomorrow I shall tell you more. There are thousands of wondrous stories about the Kingdom of the Ancient Progeny."

Ulu entered the large living room, and allowed himself the luxury of relaxing on his comfortable, soft chair. The pleasant evening events offered only a temporary distraction for Ulu. Now his thoughts returned to the sharply contrasting, serious events occurring beyond King's Valley. Eyes closed and deep in thought, he was unaware of his wife's gentle presence. She sat down next to him and whispered his name. Her voice brought him back to reality. Opening his eyes, he gazed at her. Even before they were married, she had known that he had been chosen to serve the Chamber. Even back then there were rumors about dangerous developments in the Land of the Green Lowlands, although these vague rumors seemed far away. She understood the risks her husband would be exposed to but she appreciated the extraordinary qualities and abilities which he possessed.

"I know that you are destined for an important mission," she had said back then, "but promise me that you will share everything with me!"

Ulu could not disclose his secret knowledge to her, but he had shared some of the details of his training in the White Desert. They had also talked about the persistent rumors of an impending war. Like most of the villagers, Ulu's wife was unconcerned about these rumors.

No one is interested in the villagers, she would say with indifference whenever the matter arose. *Why would anyone threaten our peaceful life? But, I do feel a vague sense of trepidation*, she would say, without consciously knowing why. With her sharp senses, she felt many things were changing in the world. The weather had become stormier over the past few years. The animals had become increasingly restless, and people tended to remain more and more in their homes. There was a general feeling that something was coming, but no one seemed to be able to define it. Although she worried about her husband's fate, she admired his brave participation in the great struggle beyond King's Valley.

Now Ulu looked deeply into his wife's eyes and announced, "I have seen the purple clouds."

Her eyes filled with wonder. She knew about the Light of the Transcendor, the source of the great power of the Warriors of Transcendence.

A warrior who begins to see the purple clouds, he had once explained, *reaches a place from which he may encounter the Light of the Transcendor.*

In the darkness, the candles flickered, the dreaming children slept, and Ulu and his wife sat in silence together, contemplating Ulu's extraordinary experience with the purple clouds.

"The Light of the Transcendor is revealed solely to those who can face the darkness bravely," Ulu explained. "All the evil in the world comes into being when entities are separated from their original form. The Light of the Transcendor causes all illuminated entities to return to their original form; the primal form in which they existed prior to any distortion or slanting. Consequently, evil is destroyed and only goodness remains in those who receive the light."

"Who is entitled to use this light?" she inquired, "and why do you fear its presence?" Ulu had expected to encounter difficulties as he attempted to conceal his true emotions from his wife, but her perception was so clear, she saw through his bravado. Had she discovered his fear of the Light of the Transcendor? For a moment he was silent, ashamed. Deep in thought, he answered softly, apologetically, "We have all distanced ourselves from the Source. We all hold inaccurate perceptions. Dark elements invade our thoughts. We are particularly prone to arrogance which causes us to feel separate and superior to others. This is considered a deep inner slanting."

"And so?" Ulu's wife did not quite comprehend his words.

"To summon the Light of the Transcendor, the Warriors of Transcendence must return to their most primal selves, the state of pure childhood. A warrior, who is not completely pure, is in danger of being harmed by the light. Excess, negative elements, waste elements like despair and arrogance need to be peeled off."

"Is that a painful process?" she asked, her understanding increasing.

"It can kill!" Ulu replied. In the silence that ensued, Ulu's wife tried to collect her thoughts. She arose from her chair and opened the window. For some time she gazed into the distant blackness, then turned back to face Ulu, her words bright and luminous.

"I know you. You possess sufficient purity. You shall not die."

Once again, silence prevailed.

"This time, our separation will be prolonged," said Ulu. "The Warriors know that something new is coming. The Emperors seem to be restless. The Tower Inviewers are beginning to appear in many places and they may have plans to begin an invasion of the villages."

"But why? Why were you chosen?" her voice faltered

"I am not the only one, my beloved," said Ulu, "The Master of Transcendence has called for my participation. I must be there."

She was silent. There? She did not ask Ulu to explain as she knew the answer would not be forthcoming.

"Are there many warriors serving the Master of Transcendence and fighting his wars?" she inquired, still yearning for understanding.

Ulu was quiet for some time.

"It is difficult to say," he finally replied. "The Master of Transcendence has men scattered in many places, fulfilling various tasks. Usually they are concealed, as I am. He alone knows our identities and our missions. The Master of Transcendence is served by many men, but the vast multitudes are ignorant of his existence."

She remained silent.

Ulu took this opportunity to inquire about the children's strange game.

"In some unclear way, things are being revealed to them," she began explaining.

"A stranger has visited the village recently. Maybe he is responsible for their new activities."

The dog arose from his resting place, shivered, and began wandering around the room restlessly.

"A stranger?" inquired Ulu. "Who is he? What can you tell me about him? Was there something odd in his behavior?"

"I do not know. Most of us assumed he was one of the toy merchants who visit the village each year."

"And you, what do you think?"

She caressed her face, as if trying to erase something. She closed her eyes for a moment, in an attempt to concentrate her thoughts, and said, "Although he wore light blue garb, I sensed that this was not his usual attire. He was tall. He walked slowly, his face was gaunt and his speech was impaired. He conversed mostly with the children. No one questioned his identity or presence, and after just one day he vanished."

Ulu was quiet, and his wife became embarrassed by his silence. Intuitively, he gazed towards the children's room. Is he worried about Saag? she wondered. The girls were too young to be drawn into a stranger's conversation, but Saag, already twelve, may have spoken with the stranger.

"Please explain to me," she said, changing the subject, "What prevents the Descendents of the Emperors from over-running all of the villages?"

"What a terrible loss of our beloved land that would be!" he replied.

"You must be joking!" she exclaimed. "Surely you do not believe that this is what interests them!"

"Yes, I do," Ulu insisted. "They are not interested in the beauty of our land, but only in its agricultural potential. They lack fertile land and want our blessed earth to serve their needs for food, provisions for the impure Tower."

"If the villages fall into their hands, they will become the masters of our bountiful land!"

"Yes," answered Ulu, "but they also desire the workforce, the thousands of villagers adept at agriculture and fishing, to continue working and sending the produce to the Tower. It is so simple..."

"What is so simple about it?" she said, infuriated. "Who would want to relinquish their freedom and work for them?"

"At the moment," he answered sadly, "very few. But as obliterations increase, and desire to belong to the Tower becomes a strong force in the hearts of many, a dynasty will be created. Why waste resources and weapons in order to conquer bodies, when it is simpler to conquer minds?"

Her face turned pale.

"Are you saying that they plan to turn us all into their slaves?"

Ulu nodded.

"Then how do you explain the rumors that are whispered around the village, about the Emperors' fear of the Master of Transcendence?"

"This story has been purposely created by the Obliterators and their adherents," said Ulu in anguish. "The Master of

Transcendence can appear in any place, not only in the villages. Their objective is to promote a false sense of safety and security amongst the villagers, so they have promoted this ridiculous idea that the Emperors are afraid to enter the villages. The same is true in reference to the Obliterator. In truth, were they to appear, the villagers would be defenseless. A gradual and covert conquest is more efficient for the Emperors. A military conquest would create a bitter, antagonistic situation leading to rebellion. Rebellious warriors would arise, capable of executing daring missions. The Descendents of the Emperors want to avoid this just as they want to avoid encounters with the Storm Dancers from the Northern Forests. A military conquest would certainly seem to take less time but the Descendents of the Emperors are very patient. They are in no hurry. Tomorrow, I shall talk with Saag," he returned to the original topic, as his wife lowered her head.

The following day, after lunch, Ulu and his son went out together. On wide paths, bordered by smooth stones, they strolled toward the shore. A cluster of boulders protruded from the sea close to the shore. Father and son carefully made their way past the sharp rocks that held many hidden tide-pools. Beyond the area of the boulders the water became deeper and darker, but the weather was comfortable, and they swam out into the sea. Saag displayed his strength, showing off his diving skills to his father.

"I hope you don't spend time here without me," said Ulu.

It was common knowledge that this spot was dangerous, and many young villagers had lost their lives in daring deep-sea swimming competitions and by diving into the narrow underwater tunnels formed by the boulders.

"Of course not, Father, you know I don't belong to Tzalaii's gang."

Tzalaii was a young man of nineteen, handsome and witty. But he had been adversely affected by his childhood as an orphan.

Although the village chief himself had taken him into his home, along with his sister Sihara, Tzalaii had a restless spirit. He became the head of a gang, comprised of boys his age and younger, who were attracted to the boulders and the stunts that could be performed there. Ulu became uneasy upon hearing Tzalaii's name. Saag wrongly guessed that his father's unease was related to the feats of courage the boys performed in this dangerous spot. But that was not the only reason for Ulu's anxiety. Each time Ulu saw the gang leader, he feared in his heart for Tzalaii's fate, foreseeing an ominous future event.

The sun was setting on the water. Small waves gently touched the shore. Ulu and Saag sat quietly, watching the sea as it took on a turquoise hue. They felt a sense of closeness and tranquility and both were deep in thought. Saag's widely-spaced eyes were large, always pondering the world, always curious. In contrast to his father, who was stocky and slow-moving, Saag was thin and his movements were rapid. He always seemed to be chasing after something. His mind, like his father's, was inquisitive, demanding and alert. He, like his father, always sought a deep understanding of situations and events. But in contrast to his father, who was often silent, Saag's speech was animated and excited and he preferred to share his thoughts with anyone who would listen

Ulu did not know how to approach the topic of concern. Had a stranger influenced his son? For now, the mystery remained unsolved. Saag had made no mention of a stranger and he continued to speak of childish thoughts and events.

The world was tinted red-orange as the day came to an end. They arose from the sand and started towards their home. Ulu began to think that all was well, his fears unfounded, but just then Saag gazed at the reddening sky and smiled strangely.

"That is the same exact color as the flames," he said. Ulu stopped walking, coming to a halt with a jolt.

"What did you say?" exclaimed Ulu loudly, mindlessly grasping his son's hand very tightly.

"Father, you are hurting me!" said the boy.

Ulu regained control of his responses, and repeated his question in a calmer tone, "I'm sorry...what did you say?"
"All I said was that the flames were the same exact color. Such beautiful, gentle flames, and they were embroidered upon the shoulder of a man's clothing. I alone noticed the flames," he said with childish pride, triumphantly, "because he wore a blue cloak, like ours."

Ulu chose his words wisely. He knew he had to maximize this opportunity without startling the child.

"Who is this man you saw, my beloved son?" he inquired calmly while sweat began to dampen the back of his neck.

"The funny, tall man who visited the village. He had a strange way of speaking."

"Did he speak to you?" asked Ulu.

"Sure, he asked lots of questions."

"What did he ask?" inquired Ulu, sensing that his suspicions were correct. His son had encountered an Obliterator. Now he was sure of it.

"Well, he asked what colors I am fond of, and which musical instruments I can play." Ulu's voice roughened, "Did he give you anything?"

The child, feeling a bit guilty, was offended by his father's tone.

"Yes, he did. But what of it?" He removed a small wooden cube from his pocket, and showed it to his father. "The man told me this is a game used for expanding the mind."

Ulu forced himself to handle the cube without betraying his anxiety. He noticed the engraved shapes and saw that each side contained a different image. Etched into one side were three warriors armed with swords. Various other warriors and animals were etched on the other sides, including an etching of a lone spider.

"Do you know how to use it?" asked Ulu, casually.

"It is very simple," answered the boy, his eyes gleaming. "One must concentrate on a certain image. This spider, for instance," he said, and pointed at the despised insect. "If it is done properly, the image 'jumps' into a different square. Each time an image enters a new part of the cube, there is a war between the images. Some 'jump' into other squares and some vanish."

"And what is the ultimate goal?" inquired Ulu.

Saag explained, "When all of the images disappear and only the spider remains, the game is over."

Ulu guessed that this game was similar to the *Game of Forces* played in the Tower. He did not know the actual goals of the game, but was sure of one thing. The goals were not what his son mistakenly believed them to be...

"I will keep this for now," Ulu said, and placed the cube in the pocket of his cape. The child began to object, but the stern look in his father's eyes rendered him powerless to protest. Saag simply did not understand what all the fuss was about.

A distant memory suddenly flashed through Ulu's mind. Why did this thought come to him now? He did not know. But this recollection served to further dishearten his spirits.

He recalled a childhood friend named Tyklah. *The men from the Chamber of Changing Colors had chosen Tyklah and Ulu for initiation training as Warriors of Transcendence, but Tyklah was always overly satisfied with himself, pretending to learn more quickly than others, to understand more than he really did. Eventually, he abandoned his studies and disappeared. Rumors were spread about him, alluding to his misusage of the knowledge which had been entrusted to him. He was even suspected of sharing it with the enemy.*

The thought of his enemies brought Ulu back to reality. His heart filled with somber fears. He knew, without a doubt, that someone had touched the heart of his firstborn son, and had planted in him the seeds of retribution. The stranger or another enemy agent could appear and cause more trouble in the future.

As they came closer to their home, a new thought came into Ulu's mind. He realized that in light of this imminent possibility, he would have to take Saag with him on his next journey. Although he was planning to go beyond the borders of the Land of Green Lowlands, where Saag's life would be in danger, they would at least be together, and Ulu would be able to protect him from harm.

I cannot allow myself, he thought, *to leave Saag in the village, exposed and vulnerable to those damnable Obliterators.*

That night, Ulu prepared himself for Unification. He wrapped himself in a warm cape and descended to the sea shore, walking on the sand towards the village border. The air was cool and the stars seemed to be very far away. A pale moon shed silver rays upon the earth. Ulu stopped, sat down upon the sand, rested his head between his knees and sighed.

"Should I take Saag or shouldn't I?" He began with a question, with no prior introduction, "Do I take him or not?"

A gust of wind blew in from the sea, causing his hair to become disheveled.

"I need guidance. I don't know what to do. He is so young, but I am afraid I have no choice…" He noticed that his words were jumbled.

He placed his hands on his face in an attempt to concentrate his thoughts, and tried to sort out his words.

"The stranger who visited the village…" he said, and his voice weakened. "Saag is my son, my beloved! I have no other. They touched him, and I must protect him! He is my very own, my son. "Saag," he said, "Saag…Saag…"

He arose from the sands and continued walking along the shore. More at ease now, he was able to find the proper words in his heart.

"Please help me! There is no one in the world but You who can help me! I feel compelled to take Saag with me. I feel I have no choice. I must protect him. Am I doing the right thing? Please give me a sign!"

A faint cloud covered the moonlight. Ulu shuddered.

"And what choice have I?" he asked, "To leave him behind in the village and wait for one of them to simply show up and take him away?"

It is riskier than you think, a thought arose in his mind.

He did not know whether this thought was his own or possibly an answer from the Transcendor.

He must be trained, his thoughts continued, and Ulu questioned himself. *How can I take a young boy to the White Desert?*

The Light of the Transcendor shall protect you Ulu felt in his heart, and he realized that these thoughts were his own and not from the Transcendor.

"Give me a sign!" he repeated his plea, refusing to accept the night's obscurity as the answer to his question.

The night remained silent. Ulu understood that the sadness which pervaded his thoughts had prevented his proper Unification.

Chapter Three

The Wall

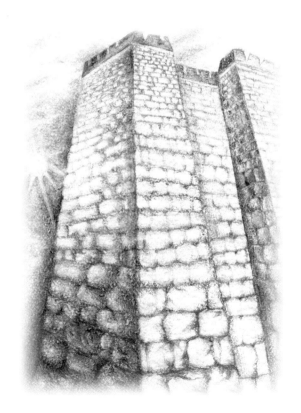

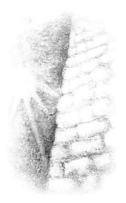

The Wall

Tzalaii descended the Southern slopes of the Northern Forests. He was tall and thin, with hair as dark as a winter night and eyes like a curious child. As he walked, he recalled the fateful conversation that had propelled him to set out on this lonely and perilous journey, which would take him many weeks' distance from his village by the sea. His mind traveled back in time to the day he had allowed himself to take this daring step into the unknown.

The members of his gang had gathered, as usual, by the beach, that fateful day, close to the stand of boulders which protruded from the sea. Some of them idly cast small stones into the water; others relaxed in the sand or etched meaningless drawings in it. They were all awaiting Tzalaii's return from his dive, down below, in the great water tunnel under the rocks. And then Tzalaii emerged, out of breath, though smiling triumphantly at the approval of his admirers. One of them, a boy much stronger than Tzalaii and always envious of his leader's achievements, spoke up boastfully. "It's no great feat to swim through that tunnel." At once all the boys laughed at his comment for it was quite clear that this was, in fact, a dangerous feat that required courage. Only Tzalaii was capable of successfully executing this stunt time and time again. Realizing his foolishness, the envious boy reddened in embarrassment as he tried to correct his error.

"No, of course it is very difficult. But still, it is just a childish stunt, not a truly brave act."

All were silent and looked toward Tzalaii who was sitting in the sand.

"Well, my friend," Tzalaii retorted confidently, "what is, in your opinion, a truly brave act; one that is not child's play?"

"A brave act entails a journey to a truly dangerous place, such as the Green Lowlands."

Everyone gasped in fear, suddenly confronted by something seriously and enormously terrifying. This conversation no longer sounded like playful, innocent banter.

But Tzalaii was not frightened. "And what, in your opinion, must one do there?" he asked.

"A particularly brave feat," the boy suggested. "This feat alone can prove a person's bravery."

"Like what, for instance?" Tzalaii asked, his interest awakened.

"For instance," he paused for a moment, "touching the wall that surrounds the Towered City."

This was going too far. Very few villagers ever mentioned the Towered City. Even fewer knew of the dangers lurking in the Green Lowlands. The boy was brazenly and publicly challenging Tzalaii to go there and to touch the wall.

Passionate, furious voices arose from amongst the gang members. The envious boy almost rescinded his dare, but Tzalaii calmed the assembly.

"It would be the most daring feat ever attempted by a villager," he said.

"And the dumbest," added one of the members, though he was quickly silenced by the others.

"I'll do it!" announced Tzalaii with certainty.

"But how will we know you speak the truth?" asked the envious boy.

"Maybe you should bring one of the guards back to testify," he added jokingly. Tzalaii remembered the Magnathought Crystal, and replied in a serious tone, "Would a shard of the wall serve as sufficient proof?"

Motivated by his friends' approval and praise, Tzalaii accepted the challenge of this reckless dare, a seemingly impossible feat which he had never previously considered. Now as he journeyed toward his quest, his doubts and fears surfaced.

He would often yearn to return home, but then he would imagine the eager faces of those anticipating his glorious return, and this vision compelled him to continue on his self-appointed mission. Many long days filled with anxiety and doubt had passed since he had ascended the tall cliffs surrounding the Valley of the King. Now, descending the eastern slopes, he knew that each step brought him closer to the Towered City.

From a distance, the City appeared as an enormous motionless beast, and the gleaming light reflecting from its windows looked like the multiple eyes of some mythological beast awaiting its prey. The great wall concealed only the base level; six additional levels soared above it.

A pale ray of light was rolling in from the east, slowly filling the skyline. The light illuminated the outline of the valley revealing scattered trees and structures, lying in disarray, in the lowlands surrounding the great City. As the sun rose, the lights in the windows faded. A vast and irksome darkness emerged from the Tower, and seemed to descend into the entire valley. Its tentacles reached the mountain slopes, driving fear into Tzalaii's heart.

Where will my legs carry me this morning? he asked himself, trying to convince himself that this journey would not be difficult. The sound of galloping hooves cut his thoughts short. Five shaven-headed horsemen, wearing dark leather attire, and sitting as upright as swords, appeared in his path, their black horses boasting the same might as their riders.

"Identify yourself!" called one of the horsemen.

The others surrounded him, confident of their strength as they questioned this insignificant passerby. Frightened yet sure of the answer he must give, Tzalaii pointed towards the mountain tops as if to indicate: "I have come from there."

"He is not marked!" announced one of the horsemen.

Like all villagers, Tzalaii wore a blue garment, devoid of a flame. And so, it was obvious that he was not one of the residents of the Tower. The horses came closer to Tzalaii but the five horsemen seemed calm and somewhat amused. This was to be an easy kill, with no risk involved. The soldier closest to Tzalaii turned to him with words that were surprisingly soft and soothing.

"The center of strength, granting goodness to us all," he said, while pointing south, "lies in this valley."

The shaven-headed soldiers murmured in agreement.

"There, in the great chamber, the holy fire is revealed; Messenger of the ancient sun, root of all strength."

A tense silence filled the air, as all awaited the words which would transform Tzalaii into an altered being.

The holy fire, root of all strength... Tzalaii considered these words. An unsettling vision permeated his consciousness. He envisioned himself as a horseman in shiny leather garb, holding the reins of a mighty black stallion, and galloping off into the distance.

The whinny of one of the impatient horses, forced to wait, disturbed his reverie. Tzalaii once again focused on the erect, poised riders, and from deep within, he sensed silent warnings. He felt trapped as though an obscure, spider-like web was holding him against his will. Fear rose in his throat. Did he have a way out? He was untrained in battle. Showing off his strength to his young admirers, his gang, had not prepared him in any way for confrontation with a serious rival.

Suddenly his hand, as if moving on its own, reached into his satchel, extracting a gleaming Crystal. A ray of light momentarily passed through it, illuminating its fine interior wooden sketches. Tzalaii, gathering his thoughts, attempted to focus on the object in his hand. The strength of his spirit was enhanced by the ever increasing fear he felt, and he struggled to produce the image of a flame in his mind. The Magnathought Crystal began to heat up, and his hand began to tremble. The warriors, gazing at the object in Tzalaii's hands, came closer, causing Tzalaii to become enraged. He had managed to disregard the words spoken by these Obliterators, but now he felt foolish trying to use this weapon against them.

Tzalaii became increasingly courageous. He concentrated with all of his might, and a narrow, blue flame emerged from the crystal, surrounding it in a threadlike manner. The horses whinnied and recoiled; the warriors retreated. "A Warrior of Transcendence!" exclaimed one of horsemen, taken aback. Tzalaii took advantage of their embarrassment and escaped into the depth of the woods. The blue flame continued to serve as a shield between him and the horsemen. He could hear their howls of fury at the loss of their intended victim. Eventually, their voices died down and Tzalaii wondered if the fire he had created had actually harmed his assailants.

Finally, after what seemed like an eternity, he felt safe and came to a halt. Here, the foliage was dense. Tzalaii knew that the horses would be unable to enter through the thick vegetation. He allowed himself to rest on a pile of damp leaves, stroking the crystal that he still grasped tightly, and breathing more easily.

"Indeed," he thought, "facing the enemy was not so difficult."

He straightened out his blue cape, overcame his remaining fear and turned back towards the valley. Now he chose a different path, farther east. From here he would make his way through the trees on unmarked trails. Hidden by the bleak woods, he descended the final slopes. All was still, and the silence calmed his spirit. He must continue to prove his strength in order to impress his admirers.

He spent the day sleeping in a field of tall cane plants. He awoke towards evening, devoured the little food he possessed, and packed his bag with red fruit from the field. The taste was bitter, but he felt astonishingly invigorated and refreshed. After eating, Tzalaii resumed his journey.

On the fourth night, he sited a massive wall softly illuminated by the moon. The closer he got, the more astounded he became by its size. The wall seemed to have no end. He was becoming consumed by exhaustion, and sadness began to enter his heart in the face of the looming force.

If this is only the protective wall of the Towered City, he pondered, *how much stronger are its inhabitants!*

But he continued to make his way towards his destination, as if an ancient command directed him and kept him on his course. No mindless nor childish thought would deter him from his mission now. These were the buds of royalty. Slumbering, ancient threads of a calling.

As Tzalaii approached the wall, a strange feeling permeated his existence. He had the odd impression that the wall was observing him, or maybe he was being observed through the wall? A dim, weak light momentarily flashed through the massive stones, crimson-yellow. As if bewitched, Tzalaii reached out his hand to touch the wall. It was cold and damp. Overwhelmed by curiosity, he stroked the wall as if he were taming a wild animal. Was it just his imagination fooling him, or could he really sense heat emanating from the wall into his hand? Once again he removed the blue Crystal from his satchel. The golden ornamental strip was hot, as if used only a moment ago, and Tzalaii wondered about this. He gazed at the shiny blue object in his hand, and noticed for the first time since it had fallen at his side, that the carved wooden etchings were fully illuminated. To his surprise, he found no difficulty in focusing his thoughts, almost as if someone else had focused them for him. He aimed the Crystal towards the smooth wall and heat was transferred into his hand and throughout his body. The broad wall, protecting the unconquerable Towered City, had cracked! A small crack, but nevertheless one which enabled Tzalaii to break off a shard of crimson-yellow stone, and conceal it in his satchel.

The night grew dark, and Tzalaii felt a heaviness overtake him, and he once again became fearful. He still felt as though someone from beyond the Tower was observing him mockingly; as if he were a tiny mosquito challenging a mighty lion. He imagined the lion stomping on him effortlessly. Tzalaii grasped his satchel tightly and began his escape. From what, he did not know. Hours later, upon arriving at a large overgrown field, he finally fell to the ground, weeping. The magic had faded. He remained a lonely, frightened boy, deep in the heart of a foreign, hostile land.

Once again, he traveled at night. During the day he slept in overgrown fields, fed on vegetation and drank from exposed pools of water. Once, while looking through his satchel, he came upon a small loaf, baked by his sister, Sihara. He was overcome by yearning for home. He would not be able to share this adventure with her, she would certainly not relate to it as an act of courage.

Finally, after a ten day trek, he found himself in the familiar, protective, forested slopes, and for the first time he dared to look back. Silence permeated the valley. The morning fog ascended from the fields and a cool breeze accompanied the waves of the green sea. The wall was out of the range of his vision. Had his experiences been just a figment of his imagination? For a moment he felt ashamed of his childish escape and strange reactions. He opened his satchel and peered inside. A crimson-yellow shard lay there, perched next to the blue Magnathought Crystal.

Chapter Four

The Memory Shield

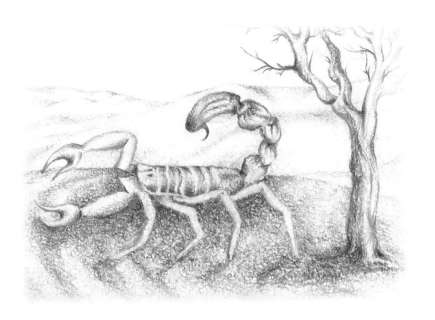

The Memory Shield

For many days, Ulu waited for a sign. Finally, one evening, as he sat by the sea watching the waves roll in, he sensed a familiar luminous Transparent One standing by his side. "It is time," said the Transparent One, with urgency. "They are waiting for you in the White Desert." He remained nearby for a long instant, as if transferring strength into Ulu, and then he disappeared. Ulu was left in the sand, deep in thought.

According to legend, the desert did not always exist. Many years ago, the desolate region was full of life. Evergreen forests flourished full of wild birds and animals. Rivers flowed, gardens and orchards bloomed, and the sunlight was bright and pleasant. Now it had become a vast White Desert, eerily silent and devoid of life... No one desired to cross the vast barren region leading to the Valley of the Shadows and to the scorching slopes of Fire Mountain. Wild beasts inhabited the depths of the white sand dunes, white scorpions as large as donkeys and enormous white snakes. Even the Shadows resided in the desert.

Shadows!

The mere thought of them reminded Ulu of his first encounter with them, years ago. His mind traveled back to a time when he viewed the borders of the Green Lowlands, watching, from a distance, as a group of men harvested the Fruits of Oblivion. Suddenly, for no apparent reason, he had experienced a feeling of discomfort. He glanced behind him and noticed smoke rising from the hill he had descended. This was peculiar, as no one had been there earlier, and the Descendents of the Emperors were unlikely to cease their work in the middle of the day to build a fire.

Ulu felt tense and searched for a hiding place. But when he turned again to face the smoke he realized that its height had diminished, and the remainder was now close to the ground, expanding and crawling towards the slopes, as if it were a living being, pursuing him. Ulu, at that time, was unaware that a Cloud Shadow was making its way towards him. His entire body became weary so he sat down to rest amidst the trees.

The approaching cloud appeared as a long, thin layer of fog hovering over the land. The Cloud Shadows would typically appear in clusters, clearing the ground for more dangerous Shadows or warriors departing for battle. But fortunately, this Cloud Shadow was alone. Suddenly, the sound of trumpets was heard from the Valley, summoning the harvesters to assemble in the City. The Cloud Shadow, assuming that he was being summoned as well, halted his search, and began to ascend and creep towards the City. Only then, when Ulu recovered his strength and his clarity, did he understand what had been pursuing him.

There were four types of Shadows known to man, but Ulu had seldom encountered any, and he lacked the skill to combat them. They were, in order of descending strength: Shadows of Illusion, Shadows of Fire, Cloud Shadows and Shadows of Light. The Shadows of Illusion were tall and thin, dark and fast. They usually wore gray capes; their faces were hollow and blank, almost expressionless.

They knew how to alter their forms and disguise themselves as humans, Transparent Ones or any other form they desired. The Whistle dialect, used by all other Shadows, was only one of the many languages they spoke; they were fluent in every language spoken in the Land of the Ancient Progeny, with the exception of the language of man. Their methods were cruel. With the use of deception, disguise and erratic behavioral shifts, they created confusion and doubt in those they encountered. The Shadows were unidentifiable and made use of this quality in order to seize the souls of their confused victims intensifying their doubts, until the hapless souls questioned their own existence, losing their minds and becoming slaves of the Shadows forever, until death.

The Shadows of Fire, with their red skin and dark capes, appeared as humans. They, too, were fast, but made no sudden movements. They had to gradually gain momentum before they could pick up speed and begin to move rapidly. When they attacked they located the natural center of warmth in their victim, and intensified it. They circled around each other in the form of spools of red and blue fire, and if their victims were unable to defend themselves the heat would cause them to dry up, with the spools of fire continuing to hover over their parched bodies.

The Cloud Shadows were large and heavy, as formless and as dense as fog. Slower than the others, they lacked the power to kill, though they had an affect on their victims even from afar. Those caught in their net would easily fall into the hands of the other Shadows, or warriors of the Towered City. The Cloud Shadows, besides having the ability to blur visibility, were able to create weakness and fatigue, even paralysis, in all who gazed at them. Recovery from paralysis was impossible.

The Shadows of Light were the smallest of all. They were shorter then men, had humanlike features and dressed in yellow garb, a light glistening from within. Their power was activated by those who gazed at them for a prolonged time. They would penetrate their light into their victims, blinding those who did not have the fortitude to escape rapidly.

All Shadows shared some common attributes: They were disloyal to each other, fearful of direct light and preferred nocturnal activity. Most of them resided in caves, crevices and hidden places in the mountains, mainly the Southern Mountains, which lacked plant growth. Their existence depended upon their ability to paralyze the growth centers in those they encountered, and they, therefore, despised all living organisms.

Ulu, still immersed in his memories, recalled that shortly after his encounter with the Cloud Shadow, he had departed for his desert training. He had walked for many weeks until he finally reached the White Desert. As he walked, the days became increasingly hot and windy, and the nights grew colder. Surprisingly, he felt no fear, only an ever increasing inner excitement. Thoughts of his ominous destination were countered by confidence that he would find Warriors of Transcendence along the way.

"Welcome!" a voice resonated.

A tall, charming creature appeared. His hair was light blond, his eyes deep and radiant. He wore a golden cape, light and airy. Visible through his cape, his human form was illuminated by an inner blue flame. It swayed in dance-like movements, and its color varied and occasionally turned lighter and livelier. Ulu recognized this creature as a Transparent One! He remembered that Transparent Ones, although not human, are creations of man's spirit and products of his thoughts. There are transparent children and transparent adults, but there are no elderly. He had learned that more would be revealed to him in time to come.

Ulu knew that the Transparent Ones gained strength and encouragement from humans, and that humans, in turn, obtained joy and vitality from them. They were fond of poetry and legend and their simple proverbs were known far and wide, though few knew of their true origin. Their existence and life span depended on their creator, though they continued to exist even after their creator perished. Nevertheless, if the inner will of its living creator were to be lost, the Transparent One would shrivel up and expire.

The hand of the cheerful Transparent One reached out to Ulu in peace. Ulu followed his lead to the desert, and together they walked towards the scorching terrain. A wondrous sunset shed its hue upon the sand, giving the exposed sand dunes a mysterious golden appearance. The weather remained mercifully calm for another hour before nightfall, when a cold frost covered everything in its path. The Transparent One told Ulu in detail about the white snakes and scorpions, and the dangers they posed.

"Because you are a man of borders, I am allowed to divulge to you that the Transcendor has appeared just once in this desert."

The Transparent One arose, shook off the sand that had accumulated on his cape, gently stroked Ulu's cheek and said: "We need you, and others like you. May the blessing of the Transcendor be upon you."

Ulu watched as the vanishing Transparent One's inner light slowly disappeared into the distance.

An inner voice advised him to arise. He gathered his cape, wrapped it around himself, and continued walking into the heart of the desert. The desert was so flat and the night so dark, land and sky seemed to merge together as one entity. A perpetual blackness filled his view as he traveled through a seemingly empty void.

Some time passed. Finally, Ulu sited a light in the distance. As he approached the light, he witnessed an astonishing phenomenon. Beams of light created a circle in the desert. A man stood within the dim light, surrounded by massive white scorpions with raised stingers. They were as large as donkeys but Ulu was not fearful of them, and watched the scene as if he were peering through a glass window into a different world. The scorpions were preparing to kill their victim! They encircled him with their venomous tails lifted in the air; their stingers, facing the center of the circle where the man stood.

Will he not defend himself? wondered Ulu. Upon further observation, Ulu realized that the unfortunate man was paralyzed with fear. The white circle was closing in, and it was too late for escape. The man's sorrow dissolved the glass wall separating him from Ulu. Without hesitation, without a thought of danger, without a plan, Ulu dashed forward, determined to rescue the hapless victim from a cruel and terrible death.

As Ulu rushed toward the luminous scene, the scorpions sensed his presence. The venomous circle was severed and they now stood in a row making their way towards him. *Why did they prefer to attack him? Why had they abandoned their original victim? A chill ran down his spine and his determination weakened. Why had he exposed himself? What should he do now?* The man remained paralyzed in place, like an inanimate object and Ulu wondered for a moment if he were indeed real. The scorpions continued to approach, their tails raised threateningly. *Borders* whispered an inner voice. What did borders have anything to do with his condition? He became annoyed at the voice in his head. His hands and legs felt paralyzed, and he wondered if the scorpions were responsible for this sensation. Did the scorpions have the power to paralyze their victims from afar?

The scorpions formed a closed circle around him, and when they were close enough to touch him, he once again heard the inner voice repeating the word *Borders*. With strength from an unknown source Ulu removed a staff from his satchel. As if guided by an invisible hand, he touched the staff to the sand, and drew a circle around himself. The moment the circle was completed, Ulu's terror dissipated. His lungs filled with air and suddenly the scorpions looked like creatures in an imaginary drawing. Death, which had clutched his soul and stared him in the face, had suddenly vanished and Ulu was once again amongst the living. The original victim had somehow disappeared, as if he had never even existed. Ulu hoped that the battle was over.

His body trembled as his entire being surrendered to fatigue and weakness. His arms fell to his sides and he breathed deeply, letting out a sigh of relief.

But the battle was not yet over.

Snakes, glaringly white, appeared from within the darkness of the desert. Mounds of sand spilled over on all sides of the writhing serpents, leaving behind deep gorges, as though they had been created by oversized pitchforks. Ulu did not wait for the serpents to reach him. He immediately knelt in his circle and raised his hands to the heavens.

In this desert, he recalled the words spoken to him by the Transparent One, *the Transcendor appeared just once.*

It was clear to the man of borders that beyond all doubt, this was his only hope to survive the threat he now faced.

A warrior of Transcendence replaces fear with light.

Ulu remembered what he learned long ago in the distant Chamber. Words, and parts of words floated into his frightened consciousness, as the serpents came closer, surrounding him, as he knelt in the sand.

"Transcendor," he finally managed to utter a single word.

An enormous snake approached him, opening its large mouth, prepared to devour him. Ulu looked away from the serpent and shut his eyes. His inner world was his border and the frightful sights could no longer enter his circle. His body still trembled, but with his eyes closed he was able to control his thoughts. The memory of the Master of Transcendence arose in his mind. Relieved by this memory, he was able to focus his powers of concentration turning his thoughts toward his Memory Shield. The snakes still slithered around him, and he was aware of their presence and of the stench of death emanating from them. But the Memory Shield prevailed, and Ulu began Uniting. The letters of the Memory Shield, like illuminated strings, threaded into words, which together were tossed as a rescue line into the heavens.

"I am an insignificant creature. Destitute, frightened and helpless.

What is my strength? What is my might? What is my life when faced with the terror of the serpents and scorpions?"

These words, when spoken, instilled confidence in Ulu. He continued speaking, his words increasingly adorned with majestic splendor: "You create and destroy worlds, Your forms are many, but You are One."

Someone, deep within, was listening. Someone, deep within, replied.

Not with speech, but by touch. Not with words, but with a deep sense of certainty.

A new voice arose from his heart, grew mighty and reached his lips. Words never before spoken appeared in his mouth and streamed forth like sunlight. Ulu drew his words from this newfound source, expressing his innermost pleas: "Only in You… Only in You do I trust…Creator of worlds and the Source of all existence. Come, my sole Protector, watch over me and remain near me. Reveal Your light to me."

Purple clouds circled above. A silver string descended and revealed a light.

The terror ceased, and morning came. Ulu, drenched with perspiration, opened his eyes. No trace of the night's terrors remained in the white sands. Once again, all was clean and pure, as if the menacing beasts had never existed. Across from him, within his reach, sat the Master of Transcendence. His royal cape created an incredible contrast with the barren desert. Ulu gazed at the Master's widening smile and even the desert seemed more hospitable…even regal.

"My dear child," began the Master of Transcendence, "there are encounters in the Chamber and encounters in the desert, and each encounter beholds a secret. Each encounter has its own special significance. I regret that this is part of your training, but only this kind of experience can prepare you for having to face the threats of the Tower and its Obliterators."

Ulu covered his face with his hands and wept. The Master of Transcendence gazed at him for a long time.

Sometime later, Ulu finally recovered his composure. The Master of Transcendence gathered a handful of sand, letting some stream out to the ground, and said: "Draw a circle for me."

Ulu did as he was told. The Master of Transcendence pointed towards the circle and said: "Look."

Ulu could not fathom what had happened; the circle had completely vanished.

"Even a slight breeze can erase this circle," said the Master.

Ulu was surprised. "I thought there was no better protection than the circle…while inside, I knew with all certainty that there was no power in the world capable of harming me."

"The first time you use it, it gives you true protection. But the next time, you will trust it too much, which will cause it to weaken. It may protect you from other scorpions or various other creatures. But there is always the possibility that you will face the risk of encountering the same creature twice. This is a risk we cannot take."

Ulu felt himself weakening. Was everything he had learned the previous night worthless?

"So what must be done?" asked Ulu, exhausted.

"When you draw a circle," smiled his mentor, "even if it is exactly the same as the previous circle, you must draw as if you are doing it for the first time, as if you are unaware of its powers, as if you have never defended yourself nor won a single battle. You must draw a circle simply because this is what is essential: To create a strong boundary between yourself and the deceptions of your adversaries. And from within this boundary, you must remember your true strength."

Ulu gazed into the eyes of the Master, his heart bursting with happiness. His true strength, his guide and the source of his light, was sitting across from him. All he had to do was remember him.

"Yes, that's it," said the Master of Transcendence, as if responding to his thoughts. "You have access to your own Memory Shield, full of moments in which you experienced shades from my Chamber. These memories are brighter and stronger when inside the circle, but at times the Shadows may transform your protective circle into a prison from which you cannot escape. When the circle is detached from its source, the powerful sensations cease to flow through you into those in need, and instead the power becomes blocked and remains in your hands. At first you will assume that you have received a blessing, but later you will become trapped in the very same enchantment which has given you strength, and your every wish will be to remain in that state forevermore. In this way, the memories from your shield are detached, and you will be unable to recall them."

"Is it possible to forget the beauty of the Master of Transcendence?" Ulu pondered aloud.

"That occurred to one of our warriors, after having been trapped in his own circle. The strength erased all of his memories, allowing the Obliterators to enter his spirit. You may need to face him someday."

"Who can confront an obliterated Warrior of Transcendence?" questioned Ulu, a shiver running down his spine.

The Master of Transcendence approached him, touched his face, and said: "A single, special warrior."

Ulu knew that the Master was referring to him.

The Master continued. "But remember, one cannot feel hatred towards an obliterated Warrior of Transcendence…because he is still one of us! He just needs to be peeled."

Ulu's thoughts of the past ceased as he returned to the reality at hand. Sitting by the sea and recollecting past experiences, he was able to rid himself of his fearful thoughts. Strengthened by the memories of his fateful meeting with the Master, he noticed that the moon had risen, brightly illuminating the sea. He stood up heavily, regaining his equilibrium after re-living the heavy memories of his past, and made his way back home. Now he felt more capable of dealing with his anxieties, though fear still lingered deep in his heart. He still pondered the question: Should he take Saag with him?

Chapter Five

Legend of the Wings

Legend of the Wings

Mahn's presence was a source of controversy among the dwellers of the Steel Level. It was common knowledge that some of his family members served in the core of the Steel Level, and several had even been promoted to the Sapphire Level. Mahn's tasks and goals were confidential. He spent his time as an Inviewer, and spoke very little. His piercing eyes were always looking beyond the apparent. He was often seen observing soldiers as they lounged around the many local inns scattered throughout the village market by the inner Wall of Fog. Mahn seemed to be particularly interested in observing the soldiers' favorite pastime, the *Game of Forces*.

The *Game of Forces* was considered a popular game at the Tower. Every child knew the rules. On the upper levels, the game pieces were composed of the same substance as the outer wall, and their prices reached as high as fifty white coins. In contrast, on the Steel Level the game pieces were simply-made of wood and were worth just one or two red coins.

The game board was marked with one hundred and forty-seven checkerboard squares, most of them empty. Other squares contained images of a crater or a thorn branch. Each player started out with forty-nine pieces: Fifteen warriors shaped like sword carrying soldier pawns carrying arrow bags, ten WireArchers shaped like spiders, six Inviewers shaped like eagles, six Infiltrators shaped like chameleons, six Unifiers shaped like Octopi, five Extrappers shaped like foxes and one piece shaped like a serpent.

According to the rules of the game, each player in turn may position one piece and move a second piece anywhere on the board except on a crater or thorn square. The movement of the pieces on the board was confined to one square per direction. One piece could not be positioned without moving a second piece, nor could it be moved without being positioned.

A warrior could destroy an enemy piece only when joined with the power of five additional warriors, together forming two triangles positioned in the same direction. Alone, a warrior was useless.

A spider WireArcher could destroy an enemy piece from up to three squares away, when he was joined with the power of five additional WireArchers, together forming a crescent.

An eagle Inviewer could only function when in a square formation. Eagles could not destroy enemy pieces, though as long as they held their form, they had the power to protect all pieces in the surrounding twelve squares.

A chameleon Infiltrator could paralyze enemy pieces positioned diagonally up to five squares away.

The five fox Extrappers had the power to create additional craters and thorns when in a star formation, and block the advancement of enemy soldiers in their vicinity.

The Octopus Unifiers prevented the destruction of all surrounding formations and attacks in their vicinity. Only when the Unifier was attacked, did the formation become compromised.

The snake, called the 'head,' was the most important piece in the game. He was usually positioned in the headquarters. Once the 'head' was defeated, the game was over.

The *Game of Forces* required a high level of concentration and strategy. Also necessary were patience, endurance and awareness. Mahn was skilled in being able to identify a player's essence through observation of his strategic moves and gaming abilities. Long hours spent sitting by the dimly lit game tables watching the players, enabled Mahn to spot Obliterator-candidates possessed of an inner resistance to being totally obliterated. He was also able to identify potential candidates for high ranking warrior positions by using this method.

Mahn wandered the market streets near the inner Wall of Fog. Colorful stands displaying various foods and beverages obscured the stone floor. He observed three warriors from the Base Level sitting at a low round table, sipping fizzy, purple drinks, deeply focused on the game they were playing. They were surrounded by other warriors who enjoyed watching the game.

A heavyset man sitting at another table conversed loudly with his companion; both were noticeably drunk.

"I tell you, there is no war!" he shouted, banging his fists on the table, "The war ended five hundred years ago in total victory. The Towered City no longer has enemies; there are no longer battles or threats!"

"You are telling me? I am telling you! I keep telling you!" grumbled his friend, "We both know that soldiers are training for war everywhere. How do you explain that?"

"It's just training," replied the man, "but not for enemy encounters, because no enemies exist, except for the lowly villagers, weak as flies…Every army needs training, otherwise how would the warriors be prepared for the marches in the Lower City?"

A warrior, overhearing their conversation, approached them and said: "No one is capable of threatening the Towered City. No one has the power to invade its walls. Our City is heavily defended and more secure than you could ever imagine."

The warrior's words caused Mahn to feel uneasy. This was no ordinary warrior. The confidence with which his words were spoken resembled the bravado of the Obliterators. Why would it be necessary for an Obliterator to be present in the lower City market? His words, too, made Mahn wonder: *Why would a City with no fear of being attacked occupy itself so much with its defense? If no enemy exists- why is so much protection necessary?* He shook his head, trying to rid himself of his confusing thoughts and he continued walking.

The stench of sweat mingled with the aroma of drinks, perfume and healing herbs. A colorful array of edibles caught the attention of the passersby. Among the lively, crowded stands, Mahn noticed a smaller stand displaying healing potions and ground herbal powders. An old woman stood behind the counter, ready to examine, for a small fee, the faces of clients in order to reveal to them details about their lives and future events. Mahn detested those healer-fortune tellers, but this one caught his interest due to the unusual crowd she had attracted. Several shaven-headed soldiers in black uniform stood there listening. This sparked Mahn's curiosity, and he approached the stand as the pungent herbal scents enveloped him.

"I shall tell you about the termination of the Towered City," he heard the words of the old peddler before he could see her. Her voice, though weak, was clear. Mahn wondered how these old hags were allowed to carry on as they wished. It was true; they added an amusing aspect to the colorful market, entertaining the bored soldiers, but at what risk?! Upon hearing her words, the warriors burst into loud laughter. They tossed red bronze coins into a bowl in the center of the stand, and waited for her to continue.

The old woman chuckled, though Mahn observed that she was not laughing with them but at them, arrogant and full of confidence, as if she knew something they did not know. She shook her head, adorned in a reddish purple cloth, shut her eyes and quietly sang a song that seemed to come from her heart and not her lips: "White is open to all hues…Open and caressing…Listening to all discoveries…The foundation of all colors…Base for all hues… Wellspring of change…The link connecting all tints…Soaring above all…Gateway to the heavens…White."

The warriors stopped laughing. The old woman continued, unaware of whether or not she was being listened to.

"In a different time, above the water, One will arrive adorned in white, a man of the heart, in the heart of time."

The words struck Mahn like sharp knives piercing his skull. His sight suddenly blurred, and he felt himself falling into a deep abyss, plunging and crashing to its depths. He reached for a small chair situated by the stand, and sat down heavily. From within his inner silence the words sounded like trembling whispers, reaching him like blinding flashes of light. Mahn understood that for the first time in his life he was hearing the greatest secret of the universe. It was the *Legend of the Wings*. This same legend, whose mention was forbidden in the Tower, was now being publicly voiced by a fanatical old woman in the open market, and she faced no dispute or opposition. The aged woman described how the fire from the Tower would be extinguished and how its inhabitants would vanish. She described how the color of the sky would change and become purple and how, eventually, a great wave of water would cover the entire earth.

"Very few mortals will survive," she continued, "and those who survive will grow wings and hover over the waters."

These final peculiar words caused the warriors to lose interest and walk away.

Mahn found himself sitting across from her, overwhelmed and embarrassed. Why did he react so strongly to her words while the others lost interest? He looked towards the upper level of the Towered City. His spirit was comforted by his hopes to climb higher and higher, become taller, more powerful, all encompassing...An irritating feeling arose in him, darkening his consciousness, causing him to feel humiliated. There he was, Mahn the Senior Inviewer, sitting like a fool across from this old, self-centered and blabbering hag. What was she whispering? He was overcome with anger. Why was he destined to waste his time down below amidst rude warriors and blathering hags?

"Pure silver...clear as a tear," she whispered, as if comforted by her own words, as if they held rejuvenating powers. As if her future and the future of others was secreted and hidden within her words.

"Stop!" roared Mahn. He felt that he must stop the nonsense forcing itself into his mind.

"Arise and follow me!" he ordered, exposing the flame on his sleeve.

The old woman was not startled. She had become accustomed to suffering throughout her long life. Would this man take her life? No matter. Nothing of importance remained for her. She followed after him as a shadow, her teeth glistening through a peculiar smile, repeatedly mumbling her mysterious tune: "Pure silver...clear as a tear."

Even after delivering her to the Base Level Interrogators, and explaining her activities to them, he remained conflicted. What did he want from her? Seated in a corner of the darkened room and listening to the Inviewers' interrogation, Mahn felt increasingly uneasy.

"Why are you frightening people?" a robust warrior challenged the old woman, a small dagger in his hand.

It was obvious that conversation was not his favorite form of communication. Crouched in her corner, the old woman did not even bother to look his way. She sat there almost lifeless, only her head moving from side to side, as if busy solving a complex matter. Two additional interrogators attempted to communicate with her verbally, though their patience quickly waned.

A shrill whistle was heard in the room. The robust warrior had snapped a long, thin whip. Still the woman was not moved.

"Enough!" Mahn uttered, rising up from his seat.

They gazed at him dumbfounded: Why was he interrupting their work?

"Leave us alone," Mahn ordered authoritatively, "I will take it from here."

The three interrogators left the room unwillingly. Mahn remained with the old woman. In the dim light, her face looked more wrinkled and shriveled than it really was. He sat across from her and spoke to her as one human being to another: "Don't worry, grandmother, no harm shall come to you."

She remained crouched in her corner, motionless.

"Are you thirsty?" He asked. She remained silent.

He was no longer angry with her. He felt overwhelmed, full of questions. After years of monitoring the inner thoughts of others, suddenly walls in his own mind were cracking, and his own thoughts were rushing chaotically. He felt compelled to elicit an explanation from her; he owed it to himself. *If there was even an ounce of truth to the mysterious Legend of the Wings, whose very name he dared not utter, and whose mere thought wrought terror in all the Tower's inhabitants, maybe she was powerful enough to unlock the gate of truth?* He suddenly became aware of his thoughts. His commanders might sense these unusual thoughts when he reported to them later! But curiosity and his intense need to discover the truth overcame his fear. His questioning became relentless.

"In a different time, above the water," Mahn repeated the words he had heard.

The words scorched his lips, and he felt the desire to believe them.

"When will this time transpire?" he asked.

The old woman's eyes opened, and they appeared to him like light-filled tunnels in the darkened room.

"Who are you?" she asked.

For the first time since Mahn first heard her whisperings, Mahn noticed that her voice was human, vivacious, full of feeling, young...She asked her question as though she had been searching throughout her entire life for someone and now she was checking: Was Mahn the one?

Who are you??? This question echoed through his mind. He searched within himself for the answer but could not find it. For a lone moment the doors of the future were opened in his mind. He heard the same question repeated again and again, asked by a young woman. And the answer was hidden in her words: *You are not who you think you are.*

Mahn shut his eyes, yearning to delve into his vision, but it suddenly vanished and the magic faded. The old woman was still in her own world, and Mahn was once again an Inviewer in a dark interrogation room, uselessly questioning a crazy old hag. He did not attempt to understand all that had occurred, and banished the bizarre moments from his consciousness. He went out into the lit hall, where the three warriors were waiting.

"Toss her out into the street," he instructed.

They looked disappointed, as if loot had been seized from their hands.

"There is no truth to her words."

But deep inside he knew how far from the truth his own words were.

Chapter Six

The Memory Master

The Memory Master

"An experienced warrior would not tread on soil of this kind. Footprints on such soft soil would leave a long-lasting impression, clearly visible to all."

Ulu had begun training his son immediately after making his final decision to take him along. Saag was still young and inexperienced and Ulu was intent on training him so that he could protect himself from danger. He would have to be as familiar as his father was with the secrets of the forests and fields, the sky and the earth. The two of them walked alongside a narrow stream, flowing down the broad yellow hills. A few days had passed since they had departed from their home at Fisherman's Village, located farthest east, closest to the great river.

They neared Potter's Village now, though they still had a long way ahead of them before they would reach the Land of the Northern Forests and its eastern slopes. They were headed towards King's Valley and the Green Lowlands. Saag refrained from questioning his father about this vigorous training program and regarded his studies and exercises as an exciting game. But

Ulu's serious demeanor and exacting presentation caused Saag to devote himself to the work and to appreciate his father's every word.

There were fourteen village located along the Shore of King's Sea, the easternmost being their native Fisherman's Village which was located closest to the shore.

Potter's Village was a three-day walk from there. The village was built upon heavy red clay earth, easy to work with and useful in creating pottery for the inhabitants of the surrounding villages. Like all the villages, Potter's Village was surrounded by heavy, high, unpainted wooden fences.

A guard always stood at the village entrance, but in light of the threats facing the Ancient Progeny, his presence could be compared to a piece of straw in the path of a beast. He functioned as a greeter, fulfilling a village tradition, welcoming people entering the gates and helping them to find their way through the winding paths and hidden cabins in the village hills.

A faint scent of smoke carried by a delightful warm breeze reached Ulu and his son as they made their way around the last hill on the outskirts of Potter's Village. The high wooden fence was visible and the sounds of voices could be heard... Several more steps led Ulu and Saag to the gate, which was arched and large enough for loaded carts to pass through it. As they neared the red clay gate, they noticed that the torches located on all sides revealed etched images of potters at work. The amiable guard wore a white linen turban around his head and a trim grey beard adorned his face.

He warmly welcomed the father and son with the traditional blessing, "A clear sky instills tranquility in the hearts of all."

He then proceeded to direct them to the visitor's cabin. The proverb spoken by the guard was such a part of the villagers' dialect that even Ulu was unaware that it had originated with the Transparent Ones.

Potter's Village was buzzing with excitement on the night of their arrival. Once a year, the Memory Master of each and every village set out on a trek to the Northern Mountains, into the depths of the tangled forest. Few people knew that the purpose of the journey was to lead the Storm Dancers to join their brothers who were engaged in battles in the north.

Ulu felt that participation in the annual departure ceremony would strengthen his son's understanding of current events, in a non-threatening way. They had enjoyed a great feast at one of the local guest cabins and then rested, following their exhausting journey. Saag fell into a deep sleep until midnight. Now they left their place of rest and walked towards the cabin of the village elders. There, in the large sandy square, dozens of men sat in silence. Their light blue capes were clean and pure. Small wooden branches crackled in the campfire in their midst, its light revealing faces filled with anticipation. Everyone's eyes were focused on the arched entrance to the village elders' cabin.

"Father," whispered Saag, without removing his gaze from the arched entrance, "what will happen now?"

Softly, Ulu whispered into his son's ear, "Every village has a Memory Master who possesses secret knowledge hidden to others. Today, the Memory Master of Potter's Village is leaving on an important mission."

The pleasant sound of a flute playing broke the silence as the cabin door opened. Ulu turned his attention back towards the cabin just as two tall men emerged from the human circle. They wore black clothes and held sharpened swords, tinted orange by the light of the fire.

"They are in costume," whispered Ulu to his frightened son who gripped his father's hand, seeking reassurance.

A third person emerged from the cabin, adorned in a blue cape with thin, white, glimmering stripes. His face displayed deep insight. On his head he wore a white turban, and his weaponless hands were outstretched. His arms moved, as if questioningly.

As the men in dark garb approached the Memory Master, they became shorter in stature. They walked slowly and hesitantly. Their swords lay uselessly in their hands. When the three of them were arms length away from the campfire, the Memory Master whispered, "Water will extinguish the fire."

"Water will extinguish the fire," echoed the spectators.

Their whispers sounded like a soaring, rising wave.

"Water will extinguish the fire," their whisper became a melodious song, gaining momentum. And then there was silence, as the Memory Master began to transcend. At first his dance was slow and gentle. As he continued, his movements became increasingly spherical, until he was dancing around himself with the force of a storm.

The spectators were bursting with excitement and filled the silence with hushed whispers, "The storm dance!"

Ulu knew all about the storm dance. The Master of Transcendence used this dance to protect free men. For years his warriors had been circling the villages, secretly training young men, teaching them the storm dance. To untrained eyes, even in the eyes of the Tower Inviewers, the dance seemed to be nothing more than a ceremonial ritual. The highly trained warriors were sent by the Master of Transcendence to the Northern Forests where their powers stalled the armies of the Tower, preventing them from expanding their conquests. The dancers were also sent to fight the Descendents of the Emperors near their Tower. No one who encountered the circle of dancers ever lived to tell about it.

None of the villagers understood the true significance of the dance, though they all knew that it was of great importance. The two sword-wielding men in black neared the dancer and pretended to attack him. Just then the song of the spectators intensified, "Water will extinguish the fire!"

It seemed as if the words hung in the air, threatening the 'attackers.' The dancer, on the other hand, obtained strength and intensity from them. He continued circling gracefully and neared the 'attackers.' The air around him filled with dust, kicked up by the speed of his spinning. As the dust entered the eyes of the aggressors, they covered their eyes and reeled around like drunkards. The dust intensified and became a dark cloud which enveloped the two 'attackers,' as if it had a mind of its own. It was unnecessary for the dancer to even touch them. Terrified, they fell to their knees, tossing their 'swords' into the fire, which consumed them. They proceeded to remove their capes and throw them, too, into the fire. The ceremony had come to an end. The Memory Master completed his transcendence appearing even taller than before.

Under the threatening capes of the 'attackers' appeared two villagers in simple pale blue garb. They knelt in front of the Memory Master. Only when he reached out his hand permitting them to rise, did they get up; their heads still lowered. On their lips was a blessing. The recitation of these words influenced the spectators deeply. It seemed as if the success of the Memory Master's journey was dependent upon this blessing.

"Be attentive to every moment. Your heart will guide the way. Have patience and the Light of the Transcendor shall protect you," the blessing was pronounced in a festive tone. The flute, playing a simple amiable tune, reminded Saag of the waves that rolled in from the sea on quiet nights. The excitement in the air made way for pure joy.

The Memory Master returned to his cabin, the fire was extinguished and the villagers prepared for a celebratory feast served on red clay dishes, the best the village had to offer. Ulu and Saag sampled the food, then left the cheerful villagers and returned to the homey guest cabin. Across from it were several beautifully carved benches, wide and comfortable. Ulu and his son sat down and watched the moon make its way through the darkened sky.

"Father, please explain," began Saag.

Ulu's hand caressed his son's arm as if to say: "slow down."

But Saag persisted. "Where is the Memory Master going? Who attacked him and later surrendered? And what is the Light of the Transcendor that defends him?"

Saag began to cry uncontrollably, a cry full of fear of the unknown and yet filled with a childish anticipation of the discovery of a new world. The knowledge his father had passed on to him and the experiences he had witnessed that night served as clues to him. These clues were coming together in his mind, and when connected formed the picture of a world war. What part did his father have in this? And why is he sharing his secret with his son?

"Why did we leave our home?" wept Saag.

Ulu caressed him and allowed the sorrow, so natural, to wash over him. His son was being forced to grow up too fast. He was being exposed too quickly to a foreign world, so distant from their village by the sea. Who knew how much time remained before he would have to face the evil powers, making his way in the world on his own?

After a two-day rest, Ulu and his son resumed their journey from Potter's Village, going toward King's Valley. They passed through Artisan's Village, where the residents created exquisite glass artifacts and musical instruments with which they performed eloquently. Next they passed through Herbal Village. With ancient knowledge handed down from generation to generation, the villagers created a wide variety of incense and medicines from the herbs and medicinal plants growing abundantly in the fields. Ulu and Saag passed through the farming regions of the villages, close to King's Valley, which supplied food to all surrounding villages.

Saag had grown accustomed to outdoor life. He could 'read' the tracks found in the sand and grass, and was becoming more and more capable of surviving on his own in the mountains. It was clear to him, based on what he had heard from his father that a great war was taking place just beyond King's Valley, threatening the lives of the villagers. What part did his father have in this war? He was too fearful to voice this question.

Ulu walked softly. Every so often he would pick up a rock found on their path and move it aside. He removed rotting tree limbs from trees. He noticed everything: A newly dug burrow near a large rock; a small red flower, freshly sprouted from the damp earth; the whispers and murmurs of small animals making their way from one place to another. Ulu journeyed through the hills as if they were his home, and his spirit was free. He felt as if he belonged in the forest, and was at ease. This made Saag feel safe, protected and happy. But beyond, the trees the slopes were coming to an end, and soon they would be overlooking the Green Lowlands. Always, when Ulu reached this point, he would be overcome with sadness. These feelings were intensified now, with his son at his side, so close to the impending dangers. In the far distance, within the Green Lowlands, they were able to see the Tower, soaring over foreign lands. Though the visibility was hampered by fog and distance, they could see the Tower which rose into the sky, topped by a white flame. Soon father and son began their descent into the valley, each step taking them closer to the Towered City.

The borders were unmarked. The Green Lowlands sprawled out as far as the eye could see, from King's Valley, beyond the Tower and reaching to the outskirts of the White Desert. Because the inhabitants of the Towered City, the Descendents of the Emperors, were so enchanted by the City, it was unnecessary to guard the border of the Northern Forests.

The Descendents of the Emperors were limited to the confines of the Towered City. No guards stood at the borders, just a wall of fear. Fear of becoming detached from the power centered in the Tower was so overwhelming, it was clear to all that it would not be possible to leave. And not a soul desired to do so. Thousands of the Descendents of the Emperors harvested the fruits of Oblivion in the Lowlands, and the green promise of freedom in the distance held no attraction for them.

Indeed, the opposite was true; the idea of freedom sowed fear in their hearts. They were in a constant state of uncontrollable desire to lift their eyes to the top of the Tower, from which they imagined they obtained strength and sympathy from the burning flame. The Green Lowlands lay before Ulu and his son. If not for the daunting black stone Tower, the Lowlands would have been attractive. Saag looked into the distance and saw the Towered City for the first time in his life. He stopped walking, frozen in place. The immense size of the Tower, which loomed into the sky, rendered its observers speechless. One was either terrified of the Towered City or passionately yearning to be a part of it, but no one could view it with indifference. Even the boy felt that its strong impression was not created solely by its enormous dimensions. The mighty visage of the City of Steel was dark and paralyzing. Its intensity was overpowering.

"Father," Saag grasped at Ulus clothing, terrified, "What is that?"

Though Ulu knew this moment was coming and had prepared his words wisely, he had difficulty remaining composed. He sat heavily upon a large rock on the side of the trail, embracing his son.

How can I expose such an innocent heart to such profound evil? he wondered.

"The city you see before you," Ulu chose his words meticulously, "is great, strong and powerful, because all of its inhabitants work for it and devote their entire lives to its Tower. The people's essence of being provides life to the flame, which leaves them empty. The inhabitants of the City are oblivious to the fact that the Tower does not give them life; the Tower actually sucks their strength and destroys their vitality. But you are still a boy, you cannot understand."

Saag moved even closer to his father, still gazing at the Tower fearfully.

Suddenly a rustle was heard in the grass. Something moved through the nearby fields. Before Ulu had a chance to discover its source, a warrior appeared before them. The gray flame which appeared on his sleeve and his crude appearance made it apparent that he had come from the City of Steel.

He extended his sword towards Ulu and asked him arrogantly, "Who are you?"

Before Ulu could even answer, a second figure emerged from the tall grass. He carried no weapons and his clothes were unmarked, but he radiated an inner strength and extraordinary intensity.

Upon noticing that Saag seemed bewildered, he smiled a terrible smile and said in a quiet voice, "The center of strength, goodness and blessing to all, lies in this valley." Saag listened to his words with utter fascination as he continued, "The ancient fire, root of all flames, seeks contact with its soul mate, the fire of your soul."

"Curses upon you!" the man of borders cried out.

His son cowered at the sound of his father's furious cry. From beneath the folds of his cape, Ulu stealthily grasped a carved flute into which he had hidden a sharp blade. The armed warrior, who had been standing on the side watching the unfolding scene, noticed the gleaming metal piece. He rushed at Ulu. Within seconds the knife was deeply imbedded in the warrior's chest.

His sword fell to the ground. Ulu looked for Saag, but he had vanished, along with the other warrior.

A wail with no beginning and no end arose from the depths of Ulu's being and finally made its way to his lips, "Saag! Saag! Saag!"

He ran frantically into the field, still grasping the knife, stained with the warrior's blood, helplessly searching for his son. He stumbled and fell to the ground. A nasty gash on his face caused profuse bleeding, the blood mingling with his tears.

"It's my fault! I took him out of the village and did not protect him…SAAG!!! MY SAAG!!!"

He remained motionless in the grass, ignoring the possible dangers in his midst.

Multitudinous images from the distant past appeared in his mind. *A son!* he remembered exclaiming upon becoming a father. The image changed, and his wife now appeared from within the fog, a gay smile lit her face. She was tired from sleepless nights, though full of the joy felt by the mother of a young baby. He could hear his son calling him *Father*, and see him take his first steps.

The images came and went. Finally, only one lone image remained. It was the image of his son clutching his father's clothing such a short time ago. Yet it seemed as if it were so long ago! Saag had gazed at the great City confused, and asked: *What is that?!* This image remained with Ulu for quite some time. The sound of his son's question echoed repeatedly, in a childish, demanding, puzzled voice: *What is that?* --and then the voice vanished and only the image of the boy's wide-open eyes remained.

Ulu had seen the reflection of the City of Steel in Saag's eyes.

Chapter Seven

A Lost Vessel

A Lost Vessel

"This material seems like an alloy of various metals," said the Village Chief after a prolonged silence. "But it seems that it is also composed of an unknown, foreign substance…"

Tzalaii stood before the Chief, feeling humiliated. This ambiguous evaluation did not give him the proof he sought to justify the dangerous risks he had taken in his daring venture. Though his friends had given him the title *Most Courageous*, this status had only brought him sadness.

After returning from his journey, he felt a need to share his experiences with a figure of authority. Despite his shame and great embarrassment, he turned to the Village Chief, the man who had adopted him and his sister many years ago and had been like a father to them. Tzalaii told him of his journey to the wall in great detail, though he said nothing about the Magnathought Crystal or how he had made use of it. The Village Chief reacted with a silence that only increased Tzalaii's feelings of shame. A strong verbal rebuke might have been easier for the youth to accept. He feared that the Village Chief's ominous silence was caused by the severity of his foolish adventure.

Puzzled, he excused himself and headed towards the sea. The afternoon breeze was calm and tranquil. Roosters crowed and a lone donkey brayed. The smell of cooking was in the air. Children gazed at him as he walked down the trail. Did they know about his journey? Restless and completely at odds with the serenity in his midst, he made his way down the paths towards the beach. Several boats were visible on the horizon. The surface of the sea was smooth, revealing the sand in its depth. "What is the purpose of all this?" he wondered. The image of the Towered City permeated his thoughts, and he was unable to rid himself of it no matter how hard he tried. *In any case all is lost...* he thought. The words of the warriors near the burning flame of the Towered City echoed in his heart, and he felt that his loss was greater than he could fathom. What had vanished was terrible and powerful.

Soon he reached the clean, white, welcoming sand. A flock of squawking birds took flight and then landed on a cluster of rocks jutting out of the water. Tzalaii felt deserted, alone with his troubled spirit. He sat down on the familiar beach, feeling tired and lonely. He looked at the water... and into the distant horizon…etched circles in the sand unconsciously as the wind blew in from the sea and comforted his soul. And then he slept. When he awoke, the sun was already setting. He shook off the sand that had settled on his clothing and sensed that he was not alone. Sihara was there. She was tall; her eyes were deep and expressed an inner charm. His sister, Sihara, with her deep eyes had brought comfort to so many. She had the power to relieve the suffering of those in despair. Despite her young age, she had been a source of hope to so many. To Tzalaii she was all that and more- his sole blood relative.

"I fell asleep…," he mumbled, embarrassed that she had found him dozing in the sand.

"That's alright," she answered simply; "I thought you might need some help." Offering comfort in time of need was her most natural and automatic response.

"No…no," he answered timidly; "Soon I shall return home."

Sihara was aware of Tzalaii's tempestuous spirit, and let him be. She turned around and walked away. Tzalaii felt well rested now. Despite his decision to return to the village, he reconsidered and remained at the shore. He sat down, refreshed, and looked at the darkening sky and sea. It was essential for him to cheer himself up with a positive thought.

A positive thought? Questioned an inner voice, mockingly, attempting to bring back the threatening memories from the great valley.

"Yes," he answered confidently, as he skipped a smooth stone in the water.

He recalled a walk on the beach several months earlier. He had gone down to the sea and wandered far away from the village, finally arriving at an ancient fortress. There was a storm at sea, and light rain filled the air with small droplets. Seeking refuge, he entered the fortress. He remembered childhood stories about an ancient battle. On several occasions he had searched this area, hoping to find a sign or an ancient artifact. On one such outing, also on a rainy day, he had approached a cave located on the Southern side of the fortress, only to find that the entrance to the cave was blocked. The rain had eroded part of the sandstone, causing an inner wall to collapse and filling most of the cave with broken stones. Only a small area inside the cave remained dry. As he tried making his way through the debris of this small opening, he stumbled upon a firm object. It was a shiny blue Crystal artifact, the size of a child's fist and almost completely flat. Next to the shiny Crystal Tzalaii had unearthed a second object- a golden piece of cloth that he rescued from the crumbling sandstone. The cloth looked as if it had been excised by a sword or blade.

How strange, thought Tzalaii, *an antiquity should look worn out, but this piece of cloth appears to be newly woven. Had someone worn this elaborate piece? Villagers in the Land of the Ancient Progeny had worn simple clothing. Was this, perhaps, a remnant from an ancient battle? The battle he had dreamed about?*

After the rain, Tzalaii had exited the cave and returned to the shore. There he washed the sand-encrusted Crystal artifact and examined the golden cloth overlay surrounding it. The Crystal piece was entirely sealed on one side, and the other side was deep blue in color. Tzalaii noticed that if he looked into the blue side for a long, long time, a delicately etched tree would appear; its thin roots widening as they reached the trunk, which was exceptionally broad, and its branches stretching upwards like aspiring hands. At first Tzalaii held the object like a child examining a new toy, then he used it to reflect rays of light onto the water. Several weeks later, when he was alone on the beach one night, he discovered an unusual feature. Fully aware of the impossibility of concentrating sunlight onto water at night, he began to play with the Crystal artifact, and a strangely ridiculous thought entered his mind: If the object is capable of concentrating rays of light, maybe it is also capable of concentrating thoughts?

Where did this idea come from? He wondered. *Did it come from the Crystal object itself?*

Tzalaii attempted to concentrate his thoughts utilizing the Crystal piece. Concentrating, he gazed at it, directing his thoughts towards a specific place on the beach. A small pebble rolled off the beach toward the water. He stood at a distance from the pebble, merely thinking about it and imagining it rolling into the water, and it happened! Shocked, he dropped the Crystal artifact and it fell to the ground but the soft sand cushioned its landing.

Tzalaii now recalled the use he had made of the Crystal during his encounter with the Tower Warriors, as well as at the wall. Memories of the Towered City returned and his mood worsened. He turned around and started walking up the dirt path leading to the village. Someone, hidden from view, was watching him silently from the hills. Someone who felt his pain, possibly even more deeply than he did. She herself was not yet consciously aware of the boy's deep dependence upon her courageous heart. It was Sihara.

In the following weeks, Tzalaii spent most of his time on the beach. He had become increasingly confused and uneasy. There had to be a way, he thought, to absolve himself of his childish act. Tzalaii enjoyed watching the fishermen sailing in their boats, and following their activities. Their faces were blistered by the sun, their arms wrinkled, and their clothes rudimentary and encrusted with sea salt. He would often join them, helping as much as possible, though speaking very little. When the weather was stormy and only the most courageous fishermen set sail and went out to battle the waves, Tzalaii joined with them in their brave feats. The sea, whether dark or pale, always sparked Tzalaii's curiosity. He yearned to see foreign lands, to reach unknown depths, to conquer obstacles and to return home with great treasures. No, not fish. Pearls maybe, or diamonds. Something valuable, never before discovered. He refrained from sharing these daydreams with his friends. They thought that his love for the sea was a result of his innate ability to manage a boat and sail it well. Only Sihara understood Tzalaii's deep grief and the comfort he found at sea.

One day Tzalaii was out fishing, when an exceptionally strong storm blew in, distancing him from the other fishermen. The sky above was dark, as was the sea. A great gust of wind carried the waves to great heights and sent them crashing down into the depths. The sea and sky growled like a creature of prey, mocking a helpless victim. Waves crashed down all around Tzalaii's small craft. The fishermen were isolated from each other by lack of visibility and the crashing sounds of the waves. Although Tzalaii usually trusted his excellent control of the sail and helm, he understood that it would be different this time. The waves grew fiercer, the darkness thickened and he was lost. The storm had enveloped him and he could no longer see the shore. At first he was stunned, but quickly came to his senses realizing that he could not afford to allow his fear to win. He gathered all his strength and skill in order to prevent the wind from tearing the sails or capsizing the boat. Drenched to the bone, breathless and exhausted, the boy fought for his life. Many hours passed, hours of black skies and thunderous waves, hours of salty tears and drenching seawater. Just as Tzalaii began to lose his strength, the storm began to subside. He dropped onto the floor of the boat helplessly. The sails were torn to shreds and the boat was carried to and fro by the wind. No light was visible, near or far. His heart felt empty, though his lips found the strength to gasp: *I want to live!*

A deep yearning suddenly overcame him. His physical strength had expired, making way for the strength of his spirit and its desires. He began to think about the ancient magical kingdom he had heard of in the village legends.

Did it truly exist? Will the world ever become a better place, full of light?

His head spun around heavily. The boat continued to drift. He felt cold in the chilly night and suffered from extreme thirst.

Maybe it is better this way, he thought in despair. *If not by storm, I will lose my life by dehydration or exposure. This is my punishment for stealing the rock from the wall...I am being punished by the Descendents of the Emperors. There is no escaping them.* He blindly felt his way around the floor of the boat, searching for something to hold on to. Wet, smooth planks were all he found. As his hands slipped and he lost his grip, Tzalaii collapsed and fell into a deep sleep.

The first light of dawn appeared and Tzalaii, awakening from a dream, opened his eyes, his dream still present in his consciousness: A tall noble man, wearing a crown, was trying to say something...words of comfort. Silvery streaks danced on the water, promising tranquility. A light breeze hovered overhead and all was silent, like at the beginning of time. The grueling night was over and in its place, such a wonderful, gentle morning. Tzalaii felt himself transported, guided and protected. His dream King still smiled at him. As he continued to think of him, he spied dry land in the distance.

Chapter Eight

The Obliterated One

The Obliterated One

The boy eyed the grey flame on his sleeve with great curiosity, noticing the subtle appearance of mingled colors. He stroked the cloth and felt the might of the steel sword strapped around his waist. It was a genuine sword, as was fit for a young man, not the sharpened stick of a child. He had no recollection of his past nor of the way had he arrived. As a young warrior on the Base Level, his only goal was to ascend, like a flame, constantly reaching upwards, to serve his masters faithfully, to enter the heart of the Base Level, and when the day arrived- to ascend to the next level. The mere thought excited him. His face was ablaze with an inner fire. He continued stroking the flame on his sleeve, imagining how glorious the sapphire-colored flame would look, the flame of the Saturn Level, the Level of Mercury.

How good it is to be here, he thought contentedly, as he gazed at the inner courtyard through the window of the steel gate. Outside was an empty world, a world in need of the healing touch of fire.

A brief call by the guard of the second gate halted his thoughts.

"You have completed your shift. You must report to Mahn, he wants to speak to you." With confused thoughts, the young warrior made his way through the long halls that led to the room of the Inviewer. Why was he summoned to this meeting?

"So, my child," Mahn began, as he tossed a wooden chip into the fireplace that warmed the room and cast its light upon them. "How was your daily shift?"

The boy's face was innocent and beautiful, his eyes large and candid.

"Nothing out of the ordinary, Sir Inviewer," answered the Obliterated One, insecure about proper protocol in addressing his honored interviewer.

Mahn was not surprised by the youthfulness of his guest. He knew that the Warriors of the Towered City were trained at a very young age. This boy had been obliterated. *Who knew his lineage? Who knew where he had been found?* The Inviewer did not know and he shook his head, trying to rid himself of these improper thoughts. Indicating the stone bench with his hand, he invited the boy to join him.

"Come, sit," he said.

The boy, feeling a sense of reward in this sudden outpouring of attention, sat down cautiously.

"How are you finding the system?" questioned Mahn pleasantly.

The Obliterated One did not understand the query.

"I don't understand, sir," he chose his words well, "I am a regular warrior and I am content with my tasks."

Mahn looked at him compassionately. There was something tiresome about his conversations with the Obliterated Ones. In some ways Mahn even preferred conversing with the prisoners of broken spirit who possessed a strong inner resistance preventing

Obliteration. His position held great honor. As an inhabitant of the fourth floor, his privileges entitled him to dine on meat delicacies and his short black blade, the weapon he was most fond of, was purchased in the depths of the main cavern for the price of just four white coins But, still, how much enjoyment could there be for an Inviewer in the Towered City?

His tasks included locating flaws in the behavior of the Obliterated Ones, recommending a repeat Obliteration if necessary, and imprisoning those who showed signs of rebellion. He loved the Towered City, and knew that before long he would fulfill the dream of all men on the Base Level, and enter the core. He did not know exactly how the level was run, but believed the words he heard from his teachers when he was appointed as Inviewer on the Base Level: "The steel strengthening fire shall strengthen your spirit and melt its locks. To ascend, as fire, higher and higher, to the peak of the Towered City."

Melt its locks? He suddenly thought. *Such a strange line…* He hurriedly touched the flame on his sleeve, feeling the outline of the gray fire, and resumed his conversation with the Obliterated One who sat across from him, shy and embarrassed.

"Well, my boy," he asked without expecting an answer, "What do you know of the world outside the Tower?"

The Obliterated One lowered his face, as if disturbed.

"A world of futility…A world of vagabonds confused and lost."

These were not the words of a young boy. They had been imprinted on his brain by powerful agents. As the boy prepared to continue with his fervent speech, Mahn's impatience grew visible. He dismissed the boy with wave of his hand, while deeply involved in his own thoughts.

A world of futility…A world of vagabonds confused and lost.

He, too, believed this, of course. How lost were those who were unaware of these facts.

The base of all is steel and the sword.

How naïve and foolish were those who reasoned that survival was possible without this knowledge. Mahn admitted to himself that he had never actually encountered vagabonds outside of the Tower. He had met Obliterated Ones and prisoners of broken spirit. The latter, he knew, did not arrive at the Tower the least bit confused or lost…

Loud cries were heard from the nearby hallways, interrupting his thoughts: "The wall! The wall!" voices of anger and fear mingled together.

Was an enemy approaching the protective walls? Knocks were heard at the door and a warrior appeared, out of breath, announcing to Mahn, "Master Elassar has requested your presence."

"It can be assumed that the stone cannot be used in any way…" said Mahn, his voice quivering.

Was he to blame for the anonymous thief who stole a stone from the wall during his shift?

"We did not ask for your opinion, we only asked for the details," one of the Inviewers uttered dryly.

Why do you regard the cursed stone with such importance? Mahn almost retorted, but instead he remained standing, quietly but uneasily as three shaven-headed men behind a long table questioned him.

One of them, Elassar, was generally disliked. He was a known antagonist. All who encountered him, during investigations or elsewhere, were made to feel guilty of some unknown crime. Mahn had always tried to stay out of Elassar's way. Unfortunately, he now had to answer to him. Many warriors silently filled the room. The air was suffocating, the light dim. Never before had Mahn undergone such a humiliating investigation.

"Do any of your family members serve in the heart of the level?"

asked the Inviewer on his left. What, in the name of the holy fire, are they getting at? Mahn thought as he dutifully replied: "Yes, three of them, as far as I know." Elassar smiled and said nothing.

His uncharacteristic silence filled Mahn's thoughts with dread. And the man's smile was not a good sign either... The three Inviewers arose and looked at Mahn. They intoned Mahn's name, repeatedly- each succeeding time with greater intensity. Suddenly he understood the unfolding chain of events. But before he could prepare himself, before he had the chance to clarify his thoughts and feelings, he found himself directed to the heart of the level. This caused Mahn great embarrassment. The situation, especially the presence of Elassar, had created a climate of judgment and accusation.

Was this the moment they had all been waiting for? The presence of the three Inviewers prevented him from delving into the meaning of his changing situation. The tallest of the men was humming; the deep throaty tune was terrifying. The others started moving towards Mahn, while chanting familiar words, as in a dream: "The base of all is steel and the sword."

"The steel strengthening fire shall strengthen your spirit and melt its locks. To ascend, as fire, higher and higher, to the peak of the Towered City."

Mahn could hear himself chanting: "The base of all is steel and the sword."

Then there was silence. The Steel Warriors exited the room. A sapphire flame illuminated the space casting a strange light on Mahn's face.

"Do you know how to ascend from one level to another?" questioned the tall warrior. Mahn still felt like he was dreaming.

"By melting its locks," answered Mahn in a voice that was not his own, as the flame drew nearer to his face.

Troops were departing from the lower City. Some moved towards the nearby lowlands, others to the north or the Land of the Southern Boulders. Skilled soldiers moved forward silently, taking their place in the battlefield. In the deep tunnels below the Towered City, the Obliterators were busy preparing the Shadows for the assault missions that awaited them. The light of day had dawned, its rays lit up the sky.

Mahn, as if being led within a transparent flame, had reached the heart of the level. Everything looked different and unfamiliar. Transparency controlled not only the people, but the objects, too. The color of his clothing was altered, and his sword became lighter. As he stood before the altar, in the heart of the level, the transparency entered his body as well. The memory of Elassar's smile continued to disturb him, and impeded his total devotion, heart and soul, to the long-awaited process.

A huge torch-lit room housed a square stone formation. The stones were red, as if heated by an inner flame, their strength a stark contrast to the all encompassing transparency. Mahn was alone. A slender flame rose above the altar, the dim sound of thunder emanating from within as if from a living creature.

"Return to us!" called bodiless voices in his midst. And Mahn repeated every word they spoke, slowly.

"My life, my body and my organs, my insides and soul, each and every thought, every word spoken, every single movement belong to the fire. In death I will give it life and with its life I shall gain eternity. You, holy fire, stay ablaze forever. And I, body and soul, shall burn within you."

"In death!," "In death!," "In death!" the nameless creatures chanted.

A great heat wave, as if emanating from the ground, arose from his feet and up through his body. The anonymous voices disappeared, the altar faded, and fire ruled all. Mahn plummeted into a dark abyss, devoid of emotions, memories and desires.

Chapter Nine

A Mission

A Mission

"My heart tells me that Tzalaii did not drown, as the fishermen believe," said the Village Chief.

Sihara listened to him, a pained expression on her face.

"The village elders," he continued, "have designated a mission for you, and I believe you will be able to find him."

Purple fields…a purple sky. She must leave this place. She must part from the beloved, familiar landscapes; forget the colorful flowers and the sea breeze. She must, for now, let the familiar paths and beloved faces fade away and disappear through the fog of time. At dawn, she must set off on her journey, a journey from which she may never return. The village elders' wishes must not be refused.

She had received a sealed box with instructions to carry it with her on the boat to Green Isle. *What did it contain?* She did not know. She was informed that an elder would greet her upon her arrival at Green Isle. He would explain the nature of her mission in full detail. From there, she would be sent to another more distant destination, but Sihara's heart was fearless in the face of this undertaking. Her entire being was concentrated on one thought: *Tzalaii.*

The sun was about to set. The purple glimmer disappeared slowly from the fields and darkness spread over the world. Sihara wandered sadly among the hills near her home. Memories of her childhood caused her throat to constrict: she envisioned herself, years ago, running on the beach collecting seashells, creating childish adornments…following the sheep herders out into the pasture, crafting garlands from the flowers that covered the valleys. Her adoptive father and mother, gray-haired but still standing tall, had provided her with a warm and cozy nest in their home. An ancient beauty and wisdom pervaded their abode, shedding grace upon all who entered. Above all, Sihara had taken great pleasure in sitting by the hearth during the long winter nights, watching the fire and listening to her father's melodious voice as he related tales of ancient times…

Our tribe derived from an ancient kingdom, he would begin. *In times of old they controlled all the lands of the Ancient Progeny. In those days, we were not wanderers, divided and scattered in isolated tribes, but a united glorious kingdom. A heroic king was our leader, and his noblemen were prominent and well known even beyond the sea.*

There was always an unknown element in these stories. Sihara had many unasked questions that troubled her. Intuiting that no answers would be given, she refrained from asking her questions.

How had the united kingdom fallen, leaving only isolated, wandering tribes? Who removed the king from his throne? How was it possible for the original builders of the dreaded Towered City to gain access to the kingdom? There was an implied hint of some kind of catastrophe, something that continued to cause deep feelings of anguish.

At times, her heart would fill with doubt as she wondered if the tales of ancient times had been invented only to entertain the children. In the stories, the characters were adorned in so much splendor and royalty. How was it possible that their descendents were but simple sheep herders and fishermen? With all the warmth and love she felt for the village and its inhabitants, such good-hearted, pleasant people, she felt strongly that their innocent simplicity was very far-removed from the grandeur described in the tales.

Sihara returned home. Her adoptive father sat by the great wooden table, deep in thought, gazing out of the window into the darkness.

"My daughter," said the village chief, his words conveying fatherly concern, "the time has come."

"Yes, Father, I know," she whispered.

He felt as always that his adopted daughter's consciousness touched something so deeply profound and hidden that it could not be named or described in words. He covered his eyes with his hand and let out a whimper. A sorrowful wrinkle was visible upon his high forehead, and Sihara felt that it was her task to comfort him. She was not the one in need of comforting. He watched after her as she walked away into the distance, ready to fulfill her mission.

Sihara left the village in a simple fishing boat. Time passed quickly on the voyage. Upon arrival, she secured the boat in a small bay, and was directed towards a narrow path that led to the heart of the island. The island's vegetation was lush, more luxuriant than anything she had ever seen. Shades of green merged with turquoise and violet, emerald green merged with shades of gold. The trees, wide grassy fields, shrubs and flowers were so full of life. Their freshness filled the air with vitality.

The atmosphere was so clear; Sihara sensed that she could gaze endlessly beyond the thickness of the forest, farther and farther into the distance. On the way, she encountered an elder who greeted her and led her to a cabin. He left her there and walked back towards the sea. The cabin was not wooden, as in the villages, but built of great, cumbersome, ancient rocks. Despite its ancient aspect, a crisp, fresh breeze blew within it, entering her heart and expanding her mind. The furniture in the cabin was simple: a makeshift wooden table, a stone bench and several trunks. Most intriguing of all were the books made of animal skin parchment, organized in long rows on stone shelves. They were reminiscent of the books she had seen, on rare occasions, amongst the village elders and she imagined that they contained great wisdom. She approached the shelves full of awe and respect. The books were soft and mysterious. She stood near them, feeling their ancient spirit.

The gentle creak of the wooden door was heard: the old man had returned, bringing with him the scent of the sea breeze. He put his small basket down in a corner of the cabin. Casually, he placed a vessel containing a fragrant beverage on the fire. Sitting on the mat, he tossed twigs and small branches into the crackling fire, casting pleasant warmth in every direction. Outside, the sound of the wind could be heard.

 As soon as he sat down, his appearance visibly altered as his body became slightly elongated. His white beard gathered neatly at his chest. His eyes shut as he hummed a little tune to himself, like a preface to something. And then he was silent. The wind died down outside as well, and a great silence hovered over the land as if the entire island was filled with mystery; as if the trees were bending down and the grass was creeping secretly closer to the cabin: as if everything expectantly awaited the old man's words.

Slowly, very slowly, the old man prepared to reveal the contents of the chest Sihara had brought with her. He placed it on the simple wooden table and opened it. A gentle, yellow-crimson glow radiated from the stone within.

"The Transparent Ones believe that I can decipher its meaning," the old man said slowly. Sihara glanced at him and her head shot up in wonder.

"The Transparent Ones? I have never heard of them."

The old man smiled his peaceful smile, put the stone down and turned to Sihara.

"If that is so, why were you chosen to come here?" he asked, "And why did you agree to this assignment with such ease? You left the village of your youth, aware that you may never see it again, and yet you were not in the least afraid…"

For a moment, attempting to respond to his query, one word alone filled her aching heart: *Tzalaii*. But to her surprise, she found herself voicing something else: "A mission."

"A mission," repeated the old man.

They both remained silent for some time. He seemed to know the contents of her heart. She began to sense a real meaning behind the hazy, vague feelings she had experienced for years. The search for her brother would only be the starting point of a hidden path, with many crossroads and destinations.

"Do the village elders know what my mission entails?" she asked.

"It is possible," said the old man, " but it is also possible that only the Transparent Ones who participated in the gathering know its true purpose."

A hidden hand, with all encompassing power, creating feelings, thoughts, situations and connections had led her to this place. She suddenly felt different, and a secret- her secret, seemed to be making its presence felt. A new path was evident on the horizon, just for her.

"So," she continued animatedly, as if she and the old man were friends in a secret order, "who are the Transparent Ones?"

The last rays of the sun illuminated the old man's face, revealing the marks of many years. His high, white forehead was illuminated and he said: "You are young in years, my child, and have seen very little- but your heart has the ability to listen. It shall understand the words and their hidden meaning- those that are revealed and those that are concealed."

Sihara listened. The air in the room was filled with a buzz of mysterious life, casting an enchantment upon the old man's words.

"A majestic kingdom stood many years ago in the Land of the Ancient Progeny," he began. "Its legendary beauty attracted many of the Ancient Progeny. Elegant towers and steeples, adorned with precious stones crowned its streets. The city dwellers wore beautiful golden cloaks, and their faces expressed splendor. The mightiest of knights were their heroes. Most impressive and wise were their kings and noblemen. Grace and truth lit their paths. Lovely and gracious were their actions."

For a moment his face was blank, and he sighed.

"I was not one of them, but I did see them."

He was silent for a while, and then spoke slowly, as if asking for the strength to continue, "I witnessed its wealth and splendor, as well as its devastation and calamity."

Fear overtook Sihara's curiosity.

"Were you there, hundreds of years ago?"

"No," answered the old man, "I was not actually there. I viewed it in the Tunnels of Time."

"The Tunnels of Time? What are they?" questioned Sihara.

"Slow down, my child," said the old man, "the day in which you shall discover them on your own draws near."

"And how do you know all this?" She could no longer restrain herself from asking.

"Those books- do you see them?" He asked as he pointed to the wall.

She nodded her head, expectantly.

"Everything is written in these books. Everything that was and everything that will be, from the foundation of the Ancient Progeny until the return of the Prince of the Ancient Progeny." He hesitated and then added, "And beyond…"

"Do I appear in the books as well?"

"Of course," answered the old man, satisfied, "But you will only read about it at the end."

"Now listen," he said solemnly. "An ancient covenant was formed between the Kingdom of the Ancient Progeny and the Transparent Ones. It is because of the power of that covenant and because of your power that I am here."

"Are the Transparent Ones timeless men, like you?"

The old man smiled.

"The Transparent Ones are timeless: they are beyond time. They are not human, but are produced by humans as products of human spirit and the creations of man's thoughts."

"I don't understand…" Sihara murmured.

The old man understood. This was all new to her. She had never before heard of such things, yet at the same time she was vaguely familiar with them.

"A person's actions are never lost. When good words are uttered, when good deeds are performed, a Transparent One is created."

"If so, everyone has their own Transparent Ones," said Sihara, suddenly understanding.

"Yes," said the old man, "and everyone has one deed, one very special deed accomplished with true devotion, triumphantly overcoming great obstacles. This deed resembles the person; it is like a precious and successful child, and it is known as the *Transparent Master*."

Enchanted, Sihara asked, "And who is my Transparent Master?" The old man smiled before answering. "I am."

Chapter Ten

Encounters on Green Isle

Encounters on Green Isle

Ulu had intended to travel to the White Desert, but his plans had gone awry. He found himself in the middle of Green Isle. He had lost his senses, impulsively desiring to pursue his beloved son, to follow in Saag's footsteps towards the Towered City. But his inner integrity overcame his longing, and he forced himself to escape by retreating in the opposite direction.

"Give yourself some time. Do not be afraid. Saag will return to you," he repeated, as he traveled farther and farther away from the Green Lowlands and towards the sea. "You must leave this place, so that you may return later, wiser and stronger, to confront your enemy."

Two Transparent Ones met him on the shore. Their presence strengthened his decision and assured him that he was traveling in the right direction for the moment. They sailed with him in a small boat, arriving at Green Isle, from whence they departed silently. Ulu was left alone on the sandy beach.

He knew that the Transparent Ones would be there for him again.

Watching over you, aware of your travails, we accompany you, he thought as the Transparent Ones waved farewell sailing into the distance in their small boat.

In the past, this type of affection would have touched his heart deeply, but now his emotions were stunted by his grief. He gathered his strength and began to explore the green, luxuriant island

Amidst the harmonious beauty of the island, the grass, trees and flowers seemed to murmur songs of delight. But Ulu did not notice that aspect of his surroundings. He kicked the stones in his path, headed towards an area of plush grass and sat down, heavily.

"I asked You if I should take him," he uttered.

His words were as heavy in his mouth as boulders. He had to use every ounce of strength to voice them.

"I could not leave him in the village... I did what I thought was right... What will become of him now?" Inundated with feelings of misery, he felt as if his will to live had been taken from him.

I cannot do anything while Saag is in enemy hands, he wanted to say, but could not utter the words. He looked ahead helplessly. The waves crashed upon the shore in constant motion.

"I cannot go on. I cannot act. I would be better off dead," he concluded.

Something cracked in his heart. He forced himself to pause and examine his pronouncements before pouring out his heart, fully.

"Saag! If you have been poisoned by Khivia's pernicious whispers…if your pure aspirations have been obliterated by the messengers of the Emperors…"

Ulu began to sob and cry out in pain, as he plummeted deeper and deeper into the obscurity of his anguish.

And the Transcendor listened.

At this moment, Tzalaii found himself on an unfamiliar beach on a green and lush island. Green Isle! He had drifted for many days from the familiar shores of his village. The morning breeze caressed his face, smelling of the island's vegetation. He was near starvation, after his long storm-tossed sea voyage. The trees were remarkably fresh and vigorous; their movements in the wind poetic. The rich soil was visible through the overgrowth of vegetation and between the great trees whose peaks reached toward the sky. Fragrant, delicious fruit grew abundantly. After nourishing himself with the fruit, Tzalaii leaned back against one of the trees, and looked towards the beach attempting to assess his situation.

People, forces, and events had been set in motion after he had removed the stone from the outer wall, but Tzalaii was unaware of these events. He wondered what he was to do here, not even knowing how he had arrived. He wondered if any of his fellow-villagers had ever been here in the past. And he wondered about his sister, left behind in the village. *What would become of her?*

Some days passed and Tzalaii grew stronger. He had access to food and water and the island was pleasant, but he felt alone, restless and uneasy. One evening, at sunset, he noticed a man on the beach. His slow pace was confident and serene, his garb as simple as that worn by the villagers. At the same time Ulu, too, became aware of Tzalaii's presence.

I am not alone, thought Ulu. But silence, devoid of thoughts, descended upon him, and from within it he felt that he must remain in place until called upon to proceed. Saag was under the protection of the Transcendor. Ulu's messenger- the Master of Transcendence- knew everything. Ulu, on the other hand, knew nothing. But it was not his task to know everything. Some thoughts mustn't be contemplated.

Even from a distance, it was obvious to Ulu that the young and dreamy villager in the distance was not a threat. When Ulu reached him and extended his hand in peace, he recognized the boy as Tzalaii- the adventurous orphan from his village. As a Warrior of Transcendence, he knew he must conceal his surprise. Surely their meeting was no coincidence. He must pay close attention to everything. The boy did not recognize Ulu even though they were from the same village. Ulu always tried to appear simple and inconspicuous, giving no reason for others to notice him or remember his features.

"Welcome, my friend of the villages," Ulu began with calming words.

Tzalaii excitedly began asking questions: "I didn't know there were people here! I thought I would remain here on my own forever! Is there a way out? Are you the only one here? Are there others?"

"Let us sit," offered Ulu, pointing towards the sand. "So many questions cannot be answered while standing."

And so, Tzalaii related his memories of the storm, and his mysterious survival, carefully omitting any mention of the blue stone. Ulu explained his presence as accidental and offered Tzalaii his friendship. The boy felt safe with his new friend and trusted him fully. He proudly removed the golden cloth from his knapsack and with childish excitement, began telling Ulu about his discovery. Ulu examined the cloth. During his training in the Chamber of Changing Colors he had learned that this type of cloth had been worn only by Descendents of the Ancient Progeny. He turned it over and stroked it. The rough surface of the material accentuated the etchings. Hidden maps of the Tunnels of Time were always etched on the royal capes of the Descendents of the Ancient Progeny. Ulu casually returned the cloth to its owner, trying not to betray his intense interest in it. In time he might need this map, and it was good to know that the boy with the gleaming eyes held this precious and critical guide.

In the heart of the island, at that very moment, Sihara sat across from her Transparent Master as he spoke. He had secluded himself in his room for many hours, bent over his books, and gazing at the red stone. Now, it seemed, he understood its significance. He invited Sihara to listen to his assessment.

"It seems to me," he began hesitantly, "that I have reached a conclusion. The Transparent Ones sent this valuable stone to me because of the secret information it contains. Until now, the villagers chose to ignore the evil spirit threatening the earth. They preferred to believe that no harm would come to them, and they mistakenly insisted that the soldiers of the Tower will not arrive on the Shore of Kings Sea. However, the battles have already begun. Shadows are being cast in all places, and the dispatchers augment their forces each day. Even if the Transparent Ones are victorious in many battles, others shall be flung into the Abyss, and the land shall blacken with Shadows."

Sihara trembled as she listened to his words. *Are men the creators of the Shadows?* She wondered. *Why would humans want to create their own enemies? And what was this 'Abyss' mentioned by the Transparent Master?*

She gazed at the rock perched on the center of the table in the cabin and noticed a glimmer of light emanating from it.

The old man continued: "If the secret of the stone is revealed, everyone in the land will rebel. Old and young, adults and children, everyone will be outraged- possibly changing the outcome of the war. The Emperors know this, and consequently will do everything in their power to retrieve it. You must avoid them."

"Do you know the secret of the stone?" questioned Sihara, looking pale.

"I think so…" he hesitated, "I think so."

Silence hovered over the cabin and the trees outside were motionless.

"The Descendents of the Emperors did something dreadful; something that will cast eternal shame on every Emperor and every soldier in his army."

"This stone," he pointed to it as if it were alive, "is no stone at all"…

Sihara was stunned.

The sound of rustling, cracking branches was heard from outside. Sihara turned her head to the door. A sudden cold light entered the warm cabin, the light of torches held aloft by furious warriors, white flames embroidered on their clothing. They noisily crashed into the interior of the cabin like a sudden storm and then fell curiously silent. They stood proudly, stiffly, as if composed of metal. The tallest one pointed to the glimmering stone in the center of the cabin as two others seized it, concealing it in a small wooden box. Sihara froze in place, not knowing what to do. She glanced briefly at her Transparent Master, but he was gone.

"Seize her!" barked one of the warriors.

Within moments she was shackled and her mouth was taped. Two warriors carried her, as if she were a small branch.

At the same time, an entire brigade from the Lead Level was moving quickly towards the beach, planning to camp before proceeding at dawn. Silently and methodically, the warriors maneuvered through the trees, like large human beasts.

On the other side of the island, Tzalaii and Ulu were still sitting together and talking, as the Transparent Master searched for help. He had been told by the Transparent Ones that a Warrior of Transcendence on the island was in need of aid. Stealthily, he made his way to the beach, searching. Maybe together they could rescue the girl. A small flame stopped him in his tracks. Within seconds it had transformed itself into a dancing, furious pillar of fire. Another flame appeared and yet another. Within minutes, he was surrounded by brightly colored flames, hands of fire reaching out from within. Did they think he was human and could be frightened by their flames? He wondered. The encounter with the Shadows was never pleasant, but as far as he could remember he had never been defeated by a Shadow of any kind.

Ulu and Tzalaii were not too far from where the Transparent Master stood. The swirling flames were visible to them as well.

"Stay here!" ordered Ulu authoritatively.

Tzalaii had not heard him use this tone of voice before. Ulu ran towards the Transparent Master and was immediately spotted by the Shadows. Some of them continued circling around the Transparent Master while others turned towards Ulu. They whirled around in circles, causing their flames to appear thin and blue. As they neared Ulu they scorched all manner of branches and twigs, weeds and thorns in their path. They illuminated the night with their mysterious light, which was visible all the way to the shore. Tzalaii, who had found shelter in the high branches of a tree, shuddered in fear.

Ulu stood in place, suffering from the heat…his throat dry. His movements became heavier and he felt his strength being sucked away by the Shadows. He took a deep breath, focused on his inner self and ignored the swirling threat. Oddly, the Transparent Master remained motionless.

Does he not have the ability to help me? wondered Ulu. *He must be capable of helping me!*

Six white-clad beings appeared from behind the trees and neared Ulu. Their faces and eyes were sharp and their movements measured and consistent. The Shadows of Fire retreated and withdrew to observe from afar. Ulu knew that these were the

Extrappers. A quick glance at their emblem revealed the mark of white flames.

"The Stellar Level..." his lips formed the words involuntarily, as if they were familiar to him. He began to dance, intending to impersonate a storm dancer from the Northern Forests. The six warriors halted their approach but they remained nearby, watching Ulu's rhythmic movements with frozen faces. A white vapor arose from his dance and surrounded him. A similar vapor surrounded the Transparent Master as well. At once, Ulu noticed, through the corner of his eye, that the Transparent Master was performing a storm dance, as well.

The Extrappers moved forward. They released thin, golden threads from their hands, and threw them, like a net, upon Ulu. His dance came to a halt. The white vapor momentarily delayed the net's action, but dissipated soon after, allowing it to affix itself upon Ulu as a cocoon. Its heat was greater than his own.

The Shadows of Fire were getting closer and closer. Behind them stood the Stellar Warriors, awaiting the exciting sound of the explosion of thousands of thin glass shards.

Suddenly, a fierce voice bellowed forth, "In the name of the Stellar Emperor!"

The voice was heard over the shrill cries of the Extrappers, "Run for your lives!" The warriors turned around seeking the source of the concealed bellowing voice.

From the distant shore, a great howl echoed, as if immense waves were rising, crashing and rolling onto the island. Petrified warriors ran helter skelter in fear until one amongst them regained his composure and shouted, while pointing towards the Transparent Master- "It's his voice!"

Those who accepted this information quickly removed their small bows and began shooting threadlike arrows towards the Transparent Master; however he had just completed etching a circle around himself. A halo of light arose from the earth, sheltering and protecting him. The arrows struck the light, melting and disappearing.

The eerie howling of the waves intensified. The Transparent Master neared the Warrior of Transcendence, still trapped in the net of golden threads. The net generated sparks, as if the Transparent Master's presence caused it to increase its efforts. He removed a thin blade from the folds of his cape, and used it to cut and loosen one thread. The thread spun around, gaining heat as it rose up, and bounced back to one of the Extrappers whose hands were still extended. The face of the Extrapper immediately became smooth, and was drained of color. His facial features began to vanish, as if a melting agent had been poured on him, distorting his form. His body transformed into a gray glass-like powder. The net of threads surrounded the powder, burning up and becoming colorless, until it became black ash. The net trapping Ulu paled and weakened, allowing the air to return to his lungs.

And then rain began to fall. At first, tiny drops of water, almost imperceptible and finally, a sweeping, murky shower of black rain. The Shadows vanished and the noise stopped. Ulu opened his eyes. It seemed to him that he had been dreaming, and in his dream he had been pinned down by a net of fire that increasingly tightened, making it difficult for him to see and breath. Now all that remained from the dream was the fog in his mind, and Ulu remained prone on the ground surrounded by white clouds. He gathered his strength and searched for his Memory Shield, but it refused to appear. The memories of the Transparent Master had been wiped out, and he did not know where he was. Just then the fog lifted, and Ulu observed the transformation of the rain into silver swords. The swords struck the Shadows and the Warriors of the Stellar Level who were roundly defeated. His eyes scanned his surroundings until he noticed the Transparent Master smiling at him.

"Where did the voices and the noise come from?" Ulu asked eagerly.

"It's simple. Voice-casting."

"You did all that?" asked Ulu in astonishment.

"Yes," answered the Transparent Master. "It is possible to create inner voices and cast them outwards in any direction you desire."

There is yet more to learn, thought Ulu to himself, regarding the Transparent Master in a new light. Until then the Transparent Ones had looked somewhat fragile to him. He had witnessed them in combat, but not at such close range…

Contemplating Ulu's astonishment, the Transparent Master became serious and he stated, "We must not forget that everything is dependent upon Unification."

"Unification?" wondered Ulu, "You mean speaking with the Transcendor?"

The Transparent Master nodded. "All the voices of the spirit derive from it."

"We learned about this in our first initiation training session," said Ulu, "But how is it connected to casting voices?"

"It is connected to everything," answered the Transparent Master.

Time did not permit a full explanation of the matter. The island was creeping with Shadows- the Shadows of Fire that had attempted to harm Ulu were but a few of the many forces present on the island. Their friends, the Shadows of Illusion, had already captured Tzalaii and led him swiftly to the Warriors of the Lead Level, as a gift to their masters, the Emperors.

Realizing that Tzalaii had disappeared in the battle, Ulu and the Transparent Master marched quickly and silently along the beach, attempting to find the dock and rescue Tzalaii.

As the sun rose in the sky, Ulu and the Transparent Master sited the soldiers of the Tower preparing to set sail in three large boats. They hurried towards the dock, exposed to the soldiers. The soldiers in the boats, already afloat, were humiliated; their swords were of no use to them, and they had no arrows.

"Where, in the name of the holy fire, did the Shadows go?" the soldier in command roared.

"Hurry! Row!" he shouted at his soldiers.

They seized the oars and the heavy boats began to move away from the shore, carrying their precious loot: Tzalaii, Sihara and the stone from the wall. Ulu glanced at the Transparent Master, expecting the powers he witnessed during their encounter with the Extrappers to re-activate. But The Transparent Master entered within himself and closed his eyes silently as the boats continued to move farther away.

Nothing happened. The earth did not roar, the thundering hooves of animals were not heard, giant waves did not rise up and rain did not fall. An irritating silence hovered, as Ulu and the Transparent Master stood helplessly on the beach watching their friends depart in captivity.

"Why didn't you cast voices at them?" Ulu asked urgently.

"I tried to," the Transparent Master explained, "But this time the Transcendor did not grant me the power to do so."

"Why?" inquired Ulu.

The eyes of the Transparent Master studied the Man of Borders deeply, wondering about his question. He gently stroked Ulu's hand and said: "He always listens. He knows everything, but He does not always respond the way we expect Him to. His Will is not in our hands. We are in His hands."

He was silent for a moment, and then added: "If this were not so, our spirits would incorrectly conclude that we are the creators, and that the power resides in our hands."

As they spoke, they noticed that the boats had slowed down, and it seemed as though something was happening. One of the boats caught fire, its sails seized by flames. The warriors tried to battle the fire and extinguish it, but their attempts were in vain. Taking advantage of the confusion, Tzalaii dove into the sea. The waters were turbulent and swimming through them was no easy task, but Tzalaii's aquatic abilities came to his rescue. He mustered all of his strength and swam towards the boat where Sihara was shackled. The soldiers, occupied with the sails, did not notice Tzalaii's stealthy arrival, as he climbed into the boat... He pulled a knife out from his clothing and released his sister from her chains. But the soldiers on the distant boat noticed and sailed rapidly towards them. Ulu and the Transparent Master stood on the beach nervously watching the tense scene.

Sihara's captors aimed their swords at him. Just at that moment, the second boat reached them and its warriors seized Sihara. What happened next was completely unexpected. The Transparent Master opened his eyes and let out a great howl, reaching the ears of the Lead Level Warriors, despite the crashing waves. From a distance, from deep within the sea, the sounds of stampeding beasts and their riders were heard, accompanied by the steady beat of drums. Rain, again, began to fall. At first, tiny droplets of water, almost imperceptible, and finally, a sweeping, murky shower of black rain. In the boats, the warriors were fear-stricken. The strong wind and mighty waves created by the Transparent Master continued thrusting the tossing boats towards the shallow water. An inner voice momentarily guided Tzalaii's actions, and he was unable to focus properly on his goals. He handed his sister the Magnathought Crystal, mustered his voice from amongst the immense noise and instructed her to jump into the water. Sihara placed the object given to her into her clothing, used all her strength to ignore her fear and jumped into the roaring waves.

The noise ceased when the Transparent Master noticed Sihara struggling with the waves, and he directed all of his strength towards rescuing her.

"The Light of the Transcendor shall protect you!" he called to her, and she felt the water fall away from her as she was carried gently to the beach.

The warriors, frightened by the voices, yearned to escape. Tzalaii, ready to dive into the sea, was captured and chained to the mast as the boat began to sail out into the stormy waters, heading towards the Southern Boulders and beyond, to the Towered City.

Ulu, the Transparent Master and Sihara remained on the beach for some time, regaining their strength while staring helplessly at the sea. The storm raged, casting heavy rain upon them. Sihara crouched in the sand, in despair, throwing wet sand into the sea. Covering her face with her hands, she wept. Ulu, hands clasped behind his back, paced to and fro on the beach. The Transparent One sat on the beach, his hands atop his bent head cradled by his knees, like one who has witnessed an unavoidable tragedy. When he regained his composure, he turned to Sihara and said: "At least we were able to rescue you. Now you mustn't remain on this island. Many secrets have been revealed to you, and you are still at risk. Tzalaii is not lost."

When he saw her tears of despair, he added: "But only you can save him. That is why you must make your way to the Chamber of Changing Colors."

Suddenly Sihara remembered the object Tzalaii had given her. She took it out quickly and gazed contemplatively at the blue colored Magnathought Crystal in her hands. What was she to do with it? The Transparent One concentrated on it and his eyes grew increasingly wider.

"Look, my child," he called softly.

Sihara looked at the shiny object closely. Ulu, too, examined it, yearning to understand the old man's excitement.

"The tree!" they both exclaimed in surprise.

Inside the blue Crystal, fine lines were revealed, creating a picture of a great tree with many roots. Sihara looked up at the Transparent Master with wondering eyes.

"All living things, apart from Khivia and his servants, exist in this tree," explained the Transparent Master, "The root of the tree is the Transcendor. It is from Him that everyone receives life."

The roots of the etched tree gleamed in a purple light, and Sihara's eyes widened.

"The servants of the Transcendor are the branches- they receive life from Him and pass their strength on to their charges, the Storm Dancers and the villagers."

The thin branches were now a gleaming, illuminated purple.

"Even the Descendents of the Emperors, unless utterly devoted to serving evil, receive life from the tree, the way weeds take pleasure in the shade of a tree, even if they are not a part of it."

For a moment, the entire Magnathought Crystal turned purple, afterwards resuming its original blue color.

Many questions arose in Sihara's heart, but time was of the essence. She hid the Magnathought Crystal among her things, full of respect for it.

"The tree shall clarify all mazes," the Transparent Master said, concluding his bewildering words. Ulu got up.

"The Transcendor never forgets. Is that not true?" he said quietly.

It was unclear whether he was muttering to himself or talking to the Transparent Master.

"He has His own ways of touching your heart and granting you strength…the tree, who would have imagined that I would suddenly encounter it?"

He shook his head in awe, and turned to the others: "May the Light of the Transcendor protect you. I, too, shall continue on my journey now."

Chapter Eleven

Conspiracies at Obliterator's Peak

Conspiracies at Obliterator's Peak

The Ocean was turbulent; waves crashed down mightily upon the rocks, leaving behind a white froth. From atop the towering Obliterator's Peak, the water below was just a blur. Only a deep blue was visible to the naked eye. Down below by the sea, the sharp cliffs formed an impervious barrier, preventing access to the castle. On the opposite side, facing inland, thousands of Shadows guarded the structure. Shadows of Fire, Shadows of Illusion and Cloud Shadows encompassed the area, obscuring visibility and casting a pall upon the scene.

Obliterator's Peak, situated atop a large stone castle, was the lone remnant of the once flourishing cities on the Southern Cliffs. During long- forgotten distant times, this structure had served as one of the castles of the King of the Ancient Progeny. The Emperors had been drawn to the site, not because of its beauty, but because of its defensive position, massive strength, and isolation from other areas. From this vantage point, they would be able to pursue their evil plans.

The ten highest ranking Obliterators gathered in the main hall on the ground floor for an urgent meeting, accompanied by

Inviewers from all levels. Two warriors, white flames etched upon the corners of their garments, stood in statuesque silence beside a heavy, convex wooden door.

The ten expressionless Obliterators sat around a gray, exposed stone table. The atmosphere in the room was ominous. The few torches on the walls cast elongated shadows upon the floor. No one spoke.

The Obliterators were not human. They were creatures of doom, the creation of the Emperors at the start of their rule. Human fragments had been cast into the Abyss of Shadows: man's desires and passions, his dreams and aspirations, as well as enslaved humans who worshipped the White Fire. The substance formed from these fragments was used to create the various Shadows in the dark Abyss. All, with no exception, were exemplary servants of the Emperors and obeyed all of their rules. However, once in a while, it happened that human desires and passions would combine to form skin and muscle. This cluster of wills, instead of morphing into Shadows, remained in the Abyss, restless and turbulent.

Upon completion of the City, The Emperors decided to analyze this curious material. Clusters of it were taken to the castle, and the Inviewers discovered that it was malleable; it could be formed in any way they wished. The Inviewers were intent on creating powerful humanoid creatures capable of entering a man's brain, casting a shadow upon him, thereby capturing him to worship the fire. The Inviewers had been successful in creating the very first Obliterators in this way.

A strong Obliterator has the ability to connect to that element in humans which represents the shadow core, and to cause growth and development rapidly until the human is prepared to surrender his entire personality. At that moment, the Obliterator brands him with a surrogate personality, thereby compelling him to become a servant of the holy fire.

Errors and blunders occasionally occurred during Obliteration. Sometimes the Obliterator lacked precision while entering the spirit of their victim. Failing to locate the shadow core he might enter another element of the spirit. In this way, unwanted forces were inadvertently strengthened in the Obliterated man, such as free will or imagination. Aspirations or imagination which grew too large to be contained would cause a loss of sanity. Resistance of any kind was a protection against being branded with a surrogate personality. Those who were branded became devoid of inner essence. They were rendered empty and hollow, like broken vessels. The active fragments of spirit were like fire flickering through extinguished embers. These fragments were taken to the Southern Quarries.

Total Obliteration failures were also possible. There were brains which were capable of blocking all means of thought invasion. The Descendents of the Emperors preferred not to speak of such cases. They believed this was just a temporary obstacle, to be resolved by the creation of a stronger and more efficient Obliterator, capable of deeper, more pervasive, invasions into the spirit of man. To this end, they relentlessly toiled in their quest to create such beings in the underground laboratories of Obliterator's Peak.

Meanwhile, at the gathering, the present situation was still under discussion.

"Well," one of the Obliterators finally uttered, "maybe we shall finally get a clear picture of what is transpiring."

"Nothing justifies the many recent errors!" declared another, angrily.

"The situation is such," began a third in a formal tone of voice, capturing everyone's attention, "the stone was found on Green Isle and brought to the Towered City. The owner of the stone, Tzalaii, is still alive. He did not lose his life, as was first believed. The stone was in his possession when our warriors captured him on the Island. The affair is not yet settled…Warriors of the Stellar Level reached a dead end. They were confronted by two Warriors of Transcendence."

Whispers were heard amongst the listeners.

The speaker silenced them and continued: "A girl from one of the villages was found with them, but she managed to escape. Despite our control over the stone, we must face the possibility that our secret has been revealed to those remaining on the island. We must prevent them from sharing their knowledge with others."

"Why is it so difficult?" An Inviewer asked abruptly "Don't we have enough forces to surround the island and eradicate this minor threat?"

"Don't be so sure the disturbance is minor," answered the speaker. "There was a delay in the transfer of information and it is possible that the two have already left the island."

"Another immense failing, in addition to that of the rock," he continued, "is Mahn."

"The infamous!" shouted another Inviewer, mockingly.

"We have no doubt that his loyalty to the Tower is weakening steadily. We have no definite proof, but it is possible that Mahn has accessed information shards regarding our secrets, including the identity of the wall's building material."

"We shall follow him," said another Inviewer, "and he shall be executed if necessary."

"Yes…" answered the speaker with discomfort, "but that is the small problem."

He was silent for a moment, took a deep breath and added: "Even if the secret of the stone becomes known among men and creates an uprising, the system will not be seriously jolted. Our task now is to prevent Warriors of Transcendence from discovering the true nature of the wall. If the secret is in the hands of that man, it could cause the destruction of the external wall."

"And possibly the end of more than that… "someone muttered.

A murmur was heard in the hall, and then finally one of the Obliterators dared to ask: "Who said that the Master of Transcendence can threaten our wall?"

"Khivia," said the Obliterator, sharply.

All the participants responded with awe and respect to this authoritative approach.

"In addition to all this," the Obliterator continued, "there is disturbing information about the Tunnels of Time. Although formed in the distant past, they are still in use. The Transparent Ones and their accomplices are preparing for battle there."

All fell silent at this news. The Obliterators felt their stature diminishing as their confidence and security was threatened. They knew very well that their true enemies were neither the lowly villagers nor the Storm Dancers from the Northern Forests. The sole force threatening them and the millions of slaves in the Towered City was the Master of Transcendence, messenger of the Transcendor from the Land of the Ancient Progeny.

After a long tense silence one of the Obliterators spoke, "The soldiers of the Towered City must not yet be taken out into the region. The City dwellers are convinced that they are living in a safe and secure place devoid of all dangers. It would not be wise to expose them to the true nature of their tenuous situation at this time. This could cause great embarrassment amongst the City's inhabitants, and sow weakness in the hearts of the warriors. Despite this, I feel that the time has come to make wider use of the Shadows of Light."

Realizing that he was not inspiring confidence, he added: "although their forces are few, only with their help shall we be able to execute a significant mission aimed at misleading the Transparent Ones, thereby extracting them from the Tunnels of Time."

"If they are indeed there…" said another Obliterator.

"Of course they are!" a third Obliterator joined in. "Be careful not to underestimate the value of the information regarding the Tunnels of Time. You must remember- He who unearthed them was none other than the King of the Ancient Progeny himself. Without a map, we have no concept of the extent of the tunnels or their methods of operation."

An aggravating silence once again settled in the hall. Two warriors from the Lead Level left their station by the door and approached the table. They listened to the conversation intently and an idea was formed in their minds. At the sight of the white flames on the corners of their garments, those present at the table remained silent and focused, listening. But the radical idea presented by the two warriors soon led to a raucous outbreak.

"If you will, honorable Obliterators," said one of the warriors, in a polite voice, " may I suggest you head for the battlefield? Your special talents may improve the situation drastically."

The Obliterators preferred to affect events from a distance, and to make use of the Shadows for the ground battle. The idea of abandoning the peak to participate in a battle in the fields was a cause for alarm. Nevertheless, once this idea was brought to light by the Inviewers of the white flames, the Obliterators actually considered it and thought it might find favor with the Emperors.

Chapter Twelve

The Essence of Soul Concentration

The Essence of Soul Concentration

The sealed gate was actually a massive stone mound on the side of the mountain. Though it was similar in every way to the stones in its midst, Mahn had no doubt that this was the place he sought. The accompanying soldiers with sapphire flames waited silently.

He touched the stone wall searching for the protrusion of the gate. The stone moved aside without a sound and Mahn and his men entered a large illuminated hall. The walls were bright, illuminated by an inner light, skillfully designed and etched with the same flames present on the outer wall. *A bit too grandiose for a mine...* thought Mahn. The stone door closed slowly and a warrior with a sapphire flame approached Mahn, greeting him and asking for identification.

"I am Mahn- Inviewer from the Mercury Level, messenger of the Holy Fire."

The warrior appeared somewhat uncomfortable. He summoned his comrades from their position by the entrance and spoke with them. Mahn pretended disinterest in their conversation and waited. Although he had never before been here, he was confident that as Senior Inviewer it was his right to visit locations of his choice in the Land of White Fire. He also had the authority to initiate inspections on his own, without the approval of his superiors.

Still, the uneasiness he had been feeling over the past few months, which had intensified following the investigation of the old woman, had not faded, despite his promotion to the Mercury Level. Now he hoped that a prolonged absence from the City would be beneficial to him. So he had decided to visit the Southern Mines, which were always mentioned with great awe and respect.

The soldier turned to him and asked: "Did you receive the password?"

Now he was in a bit of trouble because his visit was unofficial. But Mahn had remarkable self-control. Without a moment's hesitation, he said the officially accepted words customary in requesting entrance: "Melt its locks."

The Warrior was satisfied. Mahn's gamble had been successful.

"Well then, leave your attendants here. Do not worry; they shall be looked after properly. We have a waiting room and food aplenty. Here is your guide. He shall accompany you on your tour of inspection."

Mahn followed his guide in the darkness, illuminated only by the light of the torches. Upon leaving the ante-room, they descended a spiral staircase leading deep into the mountain core, and Mahn's heart filled with fear. He strengthened his grasp on the sharp sword he carried and stroked the corners of his garment.

What is so secret about these ancient mines, in the name of the holy fire? He wondered to himself.

They passed through seven stone gates as they continued on

their way. The guards, their swords extended, were not typical warriors. Their faces were hidden, and the man accompanying Mahn communicated with them in the Whistle Dialect. Mahn's curiosity was dampened as he felt a strong desire to halt his adventure. But he did not know how to do so, and remained silent. A faint light began to appear through the dark walls. Now they entered a large hall, similar to the ante-room. Dozens of unmarked caped warriors stood before a luminous stone wall. Their whistled 'conversations' with his guide were piercingly loud.

"I must beg your pardon," the guide explained. "We may not enter at this time."

They waited in a room and were offered hot food, but Mahn's spirit was uneasy. Facing the man in the lit, spacious room, Mahn once again examined his fair face, and in an attempt to fill the irritating silence, asked: "What is your position here?"

The man appeared to be happy with the question and answered boastfully: "I am Manager of the Essence Division."

Mahn realized that he must take precautions in formulating his questions. He had never heard of a division of this type in the mines he had visited.

The guide, eager to share his knowledge, spared Mahn the trouble of asking questions, saying, "I shall explain everything upon arrival at our destination."

Passing through the final gate, Mahn found himself in a huge hall. Through an opening in a wall he saw large carts filled with a vaporous substance slowly seeping out. Workers unloaded the sizzling contents of the carts into a large boiler situated in the center of the room. Despite the oppressive heat, Mahn noticed that none of the workers were perspiring, nor did they appear to be tired. The workers toiled rapidly and effectively, and were light on their feet. Every so often, one of them let out a short whistle. So, the Whistle Dialect was used here, too.

"This is the first boiler," explained Mahn's guide.

"Here, as you can see, the red substance is brought to an exceptionally high heat, after being transported in carts from the lower mines. It is already being heated up as it is carried here."

They continued walking together towards another part of the hall. There, the crimson metal flowed through open stone pipes into a large basin. The agile workers- Whistlers- were busy accurately measuring the yellow clusters. These clusters sizzled as they were tossed into the basin.

"Here," the man continued excitedly, "we add a small amount of yellow glass to the crimson substance, which gives it its unique transparency. This, of course, explains the changing colors in the wall's bricks."

Suddenly, Mahn realized he was actually in the wall's brick factory. A sudden exhaustion spread over his limbs and he became bewildered as he thought about the heavy secrecy surrounding this process.

What is the secret of the wall's bricks?

"Now," the man continued, a serious expression on his face, "we reach the most important part."

They passed through a large stone arch into another hall. The room was freezing cold. They were alone, and all was silent. Just a slight sound resonated from time to time, like dripping water. Here, the bricks were cooling off in small stone molds.

"This is the location of the most confidential secret in the system," intoned the man solemnly, though Mahn had begun to think this must be an exaggeration.

The cold began affecting him and he lost his patience.

"Oh, I see you are cold my friend. Take my cape."

The Division Manager offered Mahn his outer cape.

"I am already accustomed to the cold," he added. Mahn was grateful to receive the cape, though what he saw next terrified him so greatly that his temperature rose immediately, the blood throbbing in his veins, his hands shaking. On the corners of the Division Manager's garment was a green flame, the flame of the Solar Level. Mahn would not have been more excited if he had seen the ancient sun itself! During his training, he had learned that the Solar Emperor resided on the fifth level, and that all of his servants bore a green flame on the corners of their garments. But to actually see one of them? He never dared to dream of it!

He must be an imposter! Is this some kind of joke? he attempted to calm himself,

My imagination may be deceiving me...but, in the name of the holy fire, a green flame really was etched on the corners of the guide's garment! It cannot be a fake. One would pay a high price for this type of fraud!

The man noticed Mahn's excitement.

"Come, come, my young fellow. Pay attention to all the details so you may fulfill your task properly."

They neared the wall of the room. Mahn noticed a glass basin moving along tracks set into the wall. The basin contained silvery liquid, almost transparent, and moved above the rows of bricks. A drop of this liquid was poured onto each brick. Clusters of the crimson yellow substance, almost completely hardened, absorbed the drop and began changing. Silvery veins, transparent and semi-alive were formed. They were illuminated briefly by a strong inner light, and then immediately hardened, their transparency turning into a cold white gleam.

It is as if one moment of life, real and pulsating, is frozen into each cluster, thought Mahn, shaken.

"This, as you can see," said the man seriously, "is the final stage. And this," he pointed to a glass container, "unites everything, and most importantly gives the bricks their powers of defense. From here, the bricks continue to the design chambers where the flames are etched into them. But this," he once again pointed to the dripping silver, "is what is most important."

Mahn felt a strong urge to escape from the mine, though the man with the green flame had not yet finished speaking.

"Pure silver, clear as a tear," he stated with unexpected poetic flair, a contrast to his usual brusque and orderly style. Mahn was familiar with these words. But where had he heard them before?

"And that, known only to very few of us, is the Essence of Soul Concentration."

Man was flustered. "The essence of what?"

"The Essence of Soul Concentration," the man repeated patiently. "When Obliteration fails, the Obliterated Ones always remain in the midst of the process, a segment of their souls remaining open. The forces that are retained within them, that have yet to be redesigned and processed, are available and ready for our use. We concentrate them and add a small amount of silver, thus creating the liquid you see." Mahn was still but his limbs began trembling again.

The Essence of Soul Concentration? He had heard of unsuccessful Obliterations, but never thought about the end result.

"It seems to me, Sir Inviewer," the man suddenly stated, "That you are overly excited."

"I don't understand what use the Emperors could possibly make of such broken and confused matter...from the Soul Essence of partial Obliterated Ones...," Mahn attempted to gather his thoughts in order to present himself in a composed and orderly fashion.

"This material is not broken and confused!" declared the Division Manager. "The segment of Soul Essence is an amazing concentration of the entire intensity of the man prior to his obliteration. Only the outer layer of the soul is marred during the partial obliteration. The Soul Essence remains unscathed. It cannot be damaged, and is impossible to re-create."

The Division Manager gazed at the transparent drops trickling down onto the bricks. "This is life itself," he said solemnly. "All they could have been, their potential, had they not been processed for obliteration."

Life itself! The words made a strong impression on Mahn.

It struck him that there might be a connection between the Emperors' campaign to gather Soul Essences and their inability to propagate. Many thoughts crossed his mind, leaving behind scores of questions, and his body began to tremble uncontrollably.

You will be able to contemplate your thoughts later, whispered an inner voice. *Now you must leave this place!*

He mustered all of his remaining strength and spoke in a stable tone of voice. "I apologize, but you see, I am unaccustomed to such cold temperatures."

"Of course," the man resumed speaking in a friendly voice. "We should leave. Your attendants await you."

Forces continued streaming out of the lower City, some heading towards the Northern Lowlands, and others towards the Land of the Southern Cliffs. Skilled soldiers, aware of the Emperors' plans, were swiftly taking their places in the battle zone, awaiting a sign. In the deep ravines, beneath the Towered City, the Obliterators were busily training the Shadows for their intended mission. In Elassar's room an expressionless Inviewer completed the delivery of his latest report.

"…And another long hour passed as he strolled along the

courtyard outside of the building, until he finally entered his room and went to bed."

"He shall be exterminated," declared Elassar silently, "before the end of year celebrations."

Chapter Thirteen
Shadow Valley

Shadow Valley

Sihara crossed the sea aided by the Transparent Ones to whom she had been introduced by the Transparent Master. She was delighted to discover the unexpected existence of these curiously charming and friendly creatures. Traveling together, they were careful to avoid the White Desert by making their way along the slopes leading towards the Land of the Northern Forests, an arduous journey that would take two weeks. But the pleasant melodies sung by the Transparent Ones and the communal meals they shared with Sihara uplifted her spirits. Her companions' inner lights revived her.

Eventually they reached a dark valley. Here, the Transparent Ones took their leave from her, warmly wishing her well. And so she was left alone.

How, she wondered, *had she come to such a place, young and alone, treading on a deserted path to an unknown destination? Yes, her Transparent Master had dispatched her on this mission. His words still echoed in her mind: She alone could release Tzalaii from imprisonment. How would she accomplish this feat?*

She did not know. *But hadn't he promised that the Master of Transcendence would explain everything to her in the future?*

The Master of Transcendence!! Sihara had learned from her Transparent Master that the Master of Transcendence had instilled his fear upon the Descendents of the Emperors, who fear no others. This pervasive fear prevents them from seeking conquest. They exist in perpetual terror, searching unceasingly for his signs everywhere, wary of his followers.

But where is the Master of Transcendence? Sihara's Transparent Master had conveyed this secret information to Sihara.

Tell no one, he admonished, as she agreed to take an oath of secrecy.

Sihara gazed upon the great valley; a gray mist hovered over it like birds of prey. The earth, the atmosphere, the tangled masses of foliage and, in fact, everything visible as far as the distant, obscured horizon, seemed gray and lifeless. She descended along the pathway hesitantly, with trepidation, moving inevitably towards an abysmal land devoid of splendor. In days of old, this valley had been the site of one of the great rivers, *The River of Profundity* as the Descendents of the Ancient Progeny called it. But now, with the river gone, the parched gray valley presented a sharp contrast to the nearby blue and awesome sea.

The dark, gray forest of Shadow Valley was covered by layers of ancient dust. Trees and gnarled trunks, rocks and shrubs, even the few leaves that had managed to survive, seemed old and decrepit. The dust covered Sihara's clothing and her face and hands took on a gray pallor.

Such a gloomy place... she mused, as her confidence and courage weakened. Thorns and broken branches interfered with her progress and large boulders blocked her path.

Nonetheless, Sihara continued to descend into the depths of the forest, bravely distancing herself from familiar territory, sinking into a deep gloom where darkness prevailed. The main path was difficult to follow as it veered off into side paths from time to time. Although she attempted to focus on her goal, Sihara's clarity was disturbed by the pervasive eerie silence and dismal gloom which affected her thoughts and cast doubt in her heart.

Many dull, uneventful and wearying days passed. Everything began to look familiar, predictable to her- the stones scattered along the path, tree stumps and boulders. But, in spite of this, she was, as yet, unaware of the fact that she had been walking in hopeless circles…

A ray of light striking the treetops attracted her attention. She looked up, awe-struck, to see green tree-tops, a surprising contrast to the infernal gray down below. Looking further, she noticed a flock of birds... Their bright, lively colors were enchanting, their songs sweet and alluring, dreamy and peaceful. The dancing rays of light came closer and a lone bird parted from the flock and flew towards her. Its wings were a luminous purple, its belly pure white, and a golden feather was perched on its head, pointed backwards. Sihara felt a sense of pleasure as she observed the bird, joyful that the creature had flown her way. She stood motionless, staring at it. *Maybe I should follow it*, she wondered. *Such a majestic bird can surely guide me forward.*

Do not be deceived by appearances, Sihara remembered her Transparent Master's words of advice. She trembled and closed her eyes. The bird's cries intensified, urging her to open her eyes and look at it. But when she did she was horrified; enfolded in the luminous purple wings she saw ominous, claw-like talons, and now the bird's beak was hideously wide open. *Why hadn't she noticed this before?*

"Do not be deceived by appearances," she admonished herself aloud, her voice echoing through the thicket of trees.

"Do not be deceived by appearances!" she repeated, this time with even more conviction as though to strengthen herself. The forest, once again, became gray and dismal. The bird had vanished!

The path began to twist and turn. Sihara focused her sight upon a stone lying on the path, noticing that it was becoming larger. As she concentrated upon a thorn bush, its stems began to thicken and lengthen, sending out rapacious, sharp tentacles towards her, seemingly hungry to destroy everything in its path. Her only chance, she quickly and astutely realized, would be to reduce her focus on her surroundings by restricting her vision, looking at things only out of the corners of her eyes.

Eventually she reached a stone well. The scent of sweet, fresh water was in the air. As she neared the well, her thirst increased. She suddenly became aware of her parched lips, her intense thirst. Although the satchel given to her by her Transparent Master held a leather thermos, the little water that remained tasted bitter. How happy she was to have discovered fresh water! A wooden pail, conveniently perched on the well, seemed to invite her to lower it and quench her thirst.

To drink…There was nothing Sihara wanted more! She leaned on the edge of the cold stone well, grasped the rope and lowered the pail into the well, deeper and deeper, but it never seemed to reach the water. Sihara could clearly see the pleasant glimmer of the water deep within the well. Why was the pail not reaching it? To drink….to drink…to drink….

I will climb down into the well to drink, she thought, pleased with her idea.

Inspecting the well's inner wall, she noticed a rope ladder leading into the depths. How strange that she had not seen it before. Sihara moved towards the well, reaching out to grab the ladder. The water in the depths seemed so cold, so inviting! But before she could place her feet on the ladder, a whisper was once again present on her lips: "Do not be deceived by appearances."

But how could she be deceived? She wondered.

Nevertheless, before descending, she gazed at the waters once more. For a fleeting moment she sensed a dark shadow in the depths, like the presence of a large beast. Terror-struck, the consuming thirst dissipating, but still attracted, she forced herself to look, once more, into the well. And the water once again seemed pleasant, sweet and clear.

"Do not be deceived by appearances!" she heard herself shout, in a voice emanating through her as in a dream. At once, she let go of the ladder, shut her eyes, returned to the path and forced herself to continue on her way. The water in the well bubbled and shrieked, letting out angry cries.

How had she been able to see through this trick perpetrated by the Shadows of Illusion? Seductive, paralyzing, captivating, designed to entrap her...Although she had escaped this time, a heavy feeling overcame her.

Would she ever find her way out of this seemingly endless forest? Would the path lead her to a clearing?

No, she suddenly answered her own question. *This path leads nowhere.*

It had taken her around and around in hopeless circles, from one illusion to another. Fear now rose in her throat.

Was she destined to spend the rest of her days wandering aimlessly? She stopped and inspected her surroundings: Bare branches, dark treetops, faint light, a faraway wail....

Who would guide her through this?

She noticed that the foliage was becoming less dense. She hopefully removed several decaying branches, discovering a clear path beyond the tangled trees. A faint green hue seemed almost visible among the trees, and if her eyes did not deceive her, fresh green leaves were visible in the distance. Life!! Life beyond the chilling barrenness! Sihara breathed deeply as fresh air entered her lungs, and the trees appeared alive and lush.

The living forest, no longer gray and ominous, sprawled out over the mountain slope, the light gradually increasing. Here and there, broken branches, Shadows and rocks still obstructed her path, but Sihara reminded herself that appearances are deceiving, and she continued walking, confidently. Gradually, the Shadows disappeared. The slopes became steeper but Sihara ascended steadily and purposefully. Shrieks were replaced with the soft sounds of a gentle breeze. The light of day increased, and Sihara felt calm as the breeze in the treetops blew the promise of redemption.

But as Sihara approached the long-awaited end of the trail, with only a few steps to go, an unexpected turn of events occurred: With every step, the resonance of life began to fade. Once again, the air became gloomy, the sunlight diminished and she felt, paradoxically, as if she fell backwards with every forward step she took.

"No!" shrieked Sihara. A multitude of echoes rang through the darkening forest.

"No!…No!…No!…"

Sihara came to a halt. *If every step seemed to take her farther from her destination, would it not be better to stop now? Perhaps I should go back in order to move forward?* a shadowy thought entered her mind. She turned around toward the last place on earth she wished to see.

"Do not be deceived by appearances," she heard a distant voice whisper in her heart. Ashamed, inert, listening to the battle of voices from within herself, and with a strength of spirit not solely her own, she turned around, away from the gloom, closed her eyes and walked one step at a time towards the illusionary darkness ahead murmuring: "I will go forward…I will go forward…I will go forward…"

Her pace increased as she found herself walking with a lighter step. She neared the forest, dark and bursting with Shadows, and announced with all her might, challenging all illusions: "I am going forward!"

The Shadows faded away. Sihara ran towards the light. Limp and exhausted, with branches striking her face, her hair in disarray, she felt confused as she emerged from the tangled trees. Though the forest was behind her, though she had emerged from the endless tangle of trees, though the sun shone brightly upon bare hills where Shadows did not rule, it was not over yet. Sihara now faced another obstacle- a wall composed of rigid, tangled, twisted shrubbery, an impassable natural overgrowth, extending as far as she could see.

Chapter Fourteen

The Marker of Tumult

The Marker of Tumult

The storm was over. Tzalaii was certain that the arrogant soldiers were leading him to the Towered City. After venting their anger to Tzalaii on the loss of their comrades and belongings, they became silent. When the second boat reached them, the warriors of the Lead Level, white flames etched onto the corners of their garments, performed their tasks flawlessly.

There were three warriors in each boat. Two were oarsmen while one observed the waters, serving as navigator. The stern, silent warriors relaxed a bit and shared their bread rations with their prisoner, but they spoke only when necessary. Tzalaii inquired about their destination, and the chief warrior pointed towards the distant shores, announcing almost kindly: "To the Tumult." Tzalaii had never before heard of such a place.

In five days time, the warriors and their prisoner prepared to dock at a small, hidden stone harbor. Long sandy beaches, dozens of gray birds circling above them, came into view. At the sight of the beaches, Tzalaii was eager to explore, but he was led to the vast front porch of a large stone cabin at the top of a hill overlooking the sea. From an old wooden bench on the porch he was able to see the entire expanse of the coast below. The warriors commanded Tzalaii to sit and wait, while they entered the stone cabin.

Is this the 'Tumult'? Such a strange name for a place so serene... thought Tzalaii.

Had he not been fearful of the future, Tzalaii would have allowed himself to relax and fill his lungs with the fresh sea air. Down below, small waves crashed onto an outcropping of rocks. The sea here was a deep, dark blue, unlike the turquoise color of the sea he loved so dearly back at home. Beyond the house, the island was covered in dense foliage. Massive tree trunks towered into the sky, their branches reaching out protectively over fruit trees.

A woman dressed in white emerged from the stone house, bearing a blue-tinted beverage. Placing the drink next to Tzalaii, she quickly returned to the house. Not one word was spoken. Tzalaii gazed at the drink, enjoyed its refreshing aroma and realized how thirsty he was. Though the water he had been given in the boat had quenched his thirst, the chilled drink before him had an altogether different effect. With each sip, Tzalaii sensed new life flowing into his body. The flavor was somewhat reminiscent of the sour crimson fruit he had eaten during his journey in the Green Lowlands, though this drink was even more delicious, and delicately spiced.

Just as he took the last few sips of his drink, Tzalaii heard a soft melody coming from the cabin. The tune had a deep, inner intensity that captivated Tzalaii completely. A pleasant sea breeze blew through the treetops, swaying them gently. The sun was setting and the air was clear. The entire landscape possessed such transparent clarity, leading Tzalaii to feel as though he could see way beyond the horizon. The waves, the melody, the wind and the sea were so full of life! The color of the sand transformed from yellow to golden, and as he watched, Tzalaii was able to see each grain of sand as a distinct picture, well defined and eternal. Life pumped through each and every grain. Profound life...

movement and desires... knowledge and understanding. Tzalaii became fearful, lest he disappear into a grain of sand! Everything he saw resembled a gate, and he felt that if he were to continue gazing, each gate would open up and he would pass through them into new worlds. *Maybe the gates would shut behind him, and he would never be able to return to his own world?*

His own world? And what is his own world? And why was it preferable to the fascinating, miniscule world of a single grain of sand? For everything was so full of life! What was the meaning of Tzalaii's life in comparison to the thousands and thousands of living creatures in his midst?

What is happening to me? a fleeting thought entered Tzalaii's consciousness and then disappeared into the eternal intensity of a grain of sand. The beverage continued to work its wonders. Tzalaii got up, tears of joy streaming down his face. He had a strong desire to embrace the immense beauty in his midst, to hold each grain of sand in his hand and nurture it, caress it, calm it, and grant it love and joy.

But how can a simple man embrace such a great multitude of worlds? How can a little, lost man be responsible for caring for so many creatures?

Suddenly images of people from the past flashed before his eyes: Friends from the village, acquaintances...and he felt compelled to embrace them, too, and protect them. *But from what?* He did not know. Overcome by the intensity of the moment, he felt empowered and with total conviction he told himself: *Nothing is beyond my reach. If I desire, I shall enter a grain of sand and lose myself inside it. If I want, I shall fly like a bird into the heavens.*

"You cannot do any of that," whispered a small voice from within, infuriating Tzalaii by this interruption of his vision. "But you can contribute your voice, and you can add another note to perfect the song." The melody grew louder, as if to swallow the voice and block out his words. Tzalaii could hear the song of the stars and the movement of the sea waves, and could sense life pulsating in distant galaxies as well as in the tiny leaves growing on the nearby bushes. Like a master surrounded by his servants, he stood up and listened.

"You too must sound your voice before the great King," the small voice spoke to him once again, barely audible, from a distance. Tzalaii could now feel life pulsating from within. The sensation struck him so forcefully that he became dizzy. Somehow, in all the intensity, he managed to let his own thoughts stream into his consciousness.

"I am the great king!" he declared, flooded with feelings of grandeur.

"You are but a vessel receiving a wondrous blessing, in song and gratitude," answered the moments of silence between pulsations. Tzalaii was being tossed around between the voices. "Make a choice!" the voice spoke to him for the final time.

"Don't choose! Allow yourself to be swept away…" the sounds of the universe tempted him.

"I am the great king!" he stood erect and raised his head toward the heavens. "This is all mine. I formed all of the creatures, and I have the power to change them according to my will!"

From deep within his powerful vision, his creatures began calling him, their spirits raging and begging: "Creator! Touch me! Grant me life!"

Winds of many variations blew past him. Winds of the sand, winds of the sea, winds of the fish, and winds of the heavens, winds of stone and winds of man, winds of the past and winds of the future.

They all pleaded to Tzalaii: "Creator! Touch me!"

Graciously, he pardoned each and every creature with the touch of his hand. A loving, regal touch. A brave, bonding caress, like that of a woman to the unborn child within her. The sun had already set, but the inner light was still visible to Tzalaii. The tune was no longer audible, yet Tzalaii could still hear it being played in his mind. The sounds opened new worlds in him, daring heights and an endless horizon of royalty.

Chapter Fifteen

All Waiting Shall Be Fulfilled

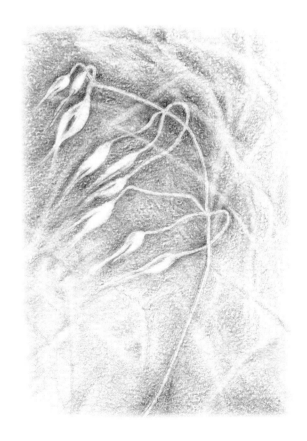

All Waiting Shall Be Fulfilled

Ulu arose at the break of dawn and prepared to leave on his journey. Two fair-haired Transparent Ones, their golden capes billowing in the breeze, escorted him to the boat anchored on the island's shore. In no time at all, they found themselves heading eastward down the tree-covered slopes of the Northern Forests. The fall foliage was at its peak and multitudes of yellow and orange leaves were visible from the mountain. Great piles of leaves were everywhere and the crunching sound created when the dry leaves were disturbed could be heard for miles.

 The Transparent Ones carried food for Ulu and were naturally cheerful and happy. Because he was a solitary person, their constant presence made him slightly uncomfortable. But he knew that being alone was not necessarily beneficial to him. While in the company of these light- footed and gracious companions, his own movements seemed heavy and clumsy in contrast, and he experienced difficulty in speaking.

The Transparent Ones were in no hurry. In the evening hours they would slowly gather sticks in the forest, patiently laying them down individually, as if the placement of each and every one was of utmost importance. Later, when it became darker and the nocturnal animals began sounding their calls, the Transparent Ones would light the fire. Cross-legged by the fire, they gazed into the crimson flames which were reflected in their eyes. Their songs, almost childish, invaded Ulu's mind and eventually brought a smile to his face.

These are the words to one of their songs:

Every tree and stone beholds a unique song

A single step launches a journey, so long

A clear sky instills tranquility in the hearts of all

And loneliness is not always painful to recall.

The wind swirled about them, listening to their song, wondering about their hope. Two Transparent Ones and one human on the way to Obliterator's Peak- Would they be strong enough to fight the darkness spreading throughout the world?

As the days passed, the forest became less dense. A lone deer passed nearby every so often, and Ulu learned from the Transparent Ones that the deer's presence was a sign that their destination was near. After the arduous trek of three weeks, the Transparent Ones finally pointed and said: "We have arrived!"

The noonday sun shone upon a large clearing in the forest, which was covered by low-lying, light green shrubbery. This was the deer's home and they were not easily startled. This time, they did not flee from the newcomers as if they felt secure, knowing that no harm could come to them.

The Transparent Ones sat down comfortably on the grass, joined by the Man of Borders. Ulu was amazed that a place so beautiful could exist in the Kingdom of the Ancient Progeny. He gazed around him and realized that this was the highest point in the Land of the Northern Forests. On his left Ulu saw huge descending cliffs, and in the East loomed a fiery mountain range. Despite its great height, fire from the mountain tops was visible from time to time, and molten lava streamed like a crimson river down the distant slopes.

A gray and murky landscape lay to the right and Ulu despondently recognized it as the Shadow Valley. He chose to look away. The sight of the White Desert caught his attention, and he recalled his experiences there. He remembered sitting in the desert, motionless, for what seemed like eons, absorbing the desert's stillness. In the heart of the valley lay the Towered City, reaching upward towards the heavens like a gigantic, overgrown weed, abundant with black stones, towers, citadels and countless levels. Those who gazed at the Tower were filled with fear, even before seeing the eternal white flame at its peak.

In the distant Land of the South, rugged mountains covered the horizon. During his first initiation training session in the Chamber of Changing Colors, when he was still a boy, Ulu had heard about the great cities, adorned in beauty, which existed during ancient times in the Land of the South. The Magnificent Kingdom of the Ancient Progeny... But the broad valleys between the mountains, once filled with people walking home from journeys to the Green Lowlands, now lay desolate, lifeless.

Will I, too, merit to cross through those distant valleys? Pondered Ulu, as he wondered about the meaning of his own thoughts.

Ulu felt compelled to look toward his homeland which lay far in the distance, to the west. As Ulu gazed at King's Sea, which appeared as a blurry, blue stain, he suddenly recalled his last visit to the village. In his minds eye he could see how the apple trees were the first to transform into a light mauve hue. His daughter, Shaii, had told him so. He could picture the patch of grass that covered the ground by the entrance to his home, and the gentle orange-colored flowers blooming on either side of the door. Ulu remembered inspecting the new carrot patch and listening to Shaii speak excitedly. He remembered sitting with his wife on a great old tree trunk by the front wall, enjoying their children at play. The sun had spread its rays generously over the world. A light breeze had carried the scent of fresh fish from the dock, and Shaii and Dorianne sat on the old swing as Saag pushed them

"I mustn't think of home!" Ulu reprimanded himself aloud. But the memory of his eldest son pierced his heart like a painful thorn, causing more and more pain with every thought, reminding him of the depth of his loss. An image forced itself into Ulu's mind. It was the image of his son during their last moments together: *Saag was gazing at the horizon, and saw the Towered City for the first time in his life. Would his innocent heart be saved from such profound evil?*

Evening fell, coloring the sky in a crimson hue. A sudden chill entered Ulu's body as the evening winds began to blow. The deer had vanished and the clearing on the cliffs was exposed to the wind. The Transparent Ones directed Ulu to take shelter among the tall trees of the forest. There, they lit a small fire and the Man of Borders, Ulu, calmed his thoughts as he listened to the voices of the Transparent Ones. To his surprise, he discovered that they were composing a song about his emotions.

"Loneliness is not always painful to recall," they sang with gentle voices.

The final words of their song led into another: "Sometimes one must listen deeply to the echoes of his own heartbeat, to the leaves cascading gently to the earth, to the voyage of the winds, to the struggle of the forces of nature: Sky and earth, chaos and light…"

Ulu found their words magical and heartwarming. He had a vivid sense that beyond the song, which portrayed autumnal loneliness at the summit of the world, there was a deeper meaning that related to his mission.

Just as before, details of his mission had not been fully disclosed to him and, instead, the Transparent Ones directed him to continue waiting in this place. For how long and why, he did not know. But his inner senses had taught him that this lack of information was a part of his trials in the mission he was to fulfill. He was well-equipped, and the Transparent Ones had pointed out the many trees which grew nearby, abundant with sweet fruit, even in the autumn.

The climate was warmer in the forest, and the Man of Borders hoped that he would be able to spend the night there safely. Completing their song, the Transparent Ones prepared to depart. Their illuminated faces and capes dimmed, as if they were aware of something casting a shadow upon their hearts. They did not share their fears with Ulu, and only said: "So says the Master of Transcendence: Be attentive to every moment in time. The voice of your heart shall guide the way. Have patience, and the Light of the Transcendor shall protect you. When all looks lost, remember and never forget: All waiting shall be fulfilled."

"All waiting shall be fulfilled"…Ulu repeated their words, as the aura of the Transparent Ones disappeared beyond the mountain

Ulu turned towards the cliff that faced Fire Mountain, unhappy about having to part with his cheerful companions. For a few long moments, he gazed at the site of their departure. Observing the distant crimson lava, he turned his ears to the inner voice of his heart, and waited.

Deep in the belly of the earth, the Warriors of Transcendence continued their training. They sat in a circle, in close proximity to one another, and listened intently to the words of a senior trainer: "Lack of precision sustains sadness, and sadness sustains the Shadows. But a precise voice has the ability to melt all Shadows. A word that conveys the strength of its speaker's spirit can overcome an Obliterator."

The cave filled with several lone sounds uttered by the trainer, which circled like birds over the heads of the warriors. The sounds waned, becoming distant, almost impossible to hear, calming in a way, but still of great intensity.

"You," the trainer pointed to one of the warriors, "Share your voice with us."

Chapter Sixteen

Abyss of the Shadows

Abyss of the Shadows

Sihara was overcome with desperation. She sat down on the exposed ground, and gazed into space. She sat motionless for over an hour, wondering: *How is it possible? Is there no way out of this road?*

She peered between the bushes, hoping to find a breach, but the overgrowth was thick, thorny and impassable, as far as the eye could see.

"You are unworthy!" whispered an inner voice, "You are an empty and lowly creature."

The wall of thorns mocked her childish hope, her innocence and faith. Did a Man of Transcendence truly exist in the world? Her encounter with the Transparent Master was now a blurred and distant memory. She sat huddled on the hard ground, her thoughts few, her hope diminished, her whole self disappearing into oblivion.

"You are worthless!" scorned the bushes.

"You are worthless!" agreed the hard soil.

"You are worthless!" echoed her pained, sore limbs.

"Worthless"! The dark woods behind her roared threateningly.

Who are you? What is your strength? What is your life? What are your capabilities? What is the power of your quest? There never was, is, or will be any meaning to your ridiculous, lowly, childish journey. Your messenger is lost, your goal has vanished, your strength has diminished, your struggle is for naught, and your will is futile.

These bitter thoughts trickled into her mind like dirty rain, sullying and damaging everything in its path, throwing Sihara into a panic of terror.

Worthless! ...

At that very moment a dark Shadow appeared, spreading out from the east and west, from the north and south. Sihara sensed that her negative thoughts had summoned it. The Shadow was in no hurry, moving slowly until it enclosed her, silencing everything in its path. An irksome silence spread all around, sending chills into her heart, freezing all emotions and depriving her of all thoughts. She sat in a shriveled, pale circle of light, not knowing what would become of her.

After some time, Sihara felt the Shadow stir and begin to make sounds, and she shook her head from side to side in confusion.

Was she hearing the voices of men? of children? She looked straight ahead and could see a deep Abyss open up from within the bushes, dark and terrifying, where Shadows moved around and bubbled within. She could see people standing on the edge of the Abyss, ordinary people, like herself, each one throwing objects, in turn, into the dark mouth of the Abyss. Their movements were heavy, and they seemed to be acting against their will. Desperation hovered in the air as the Abyss consumed the objects with a revolting shriek. Sihara recalled the words of her Transparent Master: *As long as people are being consumed by the Abyss of the Shadows, the forces of darkness will be strengthened and the war will not end.*

This must be the Abyss of the Shadows! thought Sihara.

She had no inclination to fight, as the Shadow had frozen all thoughts regarding her mission. She clenched her fists helplessly as the people continued tossing their strength into the Abyss, granting existence to the creatures of darkness. Through the shrieks of the Abyss, words began reaching her ears- fragments of sentences accompanying the tossed objects.

"I am unworthy," said a young man.

"I am better off dead than alive," a boy muttered.

"We will never make it"! a chorus of voices echoed in a sudden burst.

"There never was, is, or will be any meaning," uttered a woman in a shaky voice.

They continued tossing assets, pieces of their lives, qualities they possessed, and personal attributes they were given, into the Abyss. Sihara could see them throwing away chances given to them, opportunities to move forward, moments of fateful choices and, finally, parts of themselves: Time, health, senses, thoughts. The edge of the Abyss was emptied, and silence lingered. Everyone had disappeared into the Abyss. By now, the Shadow had reached her feet. Suddenly, Sihara saw her own image perched on the edge of the Abyss of the Shadows, leaning in, tossing words into the blackness of death.

"You are worthless," she said, as the Abyss swallowed her faith.

"What is your strength? What is your life? What are your capabilities? What is the power of your quest?" Her hopes vanished into the depths of the dark earth.

"No, there never was or ever will be any meaning to your ridiculous, lowly, childish journey!" The path shriveled away, and Sihara realized that she had no way out.

"Your messenger is lost, your strength has diminished, your struggle is for naught, and your will is futile."

Pieces of her heart were torn and lost and her legs failed her. The Shadow had nearly reached the last, remaining spot of life within her, but as it reached its claws towards her inner roots, a sudden, unfamiliar light stirred from within.

The hesitant, ashamed and humiliated Sihara had vanished, and in her place stood a brave, decisive Sihara. A flawless warrior burst forth from her inner depths, taking form and fighting for life. She jumped to her feet, broke out of the pale circle of light, ignored the enveloping cold and exclaimed with all her might: "I am worthy! I am worthy of this journey, regardless of how long it takes! I shall remain hopeful, even if the sky looks down upon me! I am worthy, no matter the cost or fight! I am ready to face the world of obscurity and all of its illusions, deceptions, barriers, Shadows and Abysses"!

The Abyss roared and gurgled like a ferocious beast, but Sihara did not succumb to its terror. She held her head erect, opened her eyes and declared in a clear, confident voice, into the heart of darkness: "I am worthy! I shall reach the Chamber of Changing Colors! I shall reach the Master of Transcendence!"

A smooth trail, backed by the wall of thorns, confronted her silently, as if the Abyss had never been opened in its midst. The luminous daylight lingered everywhere, as if the Shadow had never covered it. Sihara took a step forward upon the solid trail, crossed over it and reached her hand out towards the wall. The bushes were now delicate, green, pliable and soft to the touch. Sihara made her way through with great ease, and eventually reached a quiet, rocky path.

Chapter Seventeen

The Kings Cloak

The Kings Cloak

Ulu remained alone at Sea Point during Tzalaii's imprisonment in the Tower. The hapless prisoner faced Mahn, listening to his words apprehensively.

"All of the world's entities undergo transformation," explained Mahn as he began his investigation, casually leaning against the wall and confidently gazing deeply into Tzalaii's eyes. "The world is composed of many circles, life and death, growth and destruction. Even simple men are compelled to adhere to the Law of Transformation, and are controlled by the great circle of change. Eventually, man's dreams, passions and disappointments vanish in the wind like fleeting dust, worthless and meaningless. Do you suppose that we, in the Tower, are evil, that we yearn to control and enslave everyone and everything? Whether you like it or not, you have already been enslaved. You have been a slave to the Law of Transformation."

Tzalaii remained contemplative for a moment before managing to overcome his fear of falling into a trap, and then he asked cautiously, "How is your regime superior to the regime you refer to as 'the Law of Transformation'?"

"We carry the message of redemption," explained Mahn. "Every man needs a higher purpose with which to live his life, and the purpose we believe in is liberation from the forces of nature. This results in true liberation from the dreadful loneliness that affects everyone."

"How is that possible?" questioned Tzalaii.

"Those in the Tower are never alone," explained Mahn, the Inviewer. "They are a part of scores of others just like them, many thousands who together are maintaining something incredibly astounding. Even death has a different meaning. They do not return to the circle of life and death, they rise upwards."

Tzalaii was silent. The Inviewer's words about the loneliness of man, his meaningless existence and worthlessness, echoed within him, causing him to feel a sense of shame. He peered directly into the eyes of this self-confident Inviewer who seemed to be able to read the thoughts of others.

In a flash, for a single enlightened moment, an image appeared in Tzalaii's mind. He 'saw' the peaceful and smiling face of a man wearing a crown on his head. The smile washed away all of Tzalaii's doubts, like waves washing away the sand. Tzalaii quickly resolved that the Inviewer was mistaken, although he could not explain his conclusion. He knew his questions were, in fact, valid, although the true answers would not be found in this place.

Once again, Tzalaii found himself in the large stone cell. Day after day, interrogation followed interrogation. Surprisingly, he was well-treated by his captors. None of his belongings were taken from him, he was given a comfortable bed, and food was served regularly. Looking out through the narrow window, Tzalaii was able to study the colossal structure of the lower City and its markets. He wondered why his captors were not concerned by his access to the view of the Tower and its activities.

Were they not worried about exposure? He did not understand the reasons for his trial. His captors continued to bring up his unfortunate act, stealing the stone from the wall.

They badgered him with the same questions time and time again: "Who sent you on your mission? Why were you sent?"

His claim that it was just a childish idea of his own, merely a failed adventure, was never accepted by his interrogators. He carefully avoided any mention of the Magnathought Crystal, hoping that it would be returned to him someday. Tzalaii's thoughts often turned to the blue Magnathought Crystal.

If only I had it now, I would use it to aid my escape. If only I hadn't given it to my sister Sihara...

Yet, in truth, Tzalaii had no idea of the actual difficulties entailed in accomplishing a successful escape from the Towered City, even if he were fortunate enough to possess a sword of the Ancient Progeny.

But deep within his great despair and frightful wait, Tzalaii had one ray of hope: He still possessed the golden fringe, which he had found next to the blue Magnathought Crystal. He had no knowledge of its origin or possible special powers. But each time he removed it from his sack, out of range of the investigators' prying eyes, its lively, luminous hue strengthened his faith. Its wondrous beauty symbolized the vanished promise of the past.

One night, Tzalaii had trouble falling asleep. He was kept awake by the maddening sounds of the soldiers' voices in the lower City. To distract himself, he began to recall his dream of the sea. *The image of a peaceful and royal face accompanied him. He 'saw' the man's gentle glance, and felt that he was trying to tell him something. In his misfortune, with nothing else to ponder, Tzalaii focused on every detail of his dream with all his might, as though it were the source of salvation, and asked, without knowing to whom he spoke, "Please, help me!"*

Suddenly, as if a window had opened in his consciousness, another detail, a hint of salvation was revealed: The king who had appeared in his dream was wearing a golden cloak but part of the fringe was missing! Tzalaii trembled. He reached into his bag, removed the golden fringe and stroked it slowly and gently, immediately charmed by its presence. His dream had merged with reality.

A new thought entered Tzalaii's mind: Surely it was no coincidence that he was in possession of the missing royal fringe. Maybe he was a descendent of the king who had appeared in his dream? He perked up momentarily, but his spirits deflated just as quickly as he wondered sadly: *Maybe this is all just a figment of my imagination? Maybe I am just a delusional prisoner, being led to a miserable death?*

Once again, he felt pursued by the guilt resulting from his original impulsive act. Resting his head on his knees, he wept.

Tzalaii fell asleep on the ground, curled up in the fetal position, and he began to dream.

In his dream, he could see himself in a lit tunnel in the center of the earth. The air in the tunnel was clear, filling him with fresh vigor. A bright light illuminated the long stone corridors, and the ceiling was so high, it appeared to be endless. As he walked, the tunnel appeared alternately as a large chamber and then as a narrow pathway between high walls. The winding path was covered in colorful stone stalactites. Water dripped from them, silently descending into pools on the floor of the cave. As Tzalaii drank water from each of the pools in his dream, he found himself gazing into the water and thinking deep thoughts. The thoughts varied from pool to pool, as if each pool was a portal to a different world.

As he trekked seemingly into the belly of the earth, his mission unknown, he took pleasure in the magical underground world that was now exposed to him. This enchanting world of immense near-

silence, broken only by the soothing sound of water dripping into the pools, engendered a deep feeling of peacefulness in his heart and, at the same time, sharpened his senses. He felt comforted by the myriad of lights and colors. The blessed silence healed his soul, though the loneliness he experienced was somewhat disheartening. He recalled his friends, and longed to share his experiences with them. Sihara's illuminated face now appeared in his dream. If only she were here, he thought in his heart, if only she were here with me in this wondrous place! He stopped walking, sat down by a pool of water and gazed into it with deep concentration. The water in the pool was motionless. A vision of the past was revealed to him.

He now saw himself walking down the street of a great city, the sun shining brightly above. The street was wide and paved with large reddish stones. Elegant stone houses stood on either sides of the road, rows of marble columns supported their porches, and wide stairs led to their arched doors. Ceramic pots, bursting with plants, stood between the pillars and beside the doorways of each house. The plants cascaded onto the earth and wrapped their intertwining vines around the marble columns. The wide balconies were decorated with stone or wooden designs, and tall turrets adorned the roof tops.

As he walked, Tzalaii encountered clear springs of water, surrounded by fences, the warm breeze carrying refreshing droplets through the air. Although the street was crowded with passersby, the atmosphere was calm. The city's inhabitants were on their way to an important affair, dressed in delicate golden cloaks trimmed with white and blue threads. Many of the people carried musical instruments, and some carried swords or bows and arrows, solely for decoration. These weapons had not been used for warfare in ages. Joy abounded.

"Where are we going?" Tzalaii asked a man near him.

The man looked at him and smiled warmly. He was not suspicious of a stranger's presence in his city, and answered: "To the King's

Palace. Today is a festive day! We are celebrating the Festival of Simple Wisdom."

As the procession continued, they crossed several wide stone bridges over streams of water. More golden turrets were visible now, and the anticipation of the crowd grew. They reached a garden, surrounded by a crimson stone wall with a gate over twenty feet high. The gate had been opened and the people walked freely through into the garden.

"The Festival of Simple Wisdom?" asked Tzalaii hoping for an explanation.

The man was happy to respond: "In our kingdom there are three halls, the hall of music, the hall of creation and the hall of wisdom. Every child in the kingdom attends one of these halls of study in order to gain knowledge. After years of study, a small number of the students advance to the hall's pinnacle, where they are able to gain knowledge through Simple Wisdom. Today, the graduates are celebrating the completion of their training. It is a day of celebration for us all!" he stated, his face gleaming with pride. The sound of flutes was heard from a distance and the crowd grew even more eager.

"We are nearing the castle," whispered the man in awe. "The graduates will speak before the king, and then the king will give them his blessings."

Suddenly the vision changed. Tzalaii now dreamed of a large illuminated room in the interior of an impressive stone home. Smoke obstructed his view but Tzalaii noticed a large, open window across from where he stood. Through the window, he was able to see the magnificent homes, marble columns and golden turrets of the city, all ablaze!!

Sitting in low chairs in the room were three elderly noblemen. Their white clothing had become blackened by soot from the fires, and they seemed to know that their end was approaching. Suddenly one of the men looked up and noticed Tzalaii. He whispered to the others whereupon they immediately arose and bowed to their visitor in great respect. Tzalaii was astonished! He closed his eyes. Now he could hear only their faint whispers, as if from a great distance. They were, at the same time, vague yet clear.

"It is undoubtedly him," whispered one with great excitement.

"It is possible," answered another, "But he is oblivious to what is transpiring."

"There is no time for speculation," said the third hurriedly. "He will wake up shortly, and then we will miss our chance."

"We must reveal the secret of the cloak to him," said the first. In his dream, Tzalaii opened his eyes wide and looked at them. The fire approached them and the smoke grew thicker and more concentrated.

"You shall remember nothing of what you have seen here," the second man said to him. "You shall only remember the song of the Transparent Ones. This song is the key to the King's Cloak. When you utter the words of the song, the golden fringe shall become whole again."

"The final verse of the song," continued the first "shall reveal the map of the Tunnels of Time on the inner side of the cloak."

At that very moment in his vision, Tzalaii realized the identity of the wondrous underground tunnel with the pools of water, where he had walked in his dream. It was, in fact, the Tunnels of Time. But as his thoughts returned to his miserable captivity in the Tower and his imminent trial, the magical revelation he was experiencing began to dissolve, dimming the clarity of his dream.

"Listen!" cried the three elderly men.

Their cry made it possible for Tzalaii to fully grasp the words of the Transparent Ones' song:

In the end of time, a man in white

Shall lift a great canopy.

A white desert, close in sight

Conceals gates within.

Tzalaii awoke. He stared at the walls of his cell, dumbfounded and confused. For a while he did not know where he was, but was brought back to reality upon hearing the voices of the soldiers from the lower City. The dream was disappearing from his memory. The celebration of the Kingdom of the Ancient Progeny was all but forgotten. All that remained were the words of the song. Tzalaii held onto them with all of his might. He repeated them over and over, beseeching his heart to hold on to them, never to forget the words. He held onto the cloak's fringe with trembling hands and his lips uttered the words of the song: "In the end of time, a man in white shall lift a great canopy. A white desert, close in sight…" Tzalaii struggled to remember the final words: "conceals gates…within!"

Light rushed into the cell, and Tzalaii realized that the entire cloak was now in his hands! It was delicate, beautiful, and luminous; an assurance of redemption. It was the cloak that had belonged to the King of the Ancient Progeny! His hands shook as he inspected its lining, and saw the map of the Tunnels of Time embroidered within.

Chapter Eighteen

Loneliness is not Always Pain

Loneliness is not Always Pain

Silence prevailed. The scattered leaves, which had cast a purple-yellow hue on the ground, were losing color from day to day. Ulu recalled the last song he had heard from the departing Transparent Ones, "Loneliness is not always painful to behold."

But his intense loneliness at Sea Point, his yearning for home and family continued, nonetheless, to cause him deep and constant pain.

The extreme elevation of the lookout and its panoramic view which, at first, had been amazing to behold, had now become loathsome.

Sometimes one must listen deeply to the echoes of his own heart, assured the song of the Transparent Ones, but the Man of Borders felt incapable of tuning in to the echoes of his numbed heart. He tried to listen deeply and purely to his heart, but it was blocked. He heard only the insistent rustle of the windblown trees, the sound of falling leaves and the distant cries of the forest animals.

Many days passed. Deer gathered nearby, but to Ulu's chagrin, the animals seemed to be afraid of approaching him. Ulu's heart yearned for companionship, even the company of an animal. He remembered the reassuring words of the Transparent Master, *All waiting shall be fulfilled.*

How long? He wondered. The mystery of his task and the uncertainty of his future caused him to become depressed and anxious. The forest and its clearing had become his home, but his heart was elsewhere, in a place of warm companionship. He attempted, unsuccessfully, to sing in order to cheer himself. He tried to recall happy times he had experienced, but eventually his thoughts wandered to distant and confusing memories.

One evening Ulu sat at the edge of the cliff peering into the distance, towards King's Sea, shrouded in fog. He wondered, *What are the higher factors, the essential things? Where are my fellow warriors? What was the purpose of my training as a warrior? Was it all in vain?*

In desperation, overcome with frustration, he shook his raised fists vigorously.

"I must act," he said.

"And why now?" he implored. "The Land of the Ancient Progeny is at war and I am stranded in this strange and desolate place. Why?"

A sudden wind swept through a cluster of weeds nearby. Ulu closely observed a simple weed, one of many, focusing on its intricate details. The weed appeared to be very plain, lacking distinction. Green tendrils sprung from its blossom-filled crown. The delicate plant swayed serenely, submissively, in the breeze as if in sync with a peaceful rhythm.

Every tree and stone beholds a unique song, Ulu recalled the words of the Transparent Ones.

He wondered about the unique song of this simple, unadorned weed, just one of so many.

Before whom does it bow its head in grace, for whom does it sway in motion?

"Where are the essential things?" he asked.

This simple weed, which surrenders entirely to the forces of the wind- is it not an essential thing? Is its dance not part of the great war?

The song of surrender was the song of the green plant that swayed in the evening breeze.

Before whom must I surrender? wondered Ulu, as he attempted to understand how his surrender would aid the victory of the Master of Transcendence.

A Warrior of Transcendence exchanges his fears for light, he recalled learning in the White Desert.

Maybe sadness and loneliness could be exchanged as well? Ulu continued studying the plant. Night began conquering the sky, and the outline of the cliff became blurred. New ideas began to form in his mind. Underlying the concept of the higher essential things was the necessity to do the right thing. To live and act flawlessly in each and every moment, just like the slender weed.

Nothing is useless or meaningless, not even waiting idly in anticipation of a sign or indication. Even plants wait. They patiently and powerlessly await water and light. While waiting, they seem to dance and smile to the world. In time, the sun will shine upon them, the winds will sway them and the rain will quench their thirsty roots. They cannot be expected to change their dwelling place. They wait patiently and with great faith for their needs to be fulfilled in the proper hour.

"All waiting shall be fulfilled," again, the words of the Transparent Ones rolled over his lips, and a smile illuminated his face. Instead of succumbing to sadness and desolation, one may dance until the time comes to move on. One may experience silence, like a plant or stone. Great things can be accomplished quietly, without movement, even if the only thing stirring is the wind.

Ulu arose and extended his hands toward the imminent darkness.

"My dear little brother," he whispered to the small weed swaying in the quiet night, "you have taught me how to transform sadness into light."

He began his first dance for the Transcendor. The deer now began to venture closer to him, as they watched him dance. They were happy to befriend one who surrendered his life to the spirit of the Transcendor.

That night, the Master of Transcendence appeared to Ulu, a broad smile on his face.

"You have won the battle," he said, "and you have liberated many prisoners from the depths of pain."

Ulu was perplexed.

"When?" he asked. "Where did the battle take place?"

"Right here, in these silent fields," answered the Master of Transcendence. "And in all the distant lands."

"But I did nothing, and saw no prisoners!"

"You did not see them because they are hidden from the eye. They are trapped, like you, in silent barren lands, struggling through the grayness of lost glory. Look…"

Ulu looked at a great big rock, cold and gray. It seemed that it was devoid of life and motion, and a chill ran down his spine.

"You were trapped in this rock, and you have been liberated, along with many others, from the silent swamps of desperation," said the Master of Transcendence.

They were both silent as he disappeared, leaving only the image of his glance.

In any case, even if it takes time, and even if loneliness increases, you are not alone, his eyes implored. *Never allow yourself to remain trapped inside a rock, no matter how immense it may be. Remember that.*

Chapter Nineteen

Fire Mountain

Fire Mountain

Beyond the vanished wall of thorns lay a silent, lifeless valley, bestrewn with dark-colored stones and deep ditches. In the distance, smoke from great blazing rocks obscured the sky. The towering inferno threatened to consume everything in its path. Immense balls of fire merged together becoming gray, molten fluids, flowing down towards the valley.

"Do not be deceived by appearances," Sihara whispered to herself.

But how can I withstand the deceptions? Her journey had taken her beyond Shadow Valley but she had not yet arrived at her expected destination, the Land of the Master of Transcendence. *Had it been utterly destroyed in a calamity? Had the Descendents of the Emperors attacked this distant region as well?*

Sihara scanned the horizon, searching for an answer to her perplexing questions. The soaring, blazing mountain obscured her view. Even from this great distance, the intense heat scorched her face.

As a child, she had heard stories about a mountain of fire.

Could anyone return from this perilous place?

Adventurous wanderers searched for it, but few ever found it and, of those, even fewer escaped. Those who survived and returned became encapsulated in a perpetual silence, their eyes burning with inner flames, while bearing their great secret. It was as if they had entered the gates of another world, after which life in the Land of the Ancient Progeny seemed dull and empty. Her childhood questions remained unanswered: *How did the survivors live through the fire, conquer the mountain and continue their journey?*

Sihara considered her desperate situation: There was an enormous fire before her and darkness behind… Tzalaii was now a prisoner and she, lost and alone, was searching for the Master of Transcendence. A sudden fury of feelings engulfed her heart.

He must come to me! She knew from her Transparent Master that the Descendents of the Emperors and their followers lived in dread and fear of the Master of Transcendence.

Maybe he is unaware of my perilous position, she thought, but her heart remained unsettled, and she found no comfort in her musings.

Surely he knows! she concluded, decisively, and then, with conviction, asserted: *I must reach him!*

"Where would you like to go, my child?" asked a voice from behind.

Sihara turned around in fright. She noticed two Transparent Ones sitting on the last hill just before the valley. How odd. Her Transparent Ones had accompanied her only until the foothills before taking their leave.

"Who are you?" she asked hesitantly.

"We," began one boastingly. "We," echoed the other, "are Transparent Ones. Who else would we be?"

"Two of the best!" laughed the first in a voice that aroused Sihara's suspicions. Arising together, they hopped over to her.

"Where did you come from and what is your destination?" one of them asked.

Their golden capes glimmered, and the hot wind from the blazing mountain blew through their hair. Fear worked its way into Sihara's heart, causing her to step slowly towards the hot, gray valley and the mountain of fire.

"I am searching for the Chamber of Changing Colors," she said in a trembling voice, "Is this not the way?"

"Great dangers await you there," snapped one, and the other quickly added: "You are too close to the flames. They are impassable. Only wandering Transparent Ones are able to reach the other side. Survival for mortals is nearly impossible."

Sihara trembled and continued moving, even more quickly now. She felt the intensity of the heat, but her fear propelled her to continue. Suspicious of their speech and their proud boastings, Sihara looked for more clues.

"You are Transparent Ones, the friends of my people, aren't you?" she asked, in a naive attempt to uncover their true identity.

They both began to laugh.

"The Transparent Ones," they mocked her voice and mimicked her words: "Friends of my people."

Their stature seemed to diminish. Their small bodies curled up. Sihara was suddenly overcome by feelings of compassion and pity for them.

Whoever they may be, they seem like two lost children, she thought.

She suddenly knew what she had to do for these two creatures, forever trapped between fire and darkness.

Sensing her change of spirit, they beseeched her, wailing "Please help us!"

They extended their arms towards her, imploring, begging. Sihara did not question her sudden, impulsive reversal of feelings. Imprisoned by her own deep compassion, she began to cry. *Could any creatures be needier than these two lost souls?* The pain of others had always touched her heart. She stopped in her tracks, extending her hands towards them.

"I shall ask the Master of Transcendence to come to your aid," she whispered.

To her great shock and amazement, the two miserable, helpless creatures became terror-stricken. At the mere mention of The Master of Transcendence, they jumped back, as if stunned by a strong light. Sihara, coming to her senses, as if startled out of a deep sleep, began to move towards the fire, unconsciously, until her foot actually touched the flames. Following closely, their faces turning red from the great heat, the two imposters suddenly turned to beat a hasty retreat. As their deceptive robes fell to the ground, the two creatures appeared to dissolve into the blackness of the valley.

"Just a jot more compassion and she would have been ours!" grieved one, his shrill voice fading away.

Sihara found herself walking in a deep and tangled forest, far from the now distant mountain, but still the colors of the fire tinted the air. Orange leaves, crimson treetops, huge, dark tree trunks, and twisting purple vines. Only the trail was green. The entire forest seemed to be ablaze, but without fire. Winds blew against Sihara's face. With each step she took into the depth of the forest, the wind became stronger and more powerful, like waves. Animals were passing in the waves of the wind, roaring, begging for their lives, laughing, crying hysterically, beseeching aid and then burning up, vanishing into the air.

Were these animals or figures from her past? She kept walking, feeling a presence.

Who is this walking near her and guiding her way? Sihara felt her body changing, melting, lightening, softening, and becoming translucent. She felt a sharp pain, an inner cry, a shock to her entire being, and then great relief, as if an old, heavy covering had been lifted.

Could this be death?

Before her image could fade into the all encompassing glow, before her footsteps could became lost in the crimson forest, full of vibrations and mysteries, Sihara noticed the presence of a girl who pointed towards the remaining light. She whispered, "Come Sihara, come…" And Sihara followed.

Her inner, illuminated foundation returned as Sihara took on a new form appearing as a lighthearted, cheerful young woman. The colors of the forest became brighter and full of life and the wind died down.

Sihara sat on the far side of the mountain, in a clearing, viewing the vast fields below. The fresh smell of spring perfumed the air. She fell to her knees and wept, her heart filled with pure delight.

Chapter Twenty

Tzalaii's Trial

Tzalaii's Trial

Tzalaii was troubled by many unanswered questions, and he had ample time to ponder them while imprisoned in the Tower. The King's cloak was now in his bag and he marveled that he had been permitted to retain his unexamined possessions even as his trial approached.

Of what use was the cloak? What was the purpose of his trial? Was there a chance he might be released from the Tower? And if not, what would become of him? Why had no attempts been made to obliterate him?

His meetings with the Inviewer seemed like fair attempts to convince and educate him, not forced invasions of his mind.

Tzalaii understood from his captors that his trial was to take place on the Tin Level, the Level of the Planet Venus. Three warriors unlocked his cell and escorted him through long, windowless, seemingly endless corridors. Torches on the walls cast faint lights, barely illuminating the path. After a tedious and silent walk through an endless maze of turns and twists leading to even more corridors and more turns and twists, they finally reached a large decorated, wooden door. Stern-faced guards, situated on either side of the door, wore simple gray clothing with a crimson flame on their garb. Each guard was armed with a short, sharp sword at his waist.

Tzalaii was surprised by the immensity of the chamber in which he found himself. Elongated benches in tiers, providing seating for five hundred people, filled the entire lower end of the chamber. The well-dressed, high-ranking spectators gazed in tense silence as the prisoner was led to his seat.

They seem to be expecting to be entertained, he thought.

How was he to know that his trial had been engineered as a show, to engender respect for the Emperors and their belief system?

Throughout the Towered City, preparations for this important event had been under way for many days. Only high officials were permitted to attend, though all awaited news of the trial.

Tzalaii was seated in a raised chair on the right side of the chamber.

Guards with crimson flames on the fringes of their garments were positioned around him and the judges sat on a higher podium. The chamber was silent as the three judges arose, and Tzalaii noticed how similar they were, as if they had been formed by the same sculptor. They wore long, dark purple robes, their faces were narrow and elongated, and their hair was long and pulled back with a black cloth band. Small beards adorned their chins, pointed and elongated like their other features.

From the silence, a tune emerged, a foreign tune that Tzalaii had never heard before. It was simultaneously threatening and harsh yet inviting and seductive. Tzalaii tried to shut out the sounds, but the tune entered his hearing against his will and erased his negative feelings about the trial. As if commanded by the sounds, Tzalaii and all of the spectators in the chamber arose. A tall, silver-haired man emerged from the audience and approached the judges' podium.

The three judges were seated, followed by the spectators. Only Tzalaii remained standing. Once again, he was filled with guilt over his childish deed, and fear of his future rippled through his bones. He tried to cheer himself up, attempting to call forth his remaining strength, but the atmosphere of severity in the courtroom cast terror upon him and weakened his remaining hopes.

As the silver-haired man spoke, Tzalaii was horrified to learn that he was none other then the prosecutor.

"In the name of the Mars Emperor," the man spoke harshly, "The villager, Tzalaii, is charged with the gravest of crimes."

He paused for a moment and then announced the accusation, directing his words to Tzalaii: "You are hereby charged with attempted assassination of the Emperor!"

A low humming sound resonated throughout the chamber, and terrifying glances were sent in Tzalaii's direction.

They are mad! thought Tzalaii, his entire body tense from the severity of the accusation.

Tzalaii had assumed that he would be tried for thievery, for stealing a stone from the wall, or maybe as a trespasser for attempting to invade the Tower.

But attempted assassination of the Emperor? Were they mocking him?

Having no advocate, he was forced to defend himself. In a shaky, hesitant voice, he began: "I am but a simple village boy. I never conspired to harm an Emperor. All I wanted was to approach the wall and examine its composition..."

The prosecutor cut him off, announcing sternly: "It is absolutely clear to us that we are not dealing with a childish prank, but with a severe and threatening mission. Who would dare to inspect the wall, were he not sent by the Master of Transcendence?"

The silence intensified. The accusatory stares of the spectators were replaced with furtive glances of fear mingled with awe. If the defendant is really a servant of the Master of Transcendence, he must be feared, and his false words are but a cover for his despicable, cynical scheme. The judges began whispering to each other and Tzalaii was not offered an opportunity to speak again.

The tune was heard once more, this time followed by the shrill beat of a drum, and accompanied by distant wails and myriads of echoes. Tzalaii felt his sight blurring as reality dimmed and he fell into a dream-like state, deep in a vision. He felt that the entire chamber was immersed in fog, out of which spirits were beginning to emerge. Spirits of the sand, and spirits of the sea, spirits of the fish and spirits of the heavens, spirits of the stones and spirits of men, spirits of the past and spirits of the future. They all extended their hands towards him and begged for their lives- "Creator, father, grant us life!"

He felt painful stings throughout his body; his throat was dry and his breathing was labored.

"For you have touched us!" insisted myriads of begging hands.

The tune was amplified and it echoed through his senses. Beyond the noise he could still hear the voices, piercing, crying and demanding, "Grant us life, for you have touched us!"

Tzalaii tried to recall the events that had occurred in the stone house on the eastern shore, but the creatures he had created and touched rose up as painful waves, and produced in him the Marker of Tumult. His hands fell lifelessly to his sides, he was just a step away from losing his senses entirely. He felt his hand touch his bag and one of his last memory shards entered his conscience; it was the King's Cloak. With his remaining strength, Tzalaii battled the scorching waves of tumult, as he reached into his bag and grasped the golden cloak.

"Sound your voice before the great king!" a soft voice spoke to him from afar, "Tell him. Ask for his mercy!"

"Touch us, revive us, be unto us a father, a creator!" called the life that pulsated around him. "Remain empty, wait for help and assistance, ask for life from he who created life," said the voice as the waves of tumult burst forth, attempting to silence him.

"You created everything, Tzalaii. The strength, might, and power of the Kings of the Ancient Progeny are in our hands…"

Tzalaii wrapped the cloak around himself and immediately order was restored. The winds died down, even the howling sounds of the tune surrendered to the golden cloak, becoming soft and sweet.

I created all of the creatures, Tzalaii felt with complete certainty. *Nothing in the world is inaccessible to me!*

Tzalaii observed the spectators in the chamber, and the judges and prosecutor on the podium. They appeared frozen, their mouths agape, small, weak and powerless. He raised his hands as a champion, as if the entire world had surrendered to him, ready to serve him.

Three of the White Emperors' soldiers arose from their seats and the smug, satisfied laughter of victory filled the chamber as each one saw with his own eyes that the prisoner was indeed a Senior Warrior of Transcendence. The golden cloak which now adorned him, and his royal and regal bearing left no room for doubt. No punishment in the world would be great enough for this transgressor.

"Take him away!" ordered the judges.

Their assessment was correct. He had been touched with royalty.

The Obliterators would be able to make advantageous use of the prized segments of his soul, now almost in their hands. A tall Shadow of Illusion, wearing a gray wavy cape, rushed towards him and removed the King's Cloak. There would be no greater gift than this to present to the Emperors- the King's Cloak itself! The map of the Tunnels of Time was clearly etched on the inner side of the garment. Soon the map's secret codes would be deciphered.

Tzalaii's vision vanished as the tune once again assaulted his brain. He found himself defeated, bereft, and destitute in the defendant's podium. Now, confused and fearful, he was dragged from his chair by two soldiers.

"Where are they taking him now? To the Abyss of the Shadows?" someone asked.

"He would beg to be taken to the Abyss of the Shadows, if he knew his true destination," replied his comrade, mockingly.

Unable to cope with this harsh situation, Tzalaii plummeted into a deep Abyss of loss and forgetfulness.

Chapter Twenty-One
Seven Gates

Seven Gates

As Sihara descended the trail leading into the valley, she enjoyed the abundance of flowers in bloom. When she looked within herself, she discovered that what had been important to her in the past no longer mattered. The intense experience of the fire on the mountain had liberated her from her previous concerns. The shell that had enveloped her had been shed, and she now felt as light as a bird in flight.

The slopes leading to the valley were in full bloom. A soft breeze, full of hope, swayed the plant life, as if in a dance. Happy and free, Sihara proceeded down the path as if she were being led by an unseen guide. Eventually, she arrived at a fork in the road. To the right were vast yellow fields, surrounded by faraway hills. To the left, she could see a green valley in the distance, its borders obscured by a light fog. Puzzled for a moment, Sihara paused and wondered: *Which road should I take?*

"Your heart is the key," words from a faraway song were heard.

My heart... Sihara covered her face with her hands and looked within herself. There, in her heart, all roads seemed futile. She looked towards the golden fields which spread as far as the horizon. This field was not in full bloom, though blue veins pulsated throughout and drew her heart towards them.

"Shall I go?" She asked joyfully. "Yes, I shall!" she replied to herself, as if calling the entire world to a challenge.

She walked into the field, ran forward, wishing to get closer to the blue lines, but they had become distant. For one hesitant moment she desired to return to the trail. Right or left, it was irrelevant, what was important was to return to a paved road. But a new determination had been born in her.

"Whatever will be, will be," she whispered. "It is the blue that I desire."

She gazed at the blue lines and prepared to continue walking toward them, but she was shocked to find that the blue veins were already in her possession! Many wide, bright, inviting veins, promising pleasure and sweetening a secret.

Within a short time, the fields were behind her. Only shades of blue filled the horizon, as she found herself on the shore of a wide ocean. Between the towering waves and deep Abysses lay a path, her path. She walked along, descending before ascending to a higher place. An elevated White Chamber, surrounded by a bright light, was revealed to her in the ocean. A deep serenity emerged from within this Chamber. She held her breath and froze in place, feeling as if she could stay there forever, as the waves crashed around without touching her. A love-infused serenity radiated from the White Chamber, which calmed her spirits, and a softness full of compassion, like open arms, came her way.

Her eyes filled with warm tears and her lips trembled. "I'm on the way," she whispered, "but even if it were for this moment alone, everything would have been worthwhile. Thank you for granting me the privilege to be here, to see your Chamber!"

Sihara walked several steps forward on the trail, reaching an arched gate that stood at her height. Golden threads swayed at the entrance to the gate, like a curtain composed of many grains of sand. Sihara took a closer look at the fine threads and noticed that the changing colors created a sequence of small pictures. In the first picture a deer appeared in a forest. In the second picture the deer appeared to be nearing the edge of an Abyss, as if planning to skip over it. In the third picture the deer lay crushed at the bottom of the Abyss.

If I only could have built the deer a bridge! thought Sihara.

The pain of the animal's demise touched her heart. She gazed at the final picture and noticed the deer standing calmly in a green field located within the Abyss itself.

Sihara extended her hand reluctantly and moved the sand-thread curtain aside. Beyond it she saw a winding, white staircase, which she quickly ascended. Upon reaching the top of the staircase, she turned right, but came to a halt, confused. She had reached the top of the staircase, but she seemed to be standing in what appeared to be an unfinished painting. Further ahead, above her, was a heavy wooden gate, the second gate. It had numerous locks and bolts, its color was faded, and it appeared as if it had not been opened it in many years.

What am I to do now? She wondered. *If I go on, I shall fall into the empty space...*

I am being fooled! the thought crossed her mind, *No man can walk through thin air, and no one can expect me to do so! Not even the Master of Transcendence.*

She felt hurt. Was it possible that she was being mocked? This was not an illusion. She knew what she was up against.

"Reality?" asked a faint voice, and Sihara realized how gentle this voice was in comparison to the other voices that passed through her.

"Yes, reality," the other voices defied it, until it was silenced.

Sihara turned back and began descending the staircase, step by step. A wind began to blow, forcing her to stop and regain her balance, and she noticed that the descending steps were becoming transparent, fading into the air and vanishing.

"I am being fooled!" she said, her fists clenched tightly. "It is impossible to ascend, and impossible to descend!"

Her anger turned into defiance.

"What do you want from me?" she called into the empty space.

She stood on a step, suspended between heaven and earth.

"What do you want?!" she called out again. Her voice weakened and fear began rising in her throat.

"What do you want?!" echoed a distant voice.

"To escape! To leave this place! To return…"

"What do you want?!" asked the voice again, as if her initial answer had been totally rejected.

The repeated question embarrassed Sihara, but she began hearing the word *you* as if it had been given life, and she pondered its meaning.

Who are you? *What do* you *want?* You *aren't who you think* you *are.*

Sihara saw herself as two beings: One, an inner being, joyful, radiant and vivacious.

The second, wrapped around her, cocoon-like, made of gray threads, gloomy…an imposter, posing as herself. She heard the imposter- cocoon respond to the questioning voice: "Return, retreat, there is no other way."

Then she heard the inner, radiant Sihara responding in a distant voice: "To carry on, to continue, to grow."

Sihara echoed the words she heard, holding onto them as if they were life itself.

"To carry on, to continue, to grow." A voice from behind seemed to emanate from a living being. She turned around and saw a deer, the one from the picture, approaching her as it ascended. Wherever its hooves landed, a step was created in thin air until the staircase reached as far as Sihara and then beyond, up to the ancient gate. From close, the gate appeared even older and more faded. Sihara examined it, knocked on it and heard a solid thump.

Someone must help me, she thought.

The deer had already disappeared, and only the gate remained.

"Open up," she called. "Open up!!!"

I must know what to do, she tried to cheer herself up. *The inner Sihara, the true Sihara, will speak to me. I will then know what to do.*

"I..." she tried to say something, but her words were blocked and she forgot what she intended to say.

"I..." something negative affected her, but what?

"I..." it seemed that her inner voice was mocking her.

"And I...and I..." her voice echoed, more distantly now.

She sat down upon the earthen floor by the gate and listened to the voice of her heart.

"On your own, you are helpless, lost and confused," said the voice. "Your inner voice, your strength, is not heard. It is silenced and swallowed up in the commotion. Only the voice of the Master of Transcendence can remind you of who you are and where you desire to go. Believing that you are capable of moving forward means believing that you belong to him, that you are with him. Only then shall you arrive at your destination."

"Is that the way?" she asked. She had been worried at first.

She hadn't known how to proceed, how to choose correctly, until the voice encouraged her to toss the weight of responsibility from her shoulders.

"Without knowing?" She asked, "To surrender, and follow his voice? Is that the way?"

"That is the only way," answered the voice.

Sihara smiled. It was the first time she had smiled in a long time. How good it felt knowing that she did not have to carry the burden of the decisions upon her own shoulders. The Master of Transcendence led the way, and she was his, with him, forever and under all circumstances. Sihara sifted the sand at the foot of the gate, and uncovered a hard, rough object. It was a key! Even before she tried, she knew that it would open every lock and bolt on the heavy gate.

Beyond the gate was a great torch-lit room, made of stone. The floor was composed of smooth white rocks. Next to the wall, Sihara found a pitcher of water and some fruit.

Who left these for me? she wondered.

After feasting to her heart's delight, she leaned on the wall and looked around the room. There were many passages leading out of the room, each in a different direction.

"This place is full of mazes," she thought to herself, amused, as if she were simultaneously playing a game with the dweller of the Chamber while acquiring true insight.

After a short rest, Sihara continued on her way. She observed the passageways and noticed that one of them was slightly more luminous than the others. She chose that path and walked for quite some time until she reached a third gate, made of transparent glass. The walls around it appeared as frozen waterfalls, with countless frozen droplets, some as fine as thread and others wide and curved. The wall was composed of changing shades of green, white and blue, with fine, intertwining silver threads. The intense beauty was so astonishing in contrast to the unadorned tunnel from which she had emerged that Sihara felt perplexed and began to retreat. As she did so, she noticed her reflection in the glass. A long time had passed since she had last seen her reflection, since she had last been in her home in the village. Now her hair was in tangled disarray, her clothing faded and torn, and she was covered with dust from head to toe.

A fresh scent caught her attention, and she followed it until she arrived at a small room to the right of the gate, where she found a well-spring. She immersed herself in the water and when she emerged, she noticed a white cape perched on a large rock nearby. Donning it, she saw that it was a perfect fit! Now she stood before the gate, waiting for guidance. Whatever would be, whatever she would experience, her inner voice would be there to guide her.

"What must I do now?" she asked confidently.

There was silence.

"I am waiting for a sign."

More silence.

"It is I, Sihara!" she pleaded.

No voice was heard. Sihara touched the glass gate; it was cold.

"I want to enter," she whispered, but to no avail.

She looked, she listened. She closed her eyes and whispered a prayer, but the gate remained frozen and sealed, as did her heart. Her spirit began to weaken, and she became impatient, restless.

"Someone must help me," she said, "just as I have been helped until now. I cannot go on alone, so I have been told. Master of Transcendence, reveal yourself to me! I need guidance."

Silence. Why did her inner voice fail to help her?

Maybe it does not matter, hesitant thoughts entered her mind. *Whether he speaks to me or not, I am in his Chamber and he knows where I am.* She knew that she was his, even when she could not hear his voice. These thoughts comforted her and once again she placed her hand on the glass gate. This time, the gate opened up at her touch.

Sihara found herself in a large room. Pools of water surrounded by small, purple rocks were full of lively, colorful fish. Most surprising of all were the two Transparent Ones awaiting her arrival. They were short, charming and cheerful. Their inner, blue flames swayed as in a dance. One of them bowed to her respectfully, and the other, who was slower, bowed belatedly and bumped into the first.

They rolled onto the ground, giggled in embarrassment, then got up, straightened out their clothing and welcomed her in unison: "Blessed is she who enters the Chamber of Glory!"

"Blessed are those who dwell in the Chamber!" Sihara responded, holding back the giggles they elicited. "Now I am no longer alone."

Sihara and the Transparent Ones walked together through the Chamber. With every step, the plant-life on the walls appeared to thicken, until Sihara found herself standing before something completely unidentifiable.

Is this another gate? she wondered.

Her path was completely obstructed by thick, twisted roots.

"Must I go through here?" she asked her fair-haired companions, as she pointed to the roots.

The Transparent Ones smiled silently. She attempted to touch the roots and move them, but they were as tough and as solid as stone. She found a place to sit and rested her head upon the vegetation. Silently, the two Transparent Ones sat down by her side, and their simple movements calmed her.

There is no rush, she thought. *We can rest, look around, and wait.*

As they sat there silently, she recalled distant memories of her childhood, old memories and questions, too many questions to number. Questions she had asked as a child, and questions from her adolescence, questions she asked in the village and during her journey, questions that pestered her ceaselessly. Forgotten questions, vanished questions. Questions of time: *When will humankind see the blessings of their labor? When will the sick be healed of their diseases? When will lonely people find families? When will man lay down his weapons, and open his heart to love? When will dreams come true? When will Tzalaii return?*

These questions are like leaves, Sihara discovered, and then questions of purpose followed: *Why is man so impatient? Why are our burdens so heavy, beyond our strength? Why are people so unhappy? Why don't they raise their heads to the heavens? Why is life so full of toil? Why does strength expire as the work never ends? Why does time pass by quickly? Why are babies in a hurry to grow? Why does their innocence give way to doubt and anger? Why is the Master of Transcendence so far away? And why is no one aware of his power?*

These questions are like branches, she said in her heart, as she caressed the roots. And just then, additional questions, piercing, different than the others, arose from deep within: *What is the goal? What is the purpose of everything? What is the meaning of life and death, despair and hope, desire and resignation, success and failure?*

These questions are the roots, she knew.

The roots of the tree trembled at her touch and began to move. Sihara felt that the Master of Transcendence had heard her questions and she felt ashamed. "I did not mean to sound ungrateful," she whispered.

"I know," said the voice, softly. "Your questions were created by belief in the existence of the answers. Only the believer asks questions."

The movement of the roots increased, and a path opened up, a path that led through the thick, twisted roots, and this was, in fact, the fourth gate. As she passed through the gate, a thought entered her mind: *How wonderful it would be to see the great tree to which these roots belong and to see what gives them their sustenance.*

A simple dirt path stretched out before her, as far as the eye could see. Sihara walked ahead, with the Transparent Ones following behind her. The winding path ascended, and a stone step was set in the path at intervals of every ten steps. Sihara kept walking and ascending, and the path went on and on.

The Transparent Ones by her side were as light on their feet as children, gleefully counting each step they took. Sihara, on the other hand, was tiring of the monotonous, winding road that seemed to have no end.

"Twenty-five...thirty-eight...forty-two..." counted the Transparent Ones, and still there was no end in sight, only grayish walls on both sides and a dusty ceiling above.

"Fifty- six!" they continued counting. Sihara felt her strength expire.

"Sixty-three!" they called out, full of wonder. Sihara's spirit was almost dull in contrast to their joyfulness.

What are you so happy about? she yearned to ask of them, but she controlled herself.

Why should I ruin their good time? Let them continue smiling for as long as they can.

"Sixty-eight, sixty-nine, seventy, and that's it!" they exclaimed, as the road came to an end in a broad stone cave.

They knew there were seventy steps, and therefore they had not become exhausted like I did! Sihara thought. Without a word to her loyal attendants, she dropped to the stone floor in exhaustion and fell into a deep slumber.

"I feel as though I have slept for centuries!" said Sihara as she awoke.

She straightened out her cape, sipped from the clear water at her side and looked around. There was nothing extraordinary or awe-inspiring in the cave, and it was silent. There were no wellsprings or plants; there were no colors and no Transparent Ones. She was completely alone. There was a door, an exit from the hall, across from her, and next to it was a large cloth satchel. Sihara inspected the bag and found it to be suitable for her. She filled it with a water flask and cluster of grapes that she found in the room, and continued along the dirt path.

How is it possible that there is such vast space within the White Chamber? she asked herself.

She recalled her first glimpse of the White Chamber, seen through the waves.

It didn't seem so big then, she thought as she walked. *How can a tree grow inside of it? And how can water flow within it? And where does this road lead?* She did not have the answers, and continued to walk. After three hours, she stopped, removed her satchel and drank from the flask

"Master of the Chamber," she said hesitantly, "Where are you? Where am I? Is there still a long road ahead of me?"

There was no reply, not even an echo was heard from the walls. Sihara continued to walk for many hours, until night fell. Her strength was totally depleted.

When she awoke, she found bread, cheese, another cluster of grapes and a flask of cold water by her side.

There is someone here, someone is looking out for my welfare, she thought, joyously, *I am not alone!*

She placed the food into her satchel, and wearily set out on her journey, continuing for three more days. She no longer felt joy in receiving the food she found at her side each morning. Sihara's spirit was becoming dulled. On her fourth lonely night, she reached a second large stone cave. When she bent down to drink from the chilled water, her legs trembled and she fell to the ground. She thought of nothing as she drank, more and more. She then reached out blindly and ate the chilled grapes, soft bread and cheese. The moments passed in silence. Across from her, at the other end of the cave, she could see the narrow, gray, dusty, dirt path, which seemed endless, like the previous one. Sihara no longer expected anything. She felt that where she walked today, she would walk tomorrow and the next day…forever.

"Sihara?" a soft voice whispered. Her eyes were shut and her thoughts vague.

"Sihara," she heard the voice call again. She stopped and listened, too lifeless and devoid of strength to respond or reply.

"Sihara," the way her name was called reminded her that she was still alive. Somewhere, far away from here, there was a living Sihara, with a will of her own, with hope and a purpose to life.

I know nothing... she thought, exhausted. *I remember nothing...*

"Sihara," spoke the voice again, "Sihara."

She covered her face with the palms of her hands.

I am too tired....I have no more strength...I have forgotten everything. Once, when I met the Transparent Master, I knew...I requested...I wanted to go on...but that is over and done with...

Waves of fog rolled through her brain. Everything was bleak, dusty, worn out.

"Sihara," repeated the voice.

She opened her eyes and looked around at the woven mat, at the flask of water, and at her aching feet.

All I want is to rest and sleep and nothing more... she thought, *but the question still remains- where did I come from and where do I desire to go?*

Beyond the fog, the thin line of the horizon became visible.

"Sihara," said the voice with compassion and understanding.

The pain of the dusty journey fell away and the web of sleep that had enveloped her was loosened. She felt alert, and opened her eyes wide.

"Somewhere there is a light that awaits me," she whispered to herself.

She was filled with longing and a fear of the darkness- The darkness she had experienced, the darkness that still awaited her.

How can I forget? For it is like dying! But how do I keep myself from forgetting, when as time passes all becomes so dreary?

Exhausted, she leaned onto the wall of the cave, her mind devoid of thoughts.

Is there nothing that you hope for? the question crossed her mind. Sihara did not respond.

"Is there nothing that you wish for?" the voice pressed on.

"I do not know…" she answered, fatigued.

"Make a wish," the voice continued, and did not let go. "What is your wish?"

Sihara gathered her strength. "Maybe…to want again. To remember what I have forgotten…to find what I have lost…to want again, from the start."

A thin crack appeared along the gray, stone wall by her side.

"The dust of the journey," said the voice, soft as a bell ringing in the morning breeze.

Sihara knew that it was the Master of Transcendence who had spoken.

"If I could only show you its true value," he said. "If I could only show you the world through which you have journeyed, and how your steps brought light to the darkness from the times of old."

Tears filled her eyes. "I have illuminated nothing. I was so weary and exhausted; I knew not who I was. I had forgotten everything…"

"That is not so," he answered. "The desires in the depths of your heart were not extinguished. They became covered by the dust of the journey, unrecognizable to you, but they guided your way and led you to me."

"I wanted to come as a victor, with a sense of purpose," she said, humiliated, "and I have arrived as a failure."

"This is it!" answered the voice with love. "This is how you were chosen to arrive."

Sihara closed her eyes. She was overcome with joy, feeling like a weary traveler caressed by a soothing breeze. The crack in the stone wall had widened enough to enable her to pass through. Sihara left the satchel on the ground and passed through the opening in the wall. No more barren roads ahead. Beyond the wall was a wide, well-lit passageway where the Transparent Ones waited for her, as if they had always been there.

A broad silver staircase led inside, as two birds welcomed her with a noble flight. Their wings were a luminous purple, their abdomens a pure white, and golden feathers perched on their heads, pointed backwards. For a moment, Sihara was overcome with great fear. These birds were identical to the fierce bird with sharp claws she had encountered in the Shadow Valley! But when the birds began to sing, she knew that the terrible bird she had seen then was but an illusion, an imitation of these wondrous, lyrical creatures. The fear slowly dissipated from her heart, and she joined their song, a never-ending song of praise and thanks, a song to the dweller of the Chamber, and to the Master of all, its Transcendor.

The birds led Sihara to the sixth gate, the gate of light, and she followed them.

The light was stronger, though it did not emanate from torches, nor from the Transparent Ones, whose blue light was weaker. After a while, Sihara had to close her eyes, the light was too bright to behold. She stopped for a moment, but the song of the birds urged her forward and gave her strength to go on. Several steps later she began to sense the white light in her brain as well. If she could have seen herself, she would have been surprised, since her body was becoming more and more radiant. Her Transparent Ones had vanished in a great light. The light, a being that spoke to her, calmed her spirit: "Walk on, my child."

The silver steps continued, higher and higher, until they reached the golden gate, the seventh and final one. The gate, supported on both sides by beautifully carved white marble pillars, was adorned with many decorations, one being a myriad of precious metal shapes joined together. Near the top of the domed gate were two silver birds in flight, resembling the birds that had escorted her as they circled over her head. A majestic tree was etched onto the face of the gate, its thin roots spread out below, its trunk was broad and its branches stretched upward like aspiring hands. Above the domed entrance, silver letters were etched into the black stone, forming the word:

'R-O-Y-A-L-T-Y.'

Sihara knew that she had reached her destination.

"It is I, Sihara," she whispered, breathlessly.

And the gate opened from the inside.

Chapter Twenty-Two

A Different Time, Above Water

A Different Time, Above Water

The small meeting room, illuminated by torches, had only a few windows, but from them the interior of the wall was visible. The wall, lifeless and dull, rose up to the middle of the Mercury Level, also known as the Sapphire level due to its blue-green color. The City of Steel was referred to as 'the Base Level' and it was common knowledge that only those who resided on the Sapphire Level and above were respected. Simple warriors inhabited the Steel Level. Even the ruler of that Level, the Steel Emperor, was disparaged on the Sapphire Level in a patronizing, condescending manner.

"Drums, that's all they know about down there," the dwellers of the Sapphire Level would scornfully say about their neighbors on the Steel Level. They, on the other hand, never tired of listening to their own splendid violin compositions.

The three fully-armed warriors in the room were not interested in music at this time. The tallest warrior's narrow, elongated face expressed permanent aggravation and discontent. He clasped his hands behind his back and walked in a peculiar manner.

"A message has just arrived directly from the chamber of the Mercury Emperor," announced the tall warrior, as he presented a scroll, placing it on the rough stone table in the corner of the room.

"What's it about?" asked one of the seated warriors, nonchalantly, as though such a scroll would not be of much interest.

"Do you really want to know?"

"Enough chattering," his comrade interrupted him, impatiently. "Let's hear what it's all about."

The tall warrior sighed as he unraveled the scroll and read: "In the name of the Sapphire Flame, to the three most excellent warriors on the Sapphire Level."

"What an unusual presentation," thought one of the warriors. "Such an appeasing introduction must be a preparation for a difficult and bitter continuation…"

The warrior continued: "It has become obligatory to present to you one of the Tower's most confidential subjects: *The Legend of the Wings*. The two attentive warriors let out an astonished whistle. They knew very little about the Legend. All they knew was that it was a forbidden topic and that those who persisted in discussing it were silenced, sometimes in an unpleasant manner.

"Since you were involved in the matter of the stolen stone, the upper ranking officials have concluded that you must be given some information regarding the secrets of the Legend, which are linked to the stone and to its carrier. You must keep your eyes open at all times and ensure that rumors about this myth are not disseminated on the Sapphire Level."

The warrior concluded the reading of the scroll and now pulled out a second manuscript from his cape. This was not a formal document from the Towered City, but an old, worn out parchment.

"This parchment was found on Green Isle, during one of the rare attacks carried out there in the past. It has been kept on the Solar Level, where the most skillful Inviewers have been attempting to decipher it."

The tall warrior walked over to the table where the others were seated. As he read from the parchment, his words escaped from his mouth like frightened birds, as if they had a bitter taste:

"Nothing in the world contained white- but Him.

The fairness needed for Unification in the faraway ages.

With no sound, a fragment began to pulsate from within,

Asking for life, desiring motion

A great darkness, the darkness of the depths, was present everywhere.

Water with no name, under the burden of its weight, and the intensity of its obscurity,

It instructed that here, only here, would be the seed of light, the line of life.

Slowly, as if placed in an invisible hand

Life giving paths were formed

Chords were created to contain the water

The keys of fifty gates were molded

White absorbs all colors. It openly embraces, listens to all discoveries

The foundation of all colors

The sub-structure of hues, the wellspring of change

> The point of connection above the colors
>
> Soaring above transformation, the gate of the sky -
>
> White
>
> At a different time, above water, a man dressed in white shall arrive,
>
> a man of the heart, in the heart of time."

The three warriors were quiet. Their eerie silence filled the space of the room with an obscure terror. It took a while for them to shake off the effect of the words, which pounded in their heads like hammers. Had they known, in advance, of this persistent pounding, they would have renounced the "honor" wholeheartedly.

"In the name of the Holy Fire!" one of the warriors finally exclaimed. "So much talk about water!"

"It truly sickens me," uttered another, heavily. The three warriors clutched the handles of their swords.

"Do you desire to hear more?" asked the tall warrior, and the two others looked at him terror-stricken.

"In essence," he attempted to speak in a serious tone, "do you understand the problem? Do you sense how it works inside?"

The two warriors nodded their heads, as he raised his tone of voice: "These fables give power to our adversaries! This is what they believe, this tale among many other tales, that a man dressed in white shall arrive."

"And what is this man supposed to do?" asked one of the warriors, hesitantly.

"The Inviewers are still working on deciphering the code," answered the tall warrior in a weary voice. "They have concluded very little so far."

"And how does this all relate to wings?" asked the other.

"I shall sum it up for you," answered the tall warrior. He tucked the scrolls back into his garb as the others let out a sigh of relief. "Additional writings were discovered in the scrolls but they have been censored… There is mention of a future wave of water that is to wash over the world and wipe out the planet."

"That is nonsense!" one of the warriors blurted out, unable to contain himself. "Besides, if such a deluge should occur, everyone would perish. What could possibly be encouraging here?"

"That leads me to the most peculiar idea, probably also the most significant," said the tall warrior quietly. "It is written that not everyone shall perish. Those that are worthy, due to their good deeds, shall grow wings, thereby gaining the ability to soar above the water and avoid the calamity."

Now, the three warriors began to laugh. What was there to fear from such madness?

"Madness or not," the warrior finally concluded, "these ideas provide great strength to the believers and could cause serious danger to the Descendents of the Emperors."

Chapter Twenty-Three

Archives

Archives

The seventh gate opened. The birds burst into the Chamber and Sihara followed them like one in a dream. The walls of the Chamber were glass, so the sea was visible from all directions. Outside, the water was in motion and inside, all of the colors, every single shade and tone, were in motion. In the center of the Chamber, a boy in a golden cloak sat on a carved wooden chair. He held his head erect like a king, and his hands rested gently on the chair's arm rests. His expressive eyes sparkled with the grace of truth beyond comprehension, and his warm smile could melt away all sorrows.

His large eyes focused on Sihara. Watching her, as though he had always known her. Watching, as though he knew all she had experienced, and understood its significance. Watching, as if saying: *I have waited for you for a long time, it is good you have arrived.*

Sihara approached the boy. The streaks of light in his Chamber created crowns around him. She was overcome with great sorrow for her past distance from this place. Her arrival aroused within her a soaring sense of great happiness beyond comprehension.

She presented herself before him, as if she had just been born, and she wept. The tears washed away years, many years of doubts and distance. Her spirit calmed. The experiences of her journey, the exhaustion and the extended time spent wandering were forgotten. Now, she felt refreshed.

She observed the boy in amazement. She had always believed that the Master of Transcendence was an old man with a white beard, causing all who gazed at him to be filled with a deep sense of awe and respect. But a child? And with a glimmer of mischief in his eyes? This was not what she had expected.

" Yes, I am a child, but I am also an old man," said the Master of Transcendence.

"But what are you, really?" wondered Sihara, "What is the true reality?"

"Reality" the child repeated with a smile, and Sihara recalled the heavy wooden gate, the second gate that she had faced on her way to the Chamber. There was an abyss separating her from the gate, and she remembered thinking that someone was playing a trick on her. But the deer had taught her that when one moves forward, the steps themselves create the path.

"Reality," smiled the Master of Transcendence, "is what we allow it to be."

The sky, visible from the windows of the Chamber, became clear, and Sihara was able to see an image of the Towered City looming in the distance. Its gates were open and a turbulent river of shaven-headed warriors streamed out. Sihara retreated, but the Master of Transcendence watched the scene as if it were unimportant.

"What you see happening now is reality," he said, and Sihara retreated farther until she reached the wall of the Chamber. "But the true meaning of it depends upon the place you assign for it in your heart."

"The Transcendor created all of this. Even evil is the fruit of his inventions," continued the child, the smile ever-present in his eyes.

"But why?" Sihara asked, shaken. The voices of the warriors, emanating from the vision in the sky, grew louder, and became aggressive and war-hungry, as they prepared to destroy the land and all of its inhabitants.

"Creating distance to gain closeness and concealing in order to discover," said the Master of Transcendence as if to himself, his whispers swallowed up by the fierce tumult of the warriors.

Why is he whispering? wondered Sihara, *And why are they yelling?*

She felt confused and embarrassed. Everything was so startling. She had not expected to see the Master of Transcendence now and in such a situation. The questions that had gnawed at her during her journey to the Chamber resurfaced, demanding answers.

What is the goal? What is the purpose of life and of death? What is the purpose of hope and despair? What is the purpose of desire and resignation? What is the purpose of success and failure? What is the purpose of it all?

The Master of Transcendence arose from his chair and for the first time Sihara noticed that he was wearing a delicate golden cloak, almost transparent, with stirring shades of blue like the colors in his Chamber. He neared the large glass windows and looked through them. The image of the distant City immediately faded and the sky became clear. Then he spoke, and Sihara knew that his voice could be heard for miles. There were people out there somewhere, waiting to hear his voice, and to them he spoke: "Before all things were created, in the depths of great waters, the Light of the Transcendor was hidden in the hearts of all. The light spread through the Land of the Ancient Progeny, illuminating the hearts that yearned for it with all their might. But then a shadow covered the earth. The lights were extinguished in their hearts and darkness concealed the Light of the Transcendor, hindering His strength."

Suddenly the Master of Transcendence strengthened his voice, like a king ordering his people to fight the greatest battle ever to take place: "But beneath all of the darkness, the light continues to shine, just as it shone and desired to burst forth at the beginning of time. There is no darkness, no obscurity." Now the Transcendor Himself was speaking through him, and His words, spoken through the Master of Transcendence, were now addressed to evil itself: "In the Simple One, you have no existence. Your eyes are dead. Your Kingdom is demolished. Your Shadows are crumbling into fine dust."

Sihara dropped to her knees in awe, shutting her eyes. The Master of Transcendence moved away from the windows, and came close to her, his voice now soft and encouraging: "The success of evil is an illusion. Do not lose faith in your heart. Even if all seems lost, do not be deceived by appearances. Life will emerge from the darkness. New life, full and radiant. Even if the Shadows multiply more than ever before, remember that they are nothing more than an illusion. Evil is destined to pass and vanish like a summer's cloud. The day is approaching!"

Gusts of wind struck the windows with great force. Dark waters gushed. Light faded. "People of truth still remain," the Master of Transcendence continued, his eyes clearer than ever. "The day is near when the Warriors of Transcendence shall transform evil depth into good depth. In the villages, in the woodlands and even in the Tower. All those who raise their eyes to the good, and make way in their hearts for hope, shall receive weapons and protection from me. One of our warriors is in the Tower, though he is unaware that he is one of us. When you meet him, tell him everything about me and my Chamber. His name is Mahn. Through him you shall find your brother."

Outside, the waves were illuminated and shades of blue began to move in the Chamber again. The Master of Transcendence spoke no more. He only gazed at Sihara and transferred thoughts into her heart like drops of water.

"All of the root questions have answers, but they take time. Have patience. Allow each root to receive life, to flow upwards, and sprout. Even when the enemy armies wash over the earth, all waiting shall be fulfilled."

"To continue, to advance, to grow," Sihara spoke from her heart.

The Master of Transcendence's eyes expressed satisfaction.

"What is good depth?" Sihara asked after a few moments of silence.

"What is evil depth?" asked the Master of Transcendence.

"Evil depth is darkness, deep and complete, that extinguishes the glimmer of light in all hearts. Evil depth is despair and resignation," Sihara attempted to describe the people she had seen being swallowed into the Abyss of the Shadows.

"Good depth is found in evil depth, only deeper," said the Master of Transcendence, "good depth is the light that is concealed under the greatest darkness. Good depth is life itself."

"I saw people whose light was extinguished," said Sihara. She did not mean to interrupt his words, as she searched for answers.

"The foundation of their lives was not extinguished, but the hope that meaning would be found was destroyed," explained the Master of Transcendence. "The good never disappears, and if evil grasps deeply at the root of the spirit, good still remains, hidden behind a curtain just beyond. But the Abyss of the Shadows is deceitful and terrifying, and one can only face it with faith."

"With faith? In what?" questioned Sihara. She felt that a rescue rope, as thin as silk, was being tossed to her, and her trembling hands could barely get hold of it.

"Faith that evil depth is but an illusion and that good depth exists forever. The Transcendor is pure goodness, goodness with no borders and no end. The shadow curtains were created for you, so that you may cast them away."

"With faith," whispered Sihara.

"And with joy," smiled the Master of Transcendence, and the light of his glance washed over her soul.

"And now, to the archives," said the Master of Transcendence. From under his transparent golden cloak he removed an ancient golden key. Sihara noticed a drawing of a magnificent white tree etched into the key. The child motioned to Sihara to follow him into a different room. "Look," he said as he pointed to the ten Transparent Ones standing there. "Do these Transparent Ones look familiar to you?" The internal flames in the hearts of the Transparent Ones pulsated strongly. They were all her height, and their features were delicate. She gasped for a moment when she understood why they were so familiar to her. All of them, each and every one, resembled her.

"These are your special Transparent Ones," explained the Master of Transcendence, the smile ever present on his face. "I would say, almost Transparent Masters."

The Transparent Ones bowed respectfully to the Master of Transcendence and smiled at Sihara. They circled around her in awe, pointing at her and then gaining courage and touching her clothes lightly. They whispered songs to her, as if their joy in meeting her was too much to contain, and Sihara felt embraced.

Now another door opened. The Master of Transcendence walked down a spiral staircase carved into the wall, followed by Sihara and the ten Transparent Ones. The more they descended the wider and more luminous the cave appeared. Finally, they stood in a small, bright room with nearly transparent white walls and a carved, decorative wooden door. Above the door the word: *Archives* appeared in golden letters and underneath a picture of a great white tree was engraved. Its roots were thin, and spread out in all directions, its trunk was wide and its branches reached upwards. The Master of Transcendence opened the wooden door and said to Sihara: "The Transparent Ones shall accompany you inside, and their light shall help you find what belongs to you. Remember, you can continue searching as long as the light of the Transparent Ones shines bright. Once their light begins to dim, you must immediately return to the door, for you will not be able to find your way out in the dark." He was then silent for a moment, extending his hand in a blessing: "The voice of your heart shall guide the way, and the Light of the Transcendor shall protect you."

The ten Transparent Ones skipped like children as they walked through the doorway, followed by Sihara. Their light was a sharp blue. Sihara was amazed to find herself in a magnificent underground kingdom. The walls looked like frozen waterfalls, their colors changing from light green to delicate blue, and strewn with silvery strings.

"Here are good intentions," pointed one Transparent One toward a blue-colored wall.

"And here are pure thoughts," another Transparent One said as he bowed towards her, as if presenting one of his own creations.

"Holy words," pointed another toward a frozen waterfall.

"And of course," a fourth Transparent One continued, "true deeds."

"The Master of Transcendence gathers them," explained the first.

"Or more accurately, exposes them," said the second.

"Even if they were extinguished, imprisoned or lost, for years or generations, by the forces of darkness," the third added seriously and Sihara looked into their eyes, attempting to understand.

Now, they were approaching a large cave.

"This is how it transpires," said one of the Transparent Ones.

The light of the Transparent Ones illuminated the cave and colored the bare walls in blue. There was a large window in the farthest wall, and Sihara slowly approached it, peering through the glass. The room, visible through the window, was illuminated brightly.

"Careful!" said a few of the Transparent Ones in unison but Sihara did not understand their words of caution. She noticed the crimson-yellow colored bricks being tossed into disorganized piles, as though someone had collected them hastily and dropped them off just as haphazardly. Farther away, Sihara noticed a silver table that held one single brick. A Transparent One with a golden flame leaned over it gently, like a shaman crouching over his patient, seeking to cure him.

He then placed his hands over the brick, as if he were fighting with it or something inside it. Steam arose from the brick as if it were heated by his hands. Sihara felt tense. "Careful!" repeated one of the Transparent Ones, and Sihara understood that they were talking to their golden-flamed companion on the other side of the window. Silvery veins, transparent and nearly alive, were now visible in the silent stone. The outer layer cracked and the stone split. The Transparent One reached inside gently, as if he were touching a new baby, and extracted something. The Transparent Ones, observing the scene, let out a sigh of relief.

"Pure silver, clear as a tear," one of them said, summarizing his friend's success.

"This is life itself!" said his friend respectfully.

"The good intentions?" wondered Sihara.

"And the pure thoughts," replied one of the Transparent Ones, "and the holy words too, and of course, true deeds." Sihara closed her eyes and pictured the daunting wall of the Tower. The crimson-yellow colored bricks that composed it were crying out to her.

"The Master of Transcendence shall collect and expose it all!" she spoke to them in her thoughts, "wait for him, he is your hope."

After spending some time in the cave, Sihara entered a small purple side-room. In amazement, she touched the objects she found there. Each object was more exquisitely beautiful than the next. Everything was made of a delicate, thin, almost transparent substance and intricately designed. Precious stones had been set into the objects, and they were adorned with a multitude of thin strings. From a distance, the strings looked like glimmering water droplets, but up close they appeared as newly budding leaves. Their inner green color seemed to almost burst through the thin veins. Sihara moved closer, touched another object and was amazed to discover that the metal strings bent to the touch of her hand, like the stem of a plant. Suddenly she realized that various colored leaves adorned each and every object in the room.

"Everything is growing here!" she exclaimed to the Transparent Ones, and then she recalled the splendorous tree she had seen etched in the wooden door. She noticed that the light of the Transparent Ones was beginning to dim and she remembered the instructions of the Master of Transcendence: *when the light dims, you must return to the door*.

She was overcome with fear! Overwhelmed by the spectacular display, she had completely forgotten her goal. Quickly, she must choose an object. But how could she make such a decision? What was truly essential to her?

The voice of your heart shall guide the way, and the Light of the Transcendor shall protect you, she remembered the Master of Transcendence's blessing. Her heart was telling her that everything had a special value. But how was she to know what to choose? The light of the Transparent Ones was growing dimmer still.

"No!" cried Sihara fearfully "I cannot go! I have not yet chosen anything. Help me!"

"Take this one," all ten Transparent Ones pointed in unison to a deep purple branch adorned with tiny green leaves. In its center was a pulsating white line.

"Its value is purity of heart," they said.

Chapter Twenty-Four

Journey to the Tower

Journey to the Tower

Sihara found herself outside of the Chamber, in the blooming fields far below Fire Mountain, accompanied by her ten amiable Transparent Ones. The Master of Transcendence had explained many things to Sihara, preparing her for this crucial mission. She was happy that her companions would be with her, at least until they reached Fire Mountain. She was relieved to know that she would not be required to pass through the blaze again and that a key to the Tunnels of Time would be found nearby, facilitating her easy entry to the City. But finding Tzalaii would be more difficult. She would have to locate Mahn, a Tower dweller. He would be able to help her.

The Master of Transcendence had taught her to use Tzalaii's Magnathought Crystal. She knew that it would play a key role in her journey. Her Memory Shield was etched onto her heart, and she recalled the great joy she felt when she had reached the fields beyond Fire Mountain: the blue trail leading to the sea, the rare moment when the final gate opened and the pure-eyed Master was revealed to her in the Chamber.

She observed the Transparent Ones with great curiosity. They were light on their feet, full of grace and deep joy. Their inner flames, swaying like dancers, were enchanting in the yellow fields. The breeze ruffled their filmy clothing as the ten walked straight ahead, one behind the other, in a line. Spotting something on the ground, one stooped to retrieve a large pinecone. Placing it on his head like a crown, he assumed a regal bearing. A small twig, tossed by another, sent the 'crown' reeling to the ground. Then laughter abounded as the game continued with all joining in, until sunset.

In the tranquil land of the Master of Transcendence, the Transparent Ones felt no fear, even in the open areas. The dimming light cast an orange hue upon the fields. As darkness fell, their glowing sacred aura became more apparent and the ten joined hands, transcending silently. From her perch on a large rock, Sihara watched their enchanting dance. They began to sing softly, but Sihara couldn't hear the words.

Turning their faces to the dark skies, their inner flames changed from blue to red, green to turquoise. They raised their voices and Sihara was now able to decipher the words of the song, a chant repeated over and over: "You are the heart of the world."

Images appeared in Sihara's mind each time the chant was intoned. She saw the village of her birth and the familiar shoreline. Many scenes flashed through her imagination: Vague landscapes remembered from childhood, figures from the past, an image of Tzalaii, the Master of Transcendence and his Chamber.

Suddenly the voices intensified, conveying immense splendor. The light grew stronger, and Sihara visualized scenes never before encountered. Familiar, recognizable locations came into view: The Land of the Southern Cliffs, the Black Ocean, the white flame at the top of the Towered City, armies sweeping through, Shadows fleeing behind the trees. Finally, she saw an immense, unending wave soar above all, but the significance of this image eluded her.

Soon, all the images were clarified as the song of her companions described them with words, pleasant and soft, tough and harrowing. All meaning would be found in their repeated refrain, "You are the heart of the world."

Sihara excitedly arose from the rock, approaching the Transparent Ones. She reached out her hands to them, in gratitude for the wondrous gift of vision they had granted her, and they welcomed her into their circle. She recalled the warm glance of her Transparent Master and their encounter at Green Isle, and she understood that 'The heart of the world' and the 'Transcendor' were one. It was to Him that the Transparent Ones transcended, and it was He who was creating worlds incessantly; Transparent Ones, Shadows, Transparent Masters and Obliterators- all were His creations. Even the ancient fire and the forces which emerged from it to become creatures of darkness, were created by Him. His infinite spirit, which roamed over great waters in ancient times, created and emanated glory and beauty beyond comparison.

And He created a soft-voiced Master of Transcendence, with eyes like an exquisite lake, adorned in a golden cloak, to reside in a high and exalted Chamber, to convey His words and carry out His commands.

Sihara's heart filled with eternal gratitude, as she remembered her humble village childhood. And now she had been honored to transcend for the first time to the One, the heart of the world.

"Transcendor, I humbly thank you for these magical moments, for this beauty surrounding me. I thank you for the sweet Transparent Ones, for their pure goodness and joy. I thank you for the life you have given me, a life so full of grace and tenderness, visions, and splendor. I thank You for the privilege to fulfill this great mission for the Master of Transcendence. I thank You for bringing me to him, whose existence had been unknown to me. You have granted me a gift I did not request, from Your treasury of wonders. You have always been good to me, like my mother, my father and my brother, Tzalaii. You have always been at my side, although

I did not know it. Please don't leave me, Transcendor, even for a moment."

A warm breeze caressed the fields in a dark and silent world. The Transparent Ones formed a circle of light around Sihara, and she raised her arms to the heavens. Softly they whispered: "So says the Master of Transcendence: Be attentive to every moment and time. The voice of your heart shall guide the way. Have patience and the Light of the Transcendor shall protect you."

Fluffy purple clouds floated high above them. Thin rays of silvery light transcended and promised: *In time we shall come to your aid.*

Pointing to the sky, the ten indicated the Light of the Transcendor, explaining that the "The Warriors of Transcendence use it only when necessary, as it is potentially dangerous. If the Light touches something worthy, it brings revival and renewal. Something unworthy will be destroyed. Difficult problems arise when the worthy falter even for just a single moment, usually due to excessive pride. The result can be deadly."

Silence hovered over them. Sihara felt gentle pulls, something slightly threatening. Something seemed to be poking through the protective shield that surrounded her, but she was strengthened by her companions' encouraging faces, which imbued in her an immovable faith.

"Do not fear," said the tallest of the lot, "remember the purity of heart."

They spent the night in the fields. At dawn, they continued making their way to the Tunnels of Time. Fire Mountain was now visible on the horizon, its heavy heat evident in the air.

"Here is the entrance," they whispered to her as they approached the side of a high mountain. A stone plank, disguised as a part of the mountain, opened at their touch. They entered through it into a large stone room, as the opening in the mountain shut behind them. Descending a dimly lit staircase into the earth's core, they inhaled the clear and pleasant air. The light-footed Transparent Ones skipped down all thirty-nine steps, quickly reaching the bottom.

Sihara was enchanted by what she found. The soft light illuminated the area, and she felt carefree and happy. All was silent, except for the sound of trickling water and occasional footsteps. At times, the tunnel widened into large halls. Once in a while the main path would diverge into a side trail where the sound of soaring water could be heard. Sihara saw pools of transparent, clear, green water, and soon discovered that a single sip could quench her thirst and renew her strength, as after a long slumber. Sihara and the Transparent Ones walked for days through the Tunnels of Time, as if in a deep and multi-colored dream.

The Transparent Ones sang as they walked, filling Sihara's heart with a great longing and yearning. Stopping to rest in the large halls, they would sit in a circle, laugh, sing, eat and tell stories. Sihara knew that the stories were meant for her and she was especially interested in hearing about the Master of Transcendence.

Born in the King's Palace, during the reign of the Ancient Kingdom, he was remarkable from an early age. His incredible eyes were piercing and perceptive even then. Already, at the age of four, he was learned and wise. His grace and beauty attracted nobles to the castle from all over the world.

Once, in a moment of splendorous awe, the King of the Land of the North had offered the boy his own crown. Fearing threatening external forces, the King of the Ancient Progeny secretly removed the Master of Transcendence from the castle and ordered a Chamber to be built for him beyond Fire Mountain, in the heart of the sea, surrounded by everlasting flowers. Far away from the eyes of man, the Master of Transcendence grew and developed.

Sihara listened, in awe, yearning to learn more.

"But our knowledge is limited. On very special occasions, when the hearts of the Transparent Masters are open, they share their secrets with us."

"But even they don't know everything," added another Transparent One.

The story continued: "Even before the great Kingdom was destroyed, even before the Emperor of the Green Lowlands arrived, the Master of Transcendence had summoned all the Transparent Ones and all the Transparent Masters to his Chamber."

Oh! The songs that must have accompanied such an event! Just the thought of it made Sihara dizzy.

"As the singing intensified, the Transcendor was revealed, and his silvery threads transformed into a glowing crown upon the head of the Master of Transcendence, the Messenger of the Transcendor in the Land of the Ancient Progeny."

The Transparent Ones fell silent and Sihara was left to wonder. One detail in the story surprised her most: The Messenger had traveled everywhere in the Land of the Ancient Progeny. He was able to come and go as he pleased, including to the Towered City!

"But the Emperors, his archenemies in the Tower, how can they allow him to enter?" she asked, as the Transparent Ones chuckled.

"He has no difficulty in entering the Tower whenever he pleases."

But this did not answer Sihara's questions at all and she continued to wonder how the Master of Transcendence was able to avoid Tower security. Even more perplexing was her curiosity about her present challenge:

Why had she been dispatched on this dangerous mission when the Master, himself, could have entered the Tower with perfect ease?

Mysteries, enigmas and puzzlements. Every revelation about the Master of Transcendence solved one mystery and at the same time created a new, more puzzling one. Soon, the Transparent Ones revealed to her that the Master of Transcendence could even visit the Abyss of the Shadows!

The Abyss of the Shadows! Sihara was overcome with terror recalling the horrors she had witnessed in the immeasurable evil depths of the Abyss.

Who could emerge unscathed? She focused her attention on the matter, trying to understand all of this.

Good depth in exchange for evil depth, the Master of Transcendence had whispered to her in his Chamber. Sihara's compassionate heart helped her to perceive the secret depths hidden in people. Constantly she searched for the inner foundation of reality, always open to the distant whisper of the Master of Transcendence. Deep inside her heart she heard faraway, obscure echoes… "Good depth in exchange for evil depth," Sihara intoned the words rising from her heart.

In awesome wonder, The Transparent Ones began whispering to each other: "The Master of Transcendence has spoken through her! Sihara is a Warrior of Transcendence, there is no question about it!"

Chapter Twenty-Five

The Heart Is the Key

The Heart Is the Key

"Who are you?" Mahn asked the girl. Through the wide windows of the Tower, she could see the movement of the passersby in the square below. The City lights flickered, a gentle rain was falling and a soft haze pervaded the atmosphere. The outlines of the walls and towers were blurred so they appeared to be shapeless.

"I am Sihara," she replied confidently.

The torches that hung from the walls of the room cast strange shadows onto the ground.

"You are aware, I trust, that this area is restricted to Inviewers," said Mahn.

Sihara was silent.

"What Level do you belong to?" he asked, getting closer.

As a skilled Inviewer, Mahn was able to decipher movements, sounds, mental states and hidden personality traits. But in the dim light, he was not even able to identify the emblem on her clothing. Radiating confidence, Sihara appeared relaxed and secure, causing Mahn to feel slightly embarrassed by his suspicions. But, persisting in his investigation, he commanded her to answer his question.

Sihara remained silent. Noting Mahn's hand gripping his sword, she suggested softly, "No need for weapons."

Self-assuredly, she asked him "Who are *you*?"

Disarmed by her serenity and poise, intuiting that the question was rhetorical, Mahn became increasingly confused by his inability to read her. Should she be arrested? Should he notify his colleagues to interrogate her?

Suddenly, after a single flash of lightening lit the room, Mahn found his thoughts returning to a previous interrogation he had conducted, long ago, in another venue. In that situation, too, the roles of questioner and questioned had been reversed. His hand gripped his sword even more tightly as he recalled the previous suspect, an old woman in a marketplace who had asked the very same question: *Who are you?*

Now, this question was posed by a confidant, soft -spoken girl dressed in simple blue garb.

Another dim and very distant memory surfaced. Mahn saw himself walking along a shore, viewing the waves, with two young, carefree men, dressed in simple blue garb. This distant, memory was unsettling, and in his conflicted state of mind he felt compelled to answer Sihara's bold question.

"I am Mahn," he replied.

Sihara's face shone as she pointed to the windows. Taken aback by her compelling determination, Mahn followed the seemingly fragile girl to a window facing east. There she pointed to the distant horizon where, through the haze and rain, they were able to see the faint and shimmering reddish glow of Fire Mountain and beyond.

"I was sent to you, traveling from the east," she confided, in a whispered voice, "to tell you that this place is not your true home; you do not belong here. You have a true master, but it is neither the Mercury Emperor, nor any of the other Emperors in the Towered City."

Now she had gone too far! Mahn attempted to focus all of his strength, as he gripped his sword firmly. Recovering his composure, he resumed speaking in an authoritative tone. "You are obviously unaware of your location!" he barked sharply.

Before she had a chance to respond, he continued, his voice growing louder, more threatening: "You are in the Towered City! The great City that generates fear in all the land's inhabitants. You will never return to your home! Your words are meaningless. Prepare to be obliterated!" His confidence grew as he spoke.

Mahn, still bewildered by his momentary loss of self-control, felt ashamed. Fearing burn-out, he felt in need of a change, a rest. Sihara, too, became a bit stressed, but she quickly gathered her strength. Very slowly, as if speaking to a young child, as if Mahn had not understood her provocative statements: "You truly do not belong here. This is not your true home!"

Tell him! the voice of the Messenger echoed in her memory, as she repeated: "The Emperors are not your masters. Your master is the Master of Transcendence."

She flushed as she mentioned his name.

Mahn felt devastated. His confidence vanished and his sword fell to the floor. He attempted to regain his strength, but fear entered his heart; a pervasive inner fear of the unknown, the obscure. Feeling stifled, in need of air, he opened a window, feeling the cold gust of air on his face. Doubts assailed him. He knew the Master of Transcendence led the rebels who conspired to wage war to destroy the Towered City. Yet, Mahn, the Inviewer from the Mercury Level, felt somehow linked to his avowed enemy.

How could this be?!

Distant voices, coming closer, disturbed his already turbulent thoughts. A tour of the halls was being carried out by the Level Guards on watch. If he were to be found in conversation with this strange girl, it would not end well.

"Hurry!" he called to Sihara, and they fled down a dimly lit staircase leading into a small stone cell at the base of the Level.

Mahn had only just discovered this little room during one of his last rounds. The unfurnished room, dimly lit by a single torch, reeked of mold. The low ceiling lent an ominous aspect to the room. Mahn sat down heavily on the ground, recovering from the flight. Sihara leaned on the wall opposite him, taking note of an etching on the wall depicting a domed entranceway.

Her memory vividly replayed a long ago conversation with her Transparent Master in the cabin on the Isle where everything had been so awesomely green, alive and flowing. Here, everything was heavy and distressing, gray and obstructed. There, the Transparent Master had seen so clearly, all of reality spread out before him. Here, she confronted a confused, devastated man, as she tried to explain herself and her mission. The memory of the Transparent Master refreshed her, giving her new strength to continue. Regaining her confidence, she told Mahn about her life and her journey to Green Isle and to the Chamber of Changing Colors, about the Master of Transcendence and his eyes, and about her present mission to rescue her brother, Tzalaii, a prisoner in the Tower.

Mahn listened. Her words hovered over him like purifying winds, and her explanations helped him to connect and understand many confusing events, thoughts and ideas. His findings at the southern quarries had upset his calm spirit and confused his faith in the validity of the Towered City and its Emperors; his encounters with prisoners and Obliterated Ones had molded a deep and subconscious doubt in his heart about his masters' goals; his conversation with the crazy old woman…all of these situations were connected to distant childhood memories amidst echoes of words and fragmented pictures, exposing something alien and obscure. Perhaps he really wasn't meant to be here? Perhaps he was a prisoner, or worse, the son of Obliterated Ones? Sihara's delicate features reminded him of Tzalaii. Yes, he remembered this special prisoner who he had totally failed to Obliterate. The prisoner had been unmovable even in the face of Mahn's strong efforts. But now, Mahn did not know where Tzalaii had been taken to, following the verdict.

He suddenly realized that the trial had been deliberately staged to manipulate the audience. Stunned by his new feelings, he despised the judges for their actions. Over the years, he had been bothered by so many doubts, some clear and others obscure, regarding the falsehood of the Towered City. But he had not connected these disparate ideas and feelings. Why? Why had the proper conclusion eluded him? He was no fool.

He was confused and ashamed, fluctuating between contradicting feelings. His thought process, his clothing, the honored emblem upon his fringes and the sword he carried were all part of the routine he had followed for several decades. His heart was affected and he thought:

You must forget! Forget everything! Alert your supervisors of the girl's presence before you face dire consequences!

He almost said to Sihara: *Your words are meaningless! You shall never return to your home!*

But an inner voice, something stronger and more decisive, commanded him to think about Sihara's pronouncements.

As if in response to his inner voice, a thought arose in his heart:

Even if I were to decide to go with her, into another reality, how would we possibly escape through the great walls of the Towered

City? I would be so vulnerable outside...so lonely in the forest, in the Lowlands, and even worse...

A sudden shudder ran down his spine.

If I am caught, I might die...I might be Obliterated...I might turn into Essence of Soul Concentration and become the binding substance in the stones of the wall...

This thought served to concentrate his anger about his aimless life, about the great hoax to which he was an accomplice, about his education and training which had molded him. He felt he had been used for the evil purpose of obliterating others.

Sihara sat silently, watching him and attentive to the voice of his heart. He seemed like a wounded child on the verge of tears. She saw what he could not see. Now he was shedding his old shell, his tough features were softening, his mighty cloak with the sapphire emblem was shriveling and sliding away from his body like a useless object, bereft of beauty and splendor.

"What now?" he finally asked.

Sihara recalled the words the Master of Transcendence had spoken as she departed from his Chamber: *When you meet him, tell him everything about me and my Chamber. His name is Mahn. Through him you shall find your brother.*

She had already told Mahn about the Master and his Chamber, and her mission to find Tzalaii. But where would she find him? Carefully, she took out the blue Magnathought Crystal, given to her by Tzalaii when he was taken captive on Green Isle. The Crystal glowed, causing its etched tree to become visible. Sihara gazed at the tree- it was identical to the tree that appeared on the gate leading to the Chamber of Changing Colors- on which the word *royalty* was written.

Her heart emptied of all thoughts but one: Tzalaii. She grasped the object that had belonged to her brother, as if it were her last hope, and she repeated his name again and again: "Tzalaii!" But nothing happened. Sihara's desire to locate her brother should have activated the object in her hand, she thought, and then she remembered: *Unification!*

Slightly ashamed, like a child who had failed a test, she covered her face with her hands and whispered: "Transcendor, You have always been good to me; You have always been at my side, since before I knew of Your existence. I am still at the start of my journey- don't leave me alone even for a moment! The Master of Transcendence taught me that Mahn would rescue my brother. Please, help him!"

She then brought the blue Magnathought Crystal to her face, looked at it and whispered, with faith in the presence of the Transcendor: "Show me Tzalaii."

The Crystal responded immediately. Its golden lines became hot, and beyond the distant fog, the image of her lost brother appeared.

Mahn moved closer and gazed into the Crystal, stunned. The two of them could see Tzalaii being led by two Shadows of Illusion into an immense room. Drops from a barely visible glass object attached to the wall, trickled down upon crimson- yellow colored bricks. The Shadows tossed Tzalaii to the ground.

"Here he is," they said to an erect, proud man. His face was pale, his eyes deep, his voice quiet and a double cloak concealed the fringes of his garb. "This prisoner is someone special," they exclaimed.

"I know," the man answered, looking at Tzalaii as if he were an object of great value.

Sihara's face turned white.

Just then, Mahn was brought back to reality by heavy knocks on the stone door.

"Open up, in the name of the White Fire!" He seized the artifact from Sihara's hands and hid it in his cloak. As he calmly opened the door, Sihara wondered about his true intentions.

"Yes, sirs, how may I be of assistance? Is this an urgent matter? You are interrupting an Inviewer's interrogation of a prisoner!"

The two warriors from the Base Level retreated with an apology. Sihara's life had been saved for the present time! But the warriors might report to their supervisors and Mahn would be asked to explain her identity. The stone door was closed and Mahn turned to Sihara.

"I, alone, know where your brother has been taken. Only I can find him."

His anger intensified as he thought of Tzalaii's hapless plight; obliteration and soul concentration. This served to shock him into action, to do everything possible to rescue the boy and escape from the Tower.

"But you must disappear," he told Sihara. "Leave the same way you came. Do not linger here for even another second!"

Opening the door, Sihara peered down the corridors in both directions. In the dim light, she appeared to have grown in stature. Mahn looked at her expectantly. She removed a small object from her garb: it was the purple branch adorned with tiny leaves and green threads. A luminous white line pulsated within it.

"Your heart is the key," she heard herself say.

What was her heart telling her now? She looked into her soul, longing to hear her inner voice. *Look around you. Your true path calls you at all times! Search for its signs!*

Once again she scanned the corridors confidently, but this time she noticed a small object in a corner. Intuitively, she approached it, stooping to examine it more closely. It was a pinecone, so out of place here, so small and almost hidden from sight. Sihara lifted it, holding it close to her heart, while gazing at the wall behind it. The marks of an ancient, blocked gate were visible in the stone. This was the passage she was to enter! Yes, The Transparent Ones had left signs for her, but how was she to pass through the thick stone wall?

The silence deepened as Mahn tried to ignore his fears. Never had it been this silent in the Towered City. The sound of footsteps, the beat of drums and people in conversation were always audible.

"Hurry! Fast!" Mahn wanted to shout, but he was unable to speak.

The girl stood as if in a dream, staring fixedly at the wall.

No one can be forced to act against his will, to accept anything against his will, the Master of Transcendence had said in his Chamber. *Deep inside, you are eternally free.*

Sihara stood facing the gate, feeling the force of her dispatcher directing her.

"Neither man nor Emperor, neither dagger nor sword can stop me! Good depth in exchange for evil depth!" she exclaimed. "Liberty in exchange for slavery! Freedom in exchange for oppression!"

Suddenly, the wall vanished, exposing a magnificent underground kingdom. Sihara offered hurried instructions to Mahn about the Magnathought Crystal.

"The Master of Transcendence said that you would be able to rescue Tzalaii," she reminded him, plaintively, as she ran.

Mahn clenched his jaws in determination, as he replied: "I shall fulfill my task."

Chapter Twenty-Six

Good Depth in Exchange for Evil Depth

Good Depth in Exchange for Evil Depth

Tzalaii had been flung to the floor by the Shadows and had lain at the feet of the tall man for some time. Now he arose. Curiously, the man seemed to be quite friendly. He directed Tzalaii towards the room he had been allotted, departing with a smile. "We shall meet again." But his smile sent chills down Tzalaii's spine. Though he was alone, imprisoned in a dark labyrinth, he was permitted to wander around the chilly rooms. He was addressed in a seemingly friendly manner but he felt weighed down, suspicious of his captors motives and oppressed by an ever-growing burden. Obsessive recollections of the trauma he had endured haunted him, almost pushing him to insanity. His daring removal of the stone from the wall…his failed escape on Green Isle…the drink of tumult…the strange trial…He was unable to make any sense of past events and he felt threatened by something far worse than even the Abyss of the Shadows. Unable to comprehend his present situation nor to predict his future in this cold, subterranean prison, his thoughts became weak, his sorrow increased, and the dull, tedious boredom in this netherworld broke his strength. Day after day, he endured the isolation and uncertainty, while the Memory Shields protecting him from soul concentration dwindled.

Not much attention had been given to Tzalaii until night, while most of the people in the underground rooms were busy at work. One of them came close to examine him. The man had hidden his face with his cape, but red flame emblems were visible on his clothing. Tzalaii identified the flames as those belonging to the Venus Level, the fourth level of the Towered City. He had noticed this man before and was impressed by the respect he received from others. The man gestured to Tzalaii to follow him. Tzalaii was confused. Was this an order or just a friendly invitation, an option?

The man gestured more urgently now and Tzalaii realized that he was being commanded to follow after him. Busy workers and soldiers with weapons respectfully made way for the man with the red flame. Only the head of the Essence Department, a man with a green flame on his clothing, the symbol of the Solar Level, had the authority to speak to Tzalaii's new acquaintance, Mahn, who was disguised as a Venus Level inhabitant with a counterfeit red flame. Down, down, lower and lower, from tunnel to tunnel, Tzalaii followed Mahn.

Finally, depleted of strength, Tzalaii came to a halt.

"Do what you want with me," he said, exhausted. "I am losing my mind…"

Suddenly the stranger unveiled his face and Tzalaii recognized him: it was the investigator who had offered him *redemption from the forces of nature!*

Tzalaii, convinced that this was a trick, took a few steps backwards coming to rest against a cold rock. Instinctively, he put his arms out in front of him, assuming a defensive stance. A trap set up by the Shadows, he thought, or a final performance of illusions before his execution. He tried to speak but he had no strength. He was unable to utter even a single sound.

"Be calm now. I was sent by your sister," said the man.

Tzalaii was convinced that he was hallucinating, that he had gone mad.

"Look," said Mahn, as he removed the blue Magnathought Crystal from his cape. Tzalaii's eyes glazed over and he pressed himself against the wall, trying to escape from this man, this deception

"I have been searching for you for many days," said Mahn in a soft voice, tinged with despair, trying to convince the miserable boy that he had come to rescue him. "Good depth in exchange for evil depth," he said, quoting Sihara's final words to him.

Tzalaii's face transformed, as he sensed the honesty within these words, and he extended his hand for the artifact, still suspicious. Now the Magnathought Crystal was really in his hands and the golden lines heated up immediately. Tzalaii's scattered desires and severe state of mind prevented him from concentrating.

"They may have gone that way!" they could hear the voices coming closer and Mahn was terrified. Death was the automatic penalty for misrepresenting the color of a flame. He was perilously endangered by his attempt to rescue this precious prisoner from the hands of the Emperor.

"Your sister escaped through an opening into the Tunnels of Time," he said to Tzalaii. "Are there other openings to the Tunnels?" he asked urgently.

Tzalaii shook his head. His senses were awakening now, and the significance of the situation brought him back to his senses.

You have a chance! One final chance! He heard the words reverberate in his head. He and Mahn held on to the blue Magnathought Crystal, and they both concentrated the remnants of their fearful desire into one goal: To escape from the cold hell in the belly of the earth.

The voices were getting closer. Mahn pulled out a short sword with one hand, and with the other continued holding onto the warm Crystal with Tzalaii. "Good depth in exchange for evil depth!" Mahn roared, repeating Sihara's words, though he did not understand their meaning. These were the words she had whispered, right before the wall had split for her.

The words entered Tzalaii's consciousness shaking his soul violently. Abysmal depths of pain cracked open from within him, layers of terror, despair and loss, exposing a single, bright and distant ray of light beneath. Tzalaii closed his eyes, ignored the darkness and focused his thoughts upon the single, comforting ray of light. "Good Depth in exchange for Evil Depth," he whispered, pleadingly, as tears slid down his cheeks. A bright cavity opened up in the wall next to them with pure, turquoise- colored water streaming towards the opening and Mahn and Tzalaii scrambled out through the luminous opening. The wall of stone behind them immediately reappeared, re-sealing itself instantaneously. The echoes of people shouting and pounding were heard for a moment, and then there was silence.

Chapter Twenty-Seven

Ten Days in the Tunnels of Time

Ten Days in the Tunnels of Time

Stunned, Tzalaii gazed at his sister, at Mahn, at the illuminated stone wall and the turquoise-colored water streaming in the crevices. He felt incapable of distinguishing between fantasy and reality. In the enormity of the events, so much had been left unsaid. Mahn, astounded by the abrupt transformation from the Tower to this place, was bursting with questions. Sihara pictured the Master of Transcendence in her mind's eye, wishing to tell the others about his closeness, but it was not the right time.

She removed bread and fruit from her satchel, arranging them in an appealing manner. Mahn and Tzalaii ate a little, and then stretched out on the ground, falling into a deep, prolonged sleep. Sihara felt encouraged knowing that there were many Transparent Ones close by, in fact, just down the road.

They shall recover, she reassured herself many times, as she watched the curled-up sleeping beings, still fearful even as they slept. *They shall recover and discover new, persistent strengths within them. They will be able to withstand any threat. They shall be cured by the Master of Transcendence.*

Mahn and Tzalaii awoke on the evening of the following day, and sat up silently. Mahn was deep in thought, recalling the events of the last few days and, in fact, reviewing the events of his entire life. Tzalaii, his soul pained and aching, played with the smooth rocks by the wellsprings, tossing them into the water, one by one, as he had done when he was a child in the village. Sihara watched him compassionately, and smiled: "Now you are protected," she said softly, "as you were before, when we were children. The Master of Transcendence himself is guiding and accompanying you."

She recounted her story to Tzalaii and Mahn, explaining her experiences in the Shadow Valley and at Fire Mountain. She told them, in great detail, about her journey through the seven gates, and about her encounter with the Master of Transcendence. Mahn's eyes opened wide, as if he were unable to digest so much information. Tzalaii listened to her attentively, speaking only once: "I have already met a man on Green Isle who knew about these things and he told me the same story. It happened just before we were captured by the soldiers."

The next day, Sihara decided it was time to give Tzalaii the instructions she had received from the Master of Transcendence. Tzalaii had difficulty understanding why she called them *healing instructions,* but as they were given by the Master of Transcendence, he accepted them without question.

"During the next ten consecutive days," explained Sihara, "you are to devote at least an hour each day to do the following: Close your eyes and imagine yourself in your most beloved place. Once you have created a sufficient image in your mind, and you appear in it clearly, you must call yourself out loud: 'Tzalaii.' The intention of this calling is to return and reconnect with yourself." Tzalaii followed the instructions carefully.

Tzalaii's experience on the first day:

I close my eyes and try to imagine myself. At first, I encounter only a dark empty void. After some time, an image is revealed from within the darkness. I see myself from behind, sitting erectly, proudly aloof, on the edge of a great cliff overlooking the sea, spread out in the distance. Tzalaii is dressed in a golden cloak. Dark clouds shift in the sky, and the weather is stormy. "Tzalaii," I call him, "Tzalaii...Tzalaii..."

I sense that he hears me, but he does not turn his face towards me. Is he angry with me? I approach him quietly and sense a tense resistance. Have I wronged him in any way?

A short distance away from him, I come to a halt, sit on the ground and continue to call him slowly, pleadingly, as Sihara advised me: "Tzalaii...Tzalaii...Tzalaii."

I intend to tell him: 'Don't be angry with me. Turn to me, speak to me!' But the barrier he erects remains between us. His apathy is an insult to me. Have I behaved so badly that I deserve such treatment? Why does he make me feel so bad about myself? I begin to tire of my pursuit. Much time passes. Weary and in despair, I consider the possibility of retracing my steps. This proud and unfamiliar being that happens to be me, will never even grant me a simple glance... But no, I shall not give up.

I take a deep breath and scream at the top of my lungs: "Tzalaii!!!"

He turns his face and looks at me. Anything would have been better than that look, even if he were to ignore me forever. His glance, full of blame, makes me shrink in place as if he had said: "How dare you even approach me, you lowly, miserable creature! We share nothing in common."

Why does he despise me so? I cannot stand it.

Fog is rolling in from the sea and blocking visibility. Tzalaii returns his glance to the water, and I catch short glimpses of him, sitting proudly, through the fog. I am filled with anger. I have never deliberately harmed him, I barely even know him! I must conquer my fears and get closer. I want him to explain his behavior to me. Rain begins to fall and my clothes become drenched. Droplets wet my face as well. No, these are not tears; my heart is too dry, too angry to cry. Humiliated and full of resentment, I walk through the fog and approach him. I notice his royal stature and admire him. He appears in my eyes as a man of great importance. The anger in my heart weakens, and is replaced by a great desire to become acquainted with this person, myself. "Tzalaii" I whisper, still fearful of his reaction.

I reach my hand out, longing to touch him. The sea in the distance is turbulent, terrifying, but Tzalaii seems to be entirely unaware of the concept of fear. Once again, he turns around and looks at me. This time, though, his gaze is not hate-filled, and he seems less resistant. But something else, something bittersweet, is apparent in his eyes. It is compassion. Compassion resulting from contempt, the compassion that can be felt by a winner for a loser; the compassion of a wise man for a mindless fool; the compassion of one who is pure, radiant, and alive towards one who is writhing in wickedness and sin, dwelling in darkness all of his days, unaware of the significance of life.

I am no longer offended. I am astonished by his glance and it pierces me painfully. Have I really gone that far? Something in me shatters. I fall to his feet as to the feet of a king, and beg for my life: "Tzalaii…" I whisper to him voicelessly as I think: 'Oh, great and almighty Tzalaii, raise me up from destitution!'

How is it possible that he and I are one and the same, when we inhabit two opposing planes that never meet?

The time is up. His image blurs and fades. I open my eyes. They are filled with tears.

The second day:

Once again, he sits with his back to me. This time he is not atop a high cliff, but on the seashore, gazing into the distance. Why does he always gaze into the distance? What is he trying to see there, in the open sea? His proud stance immediately agitates me. True, at the end of our last encounter I felt admiration towards him, but why is he so arrogant? Perhaps I am mistaken, perhaps he is not arrogant. When I look at him from a distance, sitting in the sand, adorned in his golden cloak, I suddenly recall my trial and the king's cloak. I am shocked to discover it is identical to the cloak he is wearing now. Yes, my use of the cloak in the Tower was a grave mistake. Does this account for his great anger? Is it because the king's cloak remained in the Tower? But during the trial, I wore it without arrogance!

Full of curiosity, I call to him. A multitude of questions storm my brain and my heart, all part of the same puzzle, painful yet intriguing: Who am I? And who is he? He himself is the answer. "Tzalaii"

I get closer to him. Will he turn to me? And what will his glance convey this time? Resistance between us is dissolving.

"You are beginning to understand," I realize. I understand that Tzalaii is speaking to me. He continues, in my thoughts: "I am not arrogant. Everything is reversed in your imagination."

I glance at him again and discover that although his stature is royal and upright, he is completely modest and submissive, precise and simple. He is so beautiful! I love him so much! If only he would grant me a glance! If only he would speak to me and accept me as his disciple! I would do anything for him! How am I to acquire his trust?

"Tzalaii," I say repeatedly, and he turns his head slightly. He points to the right, an undecipherable expression on his face. On the beach, in the distance, I notice a large tent. It is composed of a transparent blue cloth, and the light of day shines through it, illuminating its interior. Is he sending me there? I desire his closeness and have no interest in any manner of mission.

"Very well," I say to myself and to him, "If you so desire."

I turn around and begin to walk in the sand towards the tent.

As I approach the tent, it appears to be larger than I originally thought it was. The penetrating light is a soft blue, and the transparent cover gleams in the sun. Inside, a small group of serenely calm people sit on large cushions. The floor is covered in majestic colorful carpets, and the aroma of medicinal herbs and incense permeates the air. In the southern corner of the tent, a boy in white garb sits cross-legged and speaks His eyes are good and pleasant. No one senses my approach and I am not noticed even as I stand at the entrance. They are completely engrossed, listening attentively to the speaker.

"Boundaries," says the speaker, "are prone to change. Look at the waves crashing upon the shore."

I realize how close the tent is to the water.

"The waves wash over the shore, conquering more and more sandy regions, time and time again," he says in a melodious voice. "The boundaries of the sea are constantly changing, sometimes exposing the tip of a rock hidden under water, other times covering and concealing them. But the constant interplay, the obscure struggle between the sand and the sea, is eternal. Every wave that conquers a piece of land, every grain of sand that is repeatedly purified, symbolizes the great conquest, the total and final purification that shall eventually change the boundaries completely."

I find myself feeling overwhelmed for no apparent reason. The boy is silent now. Some of the men play musical instruments. One beats a small drum, another sways wind chimes, and a third plays a delicate tune on a stringed instrument. The melody lures me into the tent as if with magical ropes. I enter and look at the people inside. Up close, I am able to see the face of the boy who is dressed in white. His eyes express a joyous elation I have never before seen. I am frightened and open my eyes.

The third day:

I am on the beach again. Tzalaii is gazing at the sea, like before. But this time, he turns around as soon as I call his name. Is it just my imagination, or do the traces of a smile appear on his face? He still refrains from speaking to me. He motions with his hand for me to sit by his side on the beach. Eagerly, I sit beside him. He points towards the depth of the sea and whispers one word to me. This is the first time I have heard his voice! It is stable, authoritative and loving. "Look," he says.

I raise my eyes towards the horizon. Fog blurs the boundaries of the sea and the sky, casting a turquoise blue-gray color on the scene. I concentrate on the colors, but Tzalaii's closeness is more important to me than the distant horizon. Next to him I feel so safe and protected, as though I have returned home after many years of waiting.

I have a deep desire to touch his hand, to express my adoration towards him. Suddenly, I want only to serve him, I want him to acknowledge me and love me. A swarm of feelings encompasses me. Still gazing into the horizon, I reach out and touch the palm of his hand resting upon his knee. It radiates so much heat!

"Tzalaii" I whisper.

The sun begins to set over the water, casting a reddish glow. An ancient covenant has been reborn.

"From now on I shall be there with you and for you. I shall never leave your side," his hand seems to say. "But what are you truly willing to do for me?" he asks.

Sadness is present in his voice and the magic suddenly ends. Does he not trust me? This question is so disconcerting to me that I have no choice but to open my eyes.

The fourth day:

"Dance for me," he says.

His cloak hangs shabbily upon his body; he faces me with his back to the sea. He smiles confidently, somewhat amused. Only now do I notice his eyes: they are as deep and as good as the eyes of the child in the tent. But why do they express pain?

"I? Dance?" I had never considered myself talented in this art.

"You asked to do something for me, did you not?"

I sense the disappointment in his voice and fervently wish to avoid disappointing him again. 'Again?' I suddenly wonder, 'when did I disappoint him previously?'

Tzalaii begins to hum a quiet tune. He is telling me about himself. He suddenly appears so human, so shy, and I sense that he longs for my closeness. Despite being greatly disappointed in me in the past, he is still willing to renew our friendship.

"Will you be my guide?" I ask.

"Dance!" his eyes are suddenly angry.

My acceptance as his student, friend and companion depend upon this dance! And then he produces a five-stringed instrument, unfamiliar to me, and in the softest, most tranquil voice repeats the words, again and again: "You are the heart of the world," as he plays. He accompanies me with his song, but I understand that the words are not being directed to me. But to whom? I do not know.

Do we both need to yearn for the mysterious Heart of the World, expressing ourselves in song and dance? This, too, I do not know, but the melody begins to pulsate within my head. My lips begin uttering his words and Tzalaii smiles an almost invisible smile, as he watches the power of his song wash over me. A profound clarity and serenity descend upon the world, as if the two of us are its sole inhabitants, as though we would live in this place eternally, participants in a ceremony ordained for us many eons ago. The wind whirls around us, and golden grains of sand dance upon our flapping capes. The waves wash over the soft, velvety sand at our feet, crashing down gently and then subsiding.

"And now," says Tzalaii in a slightly louder voice, "you are to be born."

His simple words invoke sheer panic in me and I desire to flee, never to see his face again. With great effort, I exert myself to keep my eyes closed thereby preserving the crucial scene. It is clear to me that my current choice is vital. I must either devote myself entirely to the unknown, or escape as a coward back to my familiar world.

"Come," whispers Tzalaii, and my fear dissipates as I rise upon my feet. It seems to me that everything around us is participating in our slow song: The sea, the sky, the sand and all else in the world that is beyond our understanding. I feel clarity within clarity. Everything is so transparent, as though I can slowly pierce through all things with my words. My hands are raised to the heavens and my body begins to transcend on its own, expressing each and every word in motion: "You are the heart of the world."

Sweetness inebriates my consciousness. Is this my dance? If so, there is nothing I would ever desire more than to transcend before the Heart of the World. Is this my birth? There is nothing sweeter. Why was I so fearful?

Sihara smiled at her brother. It was an empathetic smile, full of compassion and understanding for the process he was undergoing. The two of them sat in a cave near a small spring of clear water. A few rays of light shone through the entrance of the cave, illuminating the depths of the wellspring. Tzalaii smiled for the first time in a while and said: "You know, Sihara, the exercise you told me to perform…"

"That the Master of Transcendence told you to perform," she corrected him.

Tzalaii ignored her comment.

"It is a strange exercise," he continued. "At first, it was quite difficult for me, and then suddenly something in my heart opened. I felt like a young boy, when I herded the sheep in the fields by the village. I can remember when I sat in the green hills. The sheep were scattered throughout the valley, grazing, and I began to play a tune on my flute. The breeze caressed my face and I was happy. Suddenly, I had no need for anything, and even the deep pain I felt as an orphan entirely disappeared. "Sihara tossed a small stone into the water and nodded to herself: "Those were his exact words: "reconnect with yourself."

Tzalaii did not understand the link between his childhood memories and his encounter with the inner Tzalaii, so Sihara attempted to explain further: "This is your healing from the mark of the shadow."

"You are already a Warrior of Transcendence," Tzalaii said forlornly. "But I don't know very much. What is the 'mark of the shadow?' Strange events are transpiring, and you seem to understand. How did you manage to learn so much during your short visit with the Master of Transcendence?"

"You too shall learn," Sihara said apologetically. "You shall learn in your own way. And if you cannot reach the Master of Transcendence, he will find you."

"I was taken to a horrible place," Tzalaii said as his voice cracked, and once again he ignored her words. He was unable to shake off the vivid image in his mind of the tall man's ominous smile, his fear of the underground soldier's ability to pursue him and find him. He was still haunted by the man's parting words: *We shall meet again.*

"I think you should continue with the exercise," said Sihara.

"Yes," agreed Tzalaii with a sudden burst of determination. "I, too, must try to acquire the knowledge you have gained."

The fifth day:

I look forward to meeting Tzalaii again. I try to imagine the beach, but nothing appears in my mind. My eyes are enveloped by darkness.

"Tzalaii," I call out in the dark, "where are you, Tzalaii?"

"The beach is for children, an unfit scenario for a warrior," a voice speaks in the back of my mind.

Where, then, am I to ask for my beloved teacher?

"This time, we shall meet between the shadows," said Tzalaii.

My body tenses, and all at once I notice him, sitting cross-legged near a small bonfire deep in the dark desert. He points commandingly towards a simple canvas carpet on the other side of the fire. He loves me, no doubt. Our shared dance to the Heart of the World united us in a covenant of love that cannot be undone.

'Is this setting necessary?' I wonder, and Tzalaii answers: "This is the Wilderness Gate of the White Desert. This is where the Master of Transcendence trains his warriors."

"I never aspired to become a warrior," I say and try to open my eyes, but even with eyes wide open, I remain with him in the desert, and the fire hissing between us is the only sound that is heard.

"Now, there is nowhere for you to escape to," says Tzalaii sharply, his image ascending and looming over me like a pillar of clouds, "for you have been born."

"Accept your destiny with love," he says, as though trying to persuade me to trust him and his words. "You are a warrior. A Warrior of the Master of Transcendence."

"Yes," I think to myself, "I asked for a guide to advise me. But I

never imagined he would be the one. I desired a leader to pave the way. Is this the path of a warrior?"

Tzalaii says: "All sadness emanates from luxury. This is the first rule of the Master of Transcendence."

Is this the beginning of my initiation training? Concern makes way for curiosity, and my heart listens to his words. Over the course of an hour, Tzalaii explains to me the principle of luxury, according to which everything that you don't really need only harms you.

"The skills of a Master of Transcendence," he says, "include being able to distinguish precisely between the necessary and the unnecessary, at all times. Even an extra word can make you vulnerable, weaken your inner strength and balance, and draw you into the shadows."

"Precision brings protection," Tzalaii summarizes. "Your life is sheltered from all evil, even in the face of the White Emperor himself. If your consciousness detects an unnecessary sight or sound, your spirit shall become cracked with a line of sadness. Sadness is the delicacy of the Shadows. Open your eyes," he finally orders.

His hand touches my heart as though he wants to carve his words there and he adds: "Remember everything and don't forget."

I open my eyes and again find myself in the Tunnels of Time. The entire vision- every word and sound uttered by Tzalaii, remain engraved in my heart.

The sixth day:

"You have already been to the Tower," says Tzalaii, as our next encounter begins. "You have been judged, and even taken to the Southern Mines. But you were an awful student, and you have not yet learned from these experiences."

I object and he corrects himself: "In any case, you have yet to learn with the clarity of a Warrior of Transcendence."

Just like the last time, his words are followed by a vision. Tzalaii paces back and forth in a yellow field, in full bloom, part of a colorful landscape flowing with scents, motion and life. "Sihara passed through here as well," he remarks, as if this fact is relevant to me, and then says: "Let's take a walk."

A soft breeze bends a row of yellow flowers and then soars again. A bird is visible in the distant horizon, soaring slowly.

"Due to the limitations of time," he begins, "we shall touch the heart of matters today."

His words remind me of our dance and of the words, "You are the heart of the world."

"The Deathliners may appear," he whispers to me as a warning.

I understand nothing, but a cloud obscures his face transforming all of the beauty around us into emptiness. "Therefore, your initiation training shall be short and harried. What more, all I shall do is remind you. We have already discussed this more than once."

A dim, unclear memory passes through my consciousness. Distant, forgotten days. Somewhere, sometime I have already been a student of Tzalaii's.

"This time I shall not disappoint him," I promise.

We sit on a large rock surrounded by red flora. The sky is clear once again as Tzalaii speaks: "The Law of Transformation rules nature," he begins.

I am surprised. Every child knows that all living things change and renew their forms and are not eternal! What is my mentor trying to teach me? Suddenly I recall Mahn's words:

'All entities of the world undergo transformation' the Inviewer had said. 'The world is composed of many circles, life and death, growth and destruction. Even simple men are compelled to adhere to the Law of Transformation, and are controlled by the great circle of change. Eventually all of mans dreams, passions and disappointments vanish in the wind like fleeting dust, worthless and meaningless.'

Mahn spoke of the belief the inhabitants of the Tower lived by: Redemption from the Law of Transformation.

What would Tzalaii say about this?

"Be calm," says Tzalaii. "There is a rationale for Mahn's words, but the Emperors' solution is false. They are all slaves to the Law of Transformation."

Anger is apparent in his words and I am amazed that such bitterness could be present in a heart so pure. The desires of man, even the strongest ones, are part of the transformation cycle. At times we desire something with all of our being, only to abhor and flee from the very same thing at another time. Our desires are revealed, destruct and are lost in the transformation oblivion. All acquisition is subject to the Law of Transformation. Such foolishness!"

"Is there another way?" *I wonder.*

"The other option," he says, suddenly seeming taller, "is the secret of resignation. According to the Law of Transformation, everything is lost. But whatever you relinquish escapes and flies from the Law of Transformation."

This is beyond my comprehension, I think.

"So what, if anything, is left to be desired?" *I ask.*

He gazes at the graying sky silently and then answers: "All things, all desires, can avoid the Law of Transformation, but first they must be transformed according to the desire of the One."

"But what must be desired?" I ask, feeling like a mindless entity faced with such deep, unfathomable wisdom. Tzalaii removes his musical instrument from his cape and answers my question with a song: "You are the heart of the world."

I refuse to join in and open my eyes.

The seventh day:

There have been so many new insights in the past six days. I am almost fearful of meeting Tzalaii again. Who knows what will come next. How can I be a Warrior of Transcendence after absconding from my last vision like a small, scared rabbit? I sit at the entrance to the cave, take a deep breath of clear air, feel the dampness of the wall and close my eyes. I see myself sitting alone on a wooden bench in a mountain forest overlooking a wide terrain. Echoes of woodland birds are heard in all directions. The sun is setting, painting the clouds in hues of bright orange and lavender. Birds fly by us in short, fast flight, seeking refuge for the night.

"Tzalaii," I whisper.

"I am already with you," is his immediate answer. "You no longer need to see me from the outside."

I smile joyfully. Tzalaii is already inside of me. I am Tzalaii. My eyes, looking into the distance, are his eyes. His voice is in my heart, and he is my guide.

"A Warrior of Transcendence," he says, and my heart skips a beat, "must transform external beauty into internal beauty."

To what could I transform the magical moments of the sunset? I wonder.

Suddenly I become conscious of the unfamiliar landscape. It is not my familiar world. It is neither the Northern Forests nor the Rain Forests. Am I observing the future?

"You are observing your inner soul, and getting to know your strengths."

I feel a great need to cry as night descends over the world, my inner world, and lights appear in the distance like the lights of a great city, buzzing with life. I cry uncontrollably, without knowing why, and feel as though I am being freed from a heavy burden. There is so much that I have been oblivious to inside of myself: birds, clouds, skies, trees blowing in the wind, soaring treetops, and grand rocks covered in moss, and in the distance-large wide expanses, illuminated with many lights. Suddenly the light appears to me as a multitude of lit candles, possibly the lights of souls I have encountered in another time?

My world is as transparent as a clear crystal ball. The darkness around me does not threaten me, but greets me with an embrace. It is full of the warm winds of hope, engendering security and courage. The tears continue to fall. I had been so lonely until now, so far away from the richness of my inner life. And now I feel comforted, yet I am ashamed. Is it fair for me to feel comfort when somewhere in the Land of the Ancient Progeny, enemy armies are preparing to attack? But despite this negative thought, the beauty of this moment is not dimmed. Lights flicker in the distance and I watch and observe. This life inside of myself, when would I merit to enter and discover it? When will I uncover the secret? If I were only able to wander around here forever...

Suddenly I sense I am in danger. These are not the words of Tzalaii! I feel a sudden sharp pain in my ribs, as if to say: 'I have come here to gain strength, not to get lost!'

"You must relinquish," I recall Tzalaii's words. *"You must be willing to forego all of this!"*

I close my eyes, and through the tears, I begin to sing softly: "You are the heart of the world."

The eighth day:

"The seventh is always special," explains Tzalaii.

I thought that he would only be found in my inner world from now on, but here he is, sitting across from me on the beach, gazing into the distant horizon, a breeze caressing the edges of his cloak.

"Why have we returned to this place?" I ask, "You told me that this was a childish scenario." "Aren't you a child again?" he answers with a smile. "Don't you desire to always be at the starting point? To relinquish means to forego everything," he explains.

Then he points into the depths and adds: "And this is the explanation of your words: Just no arrogance."

Again, I do not understand. I expect him to continue talking, but he arises, ensconced in silence and gestures for me to follow him. The wind grows stronger and gray clouds fill the sky. The sand feels soft and smooth. A cliff can be seen in the distance, and after a long walk we reach its base. He sits down, points to the sand, inviting me to sit by his side. He places his finger over his mouth so that I remain silent, and gazes at the stormy waters, guiding me to look in the same direction. I see nothing. The whistling wind causes his hair to become disheveled, sand is scattered through the air and the waves wash up by our feet. A white dot appears in the sea and gets closer to us. It is a boat. Where did it come from in such stormy weather? As it nears us, I notice a child aboard. It is the boy I had seen in the blue tent. He sits in a royal manner, his eyes exquisitely beautiful.

I recall my sister's words: 'If you cannot reach the Master of Transcendence, he will find you.'

Tzalaii points to the boat, and then boards it as soon as it reaches the shore. All is silent, and I understand that I am not to speak.

"Come," Tzalaii says, motioning to me with his hand. I am momentarily fearful, but the eyes of the Master of Transcendence are focused on me and I know that I will soon be safe and protected even in the heart of the most dangerous storm. As we sail out to sea, the winds calm. The Master of Transcendence tightens his golden cloak, with its delicate light blue embroidery and gazes at the water that surrounds us.

"Just no arrogance," he says as I look into the black waters.

"All of this eternal depth, all of the great, deep abysses," he adds melodiously, "do not contain even a drop of arrogance. They will eternally allow the wind to carry them and cast them in any way it desires. They will forever hold in their innards myriads of fish, aquatic plants and corals. Accepting all of this, accepting and asking for nothing."

'Water will extinguish the fire,' a thought crosses through my mind from somewhere.

The Master of Transcendence continues: "The same is true for you. The moment you relinquish your existence, you will become worthy of the crown of royalty. He who foregoes his arrogance, his false royalty, becomes a tool of service to the Light of the Transcendor."

I raise my eyebrows in wonder. What is the Light of the Transcendor?

As if able to hear my thoughts, the Master of Transcendence explains: "When the Light of the Transcendor shines, it causes the illuminated entity to return to its original condition. It destroys the evil that had gathered in it and leaves it with its primary goodness. Feelings of superiority, of being better than others, are a distortion that can be harmed by the Light of the Transcendor. You must be wary."

He is silent now, allowing his words to settle in my heart. Then he continues: "Soon your initiation training shall be complete. The places visited by Sihara- have now been visited by you."

He pauses for a moment noticing the look of awe on my face, and adds with a smile: "From your side."

He holds my hand affectionately, and I feel his strength and warmth infusing my being. The sea is now completely calm as we approach the shore.

The ninth day:

"Tzalaii," I whisper with my eyes closed. "My dear friend, Tzalaii..."

A great darkness covers the earth. Tzalaii does not answer me, but the sense of his presence imbues me with confidence even in the heavy darkness. I am sitting on a wooden bench in the deepest darkness. Only the distant sounds of the woodland birds provide a clue to my location, it is so dark!

"Tzalaii," I call out.

Distant echoes reply: "Tzalaii...Tzalaii...Tzalaii..."

I hear the rush of the treetops swaying in the wind, instilling fear in my heart. What am I to do here?

"Be calm," whispers a voice at my left.

I breathe a sigh of relief as I turn towards the voice, but I am only able to see a faint outline.

"Look," he whispers in his usual way, and directs my gaze forward.

Very far off, in the distance, I now notice small, faint lights, the lights of a city. I concentrate my gaze upon the distant lights. To my surprise, the more I look, the closer they become. I regain my confidence as I began to sense that I am about to learn something new today, something more beautiful than I had ever learned before. When I approach the lights, I notice that they are in fact thin, white candles. Their flames flicker as though they will be extinguished in a moment.

"Tzalaii," I call again.

"I am with you, always," whispers Tzalaii.

Next to him, I notice a being of short stature. I suppose that it is the boy who had been with us in the boat. He advances and takes my hand. All at once I recall the warmth transferred to me through his hands the last time he touched me. Now, too, his touch imbued me with hope.

Now you may enter," says the boy pleasantly, indicating the flickering flames.

"Enter?" I ponder the meaning of this in my mind, "but where?"

One flame, brighter than the others, catches my eye. I fix my gaze upon it, and its light begins to grow immensely. I am able to see many shades of various colors inside. Purples and blues blaze and ascend and strings of white light curl and shine, greens twinkle and flicker within the fire. I watch the colors, transfixed. Deep inside I now see the deep, black, worrying darkness again.

"Look inside," whispers Tzalaii, still at my side.

"Into the darkness?"

"Inside," he repeats.

Encouraged by the presence of Tzalaii and the Master of Transcendence, I gaze into the blackness within the light. The colorful outline disappears, and I find myself again in an icy world, where the wind scatters fallen branches, and I feel threatened by the terror of what is to come. I focus my gaze as well as I can, and manage to notice a fine flame inside of the blackness. Its beauty is astounding beyond words. It consists of all the colors and they glow and manifest themselves with such sharp clarity, beyond anything I could have ever imagined. Changing, shimmering colors, bringing joy and carefree laughter, like children at play. These are the colors of total, eternal liberation, with not even a hint of darkness and fear. I look even deeper and notice how, amidst the dancing flame, the colors transform into the petals of an opening flower, retreating from the heart of the fire, exposing a white light in its midst. I look into the center of the light and see a newborn baby! His hair is fair, his eyes are clear and a blue flame is visible through his transparent body. The scene is so beautiful, I begin to cry. I am overwhelmed and want to open my eyes.

"Wait!" whispers Tzalaii. "You must first understand what you have seen."

"Few people merit to witness such a wondrous event," whispers the Master of Transcendence. "The birth of a Transparent One!"

"Was all of this born inside of me?" I ask.

The Master of Transcendence nods, a smile illuminates his face, "Inside each and every one of my men."

I open my eyes.

The tenth day:

"Is this where it all ends?" I ask Tzalaii despondently.

"No, this is where it all begins," he answers with a smile.

He sits upon a great cliff, like the first time, dressed in a golden cloak and gazes at the sea, spread out into the distance. A light breeze is blowing. Everything is a deep blue- the sky and the sea, and even his cloak. I sit by him silently. Tzalaii gazes at me expectantly, and then I hear myself involuntarily intoning words of an unknown origin: "Teach me how to cry!"

Why is he smiling?

His smile seems to say: "You've got it. You finally understand!"

Arising and removing his musical instrument from his cloak, he looks at me and asks: "Are you ready?"

I nod.

Tzalaii plucks a string gently, sounding a single note. The sound reaches ancient, locked gates within me, breaking through them all at once and melting blocked pieces of stone inside. I cry. Not a usual cry, but a deep cry of immense yearning, a cry that makes my entire body tremble uncontrollably. A cry that cleans and purifies, removing that which is extraneous, unnecessary. I am unable to stop crying! Fortunately the music comes to an end, or I would surely be lost for all of eternity in a nameless world. As my cries wane and weaken, they become powerless, like something discarded. I search inside of myself and sense that I have achieved a child-like clarity. A thin thread of joy is present, delicate but promising, like the transparent baby that was born in the flower of fire.

"Look," says Tzalaii, and I know this will be the last time I will hear this word.

In the distance, in the heart of the ocean, something is happening. It seems like a battle among large sea animals is taking place beneath the surface. I am curious to discover the meaning of this, but I cannot see enough.

"This is the dance of the waves," says Tzalaii.

But I still don't understand.

"They are getting ready," he adds. "When you cry with all of your might," he says sadly, "you express the cries of the flames that have yet to burn, and the longing of the fire flowers that have yet to bloom, and the desires of the Transparent Ones that have yet to be born."

His voice begins to tremble, but also fills with fury: "and the deep pain of the prisoners."

"The tears are collected," he says suddenly, pointing towards the sea. He arises, stands on the cliff and calls out, as though to unseen listeners: "Your time has not yet arrived. Transcend! Transcend until the great day arrives! Soar and ascend and our tears, too, shall come to your aid."

For a passing moment, I recall the stone I had removed from the outer wall. Is it just my imagination, or do I really see a similar crimson-yellow glimmer in the depths of the sea?

"You have seen very well."

Tzalaii turns to me and we embrace.

"Cry!" says my guide to life. "And wait for the day when your ears will hear other sounds."

I open my eyes and know: My Initiation training is complete.

Chapter Twenty-Eight

An Initiation Discussion

An Initiation Discussion

During Tzalaii's healing process prescribed by the Master of Transcendence, two slender Transparent Ones arrived at the small cave to invite Mahn to participate in an initiation discussion. Mahn had been with Tzalaii and Sihara for a few days and the revolution that began in his heart was now reaching completion. The magical surroundings and the recent events dissipated his fear that the Emperors would seek revenge. Sihara captivated his heart with her disclosures about the Chamber of Changing Colors and the Master of Transcendence. But time was of the essence. There was so much to be learned in preparation for joining the Warriors of Transcendence.

Mahn enjoyed an awesome meditative, silent stroll with his new friends. Soon they reached a large illuminated cave. Chilled air cooled the interior and sounds were heard with great clarity. Mahn admired the decorative blue stone pillars found inside, so different from the gray and dismal scenes to which he had become accustomed. In the center of the room, on a floor constructed of thin, flat stones, sat twenty men awaiting his arrival. They made room for him, and as Mahn took his place, he felt a deep and satisfying feeling of belonging.

This exact spot is uniquely mine. This is where I belong! he thought.

"Friends," began one of the men, and Mahn took note of the embroidery work on his white cloak, sewn with ultra-thin blue thread. "Let us welcome our friend, Mahn." The men whispered to each other, and as their voices grew louder, Mahn noticed that they were singing a tune; he was able to hear the words: "You are the heart of the world."

Like flowing water, the words washed over him, dissolving and cleansing him of all impurities and barriers, all flaws and fractures. He closed his eyes, allowing himself to be transported by the tune. The flowing water in his mind transformed into tears that rolled down his cheeks. Soon, the tune was completed, and the men remained silent for a while in the clear atmosphere.

"Warriors of Transcendence," said the man in the white cloak, addressing the men. Mahn felt exhilarated by his inclusion in this special group. The men began to converse with each other and the richness of their well-chosen precious words, so full of meaning, was as satisfying as the most wonderful feast. Mahn was moved by so many memories and feelings arising in him as he listened. The men summarized their encounters with the enemy succinctly and clearly. One by one, they related events, but with such modesty! Never before had Mahn encountered people of such humility. He understood that all were the disciples of the man in the white cloak, who observed them carefully, taking note of every word they uttered. Mahn wondered if other groups of this kind existed. He was impressed by the great respect given to this teacher of twenty men. How awesome must be the honor shown to the Master of Transcendence! Respect beyond comparison!

The warriors discussed their skills and actions in simple terms, without bombast, as if they were not matters of life and death. They seemed to be fearless, confronting challenges during their missions for the Master of Transcendence with bravery.

How is it possible that they have no fear in their hearts? he wondered, amazed. *They are but human beings, flesh and blood!*

As the discussion continued and broadened, Mahn, no stranger to methods of warfare, suddenly discovered a new and intriguing world. He was amazed by the techniques employed by the Warriors of Transcendence. They were skilled in transforming darkness into light and in radiating fear upon their enemies. They were trained to concentrate great powers into a tiny movement, becoming vessels for the Light of the Transcendor to pass through. Listening to their words, he realized that their abilities depended upon their proximity to the Master of Transcendence, their leader. The closer they felt to him, the more powerful and accessible their Memory Shields became, in times of need.

Relinquishing their natural understanding helps them to accept and apply the profound and wise principles they acquire in their training, he learned. Each battle debriefing was followed by the warrior's summary of the knowledge he had gained from his experience. The leader of the group, exceptionally alert, continued to listen intently to each man's words. The first warrior to summarize had closed his eyes for some time, finally saying: "Water will extinguish the fire."

He used simple words known to all, but his method of speaking was unusual. He conveyed total simplicity, like an innocent child explaining something clearly known. The speaker opened his eyes, viewing his teacher's radiant and satisfied visage. Mahn intuited that this summation was some form of test.

The next warrior closed his eyes and thought deeply before summarizing.

"All waiting shall be fulfilled," he finally said.

His words carried a message of hope and calmed the hearts of all, the significance of his words conveying the thought that everything is destined to return to its proper place. Each warrior chose a summarizing statement in which he truly believed, and therefore all the spoken words entered the hearts of the listeners like solid truth, lucid and absolute.

The eleventh warrior hesitated for a long time before speaking. He seemed to be embroiled in an inner war inside of himself. Finally he opened his mouth and said simply: "The Shadows are multiplying more than ever!"

Silence descended upon the cave, and no one spoke. The words were absorbed silently, awaiting resolution. The warriors looked expectantly to their teacher, but he only nodded. He seemed distant and remote.

An unexpected noise was heard and a side door opened all at once. Two weary warriors staggered inside, their rag-tag appearance conveying distress and grief.

"The Shadows are multiplying more than ever!" said one, his voice trembling. "The battle to protect the opening to the Tunnels of Time at Fire Mountain has failed. Dozens of our warriors have been lost and disguised Shadows wait to strengthen their accomplices and enable them to break through the passage. Even the attempt to transfer a message to the warriors in the eastern tunnels has failed! Three of our men were taken captive, and the message was not received. Any Transparent One that goes out through Fire Mountain shall be captured, and every warrior arriving from the east shall be trapped! We are the only survivors, as we went through the forest and were able to come from the south."

Mahn sensed different pathways crossing through the united circle of men that now included the two surviving warriors. They were joined in a comforting unity that eliminated some of the pain of this fresh loss. All awaited a solution; all eyes were turned to the teacher, as he began to speak: "Warriors of Transcendence."

He paused, as though these words were intended to remind them, on a deep level, of their identity and of their mission.

"Sadness is a delicacy for the Shadows. Sadness cannot spread in the heart of the Warrior of Transcendence if he is precise. If you are precise- you are protected."

"And the warriors that were lost. Were they not precise?" Mahn asked, unable to control himself.

The teacher gazed at him steadily and said: "The Transcendor and his great messenger know what has been done. We see only a narrow shard of time and place. It is written in the ancient scrolls that the entrance to Fire Mountain will be blocked prior to the end of the battles, and that those who block the entrance shall be trapped. All those responsible for the activity in the Tunnels of Time knew about the changes even before they occurred. It is no disaster; it is part of the plan."

"And our fellow warriors?" asked one of the survivors, his voice trembling.

"Your friends have performed the tasks of the mission for the Master of Transcendence, and their selflessness shall have a great impact on the final battle. Do not be deceived by appearances."

The teacher arose and approached the eleventh warrior who had mentioned the multiplying Shadows. The two newly-arrived survivors stood on either side of the eleventh warrior. Kneeling in front of the three warriors, covering his face with his hands, the teacher began to cry bitterly. The sound of his cries, though wordless, was more precise and illuminating than the words of the warriors, and on a higher level. His cries contained elements of certainty, but Mahn was unable to grasp the meaning and significance. The eyes of all his disciples were shut, but only three of the warriors wept. The intensity of the display caused Mahn's entire body to tremble. The circle of pain, healing and comfort, all combined in complete unity, protective, supportive and abundant with love.

Finally, the crying ceased, and the teacher spoke softly: "Transcendor," he said, as though He were by his side.

Mahn was unaware that the teacher was performing Unification, in front of many spectators; a rare talent that few could duplicate.

"The Shadows are multiplying more than ever before. Our warriors are few and our strengths scarce. Without You, we don't stand a chance. Evil armies are washing over the earth. But," he said, his voice rising and becoming determined, "the Master of Transcendence has taught us that Your strength exceeds everything. Without You we are lost. With You, we shall overcome all obstacles."

"Transcendor," he said pleadingly, "Enter our hearts! Flow through the blood in our veins! Accompany our steps, for you have chosen us to be your messengers, to carry out your word. Remove from us all sadness; enable us to carry your light, reveal yourself in our midst in all of your glory."

He then ended with one sentence, as sharp and clear as a diamond, piercing through hearts, adorned with splendor and clarifying humility.

"Do it- for Your sake."

The silence now was so deep, even the water droplets descending from the blue stalactites into the pools in the depths of the Tunnels of Time did not make a sound. The leader now returned to his place. All eyes focused on Mahn, the survivor from the Tower. What would he add to their words? The leader of the group extended his hand to Mahn, inviting him to speak and granting him strength to do so. Mahn felt so small, so insignificant.

The teacher spoke to him: "Warrior of Transcendence, you have heard everything. The light has touched your heart as well."

But the teacher made no formal request, speaking as if to himself: "Precisely because you have come from there, precisely because the seeds of retribution have been planted in you, and you crushed them into dust out of the agonies of your soul- you may join our warriors. There is a part of your soul that is protected and shielded from even the darkest Shadows."

Mahn arose, approached the outstretched hand of the teacher, and touched it.

"Speak," instructed the teacher with a glimmer in his eyes.

Words flooded Mahn's heart, words that now seemed black and morose. He was unable to imagine ever uttering them again, especially not in such a sacred place:

The steel-strengthening fire shall strengthen your spirit and melt its locks. To ascend as fire, higher and higher, to the peak of the Towered City.

The mark of the shadows still bubbled in Mahn, deep within, and was now becoming exposed. But Mahn listened to the words, and managed to oppose them with an inner cry that remained internal: "The Fire of the Tower did not strengthen my spirit, and did not melt its locks! I have no desire to serve the forces of darkness! I have no desire to rise to the peak of the Towered City!"

For a terrifying moment, Mahn felt that he had lost all desire. Like a driven leaf, tossed into an abyss, his soul felt empty. He gazed helplessly at the Warriors of Transcendence. A moment later he was relieved, as though a layer had peeled off of him, a sealed, heavy layer that had enveloped him for years without his knowledge. Now a new desire surfaced. Although it was only the seed of desire, soft as a sprout, small as a blossom, it was full of certainty and everlasting joy. It was the desire to serve the Master of Transcendence. A desire that embraced him the way a mother embraces her only child, who returns her love, always.

Mahn gathered all of his strength and searched within his soul for his deepest certainty: The words he had first heard upon arrival: *You are the heart of the world.* Honor and adoration were evident in the Warriors' faces, and the teacher nodded his head approvingly, as though he had already known what Mahn would say.

This was Mahn's first Memory Shield.

Chapter Twenty-Nine

Melodies of the Master

Melodies of the Master

When the sign was given, the Great War began. News of Mahn's successful escape with the convicted prisoner Tzalaii ignited the spark that the Descendents of the Emperors had awaited. The astounding rumor spread quickly in the Towered City- one of the Mercury Level Inviewers had abandoned the Towered City, absconding with the Warrior of Transcendence who had been convicted of attempted assassination of an Emperor. The warriors' pride was set ablaze as they were ordered to prepare to avenge these crimes and protect the honor of the City.

"Failure to respond to this audacious act," the inhabitants of the Tower said to each other angrily, " will result in an uprising by the prisoners. Who knows what havoc a rebellion might cause?!"

But, in truth, the Emperors' desired to locate and defeat the Master of Transcendence and his men. The Shadows rose from the deepest burrows of the Towered City, like a black river flooding the earth. Soldiers from the Tower invaded the Northern Forests. The ten Obliterators had already planted the seeds of retribution in the Land of the Southern Cliffs.

Many Warriors of Transcendence, Tzalaii among them, scoured the lowlands, slaying hundreds of Shadows. The Master of Transcendence, escorted by his most loyal men, advanced towards the Towered City, which loomed before them. The secret of the stone, stolen from the outer wall, was common knowledge among the villagers, and the potential danger disturbed their peaceful lives. The fact that evil forces were aligned against them, intending harm, pervaded their thoughts. It was a rude awakening for the villagers who were unprepared for warfare, and unable to channel their anger and fear into a proper defense. They could offer fierce resistance to obliteration; they were capable of evading the illusions of the Shadows, for a time, but in the end, they would be captured. And so, the Master of Transcendence decided to enlist a new force to his aid.

A fresh breeze accompanied the Master's troops as they walked through the valleys along with hundreds of Transparent Ones, heading towards the eastern slopes of the Land of the Northern Forests. Only the Green Lowlands separated them from the myriads of Tower soldiers gathered in the valley. Night fell. The master's cape flapped in the wind, its radiance warming the hearts of the warriors and the Transparent Ones. He stood silently for a while, and then began Unification. His voice was so simple and he spoke with such grace; many felt certain that the Transcendor was with them, at their side.

"Unique, primary, first and last One," began the Master of Transcendence. "Your light is concealed in the heart of all things. All is covered by a dark disguise, but beneath the darkness, Your light shall forever shine, yearning to break forth and shine like at the beginning of time. Reveal Your light in us, Transcendor; do not leave us."

He shut his eyes, remained silent for a while, and then finally ended his Unification with a sharp, decisive declaration: "There is no darkness and no shadow of death!"

"There is no darkness and no shadow of death!" repeated the Transparent Ones. "There is no darkness and no shadow of death!" echoed Sihara.

Silence enveloped the valley. Some time passed, and then a sudden gust of wind burst forth as the Master of Transcendence bowed and stepped backwards in surrender, as though departing from a powerful master. The Unification was over and the Master of Transcendence's Warriors sensed an infusion of heart-warming strength.

Trumpets were heard from the City, signifying a gathering of great forces, and the Transparent Ones were directed by the Master of Transcendence to surround the warriors in a luminous circle. The whole world seemed to hold its breath, as though all anticipated some long-awaited event. The Master of Transcendence raised his hands to the heavens, either requesting permission or receiving strength from the Transcendor. He closed his eyes again and began to sing. He sang a story, without words, ancient as the beginning of time. It was the melody of primordial hope, of the incessant will of each and every soul to return to its place, reach its destiny and correct itself, even if it had lain dormant, even if it had been held captive for years, even for generations, by the forces of darkness. At first he sang a quiet melody, alone, but later his voice became so inviting that each and every one of his companions joined the song, as though they had always known the melody. Their music spread over the Green Lowlands towards the Tower wall. Thunder was heard in the distance, sounding almost like the muffled cries of stifled voices yearning to break free.

"The wall! The wall!" shrieked Sihara, covering her face with her hands, as if to protect herself from this cataclysmic event. The Transparent Ones stood in their long cloaks, their hands stretched forward, as if yearning to either receive something or to shield themselves from a future threat.

At first only a growl was heard, like the call of an immense wild animal trapped in a narrow maze. Then strands of silver began to appear in the distant wall, heating and rising, merging in white and burning in red, as though an ancient buried sun was now being resurrected. The great, wide wall, which had always been impenetrable, began to collapse and crumble before their very eyes! It began to sink, like soft quicksand, and then it erupted and fell over. Black, molten ash spurted from the ground, flooding the valley with searing hot steam and rising smoke. The silvery strands separated from the stones, but they did not sink into the ground with the dead substance. They became intertwined and created a silvery wall of light that spread out over the great devastation. Myriads of Soul Essences had been set free, escaping from the stones in which they had been held captive against their will. Now they united. Crimson-yellow colored crumbs, powder blowing in the wind, was all that remained from the great wall. The Shadows fled like cowards into their burrows. A new strength had been revealed to the world- the union of the Soul Essences.

Chapter Thirty

Battles in the Green Lowlands

Battles in the Green Lowlands

"They appear to be quite real!" said Tzalaii in surprise. "Why are they called Shadows?"

The Master of Transcendence sat upon a flat rock in the center of a large clearing in the forest. His warriors had performed their tasks loyally, and the Land of the Northern Forests was free of the Shadows. The Storm Dancers were now scattered along the eastern slopes and the Descendents of the Emperors had been struck repeatedly. Their pride was shattered; they had lost their ability to attack. During a short respite, the Master of Transcendence, Sihara and dozens of Transparent Ones gathered together in the heart of the forest. A soft green light emerged from the vine-covered trees. The forest was so tranquil; one could almost forget the battles taking place down below, in the great valley.

"A Shadow," answered the Master of Transcendence, "is the lack of light. It is a place that conceals and inhibits the light from being revealed to us. The Shadows are composed of dark places, of light-inhibiting spirit fragments. They have life and motion, and their movements are a replica of their owners' movements."

Sihara was curious. She inquired, "The Shadows are created in the Abyss of the Shadows, but are they created in any other places?" A shiver ran down her spine.

"In the Towered City, of course!" answered the Master of Transcendence. "Most of the Shadows are created from the fire-worshipping slaves of the Tower."

"If fire has no shadow," pondered Tzalaii, "why would its worshipers create Shadows?"

"That is a good question," the Master of Transcendence answered, smiling.

He closed his eyes in an attempt to form a clear answer to this complex matter: "Fire has no shadow because it is not concrete. But its worshipers, flesh and blood like us, are concrete, material beings. Worship of the fire causes bodies to be sealed, and the Light of the Transcendor can no longer enter their hearts, thereby creating Shadows within them."

"But the fire-priests promise liberation from the Law of Transformation and all other forms of enslavement!" Tzalaii stated. "Truly, they are liberated from them," answered the Master of Transcendence scornfully "like a silent stone, they freeze the strengths of their spirit, like dead dust in which the seeds of light lay dormant, and transformation is unable to shake them of their inner frost. Only the Transparent Ones, by melting the Shadows, can enter the hearts of the fire worshippers, remove the dust covering the seeds of light, and train them to open up to the Men of Borders."

Tzalaii and Sihara were unable to thoroughly comprehend his words, and when the Master of Transcendence noticed this he added: "The only way to gain control of the Shadows is by uncovering the inner light in the hearts of their creators. But those who have the power to uncover it are few, so very few…"

The tall trees swayed silently in the wind. "Have you wondered about the significance of the tree and roots engraved upon the blue Magnathought Crystal?" the Master of Transcendence asked them. Tzalaii became utterly embarrassed by the question. Not only was he unaware of the meaning of the Crystal etching, he knew nothing at all about it: To whom did it belong? Who had used it and for what purpose? Why did it end up in his hands? Sihara, in contrast, sensed that she knew the answer to this question, but was unable to recall it. The Master of Transcendence smiled and said: "There were many holy artifacts in the palace of the King of the Ancient Progeny. Their sanctity was created through their use- pure holy use, devoid of arrogance."

Tzalaii recalled the King's Cloak and blushed with shame.

"The image of the tree was etched upon every holy artifact in the palace of the Ancient Progeny," explained the Master of Transcendence. "Sometimes revealed and sometimes concealed. Everything yearns for its roots. Children yearn for their parents, as do the animal young, the earth yearns for the sky and everything in it yearns for the celestial bodies. When the holy tree and its many roots are engraved upon the sacred artifacts in the palace, they all become united, testifying that sanctification connects everything to its roots. Branches, trunks and leaves. The heavens and the earth. All and nothing.

A cluster of sunrays pierced through the treetops, illuminating the Master of Transcendence, who was sitting on a tree stump. Under the nearly transparent golden cloak, Tzalaii and Sihara witnessed an amazing sight of great splendor; they could only bear it for the blink of an eye: They saw the tree, shining and glowing, its roots, branches and countless leaves united. The Master- the Master of Transcendence himself was the tree! Sihara recalled, with great clarity, the words her Transparent Master had spoken as he held the blue Magnathought Crystal and gazed at her: "*All living things, apart from Khivia and his servants, exist in this tree. The root of the tree is the Transcendor. It is from Him that everyone receives life. The servants of the Transcendor are the branches- they receive life from Him and pass their strength on to those dependent on them, the Storm Dancers and the villagers. Even the Descendents of the Emperors, unless utterly devoted to serving evil, receive life from the tree, the way weeds receive pleasure in the shade of a tree, even if they are not a part of it."*

There she was, one of the branches of the majestic tree, witnessing it with her very own eyes! The Transparent Master ended with these words: *The tree shall clarify all mazes.*

While the three of them sat in the clearing, the Transparent Ones continued their battle in the valley. Near the Land of the Northern Forests, on the western front, hundreds of them created an insurmountable wall. Their golden capes gleamed and their inner flames were illuminated with sharpness and clarity. Farther down in the valley, troops of courageous Transparent Ones advanced, and it was there that the Shadows appeared. The movements of the Shadows were as fast as lightning, sharp and sudden, flashing forward all at once, as if tossed by a storm. They appeared in groups, suddenly exiting their deep burrows in the valley, and approached the Transparent Ones and the golden wall that had been created along the forest slopes. Shadows of Light flickered here and there in the great valley, but the danger to the Transparent Ones was minimal.

Fog covered the sky, concealing the sunlight and disturbing visibility. These were the Cloud Shadows. They concealed even greater forces behind them; the Shadows of Fire, too, spun around and provoked, igniting, burning red. But the most dangerous of all were the Shadows of Illusion. These Shadows were able to liken themselves to the Transparent Ones, and only the Master of Transcendence and several of his warriors were able to perceive the counterfeits. They appeared as a single Transparent One, or as a lost villager, and they would slowly approach a troop of Transparent Ones or a lone Transparent One, gaze deeply into their eyes, and whisper voicelessly: *Come.* This calling invoked excitement in the Transparent Ones, and even worse- compassion. When one would become trapped in the confines of his compassion, segments of his body would be torn off and gathered into the outstretched hand of the Shadow and lost forever. More experienced Transparent Ones, sensing the trap set before them, would close their eyes immediately and enter within themselves, like the finest Warriors of Transcendence. The light surrounding them would grow brighter and the outstretched hand of the Shadow would fade away, involuntarily shedding its human costume, and its body would shrivel up like it had been consumed by fire. When encountered by a Transparent One with great inner light, the Shadow would turn into black ash and wither away.

Meanwhile, the ten Obliterators hid in the distant part of the Land of the Southern Cliffs, not far from the copper mines. Their presence sustained their joint creation, wandering far below in the distant villages. No one knew where the old man had come from, but the few who merited seeing him reported that they had never seen a face with such a glow. His gait was slow and royal, his clothes and beard were white.

The children were the first to see him. He told stories, with gleaming eyes, of a wondrous man whose voice was soft and whose words were magical. Slowly, his presence became known amongst the dwellers of the villages by the sea. They, who hoped with all their heart for a better world, sought his presence and awaited his words. Considering the fact that the war in the Lowlands had been raging in full force for several weeks now, various threatening reports constantly streaming in, what could have been more natural than for the villagers to view the enchanted old man as a savior? The old man kept his identity concealed. He was full of mystery. His stories always described the coming redemption.

Gradually, an idea took hold and then spread like wildfire in their hearts: *He is the Master of Transcendence!*

When the youngsters mustered the courage to ask him about this, the old man remained silent, a modest smile on his face.

Chapter Thirty-One

Silver Swords

Silver Swords

Only a few Transparent Ones remained on the eastern slopes of the Land of the Northern Forests. The Storm Dancers did not come to their assistance because they could not afford, under any circumstances, to leave their watch over the southern slopes. However, in their place came several Warriors of Transcendence, joined by Mahn who had undergone a swift training in the Tunnels of Time. This small troop spread out among the trees overlooking the border of the White Desert and the Lowlands, waiting.

There was no need for scouts to inform them of what was to come, since their enemies were audible, even from a distance. Thousands of human soldiers, mainly from the Base Level, were advancing from the Towered City, to the beat of a deafening drum. The warriors moved north, towards the more distant slopes, where the trees were sparse. Their intention was to invade the forests and encircle the Transparent Ones who had conquered the Southern Slopes from behind. The soldiers moved in disorder, waving their swords in the air, grunting and rumbling, trusting in their great number. The rear guard was composed of small groups of trained soldiers from the Mercury Level, sapphire flames etched upon their uniforms. They advanced silently and in an orderly fashion.

As the rude, rambunctious voices approached the outskirts of the forest, the Warriors of Transcendence rushed towards them. At first they pretended to be villagers armed with swords; they waved their weapons and engaged in fierce battles, slaying many men. But then the leather clad, shaven-headed soldiers outnumbered the Warriors of Transcendence, surrounding them like a pack of hungry wolves preparing to attack an easy kill. The circle of warriors tightened around the ten Warriors of Transcendence, each with a drawn sword, cries of battle upon their lips. And then, for just a moment, it was silent. Just as the Warriors of the Tower planned their final attack, the Warriors of Transcendence began to transcend. At first their dance was slow and gentle, as if they were preparing for death and parting from the world. But then their movements became circular and more rapid, until each of the Warriors of Transcendence spun around in place, kicking up dust in the process, thereby concealing themselves from the enemy.

"Kill them! Now!" ordered one of the Tower commanders.

The sword -carrying soldiers burst forth with all their might, but the Warriors of Transcendence performed their duties well. No one was able to invade the perimeter of their strength, and their swords repelled all who approached them. But still the men of the Tower did not retreat. Wave after wave of warriors trekked over the bodies of their comrades, and with the sound of drumming and high pitched shrieks, continued to attack.

When the Warriors of Transcendence sensed that they were no longer moving forward and their men were weakening, they retreated slightly, in an attempt to search for their enemy's weak spots. The warriors ceased to dance, and the Soldiers of the Tower interpreted their rest as surrender. Six of the Tower Warriors advanced in a crescent formation.

"Their dances will be of no use to them when faced with the WireArchers," thought the furious Tower Soldiers, but just then something occurred that shook their confidence: The Warriors of Transcendence formed a circle, and one of the warriors began to move his hands gently through mid-air, as though tracing the form of a wave. The earth below the Tower Warriors simultaneously began to move accordingly, causing them all to fall to the ground. Before they could recover, a second Warrior of Transcendence reached out his hand, clenched it into a fist and moved it through mid-air, as though he were squashing something. Immediately, the six WireArchers collided together, as though a great gust of wind crushed and squeezed their bodies almost to death.

Terror enveloped the Tower Warriors and they retreated. A third Warrior of Transcendence reached out his hand, as though collecting their terror and transforming it into a thick rope. The imaginary rope grew longer as the warrior began to wave it above the heads of thousands of his enemies. The force of the pull transformed their terror into paralysis and they became helpless. Thousands of warriors tossed their weapons and escaped in every direction; their weakened legs carrying them, falling and trampling over one another, shrieking and crying as though they had witnessed the most horrifying sight. This was caused by their fear alone, which each and every Warrior of Transcendence amplified and intensified. The strength of a thousand soldiers was destroyed, and only two hundred of them managed to retreat and escape to the Towered City. Among the Warriors of Transcendence, not a soul was harmed.

Mahn's participation in the battle was a gamble that ended with a miracle. In a creek, hidden from all eyes, he encountered a Warrior from the Base Level. As the soldier approached him, Mahn recognized him as Elassar, the Inviewer from the Tower who had pursued him, intending to kill him. Mahn pulled out the short sword hidden within the folds of his cape, but Elassar was faster, knocking Mahn's weapon out of his hand and onto the rocks. Elassar pointed his sharpened sword towards Mahn's neck, and Mahn was certain that his end was near.

"Ha! Who do we have here? It is Mahn, the new friend of the golden rats! What a rare coincidence!" mocked Elassar. "It was precisely you whom I was searching for, and I am not alone! Every Warrior from the Tower is searching for you and for the prisoner you kidnapped! Do you know what punishment awaits you for such a foolish deed?" Mahn did not speak. Battle cries were heard from nearby, and he wondered if any of his fellow warriors would take notice of his absence and come to his aid.

"Your warriors pose no threat to us," continued Elassar, "and if you haven't noticed- only Warriors from the Base Level and a few Warriors from the Mercury Level were sent here."

"Warriors from the Base Level, warriors from the Mercury Level..." These words reminded Mahn of his days in the Tower and elicited mixed feelings of paralyzing fear and familiar distant memories.

"That is to say," Mahn's enemy summarized victoriously, "that the Emperors do not deem it necessary to send out soldiers from the upper levels. This ridiculous uprising of yours, headed by the Master of Transcendence, is about to end!"

Mahn was astonished by the ease with which Elassar uttered the name that was not to be spoken, and this heightened his anxiety. Had something changed since his escape? Had the strength of the Emperors intensified so greatly that they no longer feared the Master of Transcendence?

"They are well-spoken, aren't they?" Elassar suddenly asked in a soft voice, "They told you the forces of good are fighting the forces of evil, and about the Master of Transcendence who would come to your aid at any moment, and you- innocent Mahn, believed their tales! Do you really believe that he needs you? You are but a lowly Man, who until yesterday served in the Emperors' City and today you are a rookie, still unprepared, fighting on the edge of the Warrior's troops. He surely knows everything about you, your identity, and your actions. What is his real opinion of you?" The battle cries grew distant and then faded away, and Elassar's sword was still aimed at Mahn's throat. Strangely enough, Mahn was not troubled by its presence. Elassar's words were true, thought Mahn. But so were the words of the Warriors of Transcendence. But if the Master of Transcendence was right, and the words of the Emperors are a lie, then what importance does Mahn have? Why would anyone care for him?

"Your betrayal of the Emperors was a choice worse than death, but you still have the ability to make amends and atone for your transgressions. There is forgiveness and pardoning in the Tower."

Forgiveness and pardoning in the Tower...these words nibbled at Mahn's brain like ravenous ants.

"As for the rest of the rats, their end is near! Behind the misleading trick executed by the armies of the Base Level awaits a small surprise. Your choice is the following," said Elassar. "Either I kill you here and now, or you return to us, but not with me. You shall remain here, among your new friends, and supply us with information regarding their plans. We will find a way to contact you. But if you betray us again," he said sternly, "we have methods to extract payment from you, far beyond the strength of my sword."

Mahn recalled the Southern Mines and the man responsible for the Essence Department, and his stomach churned. What threat was Elassar referring to? Would he be turned into a stone in the wall? This was impossible, the wall had just collapsed and crumbled to the ground! A crimson-yellow colored brick flashed across his eyes, imprisoned, begging...and a terrible rage filled him. Even if he were to remain in the final row of warriors, even if he would forever be unimportant, worthless, of low status, he would never return to serve the Men of the Tower! The Master of Transcendence mends the destruction of the Emperors, and he, Mahn, was devoted to him- Always!

Mahn quickly rolled aside, and scrambled towards his fallen sword. In the flash of an eye, Elassar missed his chance to react, and Mahn overpowered him. He fled the scene as Elassar's body fell to the ground.

When Mahn returned to the battlefield, he noticed that the situation had changed. The Soldiers of the Tower were gone and the Warriors of Transcendence encircled the Lowland borders, gathering apparel and possessions lost by the retreating Tower Warriors. It seemed as though the battle had been won, but just then a cluster of darkened clouds began rolling in from the distant horizon, moving towards them. The Warriors of Transcendence quickly became alert. They spread out among the trees in the slopes and watched. On the edges of the approaching clouds, blurry figures were visible, clad in black capes. As they approached, it became apparent that the cloud was indeed composed of these creatures. Their slow movement created a feeling of fatigue and sleepiness in the warriors, but they were not fearful of the Cloud Shadows. As their visibility became blurred, it became clear that the Shadow 'wall' concealed other forces, advancing behind it. The attack of the Base Level armies was but a preliminary trick aimed at weakening them. The real battle was only now about to begin. Convinced of the intensity of the force about to strike, the Warriors of Transcendence entered within a protective circle etched in the sand and waited. When the cloud was close enough to touch, swarms of Shadows of Fire emerged from within. Burning and revolving in the fire, initially red and then blue, their movements were fast and sharp, and their flames heated the air.

A sudden intense heat was felt. Mahn felt his throat tighten as he gazed, terror stricken, at the ring of blue fire tightening around the circle of warriors. The Warriors of Transcendence entered within themselves, ignoring the flames. They were protected for now, but the path to the Land of the Northern Forests remained exposed. Many forces swiftly made their way towards the slopes. Although the Emperors' strategies were deliberately and meticulously planned, they had neglected one important detail: The Essence of Soul Concentration!

A subtle howl rolled down from the mountain tops, as though voiced by myriads of mouths, screaming into the valley with all of their might. The trees in the slopes swayed uneasily as strong gusts of wind cast terror upon them. Warriors from the Solar Level, climbing up the slopes, slowed their pace, and they summoned each other to gather, in an attempt to understand what was transpiring. The blue ring of fire around the Warriors of Transcendence weakened slightly.

The howl grew louder, and the gusts of wind became a great storm. Despite their fierce power, the Soul Essences treated the forest trees with great tenderness. Although they were blown in all directions, no tree was uprooted. The Soul Essences were familiar with the pain of the uprooted, and despite their raging fury, they were cautious of harming defenseless beings. The Warriors of Transcendence watched in awe. A strong wind now struck the heavy, black clouds, and shrieks and cries emerged from within them. The Shadows of Fire persisted and refused to relinquish their victims in the ring of fire, but the Warriors of Transcendence already knew that the Master of Transcendence had come to their aid. A strong wind circled around the ring of fire, striking the Shadows with great force. As the Soul Essences howled loudly, pure silver swords, clear as a tear, emerged from within the wind. The myriads of swords struck the flames in an all-consuming force. A short time had passed from the time the howls were first heard on the mountain tops and the strike of death by the silver swords. On the border between the White Desert and the Green Lowlands, all that remained were countless heaps of blackened ash.

Chapter Thirty-Two
Enigmas of the Wastelands

Enigmas of the Wastelands

Ulu would have preferred to travel through the Tunnels of Time, but he would have encountered difficulties in traversing the unfamiliar paths without a map. So, instead, he made his way through the lower parts of the Land of the Northern Forests, unaware of the terrible events transpiring in the world; not knowing the outcomes of the battles.

An eerie silence pervaded the valley.

What is the reason for this silence? he worried.

Advancing swiftly through the elongated crevices between the cliffs, heading towards the villages beyond, Ulu wondered if he would find empty fields and a strange silence there as well?

And the Shadows- where were they? Just then, he noticed dark clouds advancing over the earth- they were Cloud Shadows! He attempted to conceal himself by walking quietly through the trees on the slope, but his efforts were in vain. A small flame appeared in his tracks, becoming a furiously dancing pillar of blue fire within seconds. Another flame rolled towards him, tentacles of fire reaching out menacingly. More and more flames approached and surrounded Ulu, setting dry grass on fire, sending embers through the air.

Ulu stretched out his hand and drew the shape of a coiled rope in the air. The Shadows attempted to nourish themselves from the foundation of Ulu's inner heat, a result of the concentration of enormous force into a gentle movement. Spiraling flames, like ropes, appeared above the heads of the Shadows and began entrapping them painfully. Coil after coil, fire against fire. But the Shadows persisted, fighting off the coiling fire and managing to sever the red ropes threatening their existence.

Ulu decided to try a different tactic. He sat down and extended his hands forward, in a tugging motion, directed at the heart of the Shadows, as if he were extracting strings. His movement concentrated the strength of the Shadows themselves to one place. Their inner flames became thin, blinding red threads, which emerged from the Shadows and suffocated their strength.

Piles of ash remained on the ground. The Shadows were defeated, but Ulu was weary and continued to worry. He wondered what other threats awaited him as he reached the gate. To his great relief, he saw Transparent Ones were stationed at the gate, protecting it. In a land filled with enemy Shadows, it was good to be in the company of friends again. He moved towards them joyfully.

"My friends!" he called. "I am a messenger of the Master of Transcendence."

The Transparent Ones were taken aback and astonished to hear about Ulu's mission to locate and defeat the counterfeit, imposter Master of Transcendence. They offered him a place of refuge in the forest.

"You should rest and regain your strength before you continue on your way," they said.

He accepted their offers of food and rest graciously. The long journey and the fears in his heart had exhausted him and he soon fell into a deep slumber.

When he awoke, he was astonished to find that his hands had been bound with chains, his feet shackled and his mouth taped. In shock and surprise, he scanned the area. The Transparent Ones, his companions, conversed with each other, ignoring his presence.

"Indeed, we have a precious treasure in our hands," said one of the Transparent Ones in a shrill voice. "It is a shame we are not permitted to amuse ourselves a little…"

Another Transparent One approached Ulu, reached out a long and bony hand and agreed: "Yes, if we could only saw him to pieces!"

"What is necessary," offered a short Transparent One with shaggy hair "is to expose our true selves to him."

They burst into squeals of laughter, and Ulu noticed how the shells of their luminous clothing began to melt, revealing Shadows as black as coal. Shadows of Illusion! They rolled through the air, turning themselves into clouds and strange beasts. They howled with carefree laughter, as though the world and all of its inhabitants were pieces in a game.

Ulu closed his eyes and attempted to enter within himself. How had he fallen into such a trap? In fear and in haste, without investigation and examination, he had trusted the imposter Transparent Ones. His throat was dry, his body drenched in perspiration.

Unbeknownst to Ulu, Warriors of Transcendence were swiftly approaching. The Shadows, sensing the impending arrival of enemies, quickly hid Ulu in the bushes. Again, they took on the form of Transparent Ones.

"Welcome, brothers from the battles!" they blessed the warriors.

The warriors responded and Ulu strained to hear their voices. He thought he recognized the voice of Tzalaii, the village boy who had been captured on Green Isle. But how had the young villager escaped his captors? How had he grown to adulthood and become a Warrior, so confident and strong?

Ulu felt the strength and intensity of the Warriors, and they too sensed his presence. "He is here, nearby," they knew, and Ulu, unable to speak, called them repeatedly in his mind, sensing that his call had been heard. "Who are you?" He could hear the mighty voice of a Warrior.

One of the Shadows of Illusion, the one posing as a short, shaggy-haired Transparent One, looked shaken and afraid. The Warriors of Transcendence noticed the Shadow behind his transparency, and one of them immediately began performing Unification and asking for help. The clothes of the Transparent Ones melted and the gang of Shadows was revealed.

Tzalaii was shocked- this was the first time he had confronted the enemy, face to face.

"Tzalaii!" he pleaded to his inner, royal self, as he had pleaded in the Tunnels of Time. He then recalled his words in his mind: *If you are precise, you are protected.*

He gathered his thoughts and said, to himself, in deep concentration: "I am Tzalaii!"

The Warriors of Transcendence burst forwards, rushing towards the Shadows of Illusion, surrounding them. Their movements were like wheels of fire striking the creatures of darkness. The Shadows attempted to fight back and their shrieks reached the heavens, summoning heavy black clouds. Cloud Shadows rolled in quickly from the distance to aid their companions. Coils of fire appeared on the horizon, racing towards the battle scene.

"Purify and retreat!" ordered a Warrior of Transcendence.

They stretched their hands out in front of them and with a light movement signaled a simultaneous strike to the ground. The ground beneath the Shadows of Illusion split and they immediately vanished into the crevices. The Warriors of Transcendence found Ulu in the bushes, unbound his wrists and released him from his shackles. Swiftly, they all ran toward the forest. Under the protective covering of the forest, they soon stopped to rest in the shade of a hidden ditch at the foot of a tall cliff.

Ulu embraced Tzalaii, praising his courage and listening to his account of his experiences in the Tower. Tzalaii sadly informed Ulu that the King's Cloak, containing a map of the Tunnels of Time, still remained in the hands of the Emperor. Ulu resolved to complete his tasks at the Southern Cliffs, and then leave for the Towered City to search for his eldest son, Saag, and for the King's Cloak.

There was no time to lose. The next day, Ulu parted from his companions and hurried to his task. He journeyed at night and during the day he hid in crevices. Beyond the Lowlands, the land was dry and rocky, and rose sharply towards the mountains, making the journey treacherous. Ulu had no choice but to opt for this difficult path, due to his fear of the Shadows swarming over King's Valley. As he advanced, the vegetation became sparse. His water supply was almost gone.

"Transcendor!" he called out, in the hot, uncomfortable evening hours. "Transcendor! See how devastated and barren everything is here. Behold how all the beauty has faded, the joy has vanished, and the warmth of heart accompanying my mission has disappeared. Transcendor, You created a perfect world, and man has demolished it with his battles. Will You ever return and illuminate this place? Shall the wilted fields ever bloom again?"

Ulu knew that he was succumbing to defeat, and did not attempt to hide this feeling.

"I undertook this journey for You, to complete the task assigned to me by Your messenger, to serve my part in the battle. But instead of prevailing, I am failing! Instead of defeating the enemy, I fell into their hands! Tzalaii, the young village boy, had to rescue me… Me! Ulu! – the experienced warrior, well-trained and knowledgeable; I am ashamed to stand before the Master of Transcendence. I am ashamed to stand before You…"

His words echoed in the silence. Ulu was deeply embarrassed.

"Yes," he said softly, "It is true, …I am ashamed of myself. I have been too proud." His Unification continued, but Ulu was silent. Only after many moments of silence did he ask in a trembling voice: "If the battle intensifies, if the dangers increase, and if Your men fall into traps due to arrogance, who shall fight for You?"

The answer came from his heart, with a clarity that left no room for doubt: *You, yourself!*

I? Pondered Ulu, *I? But...* he lifted his eyes to the surrounding wastelands, felt himself overcome by fatigue, and the shame of his pride caused his heart to ache. *I am weak...a failure... defeated....how am I to fight?*

If you are true to all, the words came to him, *If you remember that you are but a messenger.*

Ulu allowed the meaning of these words to sink in deeply. The Transcendor did not promise him that he would be victorious from now on, He only chose him to continue the mission.

"Thank you," Ulu whispered.

Tears formed in his eyes, and consolation filled his heart. The burden of the last few days vanished, and Ulu once again set out on his nightly journey.

In the morning, Ulu found a cave to hide in, ate to his heart's content, drank the last drops of his water, and went to sleep. He did not know how much longer he had to journey, or how he would quench his thirst upon awakening, but these questions did not disturb his peace. He awoke when the afternoon sun illuminated the cave.

Sensing movement nearby, on his guard for danger, he saw a tall, silent being standing at his side. The being wore a white cape with a delicately detailed drawing of a deer, its crushed body lying at the bottom of an abyss. The deer had unsuccessfully attempted to jump over the Abyss. This picture was so alive, so real; Ulu felt compassion towards the deer. Now a second being appeared and approached him, a picture imprinted upon his cape as well, of a frozen waterfall, with countless droplets, thin as threads, swirling and growing larger, in shades of light green and soft blue. The drawing was astonishingly beautiful. The grayness of the surrounding cliffs appeared so dismal in comparison to this luminous beauty. The glorified being touched his heart and for a moment he felt a desire to be a part of it.

Now more beings began to appear in the cave. One wore a cape with a drawing of a radiant purple-winged bird, with a white belly and a single golden feather pointing backwards on its crown. Ulu gazed at the picture of the bird; it seemed to be alive! Who were these beings of illusion, fooling with his emotions?

"The center of strength, granting goodness to us all" said the tallest being with the crushed deer upon his cape, "has been awaiting your soul for a long time."

His words were as sharp as diamonds and as deep as an abyss.

"The inner fire requests the touch of its partner, the great fire, that shall help it increase until it becomes immortal."

Something in the way they moved reminded Ulu of the scorpions in the White Desert. He detached himself from the magic and sensed he was in danger.

Borders! he reminded himself. He entered within himself, enlisted his strength, and while etching a circle around himself realized that these alluring creatures were Obliterators. All was silent. Ten beings clad in elaborate capes surrounded him closely. One of them repeated: "The inner fire requests the touch of its partner, the Great Fire."

His accomplices echoed his words with voices so sharp and piercing, that even though Ulu resisted, the voices still entered his brain with a shattering force. Ulu did not know how to contend with the 'Marker of Tumult,' and the etched circle around him faded like smoke.

"Come, my friend, we have no intention to harm you."

The ring tightened around him forcing him to arise and walk deeper into the cave. A faint light illuminated the high walls, and Ulu trembled from the bitter cold. Now one of the Obliterators tossed a piece of cloth towards him, and Ulu was compelled to wrap it around himself, becoming entrapped in their charms.

"Now," said the Obliterator wearing the waterfall image, "we shall present you with the most complex of our questions. For many years, we have been waiting for a wise person who could answer them. Each of us shall ask you a question, and to remove suspicion of our intentions, we shall tell you now that if you manage to solve our enigmas, we shall set you free."

Ulu was convinced that this was true, but he also knew that he had to try to find an escape route.

"Tell us a lie," said the tall one, surprising Ulu.

One could think, pondered Ulu, *that they spoke nothing but the truth…*

He thought first, and then responded: "The center of strength granting goodness to us all resides in a Tower, in the great valley."

As he uttered these words, Ulu suddenly sensed that this was no lie, it was the whole truth! The Obliterators burst into laughter and Ulu became confused and embarrassed. The questioner removed a small drum from his cape, and his colleagues watched him in deep silence and concentration. The Obliterator beat the drum once, causing Ulu to feel a sharp pain in his chest, as though a thin knife was being thrust into his heart. His vision blurred and he was filled with fear.

A second Obliterator approached him, and asked the next question before Ulu had recovered from the pain: "Where is the center of the world?"

Forced to answer, he made a great effort. The pain in his chest faded as he replied: "I know not."

Again, the Obliterators burst into laughter, terrifying Ulu. The second Obliterator removed a fiddle from his cape, and just once ran the bow over the strings, causing Ulu to feel his heart crumbling. The pain returned now with more intensity, and again his vision blurred for an instant.

"Describe to us an object whose absence is greater than its benefit," a third Obliterator tossed another question his way.

What could it be? Ulu searched his thoughts, and then pointed towards them and said: "You yourselves!"

Now they stopped laughing. The third Obliterator took out a set of cymbals. When he struck them, Ulu felt the sounds pervade his brain and cut through hidden threads. Question after question, sound after sound, his senses numbed and his strength diminished. He no longer responded to their questions, petrified of the sounds of the musical instruments.

"If a chick dies in his shell, how can his spirit exit?" asked the fourth.

"Build us a house in the air of the world," ordered the fifth.

"If a man wants to marry a woman he is not permitted to marry," asked the sixth, "why would he think that someone of higher status would want to marry him?"

"What would one use to harvest a field of knives?"

"We have a hole in our field- raise it up to the city!" ordered another.

"If a treasure is located behind a mountain of fire, how would one reach it?"

A mountain of fire…a mountain of fire… these words pulsated through Ulu's mind and he attempted to find encouragement within them, but the Obliterators did not allow him time for introspection.

"Now," exclaimed the tall Obliterator in a shrill voice, "for the final wasteland enigma."

Ulu's mind became clear for a moment. The wasteland, which was the White Desert, returned to his mind, and he recalled his extensive training there: The threat of the scorpions, the circle of defense, the fury of the serpents, and the smell of death oozing from them all. He recalled the words of the Transparent One who had prepared him for his mission in the White Desert: *The Transcendor has appeared just once in this desert.* And he recalled the Memory Shield: the eyes of the Master of Transcendence, his great mentor, and the way his hands caressed his face.

"A Warrior of Transcendence replaces fear with light!" he whispered to himself. The shadows cast by the Obliterators onto the wall of the cave terrified him, and his heart was full of pain. Despite the fact that the tenth Obliterator was preparing to present the final enigma, the Memory Shield in Ulu's heart intensified: He recalled the gaze of the Master of Transcendence, and the memory of his eyes calmed his distressed soul, diminishing the pain in his heart. Slowly and hesitantly, he drew a circle upon the black sand at the bottom of the cave. When the Obliterators realized what he was doing, they tackled him, reaching out with their long arms in order to stop him.

Outside, the cloudy sky changed to a clear, deep blue. Something was transpiring in the heavens. Light feather clouds danced, in shades of purple and blue. From inside the clouds, bright dots like eyes appeared, from which descended a line of light, gleaming like a thin thread, pure as silver, clear as a tear. The line descended towards the heavy, gray mountain, and continued making its way into the cave, illuminating the interior with an intense glow, shocking the Obliterators who shrank back in fear.

The line of light summoned the Man of Borders, caressing his head as though he were a lost child, and then entering within him. Ulu felt a wave of heat spread through his body, and the bountiful light in the cave vanished as it was absorbed into Ulu's organs like healing waters. He felt light as a feather, as if he could rise to the ceiling of the cave and even beyond…His vision became clear and he was able to see everything around him in minute detail, even the fine cracks in the walls. His auditory perception sharpened, enabling him to hear the dim sound of water trickling, deep down in the rocks. His heart was full of laughter.

The ten dark, terrified, shrinking figures seemed so meaningless and helpless to him now! Despite his inner laughter, he knew that these creatures were the root of evil, and it was his task to remove them from the world. The Warrior of Transcendence reached out his hands, allowing the sharp, lethal Light of the Transcendor to flow through them while balls of fire transformed the Obliterators to ash.

The ten creatures of darkness were lost forever.

Chapter Thirty-Three

The Thousandth Leader of the Deathliners

The Thousandth Leader of the Deathliners

All was silent in the great hall of Obliterator's Peak. Torches cast a dim light upon the room. Around the table sat seven men. They appeared as simple soldiers from the Base Level; their clothes were devoid of splendor, their faces almost expressionless and their movements slow and heavy. But the passion expressed in their eyes could not be concealed behind their simple façade. It was clear that their identity was disguised and that they trusted no one, not even each other. After some very tense moments, one of them broke the silence. "In order to understand the reasons for this meeting," he said, "we must review the past. As we all know, the great Ohn Mountains are situated on the eastern side of the Land of the Southern Cliffs. In ancient times, four rivers emerged from the lower range, flowing through the entire Kingdom of the Ancient Progeny, the Land of the Northern Forests and beyond."

His words carried the listeners off to a different time, and they settled into their seats comfortably.

"Khivia, our great master,"- at the mention of this name, the men arose, and bowed down to the ground on all fours. When they returned to their seats, he continued speaking: "Acknowledge his wisdom, for he can affect the thoughts of all the inhabitants of the land through the waters. He proclaimed the source of his influence in a mighty stone house atop the Ohn Mountains, from whence he whispered his thoughts. All throughout the land, men drank of Khivia's waters, drinking his thought and thereby thinking his thoughts. This led to their surrender and subjugation to the Emperors of the Towered City. Today, as a result of the actions performed by the Master of Transcendence, the rivers flow below the ground and not on its surface, but this has not prevented our Master Khivia from prevailing. The mighty cities in the south collapsed one by one, and the Towered City was built from the multitude of precious raw materials we seized. In order to nourish the Towered City and provide for all its inhabitants, Khivia drilled a passageway to a deep gas well, using it to light his fire. The water, carrying his thoughts, ensures his influence over the inhabitants of the earth, and the eternal fire in the heart of the mountain provides sustenance for us and our City."

The men sat stone-faced, concealing their emotions.

The speaker continued: "However, since the Master of Transcendence proclaimed war against our ancient Father, the Ohn Mountains have been obscured by a heavy cloud covering, and Khivia's footsteps have been lost. But the fire ignited in the heart of the mountain nourishes the flame at the top of the Towered City, and the connecting path between them is completely hidden, known only to us."

He was silent for a moment, and then admitted reluctantly: "Though it is written in the ancient scrolls that at the edge of the Tunnels of Time, dug by the Ancient Progeny, there is a gate leading to the mountain core, that gate is eternally sealed."

"So," one of the men interrupted impatiently "have we gathered here to review ancient history?"

The speaker looked at him patronizingly and continued: "Since the outer wall collapsed, we have become more apprehensive about the Master of Transcendence. It is clear that the aggressive defense of the Northern Forest villages must be attributed to the support the Master of Transcendence. We do not have enough information about their methods of defense and retaliation, but the results of their techniques of warfare are quite clear; thousands of our men have been destroyed by them."

His voice grew louder as he added, angrily: "Our men have met defeat not only close to home, but even in the valley of the Lowlands and near the City walls! Although there is no reason to assume that the Master of Transcendence will find the key to the mountain core, or discover the secret fire in the mountain, it is time to stop pretending our victory is ensured. We have been busying ourselves with childish attempts at conquering the northern lands, and I have the feeling that what is transpiring there is nothing but a trick of distraction. We must protect the path to the flame in the Ohn Mountain. It is dangerous to pretend that it is impenetrable. And, furthermore, we must discuss the *Legend of the Wings*."

This was going too far! The men arose from their seats, tossed their simple capes aside, revealing royal, glorious garb underneath. The seven Emperors called out to the speaker, insulted by his words:

"What are you talking about?"

"Why even mention such a senseless mockery?"

"It sounds as though you believe all of this!"

Only when the Emperor of the Crescent Level stretched his arm out toward the center of the room and a thin blue flame emerged from it dancing through the air, did the noise die down.

"My friends," he hissed, "we have not gathered here to argue. It seems that you do not comprehend the enormous power of the Master of Transcendence. If we miscalculate his enormous capabilities and the strength of his damnable army, we shall be lost. I want to show you something."

The Emperors were unimpressed by his decisiveness and authority. They still felt strong and empowered, capable of great conquests.

The Emperor directed the thin light that had emerged from his hand towards the dark wall, thereby illuminating the entire room. A vision appeared: Enormous scorpions surrounded a lone man in the White Desert. He drew a circle around himself in the sand, causing the scorpions to retreat.

"Here you see one of their warriors in a preliminary training session," said the Emperor with contempt. "We lack knowledge about their abilities and the source of their strength. But if this is a sample of their early accomplishments, we must assume that their potential is unfathomable."

"It is all vanity and emptiness," uttered another Emperor. "Khivia's whispers continue flowing beneath the ground at this very moment, filling the minds of all who thirst for water in the Land of White Fire with thoughts of surrender."

All of the Emperors agreed. As long as the core of Ohn Mountain was protected, there was no need to fear the powers of the Warriors of Transcendence.

"The Obliterators are more than competent to handle all problems that may arise," added the Steel Emperor. "Three days ago, they left for battle with a big surprise for the Master of Transcendence."

"There are some things that you do not yet know," said the Crescent Emperor. He opened the door of the room and whispered to the warrior standing guard outside. Returning to the room, he left the door open and a tall, erect man entered the hall; his eyes were dark like his hair, which cascaded down his neck. A white band adorned his forehead, its color the same as his skin. His rugged, colorful cloak concealed his entire body, deeming it impossible to ascertain whether or not he carried a weapon. The man was unimpressed by the metallic-colored cloaks of the Emperors,' by the flames on the fringes of their garb, by the sharp glances they sent his way

He approached their table with utter confidence, waved his hand in blessing and said: "I am Ukhma, thousandth leader of the Deathliners. I was summoned to this meeting by the Crescent Emperor to discuss with you issues of utmost importance to us all. But before we begin, I must inform you of alarming information I have gathered during my journey: Your ten Obliterators have been annihilated. They were defeated by the hands of a single Warrior of Transcendence, in the cave in which he hid."

The mask-like faces of the Emperors instantly contorted as their eyes filled with shocked disbelief. But quickly they regained their self-control, intent on hiding the deep disappointment, humiliation and anger they felt on hearing this strange nomad's horrendous report.

…This is what the Emperors knew about the tribes of the wild nomads: The water from the river, carrying Khivia's thoughts, reached the north as well. In certain places, the rivers deviated into small pools. Day after day, year after year, the water in the pools became concentrated with thoughts. Even their color changed from a light blue to a deep bluish-black and those who approach the waters sense their intense presence. Both the villagers and the inhabitants of the Towered City consider this phenomenon a dangerous threat. They built high stone walls around these pools, and kept their distance from them. However, a few lone tribes regard the pools as sacred. Not only are they unafraid of them, but they dig under the stone walls and drink of the black waters during long ceremonies. These are the Deathliners.

Those traveling from the Land of the North relate that the Deathliners are the strongest and most powerful of local tribes.

They are nomadic, living in tents, and deliberately moving from place to place. The Tower dwellers, who esteem stone walls, weapons and homes, look down on the lifestyle of the Deathliners. These nomads stayed far away from the Towered City, living completely independent lives, throughout history. The inhabitants of the north supply the Deathliners with clothing and tools, as well as slaves and maidservants, all in exchange for the ironic promise of peaceful relations and cooperation in defense against their enemies, although the only enemies, until now, were the Deathliners themselves.

Ukhma began to speak confidently, as though his sources were clear to him beyond all doubt.

"Your prisons are unusually crowded and the number of semi-Oblitcrated Ones is increasing, more than ever."

The Emperors became extremely agitated and held their swords at the ready. This man had divulged information that was new to them.

The man continued: "The collapse of the outer wall and the increased number of Warriors of Transcendence in the Land of the Northern Forests has not been favorable to the reputation of the Warriors of the Towered City. The fear of the *Legend of the Wings* invading all levels of the Tower does not bode well. This threat will affect all of you. Your situation is very grim.

I shall not deceive you. We have not joined forces with you out of love for the Towered City. We have also lost men. They were either captured or annihilated by troops of the Master of Transcendence. Until now, we have never needed your feeble help."

Ukhma continued: "Khivia's creatures that drink of his waters in the Land of the North are his creations, and his strength pulsates within them. And you- you feed off of memories or of diluted waters, which contain only fragments of thoughts. Even the best of your Obliterators, the essences of the Shadows, were unable to resist us."

The Emperors glanced at each other, insulted, mortified. Was it possible that this lowly tribe had such immense strength? Did Ukhma speak the truth? He stopped talking as if he could read their minds, shifted his colorful cloak aside and removed a small square, silvery box from his cape. It held dark bluish-black waters. He approached the table and trickled a few drops into a large stone bowl.

"Taste!" he commanded.

The Emperors reluctantly dipped their fingers into the black liquid in the stone bowl, and tasted. Their faces became distorted by the awful, bitter taste, but immediately an immense inner fire was ignited in them, causing the flames etched upon their cloaks to heat up. They felt as though Khivia himself was pouring rivers of fire into them.

"We have been drinking from these waters for centuries," smiled the Deathliner when the men regained their senses. "This is not about red heifers, with which you fatten up your slaves," he said with contempt, "or about the purple drinks that paralyze the brain. Even the blue liquid, which was granted to you alone, is nothing but a poor imitation of the real thing. We," he continued, pointing to the black waters proudly, "we, ourselves, are the thoughts of Khivia." "I am willing to pay for it!" the Venus Emperor suddenly cut off the Deathliner's speech. He hurriedly produced ten golden coins from his cloak, laid them on the table and waited for the man's reaction. His offer was very generous. The other Emperors followed the proposal with interest, but Ukhma just glanced at the golden coins, as though they were grains of sand, bursting into loud and raucous laughter.

"Money?!" he exclaimed in amazement. "You think you can buy black water with money? Our most exalted scribes described to us the love the Descendents of the Emperors have for money, but

I never imagined you would attempt to desecrate the sacred black waters with such an offer!"

The Venus Emperor gathered his golden coins from the table and slunk back into his seat. Ukhma seemed content with the humiliation he had caused and continued provoking the men: "Do you not wonder why you are barren? Do you truly think that your decision to become immortal was correct? Don't you ever think that the stars you worship are actually enslaving you?"

His speech intensified and burst forth exuberantly, without clarity, as though an inner madness was compelling him to speak these words.

"Do you think that the drums shall overcome the base that supports them, that the stringed instruments shall smother the chest of those they face, that the woodwinds shall seal the mouths of those that blow into them? You should know that just a few melodies played by the Master of Transcendence crumbled your outer walls to fine dust. Your command over your melodies is very far from perfect, and you have never received any form of weapon to protect you from the reality of the *Legend of the Wings*. When the time comes...." He began to stutter, as though he had uttered words that were not to be spoken, and he stopped speaking.

The Emperors raised their eyes as they sat in the deep silence of the great hall. Their own humiliation, as bad as it was, paled in contrast to the disgrace of the sacred principles of Khivia. The first to speak was the Solar Emperor. He approached Ukhma very closely, and as he carefully formed each word said: "Do your ears hear what your mouth speaks?"

The Deathliner stood up proudly and spoke confidently: "You need to know that occasionally, the parts responsible for Khivia's strengths in the inner system lose control slightly."

The Emperors were baffled.

Ukhma continued speaking, as arrogantly and egotistically as before, as if he had not faltered and lost his clarity.

"If we so desired, we could conquer the Towered City and destroy it for our amusement, needlessly, without reason," he said with a gleam in his eyes, like a murderer who enjoys slaughtering others for the sake of killing.

"You wouldn't survive a single day. But what would we do with such a great pile of rocks? Our northern winds, our tall mountains and our gushing rivers are enough for us in our Land. But unfortunately, only you know the exact location of the entrance to Ohn Mountain. For that reason we have come to offer you a chance to cooperate with us. We cherish our freedom above all and shall maintain our independence. You shall carry on waging the war, and do all that you can to deter the enemy from the source of our strength at Ohn Mountain, while we shall protect the entrance to the Mountain, preventing an invasion. Understand that if anyone even touches the fire there, we shall all collapse instantaneously."

"I don't understand!" exclaimed one of the Emperors, in response to Ukhma's word, ignoring his offer to work together. "Are you trying to say that you believe in the so-called tale of the '*Legend of the Wings*'?"

Ukhma smiled mockingly. "On the one hand, you don't believe in the Legend," he began slowly "and on the other hand, you are so afraid of it, that the mere mention of it is utterly forbidden! The reason for this obvious contradiction of yours is that in the depths of your hearts, you know that it is the truth, but you are not willing to admit it even to yourselves. The clumsy City you built in the Lowlands is so dear to your hearts, that you cannot bear the thought of its imminent destruction."

Frozen faces stared at the speaker; no one made eye contact. The Deathliner continued to speak his words confidently: "And so, my friends, the great wave shall come, but even prior to this, no bricks in the *Land of the White Fire* shall remain intact."

His face became distorted as he mentioned the name they gave their land. The White Emperor arose and approached Ukhma. No one had ever dared to address the Emperors this way before! Although he himself had summoned the Deathliner to the Tower, he was shocked and dismayed by of his words.

"Tell me, son of the Deathliners," the Emperor began, "do your ears hear what your mouth speaks? If you accept the words of that Legend, and believe in them," he said to the Emperors as well, "then you too shall be lost in the….in the…" he had difficulty uttering the words, "in the waters that have no end…"

Ukhma took several steps back, distancing himself from the furious Emperor. He gathered the silver box containing the black waters, as though desiring to gain strength from it, and said: "You don't believe, and you care only about your own world, while we believe and don't care. The end is near," he declared, "but until the end comes, we will ensure that no man in the Land of the Ancient Progeny shall rest or feel secure. We shall make use of our remaining time playing with fire and blood."

The White Emperor did not give up. He approached the man. Both held onto their hidden swords, under their cloaks.

"Does it not seem unnecessary to you, in your plan of fire and blood, to seek the Master of Transcendence or protect Ohn Mountain? For either way, according to you, the great wave will arrive and destroy everything, and the deserving humans shall grow wings and be saved. So what, in truth, is the meaning of your battle?"

Ukhma's eyes shone, as though someone had touched his deepest secret.

"As long as Khivia's thoughts flow from the heart of Ohn Mountain into the waters of the land, none of those who drink of the waters shall fly. The spirits of those who drink from the waters shall fall, and they will no longer believe that they can be saved by ascending above the wave. As the number of people drinking from Master Khivia's waters grows, and as time passes, weakness shall spread through the hearts of men. Even if they grow wings as mighty as the wings of an eagle, they will lack the strength to rise up and fly when the wave eventually arrives."

He smiled a victorious smile.

"So that is what we are fighting for. We fight so that along with our people, everyone else shall be lost, and no one shall remain alive after us. We shall protect the opening of Ohn Mountain and ensure that until the final moment Khivia's thoughts shall oppose the winged men. Afterwards, it will be too late…"

Chapter Thirty-Four

The Imposter

The Imposter

Ulu continued on his journey until something stopped him in his tracks: the sight of many torches, and the sound of singing. Was this a dream? He had trekked along a gray and barren hill for many days, losing his way as he tried to find a pass through the mountain, determined to locate the Imposter.

The days seemed to grow longer and Ulu sorrowfully regretted his inability to be of assistance to his warrior brothers. Instead, he felt he was wandering farther and farther away. Lone turtles making their way between the rocks at night were the only living creatures he encountered. Sometimes he would kneel and pet their hard shells, trying to shake his deep loneliness and despair. It seemed that even these lowly creatures knew their destinations while he wandered lost and alone.

Reaching the end of the mountain range, he noticed a wide pass. In the valley below, he could see men carrying torches, and he could hear their songs echoing. They seemed to inhabit a different world, a world in which war was not hissing at their heels, a world without battles. The light of the torches illuminated their light blue clothing. Yes! They were villagers, and there were thousands of them. But why were they marching at night? Where were they headed? Who was leading them? Why weren't the Shadows attacking them?

Ulu decided to investigate, as he moved quietly and carefully towards the procession. He, too, wore light blue garb. He would be recognized as one of them if he were spotted. The procession stopped to rest, and the flicker of the torches began to fade in the early light of dawn. At the edge of the camp, Ulu noticed two villagers who seemed to be preparing an encampment. He listened as they arranged their food and conversed with great enthusiasm.

"Did you hear what the Master of Transcendence said yesterday?" one of them asked.

"I have not been able to close my eyes ever since!" answered the other. "And his words are echoing in my head, over and over."

"He promised that the end is near. Within a few days we shall reach the chosen place for the revelation, and we shall be the first ones to arrive. What great honor!"

"Did you notice his eyes? Fire emerged from them!"

"He hears and knows everything, even our words at this very moment."

"He knows everything about us, from birth until death."

Ulu listened carefully to the villagers' conversation for quite some time, learning about their leader's purported powers and abilities. They described him with great admiration; every facial feature, his apparel; his voice and his gait, all in great detail. The man was old. His beard was white, as were his clothes, he walked slowly and his piercing eyes commanded deep respect. Ulu realized that they were describing the Imposter!

It was morning. The valley between the cliffs was crowded with tents. Today, the *Master of Transcendence* was to speak. At the northern edge of the valley, on a flat-topped hill, many villagers were hard at work building a stone podium. Within a short time, thousands crowded around the podium. A murmur of anticipation rippled through the crowd. Ulu tried to get as close to the hill as possible while remaining under cover. The crowd suddenly split, creating a wide path and the old man walked through it, alone. Ulu felt a sharp pain in his heart, like the pain he had felt when he faced the challenge of the Obliterator's enigmas. Although created by the Obliterators, the Imposter had managed to survive even after his creators' destruction, sustained by the belief of his followers. Ulu knew that the Imposter's strength depended on his believers' faith and would weaken if a separation could be arranged.

The Imposter began to speak, immediately capturing the rapt attention of his deluded audience. Ulu was disgusted by the adulation and respect paid to this fraud. Scanning the area and spotting the Shadows of Light observing the scene from the mountaintops, he wondered why they refrained from attacking the crowd.

"You have been greatly honored," began the man, his voice amplified and his arms reaching upwards. "Soon we shall arrive at the place to which all eyes have been turned since the beginning of time."

He was silent for a while, and then continued: "The war has already ended. The Towered City no longer poses a threat to anyone. We are all free men!"

Loud applause was heard, preventing the old man from continuing.

"Fools! Fools!" Ulu whispered to himself, attempting to calm himself, knowing that anger would be counterproductive. The old man hushed the crowds with his hands, and continued: "If you obey me, your welfare shall be assured. Abundance shall be yours, the blessing shall linger, and the sick shall be healed.

You must trust in me. But know that your thoughts and deeds are exposed to me like an open book. If you do not obey me, you shall be punished with misery. Even if you fly away or hide at the edge of the world, I shall always be able to find you."

An awesome silence hovered over the entire valley. The Imposter's voice was a whisper now, full of compassion: "You are like sons to me. I love you as if you were my children. You are confused and misled, you have been blinded, and you cannot discern the truth. Who shall decide what is good and what is bad for you? Who shall devote his soul for your own good? Wherever you go, and whatever you do, I shall be with you."

He continued speaking, and Ulu feared in his soul for the deluded villagers. He made his way to the outskirts of the crowds and sat down to plan his next move. How would he convince the brainwashed multitudes of the trap they had fallen into? It was almost noon now, and the people had gone to their tents to eat to their hearts content and then rest from the night's march. Ulu decided to visit and to speak to the hearts of the villagers.

"This man is deceiving you," he said to people he encountered. "The true Master of Transcendence is not an old man; he is a young child. The war is not over, it is at its peak, and so far the Warriors of the Tower have been victorious. They have burnt fields around the villages, demolished homes and murdered thousands. If they were to find you right now, they would kill you too. Your lives are in grave danger!"

His attempts were in vain. The villagers mocked him and treated him with disdain. They supported each other, and refused to discuss serious matters, laughing at his attempts to explain his views.

He befriended one young man who seemed interested in his ideas. They walked together through the barren hills, opposite the great encampment. Ulu spoke.

"Do you understand what is happening here? This is the greatest deception ever perpetrated! The old man offers you support and protection but he threatens all who want to withdraw from the group, and promises happiness only to those who maintain their faith in him. Questions are forbidden and, in fact, all independent thought is prohibited. He damages the strength of your soul and proves to you, night and day, how insignificant and meaningless you are."

The young man listened. His voice trembled as he asked: "Who is he, then?"

Ulu was unable to explain so he just said softly: "He does not love you, and you do not interest him in the least. Your welfare is not important to him, and he is exploiting your strengths for his own purposes."

"And the promises?" questioned the young man. "What about the promises of happiness, of power?"

Ulu gazed at him fondly.

"Are you happy?" he asked.

The man's eyes were filled with tears, and Ulu turned his gaze to the mountains. He had experienced difficult moments like these during his past attempts to speak with villagers who had fallen under the influence of Obliterators. The crucial moment of uncertainty, the self-doubt and finally the admission of error, truly a torturous, painful process beyond compare.

Ulu waited. He knew that the heart of the young man had opened to his words, but his physical reactions were strange and alarming: He sat upon a flat rock and his body began to tremble. He held his head between his hands as his body suddenly froze and he ceased moving. Ulu noticed tiny white creatures emerging from the young man's brain, bursting out of his head, quickly descending to the earth and enlarging to the size of a hand. They were white scorpions! Ulu, recalling his struggle with the scorpions in the

White Desert, prepared for battle. The scorpions surrounded the young man like a fence, desiring to keep him and protect him from Ulu's words. Meanwhile, life returned to his frozen body.

"Look," he said to Ulu, the gleam in his eyes now gone, "your ideas are interesting, but after all, most people believe otherwise. It seems that there are many differences in the world, and each individual perceives the facts in his own way." Ulu emitted a sigh of grief. What was happening here? Had the tiny scorpions robbed the man of his wisdom and understanding? He looked at the tiny white creatures and saw that they were transforming themselves. One became a sweet, little boy, another a young woman, yet another a line of red fire, and the largest of them all transformed himself into an old man with powerful eyes, a transparent cloak and a white beard. Ulu was filled with pity for the young man. These creatures filled his brain and confused his mind!

Ulu reached out a loving hand, hoping against hope that his young friend would see the truth. If only he would reach out, too, then the evil circle would be broken and the cruel creatures would disappear for all of eternity. And then, the young man extended his hand like a drowning swimmer, as if this were life and death! But the scorpions were quicker. His outstretched arm threatened them and they leaped towards it.

"I did not summon you!" roared the Warrior of Transcendence angrily, heat emerging from his hand towards the scorpions.

The scorpion that had transformed itself into an old man was suddenly struck, and emitted a horrid scream. The remaining scorpions escaped by returning into the young man's body, climbing all over him and entering his brain one by one.

"Now the scorpions will be unable to protect him," thought Ulu, "but, alas, his brain is full of them."

The young man wept as Ulu tried to comfort him.

"My savior and my keeper." wailed the young man, "your words are all truthful. But what shall I do now? My wife and son are at the encampment…they admire the old man wholeheartedly. They shall never be able to resist."

"Have no fear, my son, you will receive help. You are no longer alone," said Ulu.

A bitter smile appeared on his face, as he remembered his own loneliness.

"Will you be a father and protector unto me?" begged the young man as he held onto Ulu like onto life itself.

"You shall possess all the strength necessary, you shall no longer be alone," Ulu said, with a sigh. Detached from the old man's circle of influence, the young man now asked for sustenance from Ulu. It would take a long time for him to heal and make his way to his true protector- the Master of Transcendence.

The evening shadows cast darkness upon the valley. The old man was leading thousands of people towards an unknown end. Who would stop him? The lone young man who had managed to escape his grasp was dependant upon Ulu's strength and his anonymity. Ulu wondered if he could defeat the old man in an open battle without disclosing his own identity.

Another night passed. As the light of dawn shone upon the Land of the Northern Cliffs, Ulu realized that he had been discovered. A group of stocky villagers made their way toward him, inviting him to a meeting with the *Master of Transcendence*. This invitation gave Ulu a spark of hope. He had been summoned. Although he had been unsuccessful with all but one of the villagers, his words had reached the old man's ears. Obviously he was seen as a threat to the old man's power. Maybe the Imposter was not as strong as he imagined himself to be!

Ulu found himself next to a large colorful tent. He was directed to the opening and understood that he was expected to enter. Those who had led him here waited outside, and Ulu hoped they would remain close by and be able to hear his conversation with the old man. In the center of the tent, on a beautifully carved wooden chair, the old man sat, smiling affably. His white beard cascaded down his chest, his body was wrapped in a shimmering white cloth, and his eyes were, indeed, penetrating.

"Come here, my son," the Imposter called to Ulu.

I wonder who he thinks I am, Ulu thought as he approached the man, concealing his inner strength. For a moment, Ulu strongly desired to concentrate his thoughts, reach out his arms and recite the name of the Transcendor, but his inner voice deterred him from doing so. He knew that if he were to kill the old man, thousands of dependant believers would perish as well. His mission would have to be accomplished in a different way. He must first unmask the Imposter, causing revulsion in his followers. Moreover, if the old man were to die before his true identity was exposed, he would become a hero, allowing other imposters to follow in his footsteps, to revive the legend and lead additional followers towards a false redemption.

"Why do you deceive my people?" asked the old man, in a threatening voice.

"I deceive no one," answered Ulu cautiously. "I speak only the truth."

"The truth?" echoed the old man.

"Indeed, the truth," said Ulu.

The Obliterators were gone, he reminded himself. There was no need to fight this creature, only to separate him from his blinded cult.

"And what is this truth you speak of?" asked the old man.

"The truth," Ulu raised his voice, "is that you are not the Master of Transcendence."

A murmur was heard outside of the tent, which raised Ulu's spirits. Now he had no doubt that the villagers were listening to the interview.

"And who, then, is the Master of Transcendence? You- perhaps?" the old man burst into laughter.

"No," replied Ulu, "but you are a creature of the darkness, deceiving thousands of innocent people. The Obliterators, your creators, have been destroyed by the Light of the Transcendor."

The old man seemed shocked.

"And even you have no existence without the sustenance you obtain from your believers."

The old man regained his confidence, and his voice once again grew powerful. He smiled strangely, reached out his arms to Ulu and asked softly: "Do you not recognize me?"

Be wary of traps, Ulu said to himself, as he neared the old man and examined his features more closely.

"Yes, yes, come close, my friend," continued the old man in a soft voice. "We are not enemies."

Ulu came closer, and suddenly, all at once, the man's face became horrifyingly familiar. It was Tyklah, Ulu's childhood friend!

As young boys, they had played together on the shore, and the men of the Chamber of Changing Colors had chosen the two of them for training as Warriors of Transcendence. Ulu had covered up for Tyklah's failings on many occasions. Tyklah had been imprecise in speech and failed time and time again to fulfill the goals of a warrior in training. Their friendship and devotion to each other had caused Ulu to improperly conceal his friend's failings from the men of the Chamber. Tyklah had always been overly pleased with himself, pretending to have mastered the learned material completely and quickly. He even regarded the sacred Unification as a means to summon the Light of the Transcendor for personal control. Ulu was too young to understand the grave significance of his improper actions at that time, trying to cover up for his friend. Now he understood how his immaturity had led to near disaster.

"Tyklah?!" Ulu whispered, feeling tipsy as he faced the man who until that moment he had regarded as his enemy. The man continued to smile in silence.

"You…you..." Ulu had difficulty finding the words to express his embarrassment. "You were a Warrior of Transcendence!" he finally blurted out, questioning and making a statement at the same time. The old man came very close to him, rested his hand on his shoulder and said, "One can be much more than a Warrior of Transcendence."

Ulu suddenly wondered why his friend had taken on the appearance of an old man; they were the same age.

The old man continued, "I do not know if you learned about this, but the protective circle can be a forceful circle as well."

His arrogant manner reminded Ulu to be cautious, and suddenly words from the past surfaced in his heart: *That occurred to one of our warriors, after having been trapped within his very own circle. The strength erased all of his memories, allowing the Obliterators to enter his spirit. You may need to face him someday.*

Was Tyklah the man the Master of Transcendence had referred to? The Warrior of Transcendence who had become trapped within his own circle of arrogance?

The old man sensed Ulu's tension, and attempted to prevent him from thinking further.

"If the hand of fate brought us together, my dear Ulu, there must be a good reason for it. Not only did Tyklah merit the force, so can Ulu!"

Tyklah's 'tempting' offer had the opposite effect on Ulu, and his mind suddenly became clear.

Whoever this man is, a mischievous childhood friend or a creature of the darkness attempting to deceive me, he is an enemy to be overcome, and quickly.

Ulu pushed away the doubts which persisted in his mind, recalling the words spoken by the Master of Transcendence in his Chamber: *One cannot hate an obliterated Warrior of Transcendence, for he is really one of us, and must be peeled.*

He recalled the thousands of believers waiting outside and pitied them. He then distanced himself from Tyklah, disconnected himself from his words, entered within himself and prepared for action.

"He must be peeled," he whispered to himself. But what seemed to him a whisper was in fact a sharp, clear voice heard by Tyklah as well.

"Silence!" shouted the old man, and Ulu was pleased to hear the old man's frightened tone of voice, audible not only to him, but to all those who were listening outside. "You are but a crazy, senseless villager! I almost pity you, but you are not worthy of my mercy. Bring me my weapon-bearers!" he ordered his attendants.

Two young shaven-headed warriors rushed into the tent. Until now, Ulu had thought only innocent villagers were present, but apparently Warriors from the Tower were there as well. He examined their clothing and noticed the color-changing flames upon their garb.

Warriors from the City of Steel... he pondered, *I should have no problem facing them.*

But when he saw their faces, he was stunned. One of them was his eldest son, Saag! From all of the Obliterated Ones in the land, Tyklah had chosen Saag as his weapon-bearer!

An image appeared in Ulu's heart, leaving room for nothing else: Ulu pictured *Saag gazing into the horizon and seeing the Tower, for the first time in his life. He had stopped moving, frozen in place.*

"Father," Saag had clutched at Ulu's clothing, terrified, "What is that?!"

Everything Ulu wanted to say was forgotten. He sat heavily upon a large rock on the side of the trail, embracing his son. How can you fill an innocent heart with such profound evil?

Another image, more distant and bitter, replaced its predecessor: *The night of Ulu's Unification, prior to leaving on his journey with his son. He had wrapped himself in a warm cape and descended to the sea shore, walking on the sand towards the border of the village. The air was cool and the sky seemed like an arc far above ground. A pale moon shed silver rays upon the earth. All was silent. Finally, Ulu stopped, sat down upon the sand, rested his head between his knees, looked towards the black waters strewn with dancing silvery rays, and sighed.*

"Should I take Saag or not?"

A gust of wind blew in from the sea, causing his hair to become disheveled.

"I need guidance. I don't know what to do. He is so young yet, but maybe I have no choice…

The stranger who visited the village…

He is my son, my beloved! I have no other…They touched him, and I am afraid…this is not about rescuing a stranger…"

"Saag," he had cried, "Saag….Saag…"

Ulu almost cried aloud: "He is my son, my beloved!" but he realized that it was Tyklah himself who was responsible for causing these memories to surface in his heart, memories that served to weaken him. Although only a fraction of a moment passed, it was long enough to weaken his resistance to this creature, who had once been his friend. If he allowed the images to flood his heart, Tyklah could destroy him in the blink of an eye. He took a deep breath and then whispered two words to his son, in an attempt to express all of his love for him: "My son."

The shaven-headed boy jumped back in terror, as if struck by a sharp arrow. His hands, holding the sword, weakened, and he fled the tent. Ulu did not follow him. He was forced to complete the task he had begun. He would find Saag later. The remaining soldier sensed that Ulu's strength was great and he, too, escaped. The Imposter shrieked at his men, the entrance to the tent was raised, and the area filled with people. Ulu etched a deep circle around himself on the sandy floor of the tent. His hands were outstretched and the memory of the Light of the Transcendor, which flowed through him, came to life, pulsating. He gazed at the Imposter piercingly, and thought: *Only a pure vessel able to contain the Light of the Transcendor is worthy of the force. The sole force in the world is the pure Light of the Transcendor.*

He articulated only these words: "You are the heart of the world."

A purple light filled the tent and hovered over the head of the Warrior of Transcendence. The flowing light, emerging from his hands, turned into shades of white and red. The old man retreated backwards in terror, but the light caught him, touching his cloak and causing him to melt. He let out a terrified cry, as his white hair vanished and his eyes were revealed as deep, dark holes. Under the splendorous, melted cloak, a jumble of images of darkness appeared, sharply illuminated by the surrounding red light.

Chapter Thirty-Five

The Game of Forces

The Game of Forces

Two weeks passed and Ulu remained with the villagers. While he had long conversations with the dozens of newly enlightened individuals who had previously been followers of the Imposter, answering their many questions, many others packed their belongings, preparing to return to their homes in the villages.

"Ulu possesses important knowledge," those interested in learning admonished.

"Stay and learn. Don't rush off."

But the majority of the villagers shrugged their shoulders in annoyance.

"The old man, too, knew many things and almost led us to our death. We have had enough."

"Ulu is not an imposter like the old man. He is an honest, truthful man."

"We have no doubt," was their answer, "but we are worn out from all of this, and incapable of proper judgment. Our expertise is our knowledge of seeds and plants. We are comfortable in our fields. Let us resume our work on the land."

"What about the Shadows lurking on the way?" Ulu asked as the villagers disappeared into the distance. Sorrowfully, he warned them of the Tower Warriors who could invade their peaceful homes. Didn't they want to know the truth? Didn't they want to know how to protect themselves? Were they not fearful for the future of their children?…

Tent after tent had been disassembled, and less than one hundred villagers remained from the original thousands. Ulu asked the Transcendor to protect those who had left, and he proceeded to teach those who remained about Unification. Grief clouded his eyes. He felt that those who had left would face many dangers, though he understood that he was unable to protect them.

"They will have to learn these things on their own," he reflected.

"We shall teach them," said the young man who had been Ulu's first student. "We discussed the matter, and decided to follow our brothers to the villages to protect them. We shall spread out in each village, armed with the knowledge you have given us. We have made notes of your words. If a Tower Warrior or Obliterator approaches us, we will know how to protect ourselves."

They had no idea how childish and inexperienced they truly were!

"Won't you travel to Fire Mountain?" asked Ulu, pleadingly.

"Maybe some day," answered the young man, "after we ensure everyone's safety."

Ulu felt powerless. He wished to oppose their plan and to tell them that a visit with the Master of Transcendence was necessary to strengthen them sufficiently so that they could be victorious in battle.

The information you have is so meager, you are inexperienced beginners, and the forces you will face are much stronger than you. You have no chance against them, you don't understand... he desired to say, but remained silent. The Imposter had always demeaned them, made decisions for them and told them what to do. Ulu had learned from the Master of Transcendence that this was not the proper way to lead his men. Each man was free to choose his own path, which would lead him to the truth if his intentions were honest and his heart pure. He looked into their eyes and knew that his task was complete. They had been rescued from deception, they had received important self-defense training, and now they were moving on, determined and free to choose.

"Go on your way," he said, "As long and winding as it may be. Your way is the only path."

They did not fully understand Ulu and their faces expressed uncertainty.

They will understand, in time, he comforted himself, and parted from them with words both simple and clear: "May the Light of the Transcendor protect you."

When the villagers left, silence returned to the valley, from the mountaintops to the deep ravines. Atop a hill of clean, white sand, Ulu etched a circle around himself with a trembling hand, and prepared for Unification.

"So many events transpired in this place, Transcendor, thousands of Your children were saved from death! But they quickly moved on, before hearing the truth about You. I am once again alone. I do not understand what really transpired here, and what the future holds. I am doubtful, and remain with no strength or faith. I am so weary from this journey, Transcendor! I need a healing touch, I desire to feel at peace."

Ulu was silent for the next three hours. The next day, he arose and contemplated his path. All he could think about was his son.

"I must find him!"

He began marching towards the Towered City, gripped with doubt. It would not be difficult to enter, but finding Saag was to be a difficult task, and getting out of the City would be even harder.

The Tunnels of Time! thought Ulu. *The exit from the City is marked there. Tzalaii told me that the cloak concealing the map had fallen into the hands of the Tower Warriors. If I can find it, I will be able to escape easily, without being discovered.*

Determined, Ulu set out on his journey: *I will approach the Tower and allow the soldiers from the Base Level to discover me. Then, they will take me into the Tower, and I will ascertain Saag's location. I will escape from them and rescue my son.*

Two days later, as he marched alone along the Eastern Lowlands in the light of day, he was approached by the shaven-headed Tower soldiers.

"Identify yourself!" ordered one, as his comrades grasped the handles of their swords.

"I...I...I am but a villager," stuttered Ulu. The soldiers did not waste time. They arrested Ulu, shackled his hands and led him as a prisoner to the City.

What an excellent way to enter the City! thought Ulu.

When evening fell, the soldiers stopped to rest and eat near one of the bare hills. They decided to entertain themselves with the captive villager. They unshackled him, offered him a drink, and then asked him, with concealed mockery: "Do you know how to play our game?"

Ulu continued pretending: "If you teach me the rules, perhaps I shall learn."

One of the soldiers produced a red, wooden box and opened it up. He handed Ulu half of the ninety-eight game pieces and kept the rest for himself. For some reason, the board seemed larger and clumsier than Ulu recalled.

"I paid no less than fifty white coins for this game," the soldier bragged to Ulu. Familiar with the coins used in the Tower, Ulu thought this price seemed astronomically high.

"You are yellow and I am purple," announced the soldier. "Yellow always begins."

There were one hundred and forty-seven squares on the open playing board, most were empty and a few had drawings of craters and thorns. One soldier remarked to Ulu, "This is the Game of Forces."

"The Game of Forces?" Ulu pretended to wonder.

"Yes," answered the soldier, "It is a game of battle between two forces."

"The purple and the yellow?" questioned Ulu, and the soldiers burst into laughter.

Ulu glanced at the yellow pieces in front of him: Fifteen warriors shaped like sword-wielding soldier pawns with arrow bags, ten WireArchers shaped like spiders, six Inviewers shaped like eagles, six Infiltrators shaped like chameleons, six Unifiers shaped like Octopi, five Extrappers shaped like foxes and one piece shaped like a serpent.

According to the rules of the game, each player in turn may position one piece and move a second piece anywhere on the board except on a crater or thorn square. The movement of the pieces on the board was confined to one square per direction. One piece could not be positioned without moving a second piece, nor could it be moved without being positioned.

A warrior could destroy an enemy piece only when joined with the power of five additional warriors, together forming two triangles positioned in the same direction. Alone, a warrior was useless.

A spider WireArcher could destroy an enemy piece from up to three squares away, when he was joined with the power of five additional WireArchers, together forming a crescent…

As the rules of the game were explained to him, Ulu's eyes widened, as he feigned amazement. In order to understand the rules and to plan moves, a player must possess basic intelligence, which the Descendents of the Emperors did not attribute to the villager, and his humiliation was to be their entertainment. In order to heighten their pleasure, the soldiers promised the winner a glass of their purple beverage, of the highest quality. The soldier was weary from explaining the rules of the game, and ended by stating sharply: "The snake, called the 'head,' is the most important piece in the game. It is usually positioned in the headquarters. Once the 'head' is defeated, the game is over."

"The game cannot continue without a 'head,'" another soldier reiterated.

"But what does this 'head' do, besides hide in the headquarters?" questioned Ulu, angering the soldiers.

"The 'head' thinks and plans, of course!" said another soldier.

"The 'head' thinks?" asked Ulu, "but it is merely a game piece!"

The soldier sensed his mistake and corrected himself immediately: "I mean to say that the 'head' cannot actually fight, it simply must remain in the headquarters, and that is that," he said apologetically, somewhat confused. "Let us begin."

"One more thing," he added. "At the start of the game, each player must place ten pieces on the board, according to his choice. In addition, he who loses either the 'head' or more than half of his pieces loses the game."

Ulu looked at his pieces, as though attempting to recall the rules of the game. After a long, focused deliberation, he placed the 'head'- the snake- at the front of the board, right in the center, next to three squares marked with craters, and behind him, in the rear row, he placed nine simple soldiers. The soldier from the Base Level was next, creating on the left angle of the board a star composed of five Extrappers, and then scattering five additional pieces in various places on the board. That was the classic opening move of a skilled player, unlike the foolish moves chosen by the hapless prisoner.

But the soldiers slowly began to see that the captive villager was not as unskilled as they imagined. He remembered the rules of the game and was able to competently escape most of his opponent's traps. He managed to destroy the structures built by his opponent with quick and surprising moves. The soldiers began regretting the promise of a prize for the winner.

Hours passed. The soldiers were fascinated with the prisoner's skills. Ulu was not afraid to expose his abilities and hoped that this would convince them to treat him like a worthy prisoner and therefore assign him special guards in the Towered City. It was possible that his guards would be Inviewers, knowledgeable about the Tower, and that he would be able to win them over and pump them for information leading to his captive son and to the cloak.

But suddenly something unexpected occurred. His opponent, who was utterly exhausted from playing, stamped the ground angrily saying, "That's it, you have angered me!"

To Ulu's surprise, the soldier proceeded to press a wooden button in the shape of a clover, embossed on the heavy side of the board, causing thin metal rods to emerge and create a complex metal mold. Ulu gazed at the complex structure in awe and discovered that the wooden surface on which he played was not really wood, but a surface made of very thin wood-like glass. Underneath, a third system appeared, containing square checkers.

Ulu controlled his breathing and attempted to regain his balance.

"The rules you are familiar with are old rules!" exclaimed the shaven-headed soldier arrogantly. "Today, the true battle is on three planes, not just one. And there are additional pieces that you are not familiar with."

Ulu continued playing dumb, while quickly contemplating his new information. The soldier opened up a small, concealed wooden drawer at the bottom of the complex structure, and removed ten beautifully made shiny red glass horses. They looked as though they had frozen in place while galloping. Ulu felt that he was watching live, dangerous creatures, despite their miniature stature.

"But who do these red pieces belong to? For they are neither purple nor yellow…" Ulu asked, pretending he did not understand. The observing soldiers laughed hysterically at Ulu's question.

"They belong to no one. They simply stand here, on the side," explained the soldier as he arranged the horses around the game board. "And you have yet to see their riders."

Something had gone wrong. Ulu's training as a Warrior of Transcendence had not included this new information.

We learned that the Game of Forces reflects the abilities of the inhabitants of the Tower, pondered Ulu, *and if this game differs from the other, then we really know nothing about their strategies! It is not possible that the Master of Transcendence is unaware of this…perhaps he didn't want to dampen our spirits with this information? It is always better to know what we might face so that we can better prepare ourselves... Perhaps this is another trial, the kind in which a warrior must understand for himself what is required of him?*

The soldier's words echoed in Ulu's mind, but he was unable to grasp their meaning: *Today, the true battle is being run on three planes, not just one.*

Only one being would be able to explain what was transpiring here, and he was far beyond Fire Mountain. Now, Ulu had to learn the new rules of game and be prepared to report them to the Warriors of Transcendence, for use in time of need. But his thoughts were slow and confused, and his concentration was disturbed. Before he had a chance to decide where to move his pieces, the darkening skies put an end to the game.

The game caused the soldiers to be late and as soon as they noticed the growing darkness, they hurriedly gathered their game pieces, shackled Ulu's arms and legs, placed him atop one of the horses and hurried to the Base Level. Ulu's mind was racing, and he was unable to plan his strategy. For a moment, he had the urge to activate his storm dance and cover everyone in a deadly cloud, but he decided to continue pretending.

With nightfall, a heaviness descended on Ulu and he found it impossible to recall any encouraging Memory Shields. The monotonous ride through the broad fields put Ulu to sleep, and when he awoke it was morning. An immense wall of fog limited visibility, and Ulu became petrified upon realizing how close they were to the Towered City.

The Warriors of Transcendence had always been baffled by the location of the entrance to the Towered City, since there were no apparent openings in the wall of fog, nor in the stone wall that had surrounded the City in the past. Now, as they approached the thick mist above the Steel Level, Ulu's senses became sharpened as he attempted to understand the secret of the entrance.

They forgot to cover my eyes, thought Ulu, as he heard one of the soldiers proclaim: "To the bottom plane!"

The soldiers arranged themselves in the shape of a clover, just like the one that had caused the game to become three-dimensional, and Ulu felt himself being sucked into an inner world together with the soldiers. He tried hard to observe, but only saw a multitude of reflections of the rocks and earth on which they stood, before being swallowed into the bottom plane.

"To the White Emperor!" were the final words he heard before losing consciousness. He did not see the blue flames that had appeared on the soldiers' capes.

Chapter Thirty-Six

The White Emperor

The White Emperor

"You are insignificant to us, " Ulu heard a voice in his mind, "You are but one of many trivial nuisances, and you are incapable of harming us or cramping our style." Where was the voice coming from? Ulu's eyes were closed and he felt a vague pain encompass his head.

Suddenly, he remembered everything: The encounter with the Obliterators, the incident with the Imposter, his meeting with Tzalaii and his naïve journey to seek the Kings Cloak. Although he had entered the Tower with ease as a prisoner, he doubted that he would be able to get out alive. The voice did not subside. It was devoid of emotion, anger.

Despite his weakness and fears, Ulu tried to ignore the voice, to be unimpressed by the power emanating from it, but just then the voice grew louder, and the words cut into Ulu's skin: "Who sent you here? Where is his dwelling place?"

Within these words, almost impossible to perceive, Ulu heard a fervor that demonstrated the speaker's weakness. This feeling relieved Ulu momentarily, and he bravely opened his eyes. He saw the large high-ceilinged hall. Through the huge windows, wide vistas could be seen: The Green Lowlands to the west, the sea glistening far beyond and Shadow Valley to the East, full of evil.

Am I at the peak of the Towered City? wondered Ulu.

He turned his glance to the center of the room, and what he saw confounded his entire being, leaving no room for anything else. In the enormous, transparent hall there were seven ascending wide steps made of glass. At the top of the steps sat a creature made of glass or ice upon a seat of fire. It had countless eyes, terrifying, intimidating and accusatory, all of them focused upon Ulu. Blue flames, blindingly bright, sharp as lightning, circled the creature like a blue cape of fire. And now, only now, did Ulu realize that it was this creature who was awaiting an answer to the question: "Who sent you here? Where is his dwelling place?"

Everything lacked clear boundaries and form. The steps became a deep pond and the windows appeared barred. White fragments, fierce and piercing, encircled the broad room, like wind, desiring spaciousness, like live creatures awaiting their prey. With strength that he did not possess, Ulu shut his eyes and tried to gather his thoughts. Battles of forces were not foreign to him. But this force?

The White Emperor arose from his seat, and the flames of his cloak scattered around him, filling the hall.

"If you do not give, I shall take," he bellowed as he neared the prone man, cowering on the ground, imprisoned by the magic of his flames.

"And what is more," he continued, "You have yet to hear the tenth enigma of the Obliterators."

Suddenly distant childhood memories appeared in the mind of the Man of Borders. What a contrast to these moments of true terror. Ulu was able to take comfort in them momentarily. During his childhood, soldiers of the Towered City had not yet pervaded the earth, and no one could have imagined how swift and total their conquest would be. When the messengers of the Master of Transcendence met him, he had been only twelve years old, the same age Saag was when he disappeared in the Green Lowlands. But, unlike his son, he had already sensed the whisper of his inner voice. It was a blocked mystery, from which only echoes of it reached his consciousness. How had the messengers of the Master of Transcendence known what was transpiring in his soul? Why had they chosen him from all of the village children?

The memory of that first encounter was clearly etched in his mind, it as if it had occurred that day. *The two messengers had appeared slightly taller than the average villager, and Ulu first noticed them on the shore. No one else seemed to notice that they were different in any way. They sat on the beach and gazed at the children at play, but Ulu knew that they were really watching him. As though forced, as though summoned by their thoughts, Ulu approached them and sat beside them in the sand.*

"How are you called, child?" asked one, with large questioning eyes.

"We mean to say, what is your name?" the second corrected the first, as though it was important for him to speak each word with precision.

Ulu felt then, vaguely, that this supposed unimportant question heralded great significance. He whispered to them as though in a secret: "Ulu."

The two were content with his answer and with the seriousness in which it was spoken. The strangers had then conversed with Ulu for some time, asking him many questions. Ulu was certain that these were not merely trivial questions...that they led somewhere...and therefore made use of a moment of silence, sat up straight and confidently asked: "What is it you want?"

This question contained a clear knowledge that they wanted something, and that there was a purpose beyond their seemingly unimportant questions. Ulu had sensed it, but was unable to define it.

"And what do you want?" they had answered as one.

He almost said: "To be a fisherman," but was prevented by an inner voice, and he understood: They are referring to the mystery that he had sensed with all of his being. 'What do you want? What is the desire that jabs at you constantly?'

He was unable to find the words that clearly expressed what was missing. He was yet to meet the Master of Transcendence with the glistening eyes, so how was he to know that it was him that his soul yearned for? Had he replied, "To be a fisherman," the magic would have faded. The two men would have ended the conversation somehow, and he would never have met them again, neither them nor their sender.

Luckily, he remained silent.

No one spoke, and their joint silence became their mutual secret. In order to ascertain his suitability, they tested him. This test entailed accompanying his new friends on a journey to a dense forest. In the forest, the tree trunks were red and the treetops loomed high overhead. It was dark and mysterious, buzzing with obscure life, and the sounds of animals could be heard all around. While walking silently on a narrow trail, the two men turned to Ulu and said: "Now you show us the way."

Ulu had never been there before, and the forest was completely unknown to him! In the years that passed, Ulu would learn to listen to the voice of his heart, which would lead him to the proper place and time, but back then he was filled with fear. He had looked into the eyes of his attendants questioningly, and they encouraged him by silently pointing towards the trail ahead. He walked forward hesitantly, followed by the two men, until he reached a small clearing, covered in dry yellow moss. Ulu surveyed the area, touched the scattered rocks and listened to the sound of the wind blowing through the treetops. Suddenly a vision from the distant past appeared in his mind: There he was, sitting with two illuminated warriors, in that very same clearing! He had expected the vision to enlarge and become clearer so that he could better understand it, but it disappeared. He gazed at the tall silent trees, and noticed one tree that was especially bent over, surrounded by wild bushes. A very narrow trail bypassed it. Ulu had pointed towards it and stated: "This way!"

To remember...Today Ulu knew that when doubts about his path appeared, he was to enter within himself and remember, but back then he was not skilled at remembering. His memories circled over many times and places and returned to his son, Saag. When Saag was born, Ulu had hoped that he would be the messenger of the Hall of Transcendence sent to train his own son, but Saag was gone, having been captured and obliterated…

The memory waves passed, and Ulu was struck by the grief of the present, as he heard the sharp, piercing voice of the Emperor: "The tenth enigma is as follows: Where is your eldest, Saag?"

Ulu trembled. Helpless anger permeated his entire being. He was thus exposed to the Emperors' might, and he was unable to use his powers to transform his fears with light. The Emperor came very close to the prisoner and reached out his hand. A flame, as thin as a sharpened knife, was hurled towards his nearly lifeless body. To Ulu's surprise, it was not a flame of death, in fact it felt like a jug of ice water had been spilled on him. He shook off the imaginary water and found himself sitting across from an ordinary looking man.

"I disguised myself as a human," said the Emperor, "so that we may amuse ourselves a little. It would be a shame to kill a tool as glorious as yourself. That behavior is fitting for a simple warrior, not for an Emperor. It was cruel of you to kill an old childhood friend like Tyklah, but Saag has recovered from your unnecessary encounter and has returned to us. I reckon that your deepest wish is to release him. Well, you can't complain that you didn't get a fair chance to do so!"

He continued: "You must have heard of the Game of Forces. I don't believe that the Master of Transcendence did not teach you about something so simple. Shortly we shall move into the large hall next to my chamber, where we shall play together. Of course," he smiled, "we shall grant you the playing freedom fit for a Warrior of Transcendence. The winner takes Saag. You shall see him before you shortly."

Now Ulu had to enlist all of his skills in order to transform his fear. Was he to see his son as a shaven-headed warrior again, dressed in a Tower cape, with a look of submissive forlornness in his eyes? The White Emperor pointed towards the wide door set in the glass wall, and Ulu walked in his footsteps. A broad, deep purple sky with no end appeared before his eyes. Down below, in a flat green valley, Ulu could see a wide structure of designed squares composed of short, crowded bushes. Without counting, he assumed that there were one hundred and forty-seven of them.

But why was this land called a 'hall'? He wondered.

"Magnificent, isn't it?" boasted the Emperor, and then added: "Here are your tools."

A silent army of shaven-headed soldiers suddenly appeared, wearing yellow capes. Upon one cape was a drawing of a coiled, hissing serpent, upon six capes were the drawings of octopi, and upon five were foxes, and so on.

"And these are my players," the Emperor said, pointing in the other direction. There, stood a silent troop of shaven-headed soldiers in purple uniform. Their faces were pale and emotionless, like the faces of the dead. And one of them was Ulu's son.

...Ulu envisioned himself standing at the top of a silver staircase, facing a golden arched gate that was set into a black rock. He

was no more than thirteen years of age, although his knowledge and training were way beyond that of the other children of the village. The gate was adorned with delicate silver and gold carvings, and at its top were two golden birds with outstretched wings. A glorious tree was etched upon the front of the gate, its roots were thin, and its trunk wide and its branches reached up like outstretched arms. Silver letters joined together to create a single word above the arched gate, upon the blackened stone: 'Royalty.'

The gate had opened, and the young Ulu had walked like a dreamer into an illuminated Chamber full of the sound of birds, their voices as clear as a bell. Opposite him, on a carved chair, sat the Master of Transcendence. His eyes invaded Ulu and supplied him with waves of comfort and hope, as he had never felt before...

Where did this Memory Shield come from, and why now? He did not know. But its intensity caused him to feel so good, that even the White Emperor and his threats seemed ridiculous to him, for the moment. Ignoring the fact that his son was one of them, he arranged his players upon the squares in the green valley beneath the purple skies. There was no need to physically move them. All he had to do was think about their designated spot, and the seemingly artificial players would move to their designated squares. The White Emperor, too, arranged his players, and the game began.

The purple skies darkened, but the playing field remained illuminated, in a way incomprehensible to Ulu. In a complex, creative move Ulu managed to pose a threat to the 'head' player, the Emperor's serpent, with his soldiers and allowed himself to smile slightly. But then something occurred that Ulu did not expect: The Emperor stopped playing and approached Ulu.

"Have no fear, Warrior of Transcendence," he said as he got closer, startling Ulu even more. "I only want to show you the source of the light. Look," he said, as he pointed to the playing field.

The sky was almost completely dark now, but a strange, reddish, light emerged from the checkered board and spread over the entire valley, coloring the clothing of the obliterated players in odd colors. Ulu concentrated his gaze upon the checkered board and became breathless: The ground upon which they played lost its opaqueness and became transparent. Under the checkered field, beneath the ground, appeared a parallel field.

Today, the true battle is being run on three planes, Ulu recalled the words of his captors.

What a fatal mistake he had made, allowing them to take him captive and not escaping from them.

Three planes, thought Ulu again, and then his eyes looked up towards the illuminated space above the playing field. An additional impressive structure appeared in front of his eyes, composed of thin rays of light. Between the light margins lay illuminated squares, upon which appeared players. The Emperor did not leave Ulu time to think. "Well, Warrior of Transcendence, this is the 'Game of Thoughts.' The 'Game of Forces' is child's play in relation to this. Thanks to your friend, Tzalaii, we have obtained the map of the Tunnels of Time, etched upon the King's Cloak, and as you can see, the soldiers of the 'Game of Thoughts' are already making their way there."

Black creatures moved though the Tunnels of Time, which twisted and turned in amazing clarity in the bottom plane of the game.

"Sihara!" cried Ulu bitterly.

He recalled the first time he saw her on Green Isle, after Tzalaii had fallen captive. He did not know where she was heading in the Tunnels of Time, but it was clear to him that she was continuing her mission in the name of the Chamber.

"Yes, Sihara," agreed the White Emperor, "Sihara who shall soon be called the 'Mistress of the Deathliners.'"

He neared Ulu and grabbed hold of his arm.

"And did you really think that we would leave the mountain core open to this naive girl?" Ulu could see Sihara kneeling down and gazing into a pool of water. Every cell in his body became enraged! He searched for a Memory Shield to hold onto, but this new information flooded him and prevented him from thinking of anything else.

The Emperor continued speaking, without mercy: "As you can see, the game is three-dimensional. It is based on the ancient rules of the 'Game of Forces,' although in essence, it varies drastically. Here, there is no point in striking the 'head' of the opponent, because there are essentially more heads than one."

The Emperor burst into a crazed fit of laughter, which rolled through the dark valley like the growl of a large beast crouching over its prey. Ulu was petrified. His entire being was shocked by the suddenness in which the Emperor rid himself of his human disguise.

"If you want him," he said as he pointed towards the frozen image of Saag, "you must defeat me."

The boy appeared as a motionless yellow, wax doll. Upon his cape, which looked like a transparent drawing upon his body, was the image of a fox.

"Victory means creating corresponding uniform structures on all three planes, located precisely one atop the other. For your information, the Octopus is the one capable of copying a structure from one plane to another. The Extrappers can dig craters which will force the player to move, against his will, to a lower plane. The Inviewers can see from one end of the world to the other, and have the ability to neutralize all structures on all planes. And now, Warrior of Transcendence," he uttered disdainfully, "can you identify any of the players on the field?"

The faces of the players began to change, transforming into Tzalaii, and then into Mahn. These images were not really Tzalaii and Mahn, it was clear, although the fact that the Emperor was so familiar with their appearances, locations, and deeds, to the point that he was capable of disguising his Obliterators into their form, caused another layer of Memory Shields to peel away from Ulu's soul. He felt more vulnerable than ever before, as though all of his heart's secrets were exposed before this creature of many disguises and schemes. "I shall help you arrange them," said the Emperor. "As I see it, your friends are currently located on the middle plane. You are welcome to place them in their proper places."

With the power of thought, the Emperor placed his players upon various squares on the middle plane. Without waiting for Ulu's response, they began to move, and built an Extrapper formation. With great effort, Ulu managed to move his soldiers as well and neutralize the Extrapper formation, but then the Emperor's players were swallowed into the bottom plane.

Can they harm Sihara? wondered Ulu in terror. *What is reality and what is imaginary?*

"Good depth in exchange for evil depth," whispered an inner voice.

With great difficulty, Ulu was able to convey his thoughts. He gathered his strength and continued playing, this time demoting a fox structure from the upper plane to the lower plane, and instructing his soldiers to plant obstacles, thereby preventing the Emperor's soldiers from touching Sihara. The Extrappers from the mountain-core stopped moving. The crater that appeared opposite them delayed their moves, although they regrouped and created a precise crescent formation and waited for a similar structure to be built above them, on the middle plane. The corresponding structures of the Extrappers, on all three planes, glowed red. Ulu noticed that the light emerged from shiny red horses, which were scattered throughout the upper plane. He moved one of his players, who was pushed into the Extrapper's formation, and attempted to physically stop their advancement with his body. Their strength was greater than his, and he was flung forward like a driven leaf.

"Complete the move of the flame!" screeched the Emperor, his eyes almost coming out of their sockets. The hall, the structures, the Emperor- all melted and dissipated, and Ulu found himself standing beside Saag, in a dark and silent valley. Around him, in the same exact places where they were located in the game field, stood a handful of Warriors of Transcendence, surrounded by Extrapper formations in all directions. They were all prisoners, on all three planes. Ulu sat down on the ground, bewildered.

Chapter Thirty-Seven

Into the Mountain Core

Into the Mountain Core

Sihara sat at the edge of a large pool. Through the clear water, the bottom of the pool was visible. Outside, many battles raged. Tzalaii and Mahn had joined the forces of the Master of Transcendence, but Sihara had been sent by him on a mission to the core of the mountain. As was his way, he had been vague about the essence of the mission. He told her that her external tasks had been accomplished and now her heart would lead her to the depths.

There, in the depths, we shall all need your strength, he told her, without explanation.

In the mountain core, Sihara felt a deep sense of security and serenity, comfort and warmth, but she knew that a war was raging not far away, above the thick layer of rocks on the surface of the earth. The Warriors of Transcendence were in need of her strength. She desired to share with them the deep serenity she had found. If only they could hear the soothing sounds of water trickling down the cave walls, and if only the clarity of the water in the pond could infuse them with tranquility as they faced the smoke-filled mountains and spiraling fires.

Sihara gazed at the water in the bottom of the pool. It was not river water and was, therefore, untouched by Khivia's thoughts. She had already seen revelations of the past in these waters. Would she be able to witness the future in them as well? She bent forward, cupped her hands and drank from the pure, chilled water, reviving her soul and causing her sight to become even more vivid and clear.

Within the water, she saw a vision of children at play, and approached them. They made a place for her immediately, and she sat down beside them. She held a pile of soft sand in her hands.

"Here's a shovel," said one child.

She gladly received a small blue spade and formed a square shape with it.

'Perhaps a tower' she thought, 'or a drawing in the sand...or maybe a deep hole in which to place my feet... but first I must be a child, and then I will know.'

The children were comfortable and focused.

"Wow!" exclaimed the boy who had given her the blue spade, but he did not look at the others, and Sihara assumed that he was keeping the beauty to himself.

"You stay here," said a timid little girl to her doll, "No one will block your view."

"Perhaps the tower is too tall?" said another, "or maybe it is just right!"

Feeling at ease Sihara thought 'Why don't I try?' She gathered the sand into a pile, scattered it, and then looked up to search around her. It was like a puzzle- she did not know what to look for, but believed that she would recognize it when she saw it. She noticed a fence nearby, covered with white flowers in bloom. Many flowers had fallen onto the sand. Sihara collected a dozen of them and carefully planted them in her patch of sand. The crumbly sand was wavy, and the flowers looked like a tiny plantation.

'They are so beautiful!' Sihara said to herself.

"They shall surely grow," said the owner of the spade. "I'd like trees, strong and as tall as the sky...Cedars with white flowers, for the King's Palace."

The boy smiled. The radiance in his eyes reached deep within her heart.

"We shall carry them together," he said. "It will be easy."

Not far away a few young girls sat together in deep concentration.

'Perhaps I should go there,' wondered Sihara in her heart.

The boy had already wandered off. "I am not who I am," said one of them openheartedly.

"And I am not what I think I am, either," said the other, empathetically.

"And not what others think I am…"

"It seems that I am what I think others think I am," explained one.

They giggled.

"That's really silly, isn't it?" asked the other.

"Confusing."

"Strange."

"Odd."

"Scary," added Sihara.

They looked at her in wonder. "Scary?"

"It is simply a milestone on the way."

"A process."

"A passage from one point to another."

"The resistance must be softened."

"You have a channel, therefore you shall eventually arrive."

One of the girls took her hand gently.

"Imagine what a bud feels when it sprouts into the world."

"My cedars..." thought Sihara.

"He does not know what he is, what he thinks or what others think of him."

Sihara was shaken to the depth of her soul.

"If you cover him, he will not be afraid," whispered a girl, as she placed her palms together like the flame of a candle.

Sihara closed her eyes and placed her palms together as well, rocking gently. She felt small as a bud, gathered and caressed.

"He puts all of his trust in you," said someone by her side.

"All of his knowledge of the world comes through you, and he feeds from the nourishment that you provide him."

"Until his cover splits. He will hurt and will come to take comfort in your arms."

"Your protection grows thin and transparent, and he goes out into the world."

"You did your best, but he is no longer in your hands."

Sihara opened her eyes. A group of young mothers, deep in

conversation, were gathered beside her. She felt confused and helpless. The existence of the bud in the great big world seemed as though it were hanging by a string.

'But even if he grew, what kind of life would he have?' Sihara asked herself painfully. "Dependence and weaning, love and disappointment, comfort and terror. What is the purpose?"

"Yes," said a hoarse voice, "the body withers, but the heart grows."

Now a group of elderly men and women sat beside her in the sand.

"The path is not measured by your years, but by the number of your footsteps," said a wrinkled woman, her wise eyes smiling. "Each step you merited to take opened new worlds for you."

"I have already been there several times," said Sihara, "which worlds have opened up to me?"

"Inside you and beyond."

"The thinnest worlds- in your heart, and beyond- countless halls of learning. You have yet to encounter them."

"The body withers, but the heart grows," repeated the voice.

"And that justifies the journey?" Sihara implored.

"My child," said one of them encouragingly. "You have yet to grow and learn that one step, even as tiny as a single blade of grass, makes the journey worthwhile. A blade of grass upon the earth of the heart, I mean to say."

"In my heart grows a bud of the ability to act," said a pale woman, and Sihara recognized her as an older version of the timid little girl with the doll she had seen earlier.

"In my heart grows a bud of the ability to cease," said an old man who had once debated the height of his sand castle.

"And these are just outlines....echoes hinting at the trees growing inside of you," said the oldest man as he handed her a blue spade. His eyes carried the deep radiance into Sihara's heart.

" Accept it," his smile requested.

"Wherever am I?" she asked the man, who had suddenly reminded her of her Transparent Master.

"In the Chamber of Simple Wisdom," he replied.

The vision in the pool faded away, and all Sihara could see was the sky; a deep, serene sky, like the sky at the beginning of time. Drops began to fall, soft, small, transparent and radiant. They appeared as illuminated rain. Entranced, Sihara gazed at the droplets of light and realized that each one had its own distinct shape.

...and there she was, in a different place and time, standing in the middle of the White Desert, looking up at the rain. As the glowing water neared her, she realized that the droplets were shaped like letters. The letters danced, descended and became absorbed in the sand, changing the color of all they touched, from yellow to green, from yellow to red, from yellow to blue. Pale blotches of color filled the empty desert.

Captivated, Sihara sensed that the shaped droplets of light were descending upon her as well, causing her to brighten and become transparent.

Each droplet created a sound, soft and pure as a bell. As they touched each other, they created words. Not ordinary words, dry and motionless, but transforming words, spreading joy, flowing, life-giving. After the drops had been absorbed by the desert floor, which had picked up their colors, the words spread out and flowed through it- first through thin channels, and then through great rivers. Sihara located a turquoise pool of water, in the depth of the desert.

She leaned over the large pool in the cave, reached her hand out and touched the deep, glimmering waters in which she had seen the visions. The illuminated water letters were not just a vision, they were really there! Again and again, Sihara filled her cupped hands with water and drank. The water from the crevices in the Tunnels of Time had brought deep serenity and clarity, but the rain of light bestowed the heart of its drinker with a deep inner understanding. The waters were wisdom, and wisdom was pure happiness. Now she understood the significance of the mission the Master of Transcendence had sent her to carry out.

Determined, she arose and began walking through the Tunnels of Time. The path curved and descended, the air became less clear and the light had lost its brightness. The water crevices on the side of the road became sparser. The tunnels grew colder and the gusts of wind caused Sihara to tremble. Sihara stopped by a large rock in one of the chambers in order to rest and gather herself together. She heard sharp, rhythmic footsteps coming from the path she had just tread upon.

Peeking out from behind the rock, she noticed shadowy figures moving in a stiff, orderly fashion, almost like dolls. They gathered in the chamber and created a crescent formation. Their great concentration cast terror upon her. Who were these creatures and how did they appear here? The idea that the Tunnels of Time were safe from the enemy was shattered.

"How was I able to walk through here in freedom and security?" Sihara trembled.

Although they did not see her face, the figures began to march in her direction simultaneously, maintaining the crescent formation with great precision. Sihara retreated. A deep hole suddenly opened up in the ground of the tunnel, separating her from the marching soldiers. Sihara began running in terror.

Unbeknownst to Sihara, somewhere in the heights of the Tower, Ulu was causing a delay in the progress of the WireArchers, who had invaded the bottom plane and posed a clear threat to the girl.

After running for a while, Sihara stopped, out of breath, and tried to regain her clarity. She easily retrieved the Memory Shields from her mind, her spirit returned and soon she was as strong as before.

They didn't even notice me, she thought.

She distracted herself from the crescent-shaped figures and continued on her way. Hours passed.

The letters she had ingested granted her a new kind of vitality, and created pure thoughts within her. A mission. The words echoed in her head, creating a new awareness. All of the missions she had known until that point, all of the tasks she had fulfilled in her life, were like nothing compared to the mission she now faced. This would be the crowning achievement of her life. She approached a smooth wall, which reminded her of the gloomy hall in the Tower she had passed through with Mahn, just before she found an escape route to the Tunnels of Time.

She looked at the wall with hope, and suddenly horses etched upon the wall of the small cave became visible to her: Horses of darkness and the shadow of death, horses of dusk, horses of fire, horses of hail, horses of steel and horses of fog- all etched in the rock and appearing alive. Sihara was shocked. She retreated several steps backwards and noticed how the etched horses formed a gate in the wall. She neared the wall again and touched it.

"There must be some thought that is suitable for this place," she said in her heart, but no matter how much she concentrated her thoughts on the Master of Transcendence and on the rain of light letters, the wall remained blocked. Her thoughts did not succeed in breaching it.

"Speak!" she suddenly exclaimed as though she comprehended something new. "Speak the words!" She kneeled on the ground and searched inside herself for the proper words.

You are the heart of the world, she desired to say.

Just then four tall, dark-skinned sword carriers appeared out of the empty silence behind her. Their hair, as black as the night, was kept in place by white cloths that adorned their foreheads. Before Sihara was able to think of a plan of action, they had chained her, and she was carried into the depth of the tunnels.

Chapter Thirty-Eight

The Crown of Darkness

The Crown of Darkness

The Master of Transcendence sat upon a flat white rock and gazed compassionately at Tzalaii, who sat opposite him. He shut his eyes and his face became very pale, almost transparent.

"Sihara has reached the entranceway," he said. But Tzalaii did not understand.

The Master of Transcendence's features hardened, causing him to look very old, as he said: "The Deathliners discovered her just a moment before she was to pass through."

Feelings of rage engulfed Tzalaii and his hands became clenched fists.

"Did they harm her?" he asked.

"Even worse," replied the Master of Transcendence. "They gave her black water to drink."

They both fell silent. As the light of the Transparent Ones faded, Tzalaii was overcome by feelings of doom and destruction. His world was crumbling.

When the Master of Transcendence resumed speaking, his voice seemed projected from a distance: "The battles continue. The Warriors of Transcendence, aided by the Essences of Soul Concentration, are attempting to prevent a mass infiltration into the Tunnels of Time. You must go to rescue Sihara. You will need to recall all of your Memory Shields in order to find your sister and you will be escorted by….."

Suddenly, a pleasant faced old man with a high forehead appeared behind Tzalaii. "Allow me to introduce myself," he said in a deep, melodious voice. "I am Sihara's Transparent Master."

The Transparent Master stood beside Tzalaii as the Master of Transcendence spoke: "Everything our warriors have done until today has been a preface to your mission. You must return Sihara to the gate."

Tzalaii understood that he would not be receiving directions. He would have to call forth all of his knowledge and devise a plan to accomplish his quest. The Master of Transcendence's hand rested upon Tzalaii's shoulder, transmitting an intense flow of heat. The light of the Transparent Ones intensified as they accompanied Tzalaii, and the Master of Transcendence's blessing became a pervasive, melodious echo: "Do not be deceived by appearances."

Tzalaii was silent. The Transparent Ones were silent. Nothing remained to be spoken.

The Master of Transcendence walked silently into the depths of the forest and began performing Unification, the most powerful since the beginning of time.

"Master of everything in existence," he began, raising his arms to the heavens.

"Your creations are very small and frightened. They ask that You grant them bread and water, a roof, protection and shelter, some serenity and rest. They do not know where they come from or where they are going. During the gray days of their short lives, they were uninformed of Your glory. But," he pleaded, as if in a song, "as small and helpless as they may be while facing mountains of evil- You have chosen them to establish your royalty, and it is from their trembling souls that you desire the return of their hearts. Receive their cries, which You have undoubtedly heard. Gather their lost words. Listen to their secret melodies. Adorn your head with crowns fashioned from their deep longings. Be filled with mercy for them. Illuminate them with Your light." He fell silent for some time, gazing toward the heavens.

Finally he said: "Sihara," as if pronouncing a sacred name, and then again: "Sihara. Remove the mask that is not your own, reveal your strength, toss away the crown of darkness. Entire worlds are waiting to hear the story of how a fragile, delicate soul with pure intentions, without weapons, transformed molten steel into still waters. Sihara- Many worlds are attentive to your teachings, to your strength, to your splendor which creates palaces from hissing ashes and shattered fragments."

He continued speaking for a long time, like water with no end, and the Transcendor answered him and spoke within him, until it was unclear who was asking and who was answering, who desired and who fulfilled.

That night twelve figures descended from the upper slopes of the Northern Forests, heading towards the concealed northern entrance to the Tunnels of Time. They walked swiftly, continuously for endless hours through beautiful trails going deeper and deeper into the earth's core. They stopped only to quench their thirst with pure water or to eat hurriedly. Tzalaii was deep in thought, his spirit disheartened since the moment he had separated from the Master of Transcendence. Even the presence of the creatures of light and the tall Transparent Master did not provide encouragement. He felt a deep responsibility weighing him down, disturbing his peace.

"All sadness emanates from luxury. That is the first rule of the Warriors of Transcendence," he recalled the sentence he had heard in the past, right there in the Tunnels of Time.

"Sadness is a delicacy for the Shadows," his Memory Shields grew and multiplied.

To the best of his knowledge, Shadows were incapable of functioning in the Tunnels of Time. But who knew how powerful Sihara's captors were?

"To relinquish means to relinquish everything," a new thought consumed Tzalaii. What must he relinquish? If he could, he would relinquish this mission, from beginning to end, and perhaps he could have relinquished his encounter with the Warriors of Transcendence, and remained with Sihara in their distant village. And then he understood: It was precisely these thoughts that he was to relinquish, these shadowy, doubtful, weakening thoughts that created fear and shame.

"A Warrior of Transcendence transforms all of his desires into the will of the One," another Memory Shield appeared, clearer than its predecessors.

At once, Tzalaii let go of his fears and doubts, and felt embraced by a sense of blessed serenity. He felt a calming, quiet acceptance. He would proceed and accomplish his mission with precision and humility.

At that very moment, everyone came to an abrupt halt. Tzalaii noticed the light in the tunnel growing faint and the air becoming murky. The Transparent Master pointed towards a bend in the cave, leading to a deeper darkness, and his voice cracked as he said: "She is down there."

Tzalaii understood that from now on he would be alone, aided only by his Memory Shields. He gazed appreciatively at his entourage, expressing gratitude to them for their escort, as they blessed him and turned back toward the illuminated areas of the Tunnels.

All was silent, but soon a distant murmur, an echo of human voices, began rolling in from the depths. The trail descended into the core of the mountain, and the light within gradually increased. Beneath the soft white light filling the upper spaces, there was a harsh, red light. As he neared the voices, Tzalaii was surprised to hear the sounds of a cheerful festive meal. He was even more astonished as he reached the end of the tunnel and saw beyond it a large, unguarded torch-lit chamber.

Ten dark skinned, white clad men sat around heavy wooden tables, thoroughly enjoying their feast. Their hair and eyes were dark like a winter night, and white cloth bands adorned their foreheads.

In an alcove sat two musicians playing drums. The tables, laden with meat and bread, were presided over by Sihara who sat dressed in white. Her unkempt hair, which was in wild disarray, was adorned with a fiery red crown. Turning her gaze away from the feasting men and towards the hall leading to the chamber, she was not at all surprised to see Tzalaii standing there. But he seemed to be astonished, stunned. The Deathliners were amused by the two of them, as if they were an expected part of a premeditated game. They did not draw their swords as Tzalaii approached them, and did not attempt to conceal or protect Sihara from him. Tzalaii looked at his sister. The delicate features he had known had become sharp and intense, and a foreign fire glistened in her eyes. Sihara arose and came toward him, but there was no gleam of recognition or gladness in her eyes. "Sihara." he addressed her, while trying to enlist all of their shared memories. "It is me, Tzalaii," he said. "*Your* Tzalaii!"

"No, you are not Tzalaii," replied Sihara. "Tzalaii is in there."

She pointed towards a closed iron gate in one of the corners of the chamber.

"They are in there," she said, "all of them."

Tzalaii felt his knees buckle. The pain caused by this event was far worse than anything the Deathliners could ever do to him. The desire to protect his sister and rescue her from this demonic fortress of evil pulsated through his being, but he felt as weak as a baby. The Deathliners carried on with their feast, not even glancing at the hapless pair.

Sihara entered through the iron gate first, followed by Tzalaii. The sharp transfer into another world left him breathless. There he was, sitting on the shore by the village of their youth, tossing stones into the turquoise sea. Sihara stood by his side like she used to, when he shared his experiences with her, as she listened with deep concentration. For a moment his yearnings brought tears to his eyes, but when he examined the figures more closely, he was shaken. Their eyes were empty and their expressions frozen like icy glass.

"*This* is my brother, Tzalaii," said Sihara, "and there is the village elder and his wife, and there in the wooden home on Green Isle where my Transparent Master resides. I am not alone. Everyone is here. But it is all over and done with. Everything is dead."

Something in the way she said 'everyone' terrified Tzalaii even further. He gazed at her.

"Everyone?" he asked. "Everyone?!" he looked around at the village, and walked deeper into the room. Farther on, in the most distant corner, stairs led to a carved door. It opened automatically as they approached, revealing a royal throne upon which sat the Master of Transcendence.

"I once visited him," said Sihara slowly, in a hollow voice, "but it was a long time ago, and now nothing more remains."

"No, Sihara, no!" shouted Tzalaii in terror. "Who told you these words? Who caused you to believe them?!"

"You see, everything has turned into nothingness," Sihara nodded her head as she pointed to the figures in the cave. "You, me, the past, the present, the future...this is reality."

"That is wrong, Sihara!" Tzalaii said, raising his voice. "We must get out of here, both of us, and never return again! Do you hear me? You must come with me!"

He rushed out, holding onto his sister's arm, dragging her along. When they reached the entrance, he guided her in front, walking behind her, slamming the gate with all his might and jamming it into its hinges. Once again, they were surrounded by the cheerful revelers. Tzalaii lost his grasp of Sihara as she approached them.

Suddenly a hard object fell from her cape. It was the purple branch adorned with green streaks and leaves, a white pulsating line running through it. The branch smashed to the ground, its fragments heated up momentarily by an inner flame that immediately became extinguished.

The purity of heart, Tzalaii recalled Sihara's words when he had first seen her holding this object in her hands.

The purity of heart? The juxtaposition of these words and Sihara's image were utterly contradictory. As if on cue, two of the darkskinned men began beating the drums. Tzalaii felt the sharp, insistent sound pervade every organ in his body, the same sound that had driven his spirit mad during his trial in the Tower. Now, too, he saw how the entire chamber filled with fog, from which spirits began to emerge: Spirits of the sea and spirits of the sand, spirits of fish and spirits of the skies, spirits of stone and human spirits, spirits of the past and spirits of the future- all reaching out to him, begging for their souls: "Creator, Father, you have touched us- give us life."

Myriads of pleading hands reached out from all directions, and above them were Sihara's hands, spread out in the red light, controlling, inviting and awaking the creatures of darkness and the waves of the Marker of Tumult.

The ten Deathliners neared Tzalaii who lay prostrate, helplessly on the ground. They tied him to the large support beam in the chamber and stopped their drumming. The waves retreated, the fog dissipated, and only terror remained.

They can do it again, at any given moment, and Sihara is helping them! Tzalaii realized.

"Well, my dear friend" said one of the Deathliners, mockingly, "since you are so amusing, we shall allow you, just for the sake of fun, to reveal your strengths. Not that you stand a chance to affect our new kingdom, but we shall give you one last opportunity."

Tzalaii looked over at the drums in terror. The speaker laughed, pretending to express concern, as he said: "No. No drums this time. Simply remain here with us. We can share experiences."

They turned away from him, returning to their wild feast. The drums were put aside in a far corner and Tzalaii, realizing that he had been granted a few moments of grace, used the time to attempt to remember.

Close your eyes, he told himself. *Remove yourself from her extinguished eyes!*

He searched for his world, for the beach where he had met his inner Tzalaii, for the thousands of candles he had seen, pulsating with life, but he found nothing. He cried out voicelessly to the Master of Transcendence, but found no answer in his heart. He rallied all of his strength attempting to recall a Memory Shield, but his mind was empty and hollow, like the drumbeat that had seared his flesh. His only remaining option was to perform Unification using the last vestiges of his ebbing strength.

"Help me," he whispered trying to verbalize his deep needs, but he found himself repeating the same words in a weak whimper:

"Help me"..."Help me."..

Finally, far away in the distance he heard an answer to his whispers. The echoes of an ancient calling made their way to his heart: *The strength of the sender.*

Many moments passed until the words trickled into his consciousness, and slowly Tzalaii began to feel that he was no longer alone in the mountain core, facing the forces of darkness threatening to consume his sister.

His existence was only a small part of the light that surrounded and revived everything: The Light of the Transcendor.

"Summon the Light, and you shall be redeemed!" he whispered to himself. "Hurry, Tzalaii!! It's now or never!"

He was filled with strength one moment, and then flooded with fear the next. He was not at liberty to summon the Light of the Transcendor. If only he could be precise and humble, he would be able to summon the Light of the Transcendor but he didn't feel capable at this point. He had worn the King's Cloak twice and sinned with arrogance, a life-threatening error. His eyes wandered to the corner where the drums had been placed, and a new wave of terror nearly overcame him. *I cannot!* he thought to himself, *I cannot ever do it! I am not worthy!*

If you can relinquish your being, said the Master of Transcendence during their last journey in the forest, *you shall become worthy of the crown of royalty.*

Sihara stood by his side, silent and frozen. The Deathliners became more and more raucous as the tempo of their drinking increased. Tzalaii forced himself to shut his eyes. He detached himself from the cave, from the danger, and with difficulty from Sihara and finally from himself.

"Whether I survive matters not, nor do the sufferings I may have to undergo. I do not ask for Tzalaii's existence, but for You,

Transcendor, for Your royalty and glory. Evil dominates here, in the depth of existence, concealing the light, suffocating hope, capturing pure souls and seizing their faith. I desire to fight Your battles, Transcendor! Send me as your messenger to purify Your world, grant me the honor to revive Your primal splendor."

At that very moment, deep in the Northern Forests, the Master of Transcendence continued his infinite Unification and now directed his words to Khivia: "You have no existence in the simple One, your eyes are dead, your kingdom demolished, your Shadows crumbling into dust!"

The forests filled with winds of purity and hope. The heavy clouds, high above the massive mountain, made way for a patch of deep blue sky in which an eye-shaped pale spot appeared, and from it cascaded a line of light, glistening like a thread of pure silver, clear as a tear. The line of light touched the Ohn Mountain and became absorbed within the stone like a raindrop is absorbed into the earth. The Deathliners, sensing danger, grasped their swords in fear. But before they were able to approach the chained prisoner, a blinding, paralyzing light illuminated the area. Unable to move, they saw Tzalaii in a great glow of light, a hazy halo encircling his head. Inside of the halo, lines and shapes glowing with diamonds and precious jewels appeared in an endless array of colors. The crown, intended for him since ancient times, now rested majestically upon his head. The ten dark-skinned warriors released their swords, and their faces paled like the light surrounding their enemy. Tzalaii reached his hands toward them and saw them immediately consumed by the Light of the Transcendor. Not a sound was heard. Only Sihara remained with him in the cave now.

Tzalaii gazed at his sister, waiting. A luminous crown hovered over his head, while a red crown of darkness hovered over hers. His begging and pleading eyes met her blank stare. Tzalaii knew he could be aided by the Transparent Master and the Transparent Ones, but he refused to summon them. He did not want his sister to be seen in this condition. He reached out his hands to her. His light surrounded Sihara but did not touch her.

"Warrior of Transcendence," he spoke to her. "Find the place where you were touched by the rain of light. Activate your Memory Shield. Your enslavement shall disappear in the line of light forever."

The light flowing through him intensified, the red crown lost its glow, and Sihara trembled

"Princess," whispered Tzalaii. "Remove from your midst a disguise that is not your own, reveal your strength, toss away the crown of darkness!"

Shadows and light flashed by her face, struggling to dominate her. Tzalaii gazed at the light with all of his strength, begging for it to be revealed, to intensify.

"Entire worlds are waiting to hear your story," he pleaded, "of how a fragile, delicate soul, with pure intentions, devoid of weapons, transformed molten steel into still waters."

Sihara was shaken, her eyes revealing a slight, flickering tenderness, a weakness and vulnerability, like a candle about to become extinguished.

"Remember, princess, listen!" Tzalaii held onto his words, drawing strength from them. "Many worlds are attentive to your teachings, to your strength, to your splendor which creates palaces from hissing ashes and shattered fragments. You must believe!" She nodded a faint, almost invisible nod, as though she had been waiting for this cue. Now the healing, protective light neared Sihara and enveloped her.

"The voice of your heart shall guide the way, and the Light of the Transcendor shall protect you."

His eyes filled with tears.

"Come, my beloved," he said as he turned to the entrance.

Sihara followed him silently. He went out determinedly, and waited for her to follow. As she passed through the threshold, her crown disappeared and her eyes became clear. She hesitantly smoothed down her hair.

"Tzalaii?" she asked weakly. "Tzalaii? What is this place? What happened to me here?"

Tzalaii tensed. He wanted to return quickly with her to the Transparent Master and the Transparent Ones in order for them to comfort her, but Sihara stopped abruptly, looking behind her, trembling.

"It really happened, didn't it?" she asked. "The creatures of darkness, the black waters, and me…they said I was a queen, that I was there alone… At first I called for you, but no one came. Later I ate and drank, and much time passed. They told me that everyone had died, that the world outside was demolished, and I believed them, Tzalaii. I had forgotten everything! How is it that you came here?!"

"To save you!" replied Tzalaii.

"What for?" she asked, troubled. "I am no longer myself. I have ceased being Sihara. I was a creature of the darkness, like them! Here, in this very place…" she hurried back inside. Tzalaii watched her through the opening but did not dare to follow her.

Sihara continued: "My life ended in this place and nothing of me remains. Why have you come here?!"

"I was sent by the Master of Transcendence."

"For what purpose?"

"He said that I must return you to the gate."

"What shall I do?"

"Keep going!"

Sihara smiled bitterly, "You want me to keep going? Me? Tzalaii, you are dreaming! You are all hallucinating…This is a mistake!"

Tzalaii did not know what else to say. They were both silent for a long while, and then he finally heard himself say: "I cannot help you, Sihara. I have no answers for you. You must turn to the Transcendor and ask him."

"Here?" asked Sihara, shaken.

"Yes, here."

Tzalaii turned his back to Sihara and walked around the bend.

"Transcendor," he whispered in a trembling voice, "You helped me to find and rescue Sihara. Now, please help her to save herself."

Sihara wandered through the cave of the Deathliners, opening and then closing her mouth repeatedly. She searched for words, but did not dare express them. She desired to turn to the Transcendor through Unification, but was filled with deep shame and anger for all that had befallen her.

Why? Why had this happened to her?

"What did You think of me, when I was Queen of the Deathliners?" she suddenly asked, "Did You despise me?" She paced more quickly now, agitated. "They gave me black waters to drink. I pretended to drink three times, but I succumbed the fourth time. I thought no one would come to help me, and I hoped that the waters would bring back my lost will to live. Something indeed did flow into me through the waters- an exciting, vivacious sensation, but it was so dark and full of despair, that I was filled with apathy and indifference. After I drank from the waters ten times, my reality had become so dark that I believed all I was told. I had become a creature of the darkness, just like them…"

Sihara sensed disagreement in the silence that surrounded her, some sort of inner objection that demanded her to be more precise.

"Maybe not dark like them, exactly," She said hesitantly, correcting herself, "but their darkness clung to me, enveloped me entirely. When Tzalaii arrived, I didn't even feel joy!" She now knelt on the floor and cried. "They took everything from me….everything! Even the hope of being rescued…When Tzalaii destroyed them, and advised me in the name of the Master of Transcendence to keep going, I did not believe him. Even now, I do not believe him. Help me, Transcendor, help me believe!"

Sihara sat on the ground for a long time, hunched over and aching. Finally, she raised her eyes to the passageway.

"The mission awaits me," she said to herself as she arose. "*My* mission. I have a task." Slowly, she made her way to the entrance. "At least I am no longer afraid of the etched horses," she said, in utter exhaustion. "I have already met their masters. And I know how to deal with them!"

"Tzalaii?!" she raised her voice. "Where are you? We must leave this place!" Tzalaii could see the light in her eyes expressing a new determination, and he felt relief in his heart.

"Are you alright, Sihara?" he asked gently.

"I will be fine," she smiled. "The Master of Transcendence shall cure me. But before I forget what I have learned here, I must pass through the gate."

Chapter Thirty-Nine

Whispers

Whispers

After a long journey, Sihara and Tzalaii stood together before the final door. The etched horses were visible on the wall: Horses of darkness and the shadow of death, horses of dusk, and horses of fire, horses of hail, horses of steel and horses of fog, together forming a gateway.

Tzalaii retreated, "From here you must proceed alone," he said.

Silently, she gazed at him. For a moment he looked to her like an old man, scathed by the terrors of war.

Do I, too, appear this way? She wondered. Their bodies ached and their souls were weary. They wanted to abandon their mission with all their might, to share their experiences with one another, to be silent, to weep and to wash away their sorrows and encourage one another. But the enemy armies continued to flood the earth, and the Master of Transcendence's mission took precedence: To carry on, each with their own mission, possibly their last...

"When shall we meet again?" asked Sihara.

Tzalaii looked down and sighed, a sigh of sorrow and acceptance.

"The Light of the Transcendor shall protect you," he replied.

Their gaze met for a long time, transferring strength, transferring blessings. And then Tzalaii turned around and disappeared into the winding Tunnels of Time. Sihara listened to his fading footsteps until there was silence.

She gathered her strength, entirely focused on her mission and moved closer to the wall. As she reached her arm out towards the etched gate, she gathered all of her strength and said: "Your threats do not frighten me, and the devastation you have brought into the world will soon cease! You create feelings of hopelessness, and I was sent to inform you that a new sun of faith shall soon rise from the darkness. All darkness shall disappear. Light shall prevail!"

The stone passage creaked and trembled; the gate spun around and opened a crack. Suddenly there was a loud clamor of roaring and howling animals, a sound so deafening! Yet Sihara opened the door with a decisive motion, and discovered a vast Abyss. A white metallic bridge stretched out into the horizon, its pillars descending into the Abyss. A thick fog, far in the distance, hid the ceiling of the cave. Beyond the heavy mist that filled the area, Sihara noticed flocks of horses in the depths of the Abyss, bursting forth, roaring, howling. Horses of dusk, horses of fire, horses of hail, horses of steel and horses of fog.

At the distant edge of the Abyss- she became aware of rushing rivers of fire, splashing sparks, from which the horses took long sips. Next to the river there were huge troughs filled with sizzling coals- the horses' food. She intuitively felt that at the other end of the white bridge the most terrifying evil of all awaited her, feeding the fiery coals and flowing in the rivers.

I must go to the end of the bridge, I must face the terror, she knew. *But how is it possible that the pure tunnels of time lead to such a dreadful place?!* she wondered, appalled.

An image appeared in her mind. It was the image of the Master of Transcendence's eyes, in his Chamber, when she saw them for the first time. His eyes were of such beauty, that the incessant neighing of the horses in the Abyss momentarily faded away.

Time is of the essence, princess, spoke the Master of Transcendence in her mind. She placed her feet on the narrow metal plank, grasped the support rope at her side and stepped forward with a quick stride, determined to succeed.

Evil has no roots, she repeated to herself. *Evil is not real, and I am not afraid of it! I am fearless. The truth is in my hands, and I can overcome deception!*

She reached the half-way point of the bridge and continued moving forward.

I must merely remind myself that the fire, the horses and the Abyss are not real. They are only imitations attempting to weaken me, but I will not be weakened! The truth is at my side, I shall be victorious - -.

A blackened burst of suffocating fog permeated the air, blinding her. Murky steam filled her lungs, and her breath became labored. Her eyes filled with tears and she began coughing violently.

She looked down and noticed that some fresh air remained on the ground directly under the bridge. She bent down and breathed deeply. For a while she waited for the fog to dissipate so that she could get back on her feet and continue her journey, but more fog rolled in from the Abyss in blackened waves, blocking her path. Sihara sensed evil eyes watching her, mockingly, from the edge of the bridge.

"Come, little Sihara, defeat me," it seemed to say

She crouched down into the strip of fresh air. She knew that it would be pointless to wait for the fog to pass. The Abyss was full of fog, and it would continue flooding her path, attacking her.

Frightened, she grasped the bridge's railings and contemplated her steps. Behind her the bridge was clear, and the air pure. Ahead of her a heavy fog covered everything.

If I return, I shall be saved, she thought, *I cannot go on. I must retreat...*

But the eyes of the Master of Transcendence permeated her thoughts, gazing at her, urging, pleading.

I cannot get up, she explained to the Master of Transcendence in her imagination, *The mist from the Abyss is suffocating me.*

Who said you must get up? Move forward, the Master of Transcendence's eyes seemed to say. *Keep going. Do not surrender!* And Sihara began to crawl.

Crouched down as low as possible, she slowly made her way forward. The tunnel of fresh air over the bridge was like a narrow strip of light amidst the gloom. The fog thickened, becoming black as tar, and hovered over her. If she would have lifted her head just slightly, she would surely have suffocated to death. Sihara lowered her head and continued crawling.

Evil is not real... her previous thought persisted. She felt ashamed, confused. *The lie is false... truth is at my side and with it I shall overcome, I am not at all afraid...*

Khivia's wild laughter echoed around her, as if in response to her thoughts: "Childish, weak and confused Sihara, they sent YOU to battle the terrible mountain core? *You*? Innocent Sihara, unable to differentiate between reality and imagination, between the possible and the impossible, between life and death... Little Sihara..."

Sihara shrunk back. She really was confused, and did not know what was expected of her. Where was she going? How would she fight? What chance had she to win?

"The Master of Transcendence," she reminded herself. "I was sent by the Master of Transcendence! He sees where I am and is always at my side. The Master of Transcendence is stronger than all of this."

"The Master of Transcendence is daydreaming," whispered Khivia, as if presenting a fact that may not be challenged. "No one has heard his cries; no one has come to his aid. His strength is powerless and weak against the might of the Tower. The Emperors have many levels, thousands of soldiers and slaves throughout the land, while the Master of Transcendence wanders the forests with a small group of followers, weak and insignificant. Who even knows of the Master of Transcendence? Who has heard his cry? Who does he influence?"

"He shattered the wall!" Sihara recalled the bricks collapsing in front of her eyes and the Essences of Soul Concentration that were thereby released.

"In place of every collapsed brick, thousands of new ones were added to the basements of the Obliterated Ones. Each day hundreds of new Obliterated Ones join the Tower, thousands of women leap into the Shadowy Abyss each week! The Master of Transcendence may have exciting dreams, but they have no connection to reality…"

"A day will come when all shall be flooded by water," Sihara held onto the last memory she had of the Transparent Ones, singing.

"That day can take its time arriving," said Khivia calmly, "No one is ready for it. The opinions of the humans are wild and shameful, and so is the faith of the believers, flickering like the flame of a tiny candle. Remember how you were overcome by the Deathliners…"

Sihara stopped crawling. She looked so helpless there on the mighty bridge, like a tiny dot between the Abyss and the distant ceiling. She lay there trapped, lost and speechless.

Remember how you were overcome by the Deathliners…

He is lying to me! Her last thought careened through her blurred mind, *I was not overcome by the Deathliners; I overtook them! Tzalaii summoned the Light of the Transcendor; it permeated the mountain and consumed all evil. They were lost and we prevailed! I, too, spoke with the Transcendor, and he answered me. He helped me go on. The Transcendor-*

"I am the Transcendor!" arose a whisper so furious from the belly of the mountain, almost knocking Sihara over. "Worlds were created by my whispers and worlds shall collapse into the Abyss with my whispers, like you- obstinate child!"

A sincere smile, small and impossible, appeared on Sihara's lips, as she closed her eyes and allowed herself to block everything out. For several moments she sank into a sweet and distant sensation, taking pleasure in the clear knowledge that no one in the world had the power to take from her the strong faith she had in the existence of the Transcendor. But then the eyes of the Master of Transcendence reappeared, their gaze so serious and severe, Sihara was shaken.

Now is not the time to rest! his gaze suggested, *each moment is crucial. You must continue going forward. Do not stop your journey!*

She resumed crawling. Her knees and hands were scratched and bruised, the narrow tunnel of air stretched out endlessly in front of her.

Keep going! she said to herself, *Keep going…Keep going- - -.*

But the end remained out of sight. Hours passed, and Sihara felt herself weakening. Warm tears streamed from her eyes and her throat ached. She shut her eyes and began crying for help:

"Transcendor, I have lost my name…I have lost my life…Do You hear me?!

My eyes have become blurred, my love has melted and my life is fleeting… I remain a twitching, bloody dot, with no place in this world! Wherever you are, tall, distant and invisible, look down and see me here, in this inferno! I am so lonely and lost. The life You gave me- that You created, has it reached its end? And the Master of Transcendence, out there somewhere, in his lavish Chamber, has he, too, been consumed by the clouds? I have lost my life…I have lost my name…Transcendor, please stay with me! Protect me in these painful, lowly paths, as I fight against an evil that has no name, as it attempts to consume me. Do not leave me alone, Transcendor, stay with me, here, now!"

She could utter nothing more. The words weakened her and she was depleted by the effort she had invested while attempting to overcome the evil in her midst. She remained empty, as she waited for the end.

Out of the shadows, as if from a great distance, she suddenly heard a voice speaking to her. She opened her heart and heard the words: "Get up, and fly away. Above the cold puddles of terror! I shall create for you clouds of blue. Go on, look away from here, beyond this place, to the silent green fields, the white sand dunes and distant skies!"

She was calmed by this, and rose up on her feet. The dark mist disappeared and clean air surrounded her, protecting her every breath. She moved several steps forward, and became aware of a stone wall ahead. She had reached the end of the bridge! She stood before a towering stone wall, also covered with etched horses forming a gateway, but she did not touch it. She closed her eyes and remembered.

The rain of letters had a tune, a tune as old as time. Its sounds were similar to the tune played by the Master of Transcendence, causing the walls of the Towered City to crumble. Sihara pictured herself in the White Desert, watching the letters of light and listening to their rejuvenating whispers.

Sing, my daughter, sing, commanded the Master of Transcendence in her thoughts.

At the final gate, separating her from Khivia's fire and whispers, she began composing songs. Her words told stories of the days of the world, from the first rain of light until the end of days.

At first the roars of the horses in the Abyss drowned out her words. The impure whispers of the ancient evil wrestled beyond the stone in her weakened voice. But Sihara's ears were attentive to the rain of letters, and in her memory- their light kept on fighting. She knelt for hours in front of the wall, whispering, her words striking the rock and entering it. The roars gradually quieted and Khivia's whispers withered away. A deep silence spread through the core of the mountain, as if the silence of the Tunnels of Time had reached her.

Sihara continued whispering. Her song struck the great rock, and a vision entered her mind. In her mind's eye, she saw the terrible Towered City, its stones cracked and gone, and the wall of fog gone too, torn to shreds, blowing in the wind. Suddenly the Master of Transcendence appeared- his cape as white as snow. Sihara gazed at him, and then at herself. Her body became invisible, and her arms spread out like enormous wings. Then she beheld a tremendous wave flood the Abyss, its great waters extinguishing the fire of the horses of darkness. The wave rose and turned toward the final wall, getting closer to the stone, preparing to enter the mountain core and invade the root of fire of the City that was already covered in water. The sky was visible through the shattered rock, inviting invisible Sihara to spread her wings and fly.

…At the same time, in the lower Towered City, the market ruckus suddenly faded. Warriors of the lower City looked up at the sky, as if sensing what was to come. Their heroic spirit weakened. They became ashamed, like children who had lost their way. A secret hope touched their hearts, a hope they had never known- they were to rise up and spread their wings. They looked at each other, each one trying to ensure the other of their simultaneous transformation.

An old woman arose from a huddled position. She gazed at the sky, a wide smile spreading across her face.

"Pure silver, clear as a tear," she whispered.

From inside the Towers reaching endless heights, this spirit spread. Obliterated Ones gazed at their capes marked in flames, and for the first time in their lives felt like strangers. As if dreaming, they hurried to the large windows to glimpse the sky. Frightened soldiers ran down the long corridors, carelessly flinging weapons as if they were worthless objects. Shame permeated the villages as well.

"Mama, why has the sky become brighter?" wondered a six-year old girl.

Her mother, gazing at the sky, dropped the tool she held in her hand and ran out to the streets. People huddled together in groups, all excitedly pointing to the sky.

"The sea, too, has changed!" exclaimed one of the children.

All looked towards the ocean and saw that it had become clearer, so clear that its depths were visible to the naked eye.

"Drink!" called out one of the fishermen who had just emerged from the waters. "The water is no longer salty; it is so rejuvenating and invigorating!"

All who drank felt like they had awakened from a nightmare. Ulu's young students, who remained behind, gathered together with the confused villagers.

"We must all unite immediately."

They did not know that the final battle was not yet over, but their hearts told them that the Master of Transcendence was in need of their unity.

Chapter Forty

Trapped in the Valley of Silence

Trapped in the Valley of Silence

It was nearly dawn. A thin ray of light rose above the hills, exposing a buzzing hive of shaven-headed soldiers in triangle formations, their sharp weapons pointed towards the valley. Between the triangles, WireArcher crescents were positioned, and behind them Cloud Shadows, blocking visibility and blurring the horizon. A red horse stood atop the tallest hill. Its rider was dressed in white and held a staff, from which white fire burned and projected a dim light all around. The horse and its rider were surrounded by warriors in a star formation.

Down below on the plains, the trapped, enslaved Warriors of Transcendence waited. Ulu and Saag, who had been cast down into the valley during the "Game of Thoughts" with the Emperor; Tzalaii and Mahn along with the group of warriors who had been touring the outskirts of the Towered City when the ground they stood on suddenly became transparent and had fallen straight through into the sloping valley; and the remaining groups of the warriors from the forest. They were all shocked by having been enslaved without a fight. During all the years of their training, they had never learned that the Emperors were able to cause the ground to become transparent and capture them in its depths. The Transparent Ones that remained from the battles had locked away their inner lights and gathered silently behind a lone rock. The only sound that broke the silence was the neighing of the horses from the hilltops.

Saag sat upon a flat rock and gazed at the armies of the Emperors. Until yesterday, he too was included in their forces, and suddenly he was now being held captive by them. He was stunned by this sharp transformation. How had he reached this rocky terrain? Was he truly no longer a part of the Emperors' troops?

He examined his father: His face was wrinkled, his cloak dusty, his hair unkempt but his eyes were full of faith. He saw Tzalaii and Mahn, their behavior and clothing simple, their eyes set on the horizon, waiting. He knew that they were awaiting the Master of Transcendence, as he had heard them speak of him.

"The Master of Transcendence knows what to do," they said to each other.

At night, before dawn shone upon the Emperors' horses and soldiers on the hills, Saag spoke with his father for a long time. Saag asked questions, and his father answered. Saag wept and his father consoled him. Saag spoke and his father listened. His father mentioned the Master of Transcendence many times, each time his eyes glistened with a light so full of love and faith. Saag felt the desire to believe like his father believed, but everything was so vague…who was he? He had been neither seen nor heard.

He sat upon the earth with his arms encompassing his knees, and with a heavy heart scanned the outline of the hills, which were becoming brighter. In the Tower, men wore capes with etched flames. The lower City was always busy and the days were lived at a dizzying pace. Weeks flew by, and then entire months…and the fire in the Tower burned constantly. Here, there was no such fire, only an anonymous Master of Transcendence and an unknown Transcendor. He moved around uncomfortably as he attempted to define his feelings. Here- there was space, some sort of empty space...a vacant space for thoughts, feelings, and listening. Saag felt lost. He had once been a soldier in the Towered City, and now he did not know what he was or where he belonged.

His father, some distance away, raised his hands to the heavens, and Saag recalled the words he had whispered to him the previous night about the Transcendor, and about the way anyone could, if he desired to, unite with Him. Unite? Saag felt detached, separated and cast off uselessly. His eyes filled with tears.

"Transcendor!" He attempted to utter the name of the entity that was so foreign to him. "Transcendor, if You can hear me, if You can see me now...tell me how it can be that if such a wondrous Master of Transcendence exists in this world, no one knows about him? Father says that those who get close to him become more alive, but I know that everyone in the Tower lives without him. It is so backwards...I cannot make sense of it all. In the Tower, I had clothes and friends and set orders. I felt protected. The troops of the Master of Transcendence have no uniform and no respectable attire. They wander around alone. Father has spent his entire life on the roads, and mother waits and waits, and the girls..."

He began to tremble. All this time, the memory of his sisters had been absent from his mind, and now, it suddenly surfaced.

"...They live in constant uncertainty, while they play in the yard under the apple tree. In the Tower, everything has a time and a place...but of course, the girls must not be taken to the Tower... they must not be taken there!"

Things were becoming clearer. His previous life began to separate from the period of his training in the Tower, and he felt surrounded by a soft light.

"Transcendor- father says that You listen to me and protect me despite having been a Soldier on the Base Level, and despite my confusion. I wanted to tell You that I am willing to try! I believe father and desire to emulate him, but have so much to learn and I desire to live!"

The hills were blackened by the multitude of soldiers they crawled with, and the fireballs on the tips of the Emperors' staffs cast a threatening glow. Saag wiped away his tears.

"Transcendor," he continued. "Please remain with us! Save us! Have mercy upon father!" For a moment, he sensed that the Transcendor could indeed hear him, see him and know him, and in an unexplainable manner, was actually *inside of* him.

The sun shone, flooding its light over the hills. A murmur was heard among the waiting armies, and an approaching sound like a storm bursting through the skies. The multitude of soldiers split as ten horses of fire appeared, twice as tall as the Emperors' horses. A dark-skinned rider sat atop each horse, dark hair cascading down necks, white cloth bands upon foreheads, and staffs of black fire in hands. Ulu recalled the words of the soldier who had been his opponent in the game, after he positioned the ten red horses atop the game board: *And you have yet to see their riders.*

Now he saw them, and rued the sight.

The White Emperor spoke and his voice rolled throughout the great valley: "Soldiers, the battle is over. The last men of the Master of Transcendence are in our hands, lonely, weary and weak. Do not be impressed by their tricks, for their end is near. In a few single moments you shall be gathering their eternally disgraceful ashes."

The White Emperor, as well as the Deathliners, knew that the Master of Transcendence himself was not trapped in the Valley of Silence, but what were they to do when their last men were to be turned to dust?

Seven white flames emerged from the Emperors' staffs, and were fired towards the heart of the valley. They arrived right above the heads of the warriors, squirming and grasping tightly onto each other like serpents in a dance of death before attacking their helpless victim. Their forms reminded Ulu of the thin metal wires from the "Game of Thoughts." This, therefore, was the 'flame move.' The whistle of the flames silenced all other sounds and swallowed up the cries of the trapped prisoners. The sharp sounds caused rocks from the valley slopes to split and roll down to the ground, where they crumbled and turned to dust.

"Sihara," whispered Tzalaii, feeling the terrible heat.

But Sihara was still in the core of the Ohn Mountain, battling Khivia's whispers.

The thin flames grabbed hold of each other until they turned into a ball of white fire. The ball rolled above the heads of the warriors, who could do nothing but stare in terror at their imminent death.

Suddenly, a new sound was heard in the distance; a cry emitted by thousands.

"The Essences of Soul Concentration!" whispered one of the warriors.

The flames slowed down, and the many soldiers stood motionless. Sharp strands of silver poured down from the sky, cascading like radiant rain, but not even one sword succeeded in piercing through the upper plane. Now a roar was heard: the neighing of the horses of fire burst forth like a jet of smoldering flames, erupting and blazing through everything in its midst. The ten Deathliners held their staffs in the air, firing shrieking black flames into the valley, grabbing onto the Emperors' white flames and consuming the cascading silvery strands.

The dance of black flames turned the white flames into a red, blinding ball that slowly approached the squirming Warriors of Transcendence.

"They are surely not expending so much strength merely to annihilate a few lone warriors here in the valley…" thought Ulu, prostrate on the ground like a fallen leaf, the red death reflected in his eyes. "They are trying to draw the Master of Transcendence here, to rescue us."

"No one may touch my warriors!" spoke a voice so confident, simple and clear.

It was impossible to understand how it was even heard among the shrieking flames. The White Emperor halted, as though his horse, too, had understood the man's words. "You have no existence in the Simple One. Your eyes are dead, your kingdom demolished, your Shadows crumbling to thin dust."

His words split minds and settled in hearts, leaving no room for doubt or objection. The Emperor raised his hands in defense, and the flames emerging from his staff dimmed and moved heavily. But then an enormous, terrifying horse of fire marched forward, and its dark rider shattered the powerful words as he spoke: "We are not impressed by your words," called out Ukhma, the thousandth leader of the Deathliners. "Reveal yourself, emerge from your hiding place."

The red ball of fire ascended to the heavens, as though observing from above, searching for the source of the voice. The Warriors of Transcendence crawled over each other and collapsed near the Transparent Ones, gazing at the red skies. A ball of light appeared in the south. Was it the Master of Transcendence? The glowing ball produced many shades of white and moved at a rapid pace. It approached the united flames of the Emperors and the Deathliners, and began to circle around them.

For a moment it seemed like a playful game between two kittens, rather than a fateful struggle. In a single motion, the ball of light invaded all three planes, touched the valley ground and chilled the wall for the warriors. It then ascended to the upper plane, surrounded the red ball of fire and distanced it from the valley.

"He is trying to stall us," shouted the White Emperor, after he recovered from the surprise. He raised his staff as a sign to charge, and thousands of horsemen began galloping towards the valley.

"Keep and protect Your world, and be kind unto us," pleaded Ulu's disciples, each in their own way, and in their usual place of Unification.

"Increase the light and rid us of the darkness, give us strength to grow and illuminate the world, Transcendor."

The Towered City was empty of inhabitants. In the early morning hours, the Shadows and Obliterators left for the Valley of Silence, accompanied by those loyal to the Emperors, who were devoted to their masters in servitude. The thousands of remaining Tower Soldiers, the Descendents of the Obliterators and of the Emperors who served their masters thoughtlessly, suddenly felt a sense of discomfort and foreignness.

"I'm leaving," each one said in his heart, and without thinking, removed his cape and left the City.

By afternoon, the Tower had been completely abandoned, not one person remained. This caused the walls of the City to crack and the levels to begin collapsing. Masses of surprised onlookers pointed to the top of the Tower, which was slowly sinking, and to the fire which was slowly dimming. Great clouds of dust arose from the ground, concealing the devastation. The Tower continued to crumble until it turned into a huge mountain of rubble, completely burying the fields of the Fruits of Oblivion.

"Will they kill us?" Saag asked his father, as the balls of fire and light continued struggling in the distance, high above them, and the soldiers continued descending the slopes.

Ulu looked him straight in the eye and replied simply: "They may."

Saag clung to him, trembling with fear. "Aren't you afraid, father?"

"No," answered Ulu. "I'm not afraid. I just grieve for all of the helpless people…the villagers….the small children…"

"And Mother and the girls," added Saag.

Ulu nodded. "Mother knows what she must do. She faces fewer dangers than the other families do. There are so many people who know nothing of the dangers lurking. I yearned to teach them the ways to summon the help of the Transcendor, to tell them about the Master of Transcendence and to teach them the tricks of war. But now, with all of us trapped here, who can help them?"

"No one can," said Saag, "and if we are not freed, the Emperors shall prevail."

"No," said Ulu. "No, Saag. Even if we all die, others shall continue our task. The Transcendor will ensure that evil will disappear and that good shall prevail, whatever may be."

The red ball of fire weakened, and its burning fire began to fade. Ukhma was the first to notice this, and his face flooded with outrage and anger.

"Khivia has surrendered! The Tower has collapsed!" he hollered to the Emperors. "We are the only ones remaining, and we must complete our task!"

The Emperors froze in place as though they were struck by lightning. They looked behind them in search of the soaring flame of the Tower, but the horizon was empty, the Tower gone…

The soldiers that awaited an order looked at the Emperors, turning their gaze backwards as well. When they discovered that the Tower was no longer soaring in the distance, they began to wail. They were enveloped with fear, their hands weakened and their weapons fell to the ground. "Attack them!" commanded Ukhma. "If you don't destroy the warriors in the valley, I shall send my fire ball after them! Go now, before I send it after you!"

Only a few soldiers heard his roaring command and realized its significance. They gathered their weapons and aimed them at the group of warriors crouched behind the small rock. Ukhma aimed the fireball, which was by now much smaller and dimmer, straight at Saag.

"The world has been saved! Sihara has fulfilled her mission!" exclaimed Ulu, who had understood the significance of what had transpired.

A smile illuminated his weary eyes and smoothed out all of the creases in his face. "Now we may all die with joy in our hearts. We have fulfilled our destiny."

Just then a sound was heard, like a short whistle, which halted the battle in the valley and drowned out all of the voices. The ball of fire disappeared, and the thousands of horsemen collapsed to the ground. The White Emperor took one last look at his body. His white clothing had become gray. The bodies of bloody WireArchers were strewn around him in great numbers, and the Emperor was unable to fathom how they had been killed. Horses with no riders leaped wildly and roared. The Deathliners shrieked in pain, and Ukhma squirmed as though struck by invisible whips of fire.

The radiance in the sky disappeared, and the ball of light hung above the Warriors of Transcendence and caressed their agonized faces like a father caressing his only son.

While diving into the terrifying darkness that had no name, the White Emperor understood: Khivia had passed from the world.

Chapter Forty-One

A New Dawn/ Epilogue

A New Dawn/ Epilogue

Everything was now more radiant than ever; the children's eyes sparkled, the flowers seemed more colorful, the sky was illuminated, even people's clothing seemed more beautiful.

"Have I changed, too?" each person asked himself.

Songs echoed from the houses and laughter from the playgrounds. Farmers looked upon their plants and trees in awe- they had grown so tall and straight. The animals were calm, and a deep sense of serenity arose from the herds. There was not a cloud in the sky, and the sun shone into the hearts of all and upon all creations. Old remnants of grumpiness, intolerance, inner stresses and impatience, faded away and disappeared.

Sihara sat at the entrance to her home and watched the people pass her by. There had been times when she had not fully believed the villagers' legends of their heritage, stories of their ancestors, the great Ancient Progeny- so few ever seemed to go beyond the kitchen, the field or the pasture. Now their nobility was revealed in all their characteristics and in every single motion. They continued to occupy themselves with their everyday labors, as though they were embroidering a tapestry of their deeds onto an immense, mysterious, complex creation. Their hearts expressed the deep meaning hidden in each action, and all conversations were inevitably linked to the Transcendor.

Tzalaii walked along the seashore, holding his young son's hand.

"Listen, my son," he said to the curly-haired boy. "If you listen, you will learn much wisdom here."

He heard many voices speaking around him: *"Hold the net well, brother, do not let your chance slip from your fingertips!"* called an old fisherman. *"And pay heed to the dark depths, the finest fish are found there."*

"When the weather grows stormy, fold your sails and don't fight the wind," another fisherman advised his fellow disciples. *"Never let the storms threaten your peace."*

"Raise the anchor," a voice echoed from beyond the pier. *"Now release and flow with the right wave, allow the boat to find its place."*

"Did you, too, learn here when you were four?" the little boy with wise eyes asked his father.

Tzalaii's eyes clouded over. "I did, but that was a long time ago, and back then everything was much more difficult."

"Aunt Sihara says that everything was confusing," said the boy. "What does it mean to be confused, Father?"

"To be confused means to forget," answered Tzalaii softly. "To forget your life, or to forget to be joyful, or to forget the great Transcendor."

Dorianne sat at the foot of the mountain facing the village, watching the red flowers in bloom. After gazing at them for a while, she realized that the flowers were not merely red; their colors were ever-changing, ablaze, joyous. They seemed to be full of laughter, like playing children with no worries. In the dance of the flame, the flowers opened, revealing a white light from within. In the center of the light, Dorianne could see newborn babies with yellow hair, clear eyes, transparent bodies and a blue flame in their center. Her eyes filled with tears at the immense beauty of the scene, and she sat for a long time, finally arising slowly and making her way home.

"Father, what shall there really be after everything?"

Ulu stopped reading and looked up.

"Hello, Dorianne," he smiled. "Where have you been?"

"I was just down at the bottom of the mountain, but yesterday I walked through the forest, and last week I visited the sea. My teacher says that we must listen to the pulsations of life. I notice so much and it all seems to be bursting with celebration. Something inside of me is about to happen as well. What is it, father?"

"What do you think, Shaii?" Ulu asked his second daughter.

"I feel like an un-hatched duckling in a swamp. Every day it becomes more and more crowded, and I know that beyond the shell awaits a vast sky. I am almost out of patience!"

Saag stood by the door, listening, with a smile on his face.

"You are both developing your wings, girls," he said. "The time for transformation is near, and those who listen can hear the changes."

"What do you know about the wings?" asked Dorianne. "What has Father taught you?"

"Saag learned a lot in a short time," Ulu answered Dorianne in a calming voice, "and I am sure that you would not want to be in his place. Besides, each person takes a different route. You, Dorianne, should be attentive to the pulsations of life, Shaii must strive to find a way out of her shell, Saag is learning to believe in his own goodness, and I am learning to let go."

"And you, Mother?" Shaii wrapped her arms around her mother as she entered the room. "What have you been learning?"

"Every day brings upon its wings a new learning experience," answered her mother with a smile. "I am learning to trust that I shall always have the strength necessary for the tasks intended for me by the Transcendor."

The white wilderness was now blooming and buzzing with green life. The slopes were full of plant growth, and a gentle breeze caused everything to sway like in a dance. Forests grew in all directions as far as the eye could see, bursting with wild animals and birds. Streams of water flowed through the orchards and gardens, and the sunlight was sweet and bright. To the right, the valley stretched into yellow fields and hills beyond. To the left was a green path, its borders covered by a light fog. The sound of rushing rivers rolled in from the distance, and a group of young men made their way through the dense foliage, finally sitting down in a circle upon a grassy area.

"Listen," their guide began. "Pay close attention and allow the Transcendor to speak."

"But Mahn, I can hear no words," said the youngest boy in the group after a long wait.

Mahn smiled. "You shall express the words yourself, after you understand in your heart what your ears have heard."

"It seems as though everything wants to burst through its frame," said the oldest boy after a period of silence. "The flowers look as though they desire to dispose of their leaves and discover the transparent secret inside of them."

"Look at that tree, soaring in the sky. It looks as though it is pleading to the heavens."

"All are preparing for the big change. All desire to touch the heart pulsating in all substances," explained Mahn quietly. "We too must prepare ourselves."

The Chambers of Wisdom buzzed with students. People of all ages joined together, desiring to learn. They all gathered together, as the enlightening Transparent Ones interpreted the content of the scrolls to them.

"Choose, believe and desire, and listen to the voice of the Transcendor that guides the way. Follow it and allow it to protect you."

The thirsty listeners drank deeply and absorbed the wisdom into their hearts.

"Will everyone be ready when the time arrives?" asked one of the participants in a trembling voice. "Those who are far and those who are near? And those who don't understand it all, what shall become of them?"

"Everyone knows what he must know," his Transparent Master said reassuringly. "Everyone shall reach the intended moment properly prepared."

***

"The time has come!" announced the Transcendor.

"The time has come!" repeated the Master of Transcendence in his Chamber.

The skies were tinted purple. The clouds retreated toward the horizon, creating a gate-like effect. The Light of the Transcendor was revealed, strands of it glimmering like thin thread and pure as silver, cascading down, each one searching for a single soul upon the earth. For a moment the multitudinous threads appeared as the roots of a mighty tree, soaring way beyond into the distant sky. As each thread reached its designated person, it split into tiny particles, like a pile of feathers, indicating the route of ascent.

Saag looked at his body and discovered that it had become transparent. He grasped the illuminated feathery strings and they became like his wings. He trembled.

"What are these strings?" he asked his father.

"Good intentions," answered Ulu, as Saag began to ascend.

"Pure thoughts," he added, and Saag ascended even higher. "Sacred words, and of course true deeds."

"Come, Father," Saag called out to Ulu as he soared to the heavens.

"I am coming, my son" replied Ulu, "on my own path. Everyone is ascending, each in his own light, and each with his own wings."

The old world emptied of its inhabitants. It was time for the world to become purified.

A breeze arose from the sea. Endless vistas of water filled the horizon. The sound of the wave, like rejoicing and trusting laughter, was getting closer, not to wash away, or to destroy. The waters of the ocean gathered and soared with supreme and utter confidence. The immeasurable surge of water was bluer than blue, sometimes light, sometimes dark as a winter night. With sheer determination, and in a movement it had stored up for many days before unleashing itself, in an attempt to gather everything into its midst, to drown the world with its joy- the wave arose and soared.

In the distance, from the surface of the earth came the rushing sound of myriads of wings in flight.

Glossary

Abyss of the Shadows- A deep abyss in the Land of the Southern Cliffs, into which the desires, passions, dreams and longings of men are thrown. Humans who agree to worship the White Fire are also thrown into the abyss. From its 'raw materials,' the Shadows are created.

Archives of the Tunnels of Time - The largest, most comprehensive library and archive, established by the first Kings of the Ancient Progeny.

Blue Beverage- A unique drink, invented by Khivia, the father of the creatures of darkness. Those who drink this beverage become immortal but, at the same time, they are left infertile.

Chamber of Changing Colors- Palace of the Master of Transcendence, located beyond Fire Mountain.

Circle of Tower Inspiration- An invisible area, surrounds the Towered City. Those entrapped in it begin to lose control over their willpower.

Copper (or Solar) Level- The fifth level of the Towered City. Its inhabitants worship the sun.

Copper Mines- The Copper Mines are located in the Land of the Southern Cliffs.

Deathliners- Dark-slienned nomadic tribesmen from the Land of the North. After drinking from Khivia's black waters, they became extraordinarily powerful.

Extrappers- Warriors from the Towered City. They can align themselves to create a star formation, one in the center and the others at the four points. In star formation, they have the ability to generate craters and thorns, in close proximity, thereby preventing enemies from advancing.

Fire Mountain- A Fiery, impassable mountain chain, on the eastern side of the Kingdom. It isolates the Kingdom of the Master of Transcendence from the rest of the land.

Five Cities- The center of the realm of the King of the White Crown, the home of the Ancient Progeny, was composed of the five largest cities in the Land of the Southern Cliffs.

Fruit of Oblivion- Red, fleshy fruit growing freely in vast areas surrounding the Towered City and supplying most of the food for the inhabitants following the descent of the rivers

Game of Forces- A popular board game played in the Towered City. Alert spectators are able to gain insight into the personalities of the participants by analyzing their moves.

Game of Thoughts- A secret three-dimensional game played in the Towered City, based on the rules of the Game of Forces, but completely different in essence.

Gold (or Mars) Level- The sixth level of the Towered City. Its inhabitants worship the Planet Mars.

Gray Coins- Iron coins used in the Towered City. One hundred gray coins are equivalent to one white coin.

Green Lowlands- A fertile land in the center of the kingdom that had been the 'breadbasket' for the Ancient Progeny in the past.

Initiation Training- The training process required of the Warriors of Transcendence.

Inviewers- Warriors from the Towered City, uniquely capable of reading human thoughts and motivations. Their intelligence gathering ability enables them to supply crucial information to the City Emperors.

Khivia- The ancient father of all creatures of darkness. He declared war against the Master of Transcendence.

King of the White Crown- The last ruler of the Kingdom of the Ancient Progeny. He was murdered by his seven advisors.

King's Sea- A vast sea to the South of the Green Lowlands. Refugee survivors of the five large cities of the Ancient Progeny built their villages on its shores.

King's Valley- A deep and long ravine located between tall cliffs, it is the only land passage between the Green Lowlands and the fourteen villages of King's Sea.

Kingdom of the Ancient Progeny- The ancient realm of the King of the White Crown. It existed for thousands of years.

Land of the Northern Forests- A forested land in the north of the Kingdom.

Land of the Southern Cliffs- The Southernmost land in the Kingdom, looming above the ocean. In the past, its five large cities were inhabited by the people of the Kingdom of the Ancient Progeny.

Land of White Fire- The Kingdom of the Ancient Progeny. The enemy Emperors mockingly renamed it in order to express the superiority of their Tower, from whose peak a white fire burned.

Legend of the Wings- An ancient widespread and well-known legend predicting the end of the world and the triumph of the Warriors of Transcendence.

Light of the Transcendor- This is a great power that can be used by the Warriors of Transcendence. The user is capable of thwarting all enemy plots but danger lurks for arrogant warriors as the force may attack them as well.

Magnathought Crystal- A special device employed to enhance focus and concentration in order to be able to reach difficult goals. It is a remnant of the Kingdom of the Ancient Progeny.

Marker of Tumult- An inner change in the state of consciousness of the victim, allowing the Descendents of the Emperors control of his or her mind.

Master of Transcendence- The leader of the Warriors of Transcendence, messenger of the Transcendor to the Land of the Ancient Progeny.

Memory Master- Each village has its own 'Memory Master' who travels to the Northern Forests once a year. Each Memory Master leads his disciples, 'the Storm Dancers,' to bring aid to their brothers in the north.

Memory Shield- Memories related to the Master of Transcendence. These memories have the power to encourage and increase the strength of the Warriors.

Mercury (or Saturn) Level- The second level of the Towered City. Its inhabitants worship the Planet Saturn.

Obliterators- Creatures of darkness, formed by the Emperors at the beginning of their rule. They are capable of invading a man's mind, manipulating his thoughts, breaking down his defenses and convincing him to join the forces of the Tower.

Obliterators Peak- A remote, secure and fortified stone castle, dating back to the days of the five great cities of the Southern Cliffs, now used by the Emperors for the launching of their evil plans.

Ohn Mountain- A high mountain in the eastern part of the Kingdom, home to Khivia.

Purple Beverage- Popular drink in the Towered City. It is a stimulant.

Purple Cloud- A celestial vision that precedes revelation of the Light of the Transcendor.

Red Coins- Copper coins used in the Towered City. One hundred red copper coins are equivalent to one gray iron coin.

Remembrance- A technique used by the Warriors of Transcendence to summon their forgotten Memory Shields.

Sea Point- The tallest peak in the Land of the Northern Forests, at the border of the Land of the North. It was named 'Sea Point' because of the two seas visible from it, the ocean in the south and King's Sea in the west.

Seven Emperors- The seven disloyal advisors to the King of the White Crown, collaborators with Khivia who gave them immortality.

Shadow Valley- The location of an ancient great sea which existed in the days of the Kingdom of the Ancient Progeny. Now it is a parched, gray valley, controlled by creatures of darkness who thwart the progress of all who approach or try to cross through Fire Mountain.

Shadows- Spiritual creatures formed by the evil deeds of man.

Silver (or crescent) Level- The seventh level of the Towered City. Its inhabitants worship the moon.

Steel (or Base) Level- The first level in the Towered City. Its inhabitants worship the Planet Jupiter.

Stellar (or Lead) Level- The third level of the Towered City. Its inhabitants worship the stars.

Stone Wall- The outer protective wall surrounding the Towered City.

Storm Dance- A weaponless martial art invented by the Master of Transcendence; in the eyes of spectators, it appeares as an innocent ritual dance.

Storm Dancers- Warriors of the Master of Transcendence, skilled at performing the storm dance and fighting aggressively against the Tower Warriors. They can be found mainly in the Northern Forests.

Tunnels of Time – A multi-branched network of underground tunnels, excavated by the King of the Ancient Progeny. The many pools of water in the tunnels create the appearance of visions from the past or future.

Tin (or Venus) Level- The fourth level of the Towered City. Its inhabitants worship the Planet Venus.

Towered City- A powerful city built by the seven Emperors in the Green Lowlands, inhabited by millions, composed of seven levels, each ruled by a different Emperor.

Transcendor- Creator of all entities.

Transparent Master- Spiritual creatures, which are formed by mans *exceptionally* good deeds.

Transparent Ones- Spiritual creatures formed by the good deeds of man.

Tumult- A designated area on the shore below the Southern Cliffs, where the Descendents of the Emperors mark their prisoners with the 'Marker of Tumult,' which causes them to lose their willpower.

Unification- A technique used by the Warriors of Transcendence to communicate with the Transcendor.

Valley of Silence- A large valley, located next to the entrance to the Towered City; Location of the final battle in the Land of White Fire.

Villagers- Thousands of inhabitants of the fourteen villages located on the shores of King's Sea. They are descendents of the survivors from the five original cities of the Kingdom of the Ancient Progeny.

Wall of Fog- The thick protective wall composed of fog, surrounding the Towered City.

Waterfalls - Two waterfalls, sources of the two largest rivers, in the time of the Kingdom of the Ancient Progeny, flowing from the Green Lowlands to the plains leading to King's Sea.

WireArchers- Warriors from the Towered City, capable of casting a lethal net of scorching threads upon their enemy.

White Coins- Silver coins used in the Towered City. One hundred white coins are equivalent to one yellow golden-silver coin.

White Desert- A broad, desolate wasteland, located between the Towered City and Fire Mountain. In the past, it had been a beautiful, fertile area, but it became a desert following the descent of the rivers.

Yellow Coins- Golden-Silver coins used in the Towered City. Most valuable coin of all, equivalent to one hundred white (silver) coins.